HEDGED

A Thriller by
S.L. Shelton

This book is a work of fiction. Names, characters, places, and incidents are products of the author's imagination or are used fictitiously. Any resemblance to actual events, locales, or persons, living or dead, is entirely coincidental.

Copyright © 2016 by S.L. Shelton

All rights reserved, including the right to reproduce this book or portions thereof in any form whatsoever.

Front cover, maps, and artwork contained in this book are Copyright © S.L. Shelton

The cover image is a modified and stylized rendering that includes portions of photos obtained through the Department of Defense photo library and photos from Creative Commons Deed, License CC0 Public Domain.

Books by S.L. Shelton:

Hedged

The Scott Wolfe Series:
Waking Wolfe
Unexpected Gaines
Danger Close
Wolfe Trap
Harbinger
Predator's Game
Splinter Self (Coming 2016)
Back story: Lt. Marsh

For Dad; Forgiven, Remembered, Missed

Dear Reader,

I began writing Hedged hours after my father was buried. And though the story drifts far (very far) from being a memoir, I found at the end that I had worked through much of my grief and come to a delicate truce with memories of my father.

Sadly, only days after sending the manuscript to the editors, my beloved wife was diagnosed with a rare form of cancer, very late in development. All projects stopped, including work on the last book in the Scott Wolfe Series.

When I penned this story, I had never set foot in Virginia Hospital Center—I was writing from pure research. It was an odd coincidence that when my Gretel fell ill at 3:00 a.m. one Sunday morning, it was the emergency room there, then the 7th floor, where she was admitted.

My gratitude to the men and women of Virginia Hospital Center cannot be adequately expressed in words. I've never seen such heroic outpouring of support as I have there. The amazing people in the ER, the inpatient wings and Radiation Oncology are a gift to the region that I had never fully appreciated until we needed them.

My thanks to those great healers. Their jobs, their daily efforts to help, touch so many people in ways you can't imagine. They're all heroes.

With sincerest gratitude and my very best regards,
Very best regards,

S.L. Shelton
Author

GOODBYE

CHASE GRANT stood over his unconscious father.

"Asshole." The word, though whispered, sounded like a scream.

He stared into his father's face hoping to see some sign of movement yet dreading it at the same time. What he had to say was best uttered without interruption—lest he lose his nerve.

He sat in the chair next to the hospital bed, keeping his eyes locked on his father's face. He stared for several minutes before exhaling slowly, realizing he had been holding his breath.

"An apology would've been nice," Chase said, his voice low. "If not to me, at least to mom… It's too late for her now, too."

No response.

A tear burned a path down Chase's cheek before dropping off his chin to his lap. His father wouldn't survive the night. The cancer had come on fast—or rather, his father had ignored the symptoms too long. By the time it was painful enough to go to the doctor, his lungs were eaten up with the murderous byproduct of a lifelong two pack a day smoking habit.

"I don't know what to say, Dad," Chase whispered. "You weren't there when we needed you and when you were, you were beating the shit out of us."

That's not fair, Chase thought. *He never hit mom.*

Chase shook his head and a hot tear rolled down his face.

But you left her, you son of a bitch. "You left all of us."

He watched his father's face, so pale, so weak. How could someone who had been so godlike, so all-powerful end up a broken, sad, pile of meat like this?

"It's not fair."

More tears slipped down his cheeks. He grabbed the corner of his jacket and wiped his face clumsily, absently.

"You spent my whole life teaching me you were always right and I was always wrong," Chase said through a catch in his throat. "How is it I learned family is everything and you didn't?"

He reached out and touched his father's hand with the intent of picking it up. But when the paper-thin skin felt cold to the touch, he withdrew and instead, tucked his hands under his legs, preempting further temptation.

He hadn't talked to his father in almost two years. He had given in to a moment of desperation and called the elder Grant for bail money. Then, like now, he got no response, no acknowledgment.

"But you always left us hanging, didn't you."

And, like now, he felt stupid for even trying to talk to his father—words meant nothing. His last words to his father before tonight were spoken to silence on the other end of the phone nearly two years earlier—*"Coward."*

Chase hadn't known what that meant when he was a child; only that it was supposed to sting, though it never did. Nor did he understand why he insulted his father in that particular manner that night almost two years earlier, except that it had been a word his father had bullied him with—it must have held some secret abusive power Chase wasn't aware of.

Chin up, asshole. You were right. I know I'm a screw-up.

Chase shook his head. He knew he suffered from serious character flaws, shoving people out of his life when they didn't seem to love unconditionally, quickly resorting to physical violence when he or someone he loved was threatened. Occasionally it had led to extreme violence. Violence; *that* was something Chase was good at.

He chuckled through his tears. "I wonder where I got that from?"

A bubbling breath caught in his father's throat and he wheezed a weak cough. Chase froze, his heart jumping at the movement. But his father didn't wake—his breathing simply became louder.

After a tense moment, holding his breath, Chase relaxed and leaned forward. "I guess I should thank you," he whispered. "You taught me better than anyone how to take a punch." Chase curled his fingers into a fist unconsciously. "Of course, I had to learn on my own how to throw one, but hey, there's always a learning curve growing up…right?"

The rhythmic rattle of his father's breath made the conversation unsatisfying. He wondered if his sister Chloe had been right—maybe it would have been better to just let the old man die and have it all behind them. But that seemed too easy, and nothing worthwhile was easy. In fact, nothing in Chase's life had ever been easy, so why start now?

"If it hadn't been for your constant need to beat me down, I wouldn't have worked so hard to prove you wrong."

A particularly loud rasp in his father's throat seemed almost like a scoff of smug satisfaction—that's how it sounded to Chase's ears anyway.

"I make good money now… It's a good job…a legal job." One that didn't involve calculating the spread on a basketball series in his head, on the fly—Chase was always good with numbers. Like little magic codes, begging to reveal their secrets, numbers had always been Chase's friend. They winked at him, sharing their secrets effortlessly. While others saw stacks of numbers in chaotic and formless flows, he saw patterns, tricks, secrets. Numbers don't lie. If they do, you aren't treating them right.

Working for the bookie let the numbers man Chase had become pursue his natural talent with math.

But he had changed all that and was earning an honest living now. The lack of acknowledgment from his father for that accomplishment angered him. He gritted his teeth, suddenly overwhelmed by the desire to punch his unconscious father in the face.

"Coward, asshole…loser," he whispered, then waited for the back of his father's hand.

Chase wanted it. He wanted that fight, the brutality…he wanted an excuse to put a pillow over his father's face and choke out the last few moments of the life he had left.

Stop it. He's your father. Bastard that he is, he's family. Protect family at all costs.

"I've done things," Chase said, leaning forward and whispering so softly even he didn't hear it fully. "I've hurt people."

No response—not even a flicker of motion in his eyelids.

"But I kept Chloe safe," he said, sitting straight and wiping his eyes again. "She's a good girl. Smart. Strong."

Chase's cheek twitched, almost as if his body rejected the comfortable lie he told himself. Like Chase, Chloe had flaws that haunted her. And like Chase, her flaws had led her into dark, violent places. Unfortunately, she was usually on the receiving end of the violence she attracted—and unfortunately, it was usually Chase who stepped in to stop it.

"Do you remember the night I called you?" He asked, his voice low and full of accusation. "Chloe was in the hospital again." He shook his head, trying to remember the name of the guy who had hurt her. "Eddie…Eddie was the guy's name."

He listened to the oxygen hissing through his father's breathing tube.

"Eddie." He shook his head. "I could've used your help that night. Chloe had three broken ribs by the time I got out of jail."

He leaned forward again and whispered. "You can hear me, can't you?"

No response.

That night he had called his father for help, the night he'd called his father a coward and hung up after hearing no reply; it had been a wake-up call—Chase had realized he was alone. There was no one out there to keep an eye on him or help him up when he was in trouble. And worse, he had been so close to being sent away for a long time. He realized he'd never be able to protect Chloe if he were in prison.

He shook his head, staring at his old man's face, angry that the tears were still falling. "I guess you think you did me a favor by not bailing me out that night," Chase said, then cleared his throat. "—and maybe you did. But it didn't help Chloe…she suffered because I wasn't there. They…they did things to her."

He had tried to clean up his life since then. He had caught a lucky break. He hated relying on luck for anything, but he was grateful for it that night almost two years ago. A smart kid with a head for numbers, trying to make a living the best way he knew how—that's how the police had seen it, and that's how they presented it to the judge. *Thank god they didn't know about the rest of it.*

One of the cops had actually vouched for him; Jimmy, the friendly cop. Jimmy had stepped in front of the judge and took responsibility for Chase's release. The judge set him free on the condition he'd move into the empty apartment next door to *friendly cop Jimmy* and get an honest job.

Chase knew a gift when he saw it and he wasn't going to do hard time working for someone else. Jimmy had given him a way out; an apartment of his own and honest work. Though dishwasher was shit work for a numbers man, it was only a few months before he found his real calling—stock analyst—a *legal* numbers racket. He started out pimping small cap penny stocks—scams, hopeful startups—and did so well, he was recruited to work at a small firm. He wore a tie to work now. *Ain't that a kick in the teeth.*

"You taught me how to hate, old man, and juvie taught me how to channel it…but I had to learn how to be a useful member of society on my own." He shrugged one shoulder up and wiped more tears on his arm.

"Fuck you for not being there for us." His words were barely intelligible, caught in his throat and pushed out through an increasing stream of tears. The conversation seemed to only deepen Chase's pain.

Sudden awareness of the time crept up his spine—he knew this was taking too long. He looked over his shoulder, half expecting to see his father's second wife walk in. The last thing he wanted was to suffer her disapproving glare. He knew how they viewed Chase and Chloe; screw-ups, losers…low class. That's why he had waited until she had left the room with her son before coming up to say good-bye to his father.

His father's second wife got the best of him—*after* the old man had grown up a bit. She had no right to cast judgment on the family who had been abandoned, allowing her to have her happy little life. Chase's family got the ruins of his father's first failed attempt at adulthood. His second wife got the benefit of those lessons, stealing him away when he got restless.

He wiped his face on his sleeve and turned back to his father. After staring at the old man for a few minutes, Chase stood, slowly, purposefully, aware it would be the last time he would walk away from a conversation with his father—and the only time he would ever get the last word.

"No do overs, Dad…sorry," Chase said as he leaned over to kiss his father good-bye. The faint smell of Old Spice wafted up—his father's iconic scent. A weak, raspy cough from deep in his father's chest startled him, precluding the kiss.

Chase straightened abruptly and looked at his dad's face again, wondering if he were waking. Or maybe it was only that his dad needed to get the last word after all—even if it was just a phlegmy roll from his cancer riddled chest.

Chase turned to walk out, abandoning the last sentiment, but paused at the door and looked over his shoulder. "Asshole."

With the last word safely on Chase's scorecard, he left, turning down the hallway before there was any chance of his father denying him the win.

At the end of the corridor, the elevator opened. His father's second wife and her son stepped off the lift and Chase diverted quickly to the stairs before being seen. His stepbrother looked over his shoulder but didn't seem to notice Chase as he disappeared down the stairwell, the slow, groaning of the closing door more likely the cause of the backward glance.

Chase was halfway down the stairs to the ground floor when he began to regret his final words to his father. He paused on the landing, letting the insult echo in his mind. He looked back up the stairs, for an instant tempted to return and correct the situation. But the idea of standing in the room with *Sarah* and her son was more of a challenge than he could stomach.

What difference does it make? He's not awake.

He continued to linger at the edge of the stairs, trapped by indecision.

But are those what I want to remember as my last words to him?

He shook his head as the tears started to flow again. He stood there, paralyzed by regret until the door below him opened and two nurses walked toward him. He hastily wiped his eyes and continued down the stairs. As he passed the two women, one of them, a brown skinned woman—Middle Eastern or Indian—gave him a sideways glance then reached out, touching him on the shoulder. The gesture lasted only a second, breaking as they crossed. But it was a welcome warmth he hadn't expected—penetrating.

The comfort transmitted through that simple gesture followed him out of the hospital and down to the street where he had parked. He got into the car feeling not as lost as he had when he left the room.

Leaning forward, he stared at the fifth-floor window for several seconds, looking at his *stepmother's* back. God, he hated calling her that. "Bye, Dad," he whispered.

Wiping his eyes once more, he started his car and drove away. He would be home by the time his father passed and deep in a bag of weed by the time he was buried. It was done—time had caught up to them both with all past regrets still lingering.

TUESDAY

A BAD DAY

Two months later in the wee hours of the morning on a Tuesday.

CHLOE GRANT looked at her watch and breathed out in frustration. The late night at the restaurant she managed had felt like a week of bullshit. She had hoped to take advantage of her chef volunteering to close up for her and unwind with some dancing and flirting—maybe a cute guy to help her burn off some sexual frustration. But it wasn't working out like that. The Step Down—the dance club she frequented in Arlington Virginia, seemed to be living up to its name tonight.

For nearly three hours, the only dance partner she'd had were the two Sea Breezes she'd been nursing and the closest thing to a sexual prospect had been the bartender who kept calling her gorgeous—Linda. And though cute, Chloe had no interest in girls—except that one time in school. But everyone goes through that phase, right?

She looked at her watch again and realized the night had been a wash; no stress relief, no cute guys, no dancing. *What was I thinking? It's Monday night.*

She shook her head and glanced over at the booth across the dance floor. The two men who had come in a short time after her weren't faring any better than she was. But then again, despite the occasional glance in her direction, neither of them seemed interested in girls anyway. She glanced over again when a new guy came in and sat with the two loners.

Ain't that sweet...boys night out.

She turned and watched them for a moment in the reflective metal back of the bar. *The new one is pretty cute,* she thought.

She checked her watch again. *Okay, cute boy... you have ten minutes, then this little girl has to get home. Work tomorrow.*

She sipped the last watery remnants of her Sea Breeze and watched the bartender as she went about her side-work, cleaning up in preparation for closing.

After several minutes, Linda the cute bartender checked her watch and looked over her shoulder to Chloe. "Last call, gorgeous. Can I getcha another before I close down?"

Chloe shook her head and looked down at the water in the bottom of her glass. "Nope...I'm done."

"Oh, don't say that," a man said from behind her. "I just got here."

Chloe turned as he slid in sideways next to her. It was the cute guy who had been sitting with the two loners in the booth—though, up close he wasn't that cute. In fact, he looked a little dirty; and not in the good way.

"Late nights and early mornings don't mix well," she said as she pulled her credit card from her purse.

"True...but you almost made it to closing. You don't want to be a quitter, do you?"

She smiled. Weakened by his persistence and the mild challenge to her stamina, she felt her resistance melt a bit.

She nodded, grinning shyly—guys like it when you give them a shy smile. "Okay...maybe one more for the road."

He turned to the bartender. "Two of whatever she was having."

"Two Sea Breezes, coming up."

A frown flashed on his face for a second and Chloe chuckled inwardly, aware that it wasn't the manliest drink to be ordering at one o'clock in the morning.

"I'm Brad," he said, turning back to her.

"Chloe."

"Oh. I like that. Chloe...Chloe. It's almost like a song or something."

Oh, Jesus. Dirty and lame. What the hell are you doing, Chloe? Does your life suck so bad that you'd stoop to this? She smiled thinly and put her card back into her purse. "I think it was a song. Maybe you're thinking of that."

Brad shook his head. "No. I think I'm just thinking of you."

Drink your drink, Chloe, then get the hell out of here, she thought.

Brad tucked his credit card in the check holder when it arrived with the drinks.

"Thank you," she said, always aware of the politics of free drinks and the boys who buy them—that constant pressure to balance gratitude with caution.

"My pleasure, m'lady."

It was all she could do to keep from rolling her eyes. When he reached around the chair, he bumped the strap of her purse slung across the back of the tall bar chair. It fell to the floor spilling its contents.

"Oh shit. I'm sorry," he said, leaning around her to help.

"I've got it." She climbed off the stool to shovel her belongings back into her bag.

When she got back into her seat, he pushed her drink closer to her and lifted his own. "To happy accidents," he said, clinking his glass to hers.

Just smile, nod, then get the hell out of here, she thought as she took a long drink from her glass. She leaned back and watched the red of the cranberry turn and tumble inside her glass. She swished her straw around, aiding the blending motion.

Brad absently toyed with the rim of his glass. "So, Chloe... you work nearby?"

She shrugged. "Not far, I guess," she replied, avoiding details as the alcohol flushed her cheeks and the pleasant numbness began seeping to her jaw and the bottoms of her ears. *Whoa! Linda saved the strong drinks for the end of the night.* Or maybe Chloe was just tired. Either way, she needed to finish up and get out before *Brad* found any more of her triggers and snaked his way into her bed. She just wasn't interested. In fact, it had been months since she had been interested in anyone at all.

"You have family around here?" Brad asked.

She looked up, realizing suddenly that she had zoned out. She felt as though she was leaning to the right, so she straightened up, trying to compensate. The adjustment caused her to tip to her left.

"Whoa, there," Brad said, grabbing her shoulder.

She giggled, embarrassed but playing it off as just silliness. *Why? Why would I feel the need to—*

Her thoughts drifted before she even finished asking herself the question.

"You have family around here?" Brad asked.

Chloe nodded, her eyes droopy. "Brother… Chase."

"Ah, cool. Where does he live?"

"Flairflax."

"Flairflax?" Brad asked, chuckling. "Do you mean *Fairfax?*"

"Yeah…that."

He nodded. "So I guess you need a ride to his house."

She shook her head. "I'm fline."

She stepped off the stool and fell forward. Brad caught her and lifted her back to her seat. "You don't seem fine. I think you may've had too much to drink."

Jesus, Chloe…how much did you drink? She wondered to herself—she suddenly couldn't remember. She brushed her eyes with the back of her hand, almost as if trying to sweep away the fog that was closing in on her brain. "Yep…a lil too mulch."

"That's okay," Brad said. "I'll take you to your brother's house."

"So sweet," she said, suddenly, oddly, grateful for the assistance.

"Where's he live?" Brad asked as he helped her from her chair.

She reached back and grabbed her purse, but it slipped from her grasp before she could tuck it under her arm. Brad leaned down and grabbed it for her, draping the strap over her shoulder.

"Um…," Chloe hummed. "Flairflax."

"Right…Flairflax," Brad replied, a little sarcastic. "How about an address?"

As they stepped outside, Chloe panicked, unable to remember Chase's address. She began to cry. "I cam remembah," she slurred as she wept.

"Shhh, shh, shh…it's okay," Brad said, looking around nervously. "Do you have his address written on something in your purse?"

Her head dipped and swooped, trying to remember. When it came to her, she stopped walking, "My dribers license… emergency contact."

Brad helped her to a car and pushed her in on the passenger's side.

After adjusting her in a seated position, spending far too much time arranging her breasts, he reached into her purse. Chloe was vaguely aware of him pulling the cash from her billfold as he thumbed through her cards.

"Nope...no emergency contact information on the back of your license," Brad said, flipping the ID over.

Chloe's brow pinched together in confusion. "No...no. Thas not right."

He held the card up to her unfocused eyes. "See...? Nothing."

"Shit," she muttered. "Hmm... Oh! Try my dress book. Is in there."

"What's his last name?"

She laughed. "Same as me, sillerd."

Brad flipped to the back of the front cover, reading her name and contact information before flipping the small book to *G*. "Fairfax Towers? Is that right?"

Recognition flashed across Chloe's face and her eyes opened wide. "Thas it! Flairflax Tomers."

"Alright then," Brad said as he ripped out the page from her book and stuffed the rest back into Chloe's purse. "Let's get you buckled up."

He again spent far too much time making sure her breasts were secure, letting one of them slip out of her bra before having to reach up under her blouse to return them to their proper places. She was only half aware that her skirt had ridden up on her thighs as Brad nuzzled her neck, reaching across her with the seatbelt.

Chloe panicked for a second, not remembering where she was. The spike of awareness was only enough to deliver a reflex to her mind—kissing the top of Brad's head as he nuzzled her breasts. A familiar pressure bloomed, pressing between her legs and her slow exhale of breath became a moan when his hand moved insistently past her panties. A mixture of shame and arousal filled her as her body instinctively released a slick dew of moisture.

"You are a very dirty girl, aren't you," Brad whispered into her ear.

Another voice snapped Brad's attention elsewhere. "You idiot!" someone said.

Brad pulled away, leaving Chloe's wetness exposed to the cool night air before tugging her skirt back in place and returning her breasts to the cups of her bra.

The door slammed shut and he got in on the driver's side. "Okay. Let's go see Chase," Brad said.

Chloe nodded. *You better be nice when you show up at Chase's house—he'll kill you if you're mean to me.* She chuckled, only vaguely aware that she was slumping toward the door. As Brad started the engine, the vibration quickly drove Chloe into a deep slumber.

►◄

CHASE woke to a knock at the door. After stretching into a sitting position he flipped the light on next to his bed and picked up his phone—two o'clock in the morning.

"Are you kidding me?"

He pulled his jeans on and grabbed his shirt from the day before as he passed the hamper. The knock persisted.

"Hold on, hold on," he muttered as he pulled the stale shirt over his head.

He looked through the peephole. "Jesus," he muttered, seeing a man with stubble on his face and deep, dark circles under his eyes. "Who is it?"

"There's a girl here who said I should bring her to you...Chloe."

Chase dropped his head and shook it back and forth. Chloe—this was not the first time she had begged some one-night-stand to drop her at Chase's house.

Chase unlocked the door. "Damn it, Chloe."

"She's pretty messed up," the guy said, trying to help scoot her through the door.

Chase glanced at the man and got a chill of discomfort. He decided he didn't want this guy in his apartment. "I've got her... Thanks."

"Uh." The guy didn't seem to know how to respond to that. He looked down the hallway and back to Chase as he pulled Chloe across the threshold.

"You got dem best brudder om—" Chloe's head lulled forward, cutting off the remainder of her profound statement.

Chase moved to shut the door. "Thanks again."

The man put his hand up and stopped it from closing. "She said you could hook me up."

"She's too wasted to know what she's saying." Chase pushed harder.

The man persisted, grasping the edge of the door and using his toe to stop it. "Come on man...just a little weed."

"Dude, I don't know what she told you but I don't have *weed* or anything else."

An angry crease folded a line at the center of his brow and he leaned in close to Chase. "Next time your sister gets an itch, tell her to go rub up against someone else."

Chase dropped Chloe to the floor and punched the man in the face sending him sprawling backward to the floor.

Chloe landed with a thud. "Hey! Whab da fung hwo—"

Stepping over her, Chase went into the hallway and grabbed the guy by the collar of his dirty denim jacket, lifting his shoulders from the floor.

His neighbor's door opened and a tall, older, black man stepped into the hallway wearing blue police uniform pants and a white tank undershirt. His service weapon hung absently from his hand. "What the hell is goin' on ou—Oh. Chase. Everything cool, man?"

It was Jimmy, the friendly cop who had vouched for Chase almost two years earlier, giving Chase the fresh start he had sought.

Sometimes Chase wondered if Jimmy regretted stepping up for him and moving him into the apartment next door. Had Chase been a different sort of person, not anxious to clean his life up, things could have gone differently when he accidentally stumbled in on Jimmy smoking a joint in the basement laundry room shortly after moving in.

Instead, Chase had said. *"I can smell that ditch weed from outside...come on up and I'll let you have some of the good stuff."* Their relationship changed dramatically after that.

It was nothing to have Jimmy knock on Chase's door after a shift change and sit with him, taking hits off his bong and joking about the wild shit that happened that day.

"It's fine, Jimmy. Sorry for the noise," Chase said without looking.

"Cool. I'll leave you to it then."

The door closed and Chase could hear Jimmy's wife, Tonya, asking what was going on. Lowered voices prevented him from hearing the reply, but he knew he didn't have anything to worry about—not if he stopped now before things got out of hand.

The guy on the floor rolled his head up, looking up bleary-eyed at Chase. "I'm sorry man. I didn't mean nothin' by it."

Chase dropped him with a thud, deciding against further brutality after Jimmy witnessed the scene. He went back through his door and lifted his sister from the floor, not bothering to look behind him as he kicked the door closed.

With little effort, he carried Chloe to the sofa and lowered her to the cushions. He looked at her and chuckled as he pulled her shoes off. "What was it this time?"

"Wha?"

"It's Monday—no...make that Tuesday—middle of the work week, and you're piss-your-pants drunk at two a.m."

"I nee a reas to hab fun?" She dropped her feet to the floor and leaned over the edge of the couch.

"Don't you puke on my sofa."

She only grunted in reply.

"You're going to fall over and split your head. Come back over here," Chase said, grabbing her by the arm and dragging her back.

In her hand was a small hand-carved box from the side table.

"No," Chase said, grabbing at the box.

She tried to snatch it back but missed. "Come on. Jus one bow to pu me to slep."

"Lay down...you'll be asleep in five minutes." He spoke "drunk Chloe" fluently, though tonight she was speaking a particularly fuzzy dialect of that language.

"Head's buzzin' too lou, Chase. Jus one...pleeeease." She was slurring her words so drastically, he wondered if she'd be able to pack a bowl.

"Whatever," he muttered, setting the box on the table in front of her.

Giddy, Chloe reached behind the sofa and pulled out Chase's bong. He tensed, watching her closely, worried she would drop and shatter it. After setting it on the coffee table, she opened the box and flipped past two small baggies of pot before seeing what she wanted. Chase glanced over and saw she was digging past the larger baggies in the front.

He shook his head in resignation. "Help yourself to the good stuff."

She deftly, though slowly, packed the bowl on the bong, careful not to let a single crumb fall.

"So who was the guy?" Chase asked as his sister clumsily produced a lighter from her pocket then lit up her prize.

Bubbles gurgled in the throat of the glass pipe, but being a loving, considerate, sister, she kept her thumb over the hole on the side before passing it to Chase. He leaned forward, carefully taking it from her, then drew deeply from the bong himself.

She let slip a silken stream of white smoke before coughing.

"Stawberry! I lub dat."

Chase held his smoke for a beat then released it. He felt lighter already—maybe a couple of hits *would* make it easier to get back to sleep. "You didn't answer me."

"Cough," she said, droopy-eyed but grinning mischievously.

Chase rolled his eyes and coughed. Chloe giggled and took the bong from his hands. "Bret." She cocked her head to the side, her lighter poised above the bowl for another go. "Or, Brad...sump like tha."

Chase shook his head again. "Please don't bring them to my house."

"I needed a ri," she said and dropped back into the cushions, her eyes closed. "I din't pomise anyfin."

He got up, his head swimming with the euphoria of the Strawberry Cough. "Go to sleep...and no looting my stash before you leave tomorrow—today."

He picked up the baggie and flicked it once before tucking it back in the box.

"You aren' gonna be here in morin?" She asked.

"It's after two...I'll be here in the morning, but I seriously doubt you'll be up."

She waved dismissively, her hand flopping to her lap.

He pulled the blanket off the back of the sofa and spread it out over her. "And don't throw up on my couch."

"I'm fine," she whispered.

"Good night Chlo."

"Night."

As he disappeared into his bedroom, Chloe rolled over, hanging off the edge of the sofa and looking up at him. It almost looked as if she were about to fall to the floor. "You don' thin he suff'rd do you?"

"Who? Bret?"

She shook her head lazily. "Dad."

Chase took a deep breath and let it out slowly through his nose. "I don't think so. But if he did, it wasn't for long."

She nodded and the tear that rolled down her cheek tugged at Chase's heart.

He walked over and nudged her back on the couch. "Sleep."

She closed her eyes and nodded. "Night."

He stared at her for a moment, wondering how he could stop her from hooking up with idiots. She seemed to find them almost exclusively as if she had a finely tuned radar that identified then steered her clear of decent guys. He closed his door and crawled back in bed. Despite the Strawberry Cough, he found it difficult to relax back to sleep. "Damn it, Chlo."

As long as he could remember, he'd been stepping in to defend Chloe from assholes and abusers. From elementary playground scuffles to that one time in middle school when he had broken a kid's jaw with a history book, Chase had always been Chloe's reckless, fiery defender.

The kid in middle school had been a big guy—big compared to Chase anyway. Chase had found Chloe under the bleachers, trapped by three guys who were feeling her up under her gym clothes. Despite her screams and angry swearing, no one had gone to investigate.

Chase had charged through the back row supports and attacked, flinging himself wildly against all three before laying his hands on the book. Without hesitation, he began smashing their faces with it. Blood, swearing, fists, and cries had not stopped his berserker like rampage until two coaches pulled him off the unfortunate attackers.

When all was said and done, two of the three boys had required a trip to the hospital, one of them with a broken jaw—and one of the coaches sported a black eye for a week, though Chase never got to see it. He was arrested, charged, tried, and sent to juvenile detention for more than a year.

When he returned home, he had learned two valuable lessons: 1. You have to be smart when playing the protector—thoughtless rage doesn't do anyone any favors. And 2. If you take someone down, make sure you take them down hard—no hesitation, no mercy, and no witnesses. Juvie had been a cruel but effective teacher.

When his alarm sounded at seven a.m., it felt as if he had only crawled in bed moments before. But by the time he showered and shaved, he felt awake enough to start his day. He was surprised to smell coffee when he opened his bedroom door.

"Morning, sleepy head. I was starting to wonder if you slept past your alarm." Chloe sat at the kitchen bar, her elbows propped up and cradling a wide coffee cup between her hands.

She was dressed, her face was made-up and she looked ready for anything. She was the spitting image of Chase—a female version of him. Thought she was a year younger and thinner, with her pale Grant skin, long straight nose and head of thick, black hair, people had always asked if they were twins.

He looked at the sofa then back to her. "You got up all by yourself?"

She nodded, grinning mischievously.

"Are you still drunk?"

She threw a dish towel at him. "No. I have work too you know...I do have the mother of all headaches, though."

"Okay. Sorry."

She got up and poured a second cup of coffee, sliding it toward him slowly, almost as if taunting. "Thanks for letting me stay last night."

"Like I had a choice...I wasn't gonna send you home with Bret." He sat and took a sip of coffee, glaring at her over the rim of his cup.

"Brad."

"Bret, Brad, Bread...it doesn't matter. They're all assholes and they all treat you like shit."

She shrugged and lifted her cup to drink again. "They pass the time."

"Damn it all, Chlo—"

She set her cup down and stared at it, intentionally avoiding eye contact. "If you're going to lecture me, then I'll just put my coffee in a to-go cup."

He shut his mouth, letting his tirade abate before it could get a head of steam. He did like to lecture his sister, though the resulting conversation was rarely positive.

She stared at him, waiting, on the verge of leaving.

"I'm sorry," he said stiffly, staring into his cup before drinking again.

She relaxed a tick and sipped her coffee.

After a moment of silence he looked up at her. "Still..."

"Damn it, Chase," she muttered, pulling a pack of cigarettes from her purse. She dug for some time before spotting her lighter on the coffee table from the night before.

Chase followed her gaze and got up to retrieve it. "You can see whoever you want—"

"Well, gee, that's nice of you."

Chase picked up the lighter and returned to the bar. "But just keep in mind when you're picking up some guy that he might be the one taking care of you—or not—if something happens."

She lifted an eyebrow as she lit her cigarette. "You think something's gonna happen to me?"

Chase motioned with his fingers that he wanted one of her cigarettes. She slid them over and he pulled one out of the pack, twirling it in his fingers for a second. "Something *will* happen to you…eventually."

"Awesome," she muttered toying absently with her lighter.

He smiled and reached across the counter, his fingertips barely touching hers. "Face it…we don't live charmed lives."

"Tell me about it," she muttered. She looked up abruptly. "You didn't hurt Brad did you?"

Chase shook his head. "No, I didn't hurt Prince Charming."

"Don't be a jerk. He gave me a ride."

"Oh…so you remember that, do you?"

She breathed out a frustrated sigh then stood, shouldering her purse. "Gotta go."

Chase got up and followed her to the door, tucking the cigarette behind his ear. "Stop getting drunk in the middle of the week."

"Yes, Dad."

"Or if you have to, get drunk at home."

She turned to him at the doorway and grinned broadly. "What's the fun in that?"

"Well for one, I'd get to sleep through the night."

She shook her head, smiling before leaning forward and kissing his cheek. "Have a good day bro…and thanks for letting me stay last night."

He stood in the doorway and watched her walk away. "I love you, Chloe."

She turned and continued to walk backward. "Love you too, Chasey."

He waved before she turned and disappeared around the corner at the end of the hallway.

"Your sister is hot," came a voice behind him.

Chase turned and saw Jimmy standing in his doorway in full uniform. He grinned. "Careful… How would Tonya take it if you had to explain getting your lip busted for talking shit about Chloe?"

Jimmy laughed and peeked inside his apartment. "She'd give me a harder beat down than you could."

"Sorry about the noise last night," Chase said, lowering his voice.

"Weren't nothin'. I can't ever sleep after a shift change anyway."

"Yeah…why are you up already?"

"Extra hours—drug task force shit."

"Speaking of which… If you can, sneak over after I get home from work tonight and I'll make it up to you."

Jimmy smiled and winked. "I'll bring the rolling papers."

Chase nodded and went back inside. "Later."

He finished getting ready for work then rushed out the door, made late by his coffee encounter with Chloe. It was totally worth it but he'd have to face ridicule and reprimand from his boss, Frank, unless he was able to sneak in without drawing attention to himself.

The commute to work drove his tension up several notches, getting stuck behind accidents twice—he would have been late even if it hadn't been for Chloe.

Twenty minutes late, he strolled through the lobby with purpose, conscious of every face that might challenge his late arrival. When he reached his desk, he breathed a sigh of relief having run into no one who might give him grief or rat him out.

As his computer booted up, someone cleared his throat behind Chase.

Oh, shit.

He turned, greeted by the withering glare of his boss. "Hi, Frank."

"Strolling in late and all you have to say is 'hi'?"

"Sorry. Two accidents on sixty-six this morning."

"I don't need excuses, Grant. I need employees who respect the job…and me."

Chase dropped his head ever so slightly. "I'm sorry, Frank. I'll try harder."

Frank stared at him with a penetrating scowl then leaned forward, placing his face within inches of Chase's. "You are on your way out, son."

A pinch in Chase's chest at being called "son" by this cocksucker was almost more than he could stand. He could feel the heat spread across his face to his ears.

"I…"

"You what, Chase? You want a raise? You want me to give you a back rub? What?"

Chase turned in his chair attempting to hide the sudden surge of rage building on his face. It was people like Frank who made it hard for him to stay on the straight-and-narrow course of a respectable citizen—in the old days, Frank would have already been bloodied on the floor.

"Don't turn away from me," Frank snapped, spinning Chase around in his chair.

Chase's hand was on Frank's wrist before he could stop himself. His grip was powerful and the anger in his eyes produced a glistening sheen he could feel and see.

The aggressive move startled Frank who unsuccessfully tried to yank his arm away. "You lay hands on me?!"

Chase released him abruptly, panicked.

"You're on borrowed time, Grant."

Chase stared at him without comment. The tense moment broke only after Frank turned and walked away.

He watched Frank walk all the way to the end of the cubicle row and disappear before turning back to his desk. *Shit, shit, shit.*

"One of these days, someone's gonna deck him," his neighbor, Tammy said, hanging over the low partition, her breasts resting on the divider wall.

Self-conscious about every action after the hostile confrontation, Chase averted his eyes. "I wish they'd promote him or something…anything to get him off the floor."

"As long as we keep producing for him they'll keep him right here, cracking that whip," Tammy said with a sweet, understanding smile. It almost pissed Chase off that she was trying to make him feel better. And to lump herself into the *producers* category with him was a bit of a slap—she barely met the floor average.

He found his gaze drifting toward the odd placement of her breasts on the divider wall again and looked back to his computer. "Trading opens in seven minutes and I still have to load my bulk buys."

"Okay," she replied wistfully, mild disappointment in her tone. Playfully impersonating Frank, she wagged her finger at Chase. "Better get on the stick, boy."

Once she had retreated to her space, he forced his stress out in a long breath. When his lungs were empty he launched into his spreadsheets, building the morning's pre-trade bids from the analytics built on his clients overnight.

His only solace after the face-off with Frank was that Chase was the division's highest producer. He made more commission for the trading firm than any two analysts combined. He was also the highest rated by his customers. Frank would have to come up with something better than Chase arriving late if he wanted to fire him. Besides, he had a trump card—Frank wouldn't be a problem if he pulled it.

"Hey, boyeeee." The greeting was accompanied by a bumper car like collision from across the aisle. Bobby Tang was a clown and one of the few friends Chase had.

"Give me a minute, Bobby. I have to load my trades."

"Well, young man. You'd wouldn't be rushing your sheets if you'd show up on time," Bobby said, mocking Frank's blustery tone.

Chase ignored Bobby's taunt and continued to work despite the rough, shoulder shaking grab.

When Chase didn't react to any of the Morning Bobby Tang Show, Bobby rolled back to his desk and sat staring at the back of Chase's head—Chase could feel his eyes boring into him.

"Five minutes," Frank said over the intercom as if every trader and analyst wasn't already preconditioned to glance at the many digital countdown clocks hanging on the walls.

"Five minutes, son," Bobby said to the back of Chase's head.

He finished loading his sheets and ran a test insert on his numbers. As always, the numbers confirmed and he inserted them into the system with three minutes to spare.

After pulling up his trading screen and logging in, he swiveled in his chair. "Morning, Bobby."

"What's up bee-otch?" Bobby said, grinning broadly and rolling forward again.

"I don't like the way the Chinese boosted Russian oil last night."

"Don't blame me. I was balls deep in a—"

"Please." Chase held up a hand and turned his head in an exaggerated display of disgust. "I don't want to hear about your bar trolling, homoerotic adventures."

"Homophobe," Bobby said, wrapping his arm around Chase's head and ruffling his hair.

"I wouldn't want to hear about it if you were crushing vagina either."

"Coitusphobe." Bobby released Chase's head and sat back, grinning. "You should come out with us tonight."

Chase shook his head while patting his hair back into place. "Work night."

"All work and no play makes Chase a dried up scrotum."

Chase laughed. "Friday. I promise I'll do it at the end of the week. But I'm not getting enough sleep as it is."

Bobby tilted his head and squinted, examining Chase's face closely.

"Yeah...you're pretty baggy under the eyes this morning... dreaming about me again?"

Chase shook his head in amusement. "Well, that would certainly be enough to wreck my sleep. But no. Chloe showed up at two o'clock this morning after a rough night."

"Now, Chloe...she's a partier. I should have linked up with her last night."

"She could have used the chaperon."

Bobby laughed. "I suck at being a chaperon. I'm usually the enabler of bad behavior."

"I know you like to victimize unsuspecting twinks, but I've seen you with your gal pals...you can't fool me. I know you're a guard dog."

"Woof," Bobby said with a wide grin and flexing his biceps. "Though I like to think of myself as an angry guard cock."

Chase laughed, shaking his head. "There is such a thing as 'too gay'."

"I'll let you know when I reach that point," Bobby replied, rolling back to his cubicle. "They give an award or something, or so I'm told."

The buzzer on the ever-present digital clocks sang out, setting everyone into motion on their phones or computers.

"Lunch?" Bobby asked as he turned to his desk.

"Yeah," Chase said before picking up his first customer call of the day.

Once in the zone, his brain went on autopilot, answering questions, responding to needs, intuitively changing market sector screens, and winning money for his customers, the company, and himself. It was just another numbers game and he was always good with numbers—the smartest guy in the room, even if he didn't see it in himself.

That's the thing about a man who was battered into believing everything he did was wrong; He makes sure he's always right—and Chase was always right.

12:10 p.m.

CHASE punched the code into his phone forwarding his calls to the queue, then stretched, pressing the stress from his shoulders.

"You ready, cupcake?" Bobby Tang said, grabbing Chase's shoulders and squeezing them.

"Yep. All set."

Just then, his cell phone rang. He picked it up and looked at the caller—it was Chloe.

He answered as he and Bobby left the trading floor. "What's up?"

"Hey…I wanted to thank you again."

"Is that Chloe?" Bobby whispered.

Chase nodded.

"Is that the fabulous Bobby Tang?" Chloe asked.

"Yeah… Did you make it to work on time?"

"No. I had to go home to shower and change. The morning crew was waiting for me outside the restaurant when I got there."

"You should keep spare clothes in your car," Chase said, getting on the elevator with Bobby. "It stops bad choices the night before from affecting the morning after."

"I do, smart-ass. I don't know if you noticed or not, but I didn't drive to your house. I had to take a cab home this morning."

"Oh. Do you need a ride to your car after work?"

"Nah. I'm on my way to pick it up now. I'm on the metro."

"I see. So the purpose of this call is to entertain you while you sit on the train?" Chase had the regrettable habit of making his jokes sound like reprimands—or rather, his reprimands sound like jokes.

"Yeah… problem?"

He laughed. "No. But I'm on my way to lunch. So I'm gonna hang up now."

"Okay, jerk. See you later."

"Later sis." Chase hung up as he and Bobby reached the garage.

"Chase!" Someone yelled from behind him.

He turned—it was his boss's boss, Vice President of Retail Trading, Jonah Harper. Though he was smiling—and a friend—he knew he was in for an ass chewing.

He looked at Bobby, but Bobby was already grimacing in disappointment. "Yeah, yeah…I'll see you after lunch."

"Yeah. Sorry," Chase replied and turned back, walking toward Jonah. "Hi, Jonah."

Jonah was a tall man in his early-fifties. Fit, trim and impeccably dressed, Jonah was who Chase wanted to be when he was that age. The gray was just starting to show around his temples, but he had a youthful and cheerful demeanor that made him seem younger. A few months earlier, as Chase got the hang of his own prediction models and started making real money, Jonah had taken an interest in him, taking Chase under his wing at work and showering him with performance rewards. One of those rewards was "guy time" with Chase—or as Bobby called it a Spring-Autumn Bromance—sometimes Bobby was a dick.

The two men met in the center of the aisle and shook hands. "Frank was in my office whining about you again this morning," Jonah said.

"I know. I'm sorry I was late."

Jonah clapped Chase on the shoulder and turned him toward his car. "I don't understand why he has such a hard-on for you."

"I think it's because I ignore the floor trade matrix," Chase replied, preparing to get into Jonah's Bentley Continental.

Jonah looked perplexed. "Yeah...why is that?"

Chase laughed. "Because it sucks. It's only right about fifty-five percent of the time...it's almost as if someone keeps the win percentage slightly above break even on purpose."

Jonah smiled and shrugged. "Well, your accounts seem to like what you're doing. I just wish I could duplicate it."

Chase's hand unconsciously went to his key chain where his thumb drive held his personal analysis matrix and prediction models. "Keep Frank off my back and maybe one day I'll tell you how," Chase smirked as he got into Jonah's car.

Jonah shot Chase a sideways grin and nodded. "Okay, I'll try. Where do you want to go for lunch?"

"That depends on who's buying."

Jonah laughed. "Okay...someplace expensive, my treat."

"My favorite."

CHASE'S cell phone rang at 3:55 p.m. with only five minutes left in the regular trading day. It wasn't a number he recognized but he didn't like missing a call. He queued his last minute buys and hit enter as he answered. "Chase Grant."

"Mr. Grant, this is Officer Deborah Ortega with Arlington Police."

Chase's back straightened in reflex. "How can I help you?"

"You're listed as the emergency contact for Chloe Grant... your sister?"

"Oh, shit...what's happened?"

"There's been an incident. She's at Virginia Hospital Center in the trauma unit."

Chase stood abruptly, pulling his jacket on. "What happened?"

"It would be better if I talked to you in person." The tension in Ortega's voice worried him.

"I'm on my way. I can be there in about thirty minutes." He looked at his watch and grimaced realizing traffic out of DC would be bumper to bumper already. "Better make that forty-five."

"I'll meet you there."

"What's wrong," Bobby asked, clicking the hold button on his call.

"Something's happened to Chloe. I have to go to Arlington."

Bobby twisted his head and looked at the trade-day countdown clock. "Do you have after hours trades to make?"

Chase looked at his monitor and froze for two heartbeats. "They'll wait till morning."

"I can do them for you. Do you have them queued up?"

Chase rubbed his face in agitation before nodding. "They're loaded. Just check the stop losses before you execute."

Bobby nodded, worry melting his angular Asian features. "I hope she's okay."

"Thanks, Bobby. See you tomorrow."

He nodded and gave Chase a supportive shove toward the door. As he reached the lobby doors, the buzzers sounded for the close of regular trading.

The doors slid closed just as he caught sight of Frank walking toward him, a sneer twisting his mouth. "Hold on you misera—"

Chase breathed a sigh of relief as the doors closed, but then snapped to attention, every muscle going rigid when they unexpectedly opened again.

"So you make up for coming in late by leaving early?!"

"Frank, the police called me. My sister's been in some sort of accident."

Frank shook his head. "If you leave, don't bother coming back."

Chase stepped forward and placed his hand on Frank's chest. "Fine." He shoved Frank out of the doorway so hard, he fell backward out of the elevator, sprawling on the floor.

Pure surprise followed by pure hate burned in Frank's eyes as the doors slid closed again. Chase hadn't meant to shove him so hard. Anxiety replaced his anger as it hit him. "Oh, shit."

His gut tightened and he closed his eyes. *No, no, no.*

He considered going back up and try to salvage the situation, but the thought of Chloe lying in the emergency room jumped to the front of his mind again. Agonized, he stepped off the elevator and ran to his car before speeding out of DC to the hospital in Arlington.

He arrived forty minutes later, pulling into a lucky empty space at the Emergency Room entrance and went straight to the check-in desk.

"I'm looking for Chloe Grant," he told the woman behind the counter.

"Mr. Grant?" A woman called from behind.

Chase turned and saw a female officer. "Yes. What happened?"

She walked over and took him by the elbow. "It would be better if we talked someplace more private."

His feeling of dread built with each passing second. *It must be bad. Is she dead?* "What's happened?" He asked more insistently.

Ortega looked down and sighed with regret. "Your sister was found in a parking garage near Ballston around two p.m. today." She shook her head. "At first we thought she was a victim of a hit-and-run, but apparently, she was moved there after she was struck by a car then beaten."

Chase felt his legs give way and he had to brace himself against the wall. That was too much information for him to wrap his head around.

"It looks like she was left for dead," she said, gently touching his elbow for support. "She's very lucky someone found her…she wouldn't have made it much longer."

His fists clenched and unclenched helping to alleviate the dizziness as anger pumped fresh adrenaline to his brain. "I want to see her," he said, his voice hardly above a whisper.

"She's not conscious yet, but I'll take you to her. They've already moved her up to the Intensive Care Unit."

He followed Ortega through the winding corridors to the elevators and they rode up in silence, all the while Chase's worry over his sister drove his fear of what he would find. Once on the second floor, Ortega led him to the ICU, stopping outside a room in a quiet corner of the floor.

She stopped him at the open sliding door with a gentle touch to his arm. "You need to brace yourself…she looks real bad."

He nodded, clenching his jaw. When Ortega pulled the curtain back, he realized how weak her warning had been. There was nothing about the bandaged, tube filled form that even remotely resembled Chloe—he had seen horror movies with less grotesque imagery.

He closed his eyes tightly, his breath catching in his throat.

"I'll leave you alone for a few minutes," Ortega said quietly as she backed away.

When the door slid shut, Chase walked to Chloe's side. The rhythmic hiss of the ventilator raised and lowered her chest several times before he worked up enough courage to take her pale, white hand. She was cold to the touch.

"Jesus, Chloe." His words were barely above a whisper.

One eye was swollen closed, black and yellow, offering no hint of who this poor woman was. The other was covered in a bandage and made Chase wonder how bad it must be to cover it.

The collar on her neck, the multiple heavy bandages across her torso and the splints on her arms and fingers produced such a feeling of helplessness, he nearly forgot to breathe.

He found himself gasping, sucking in tears he wasn't even aware of until they choked him. "It's okay, sweet girl," he said, his voice shaking and weak.

He leaned over and kissed her bandaged forehead, squeezing her hand gently. "I'm here. You're safe now."

Is she? Will she live?

The urge to have that question answered spun him around and propelled him out of the room. Ortega was waiting.

"Is she going to live?"

Ortega turned and looked around the corner. "Doc?"

A middle-aged Indian man in a white coat came around the corner and joined them. "I'm Doctor Kapur. You're Miss Grant's brother?"

Chase nodded and shook his hand. "Chase Grant."

"I'm sorry. I know this is very difficult for you. We are doing all we can to help your sister, but she has sustained severe trauma to the head as well as deep laceration trauma to the chest…we'll know more in the morning if we can get the swelling in her brain to go down."

"Will she live?"

"It's too early to say," Doctor Kapur said with genuine sympathy. "The swelling is our biggest concern right now. If we can reduce it, her chances of survival go up markedly."

Chase nodded, unsatisfied but knowing that pressing the doctor further wouldn't change the answer. "Is there anything I can do? Blood or something?"

"I know it's difficult, but all any of us can do right now is wait. Everything that can be done is being done."

Helplessness welled up in his chest and he flexed his jaw to keep from crying more. He nodded and shook the doctor's hand again. When the doctor left, Ortega guided Chase to the small waiting area across the hall—nothing more than a recess in the wall with several chairs.

"I'd like to ask you some questions," she said, gesturing him to sit next to her.

He looked toward Chloe's room, torn and wanting to return to her side.

Ortega touched his hand. "It'll only take a few minutes."

He nodded and sat. "Did you catch them?"

"Them?"

"Whoever did it."

Ortega shook her head. "Not yet. That's what I want to talk to you about."

"Okay."

"Do you know of anyone who would want to hurt your sister? Anyone in her personal life? An ex-boyfriend, a husband, or someone from work?"

He stared at her. "So you don't have anything?!"

"Mr. Grant, I know this is hard. But please, the faster we can get some leads, the faster we can catch the bastard."

Chase took a deep breath trying to swallow the agitation. "She goes out at night sometimes and meets guys… Some of them aren't always real winners."

Ortega nodded. "Anyone recently who you might have a name for?"

Chase shrugged. "Last night there was some guy name Brad…or Bret. I don't know his last name."

"You saw him?"

He nodded. "He brought Chloe to my apartment in Fairfax around two o'clock this morning."

"Can you describe him?"

"White, five nine or ten, a little on the skinny side but in shape," Chase said, his head down and eyes closed recalling Bret/Brad's face.

"Dark hair; kind of a bump on his nose."

"Like it'd been broken in the past?"

Chase shook his head absently. "I don't know. Maybe."

"Any other distinguishing marks?"

Chase shook his head again, but then a thought occurred to him. "He'll have a swollen, split lip."

"He had a split lip when you saw him?"

"He did after I hit him. He tried to push his way into my apartment after he dropped Chloe off." He thought it best not to mention the insult that actually resulted in the altercation.

"Was there an official complaint filed?"

"No. He got up and left so I didn't think anything of it," Chase replied. "My neighbor Jimmy saw him too… he's a cop in Fairfax."

Ortega lifted an eyebrow. "What's Jimmy's last name?"

"Hall."

"I'll check with him if you don't mind. He may have noticed something you didn't."

Chase nodded. "Fine with me."

"That sounds like a promising lead. Anything else?"

Chase thought but couldn't remember anything else.

"What was he wearing?" Ortega asked as she made notes in her pad.

"Blue jeans, a black T-shirt and a dirty denim jacket…blue."

"Dirty how?"

"It just looked like it hadn't been washed in a while. Like food stains and dingy."

Ortega nodded. "Did he make any threats?"

Chase shook his head. "He tried to push his way in when he dropped Chloe off…that's it."

"Did he say why?"

Chase hesitated.

"Did your sister owe him money or something?"

"I don't think so. He said he wanted me to 'hook him up'… I didn't know what he meant so I told him to leave. That's when he got forceful."

"Hook him up? As in drugs?"

Chase shrugged. "I'm a trade analyst…I don't deal drugs, but that's what I thought."

She squinted. "You just said you didn't know what he meant."

"It didn't occur to me until after he was gone… Do you think it would be okay if I went back in with my sister?"

"Just a couple more questions."

Chase could tell Ortega was suspicious now. In the grand scheme of things an ounce or two of pot wasn't a big deal, but he certainly didn't want to invite the police in to inspect his stash—it was still illegal in Virginia.

"Is there any camera footage at the garage, a witness where she was run down, or any trace evidence?"

Ortega shook her head. "We're still looking but it appears like blind spots were intentionally found to dump her. So far no witnesses either."

Chase tilted his head, not sure he understood. "No trace evidence?"

"I know this is hard to believe, but there isn't always a pool of fiber and DNA at a crime scene. Television makes it seem like there is but…"

Chase stared at her for a few seconds before standing. "Let me know if you find anything or if I can help you more." He turned and went to Chloe's door.

"Jimmy Hall? Fairfax PD?" Ortega asked, standing.

"Yeah…he lives next door to me," Chase said, his hand poised on the door. "Thanks, officer."

She nodded. "I'm sorry this happened, but with any luck, your description will turn something up."

The last of her statement was said to his back. "Thanks," he replied as he opened the door. Chase went in and pulled a chair closer to Chloe, taking her hand in his. "Don't you die on me, Chlo."

He looked around the room and realized how much it looked like the one his father had died in—only three floors up. He wondered if he'd lose another family member in the same hospital.

After sitting and staring at Chloe for a few hours, he drifted off to sleep in his chair. As anxiety and anger twisted his subconscious, he dreamed of an anxious moment at work.

With buzzers and alarms going off all around him, he searched furiously for files on his computer that would somehow mitigate a crisis. He wasn't sure what he was looking for but was certain he'd know it when he found it. Behind him, his coworkers were screaming at customers and other traders over the phone to "sell."

The tension in his chest built, and he suddenly wondered if he was wasting his time searching when he should be busy unloading stocks. As he was about to stop his search, he found what he was looking for—a file with an icon that looked like an egg. He clicked on it and was rewarded with a stash of data that would somehow save him.

As he opened the file, Frank appeared behind him. "You're busted, Grant. Pack your shit. You're gone."

"I have to close out these trades," Chase replied, not turning to face Frank.

Chase felt a hand on his shoulder and spun around to grab Frank by the arm. Frank released him faster than Chase thought possible and before he knew what was happening, they were in Chloe's hospital room. Frank was trying to unplug Chloe's life support.

"Get off her you piece of shit!" Chase reached for Frank as the alarms started going off on Chloe's monitors.

"No!"

Chase woke with a sudden jump and blinked his eyes several times trying to get his bearings. His phone was ringing and vibrating in his pocket.

He looked at Chloe and her rhythmic, machine aided breathing as he fished the phone from his pocket. He caught a glimpse of the time as he answered—it was about 11:30 p.m.

"Hello," he whispered, momentarily concerned the noise might wake Chloe before realizing the ridiculousness of the thought.

"Chase, it's Jimmy. I heard about Chloe. How's she doing?"

Chase shook his head and looked at Chloe's battered face. "It's not good Jimmy. She's in bad shape."

"Shit…I'm real sorry to hear that."

"How'd you hear?"

"Officer Ortega from Arlington PD called me. As soon as she told me what happened, I got with our sketch artist and had him draw up the guy from last night…The picture went out in a statewide BOLO an hour ago."

"Thanks, Jimmy."

"I told Ortega I'd have our forensics guys try to lift prints from your door…it's a long shot but we might get lucky."

"Yeah, he did grab the door."

"That's great. Our odds just went up."

Chase wiped the sleep from his eyes and leaned over to look at Chloe's monitors. The dream had left him troubled. "If there's anything I can do to help find him, just let me know."

"When you get a chance, you should meet up with Ortega and go over mug shots unless forensics turns up something before then."

"I'm just worried we're wasting time on this 'Brad' guy." Chase sat back, letting some of his foreboding abate. "The only reason he's a suspect is because he showed up with Chloe last night."

"Hey…it's a start, man. That's better than nothing and doesn't stop us from looking other places."

Chase nodded. "Thanks, Jimmy."

"My pleasure, man. Anything for a friend."

"I'll talk to you later."

"Later, pal. And Chase…she'll be in our prayers."

"Thanks."

When he hung up, he felt worse. It felt more like a wild goose chase now than it had before.

"Who did this to you, Chlo?" he said, his voice barely above a whisper.

He leaned forward, elbows on his knees trying to fight the building nausea when he realized he hadn't eaten since lunch. He got up and leaned over Chloe, kissing her on the forehead before leaving the room.

On his way down to the cafeteria, he thought hard about what he could do to help find the person responsible for hurting his little sister. There would be hell to pay if he found the guy before the police did. New life or not, this was a deal breaker—the old Chase would step in and make things right his way.

He was so lost in thought it wasn't until he had been standing alone at the empty counter for several minutes that he realized the cafeteria was closed. He turned around and walked back up to the second floor where he had spotted a line of vending machines on the broad balcony overlooking the ground floor lobby. The thought of getting food from a machine turned his stomach more, but he needed something.

After two failed attempts, he got the candy machine to take his five dollar bill and punched the buttons for a Snickers. When a bag of peanuts dropped instead, he gently knocked his head against the glass in frustration.

He sensed someone behind him just before she spoke. "Not what you wanted?" She asked.

He turned and had a rush of déjà vu. It only took a second for recognition to crawl to his stress addled mind—it was the nurse who had touched him on the shoulder the night he came to say good-bye to his father.

The stress in his chest melted slightly. "No...not exactly. I got the peanuts but not the chocolate and nougat."

She laughed. "I don't think you're supposed to buy the individual ingredients."

"Now you tell me."

"Here," she said, nudging him out of the way before reaching behind the machine. When she emerged, she had a key dangling from her fingertip.

"Nice...I picked the right night to carb load."

She glanced at him sideways with a sly grin as she popped the lock and began to unscrew it. "Watch out." She swung the door open and stood in front of rows of exposed candy and snacks. "What'll it be?"

"I was going for a Snickers."

She reached in and pulled out two bars and a bag of salt & vinegar potato chips. "Anything else?"

He shook his head. "I actually came down for real food. I guess I lost track of time... the cafeteria was closed."

She nodded and dropped a couple of bills into the money bucket before closing the door.

Chase felt lighter by the second as she locked the door. *Who pays for snacks when they have the key? I like this girl.*

He watched the curve of her neck as she tipped her head to the side, clicking the lock into place. When she leaned between the machines to return the keys, he tried in vain to *not* look at the rounds of her breasts and hips beneath the pastel purple medical scrubs.

She turned and caught him looking when she straightened up. "There's real food across the street, open 'till twelve thirty," she said with a "gotcha" grin. "If we hurry, we can make it."

His stunned expression must have been obvious.

"I know you've been sitting watch with your sister," she said awkwardly as if stumbling over an excuse. "I'm not hitting on you."

He smiled and nodded, searching for something to say but she didn't give him a chance. "I'm Val," she said, shaking his hand.

"I'm Chase."

She hooked her arm through his. "Nice to meet you, Chase. Come on. Let's get something to eat."

She led him down the stairs to the ground floor and wound them through the hallways to the receiving dock for ambulances. After crossing the street she tugged him toward a pizza shop. "Are you driving tonight?"

He shrugged as they entered the restaurant. "I hadn't thought that far ahead."

"Should I order a pitcher of beer?"

He looked at her, trying to pierce the veil of her intentions. "I'm okay with tea."

She smiled and nodded before turning to the man behind the counter. "Large pepperoni and extra cheese, and two iced teas, please."

It wasn't until the man was writing the order down that she turned back to Chase. "Is that okay?"

He nodded, reaching for his wallet.

"I've got it," she said, slapping a twenty down on the counter.

He thought about protesting but realized he wasn't in the mood for the *"I've got it, no I've got it"* dance. "Thank you."

They went to a table with their drinks and she continued to smile, staring at him while their order was being prepared.

"What?" Chase asked after a moment of enduring her curious expression.

She shook her head slowly keeping her eyes locked on his face. "Nothing," she said. "You just look familiar."

"We've met before."

A crease formed on her otherwise smooth, cocoa brown brow.

Chase grinned. "It was a couple of months ago. I was here saying good-bye to my father... We passed on the stairs."

Her eyes flashed wide in recognition. "Oh, my god! I remember that."

"It made a difference. I don't know if you knew it or not...thank you."

"You just seemed to need a human touch," she said, grinning warmly.

"I'm surprised you remembered. It was such a small gesture."

She winked. "Not too small...you remembered it."

Chase could feel his cheeks flush, but was taken over by a moment of panic—Chloe was still in her room, barely clinging to life and he was across the street having pizza, flirting with a cute girl. He looked through the window to the hospital across the street, worry gripping his chest again.

Val touched his hand, cupping it softly. "She'll be okay. She's a fighter... I can tell."

Chase nodded. "She is."

"Do the police know anything yet?"

He clenched his jaw and shook his head.

"Don't worry. They'll find him... I have a feeling."

Chase smiled and looked up at her face. "You're hopelessly optimistic, aren't you."

She shrugged and a sparkle flashed in her eye. "I'm optimistically realistic."

He chuckled then breathed out some stress. "Thank you."

Just then their pizza arrived.

They ate and talked about simple things, stress free things, like vending machine conspiracies and wild caught mozzarella cheese.

"Wild caught?" He tipped his head sideways, grinning curiously.

"Well yeah," she replied, incredulous. "I'd never eat farmed mozzarella... it's inhumane. It's best to catch them in the wild."

He laughed.

"It's not funny," she said, holding his gaze in mock seriousness. "Those poor caged mozzarellas never get to run free or see the sky. It's a tragedy."

As they laughed, he stole glances at her. With her hair pulled back in a ponytail, he felt it was almost an invitation to trace the edge of her heart shaped face with his eyes. Her skin was the lightest of chocolate in color, leaving a smooth, blemish free surface to paint flashes of blush to when she smiled. He wondered if she was Indian, but Val didn't sound like an Indian name. He decided it didn't matter enough to ask, risking the moment with multicultural awkwardness.

The soft rounds of her cheeks and her naturally pouting lips seemed in perpetual preparation for a kiss. But her eyes were sorrowful, glistening as if always on the verge of crying. Something about her made him feel comfortable and sad at the same time.

When they were done eating, he insisted on dropping the tip and thanked her several times as they walked back to the hospital. She accompanied him into Chloe's room when they got back.

Val nudged him aside. "I need to get to the COW," she said, grinning.

"COW?"

"Computer on wheels," she said, her cheeks stretched wide as if some inside joke had just been shared. She logged into the computer and checked Chloe's status. "Oh, that's much better," she said, enthusiastic.

"She's ahead of schedule with the swelling…it's down a lot already."

"That's good, right?"

"That's the best. As long as her vitals continue to improve I think she'll be fine."

Chase breathed out in relief. Gone with the rush of air was any lingering guilt he felt over sharing a pizza with her—Val was a real bonus on a day with few of them.

"I have to get back to work, but I'll check in on you when my shift is over…okay?"

Chase smiled and awkwardly accepted the spontaneous hug Val delivered around his waist. When she stepped back, her cheeks were flushed with red again.

Chase grinned prompting her to blush more.

"Stop," she said, grinning.

He looked down. "I want to thank you for making my day better…twice."

She bobbed her head back and forth as if debating something in her head. "You made it easy," she said quietly before raising herself up on the tip of her toes to kiss him on the cheek.

She ran out before Chase could wrap his thoughts around it.

As his gaze fell back on Chloe, he dropped heavily into the chair next to the bed. He stared at her for a few seconds before sinking back into a funk, though less of one than he had been in earlier.

"Who did this to you, Chlo?"

WEDNESDAY
ANALYSIS

CHASE's phone rang at 6:30 a.m., waking him. He sat up with a jolt and instantly regretted it. A painful kink in his neck made him wince as he reached for his phone to silence it before it could ring again.

"Hello?"

"Dude, we didn't hear from you…how's Chloe?"

It took a second for the cobwebs to clear and he recognized the voice as Bobby Tang's. Chase sat up and looked at his sister. Her eyes were still closed but her monitors all showed strong readings, much better than the night before from what he could tell. "She's still unconscious but she looks better."

He reached over and touched her hand. It was warm to the touch and had more color. "I haven't talked to the doctors this morning. I'll let you know as soon as I find out."

"Do you need me to do anything on your trades?" Bobby asked.

Chase looked at his watch then back to Chloe. "No. If I'm not there by nine o'clock, they'll spool up with the default matrix. You loaded my script last night…right?"

"Yeah. I got it. What about your customer calls?"

Chase sighed in resignation. "Dump 'em into the queue. I'll log in remotely later and take care of anything that doesn't resolve."

"You're sure? Frank was hot yesterday after you left. We could hear him in Jonah's office screaming for your head even with the door closed."

"Screw Frank."

Bobby chuckled. "I have higher standards than that."

"I'll send an e-mail to HR and copy Jonah and Frank. If they want me gone, then they can fire me. I'll be back as soon as I know Chloe will make it."

"So…what happened to her?"

Chase clenched his jaw as anger began seeping back into his chest. "I'm not sure. It was a hit-and-run except they beat her up afterward and dumped her in a garage…they left her for dead."

"Holy shit, dude. Have the cops found the guy?"

Chase closed his eyes and sat down. "I don't know. I've been here in her room all night so I haven't heard anything new from the police."

"Man, that's just…I can't even…"

"I know. I'm trying not to dwell on it until I know for sure she'll be okay."

"What then?"

Chase clenched his jaw again. "I haven't thought that far ahead. But if he's not in police custody when Chloe wakes up and can tell me who did it, God help the son of a bitch."

"Count me in."

"Thanks." Chase's voice just above a whisper.

"Okay. I just wanted to check in. I got worried when you didn't call for the report on your after-hours trades."

"Not a top priority. I'll check everything later."

"There weren't any problems," Bobby said. "And I hope you don't mind, I used your prediction matrix to build my script last night."

"That's fine," Chase replied as a chill worked its way down his spine. "Just don't tell anyone else."

"Your secret is safe with me."

You don't know my secret, Chase thought. "Cool. I'll call you later."

"Later."

As soon as the call ended, Chase tapped out an e-mail to human resources on his phone, explaining his early departure yesterday and informing them he wouldn't be in that day either. In the note, he mentioned that he informed Frank of the situation with Chloe before he left. Though he omitted the details of the confrontation he wrote, *"Frank didn't seem to approve of my departure and for that I'm sorry. If my absence causes irreparable harm, I take full responsibility and accept the consequences."*

He tagged Jonah and Frank for CC then sent it. "Frank should like that." He leaned over Chloe and took her hand again. "Good morning, sis."

One of her monitors beeped and Chase looked at it excitedly wondering if it had been his voice and touch that had produced the response. "You're gonna have to get up if you want coffee. I can't just pour it in your tube."

The tone sounded again and her heart rate monitor picked up its pace. Chase ran to the door. "I think she's waking up," he said to no one in particular.

Before he could return, the monitors began squealing loudly, one after another and Chloe began to spasm. He ran to her side followed immediately by two nurses.

Chloe shook and twitched, her splinted hands flying to her throat.

"You'll have to step back," a nurse said as he pushed Chase aside.

Chase watched, his panic building, abruptly wondering if he had done something wrong trying to communicate with her.

A female doctor walked in and flipped off the alarms before grabbing a pad of gauze from a drawer. "It's okay," she said gently to Chloe. "This is coming out now."

It then dawned on Chase that the commotion was set off by Chloe waking with a breathing tube in her throat. It was panic.

"This is going to be a bit uncomfortable," the doctor said, holding the base of the tube with the gauze. "Your jaw was dislocated and we've wired it stationary as a precaution. Try not to fight against it too much." The doctor pulled the tube out, producing a heavy gagging reflex and a fit of weak coughing. Chloe was awake.

"Hi sis," Chase said from the corner, looking over the nurse's shoulder. "I'm here, sweetie. I'm here."

Though clearly confused, her head twisting to one side then the other as far as her collar would allow, her eyes locked on Chase. She started to moan and cry.

"No…it's okay. You're gonna be fine. I'm here and I'm not going anywhere," Chase said, fresh tears streaming down his falsely smiling face.

In a matter of minutes, the doctor had Chloe calmed and was examining her. After noting her observations on a tablet, she gave instructions to the two nurses then looked back at Chloe with smiling eyes. "You did well, Chloe. We were very worried about you yesterday. I think you're going to be just fine now."

Val had been right.

Chloe nodded and opened her mouth to speak. A dry croak came out instead.

"Your throat's going to be a little rough for a few hours. Here, take a sip." The doctor held a cup and straw up to Chloe's lips.

Chloe drank thirstily, nodding when she'd had enough. "Thank you," she rasped.

"I've ordered an anesthetic spray for your throat if you want it."

Chloe shook her head slightly, making her flinch in pain. A fresh surge of anger welled up in Chase. He stepped next to her as soon as the nurses made room for him.

The doctor looked up at him. "I'll let you two have a moment, then you should go home and rest and get cleaned up."

He nodded as he peered into Chloe's face.

"Here all night?" Chloe asked, her voice not more than a weak rattle.

He nodded, crying in ragged gasps that turned into a laugh and a thin, pasted on smile. "Someone has to keep an eye on you."

She began to cry too.

The doctor walked out, leaving the door open. Chase looked over his shoulder then back at Chloe.

"Was it Brad?" he asked, his voice barely above a whisper.

"No."

He did his best trying to hide his disappointment—the police would be no closer to catching the guilty party than they were yesterday. "Did you know him?"

"Saw him," she said rasping her answer through her tears. "With Brad…"

"So it *was* Brad?"

She tried to shake her head but she winced at the motion and the collar prevented anything but a sideways tremor. "With Brad at club."

"The Step Down?"

She nodded, crying louder. "It hurts."

"I know, I know," he said, comforting, wiping the tears away. "You're gonna be alright now. I'll make sure of that."

The doctor walked back in. "I'm going to give you a sedative," she said, pushing a syringe into Chloe's IV line. "It'll help you sleep more soundly."

"I'm right here," Chase said again, looking into her crying eyes and patting her cool hand.

As soon as Chloe started to drift, her sobs settled and the doctor looked at Chase. "It would be best to deal with her physical injuries first and that's going to be difficult if she's upset."

Chase nodded.

"She'll be out for several hours," the doctor said, chucking the used syringe into a medical waste bin with a small amount of agitation. "I suggest you go change, get showered, and get some rest so you can be here for her when she needs you."

"I'll stay here a while longer."

The doctor frowned. "I won't order you to leave, but you're emotional right now...angry. If you haven't calmed down by the time she wakes, I *will* ask you to leave."

"I understand."

"I think you should go now while she's sleeping. Get some rest...she won't know you're here and you need to get your head straight."

He breathed out a frustrated sigh then nodded. "Okay."

She smiled and nodded in return. "Okay."

He went back to Chloe's side and kissed her forehead before grabbing his jacket from the back of the chair. On his way out, the nurse at the station called to his back. "Oh! Mr. Grant?"

He turned and went back.

She handed him an envelope with his name neatly handwritten in the center.

"What's this?"

The nurse shrugged but smiled coyly.

He opened it on his way down the stairs...the same stairs he had left by the night his father died. It was a note from Val.

> *"Chase,*
> *I stopped by after my shift but you were sound asleep and I didn't want to disturb you. Thanks for sharing a pizza with me. I hope we can do it again when your sister is better...or sooner.*
> *Hugs, Val."*

Beneath her signature, her phone number was underlined twice. It made Chase smile.

On the drive back to Fairfax his phone rang.

He touched the answer button on his steering wheel. "Hello?"

"Chase?"

Chase recognized Jonah Harper's voice. "Hi, Jonah. I guess you got my e-mail."

"I did. I'm sorry to hear about your sister. I want you to know you can take all the time you need. Your job is safe."

Chase blew out his stress in one breath as he rolled to a stop at a traffic light. "Thank you."

"Is there anything I can do for you? I mean, I know this has to be hard."

"No, thank you, Jonah. I appreciate it, though."

"Alright. But if you need anything, don't hesitate to ask. I think you know I'm there for you if you need me. You aren't just an analyst to me."

Chase closed his eyes, grateful for the support.

"I know," Chase said. "Believe me, I noticed. Thank you again."

"I do have one question for you, though."

"Shoot."

"You left before after-hours trading began yesterday but your matrices are logged as run...how did you do that?"

Chase tensed. He didn't want to give away too much information about how he was beating the company averages, but he also didn't want to get Bobby in trouble for running another analyst's numbers on his own clients. "I usually have my matrix feeds built before the close of regular trading. I spooled them before I left."

Jonah laughed. "You are a killer, aren't you. I better watch out or you'll be coming for my job."

"Nah...I like having my nights and weekends free."

Jonah laughed again, louder. "Okay. Well, call if you need anything."

"You have no idea how much that means right now."

"I think I do. Take care pal and don't let it get you down. Everything'll turn out alright."

"Thanks."

The phone clicked off and Chase relaxed his grip on the wheel. As the stress over the thought of being fired abated, his mind turned once again to Chloe and her attacker.

Someone who was with Brad at the Step Down?

An impatient horn blast from the car behind him shook him from his thought and he pulled forward. At the last second, he turned right, eliciting another angry blast from the driver behind him.

He drove to the Step Down Club. That's where she had met Brad—or Bret or whatever the hell his name was. He arrived hours before anyone else, it still being fairly early in the morning. He parked his car out front and walked around to the back of the building. On the wall next to the rear entrance hung a plaque with after-hours emergency contact information. He pulled his phone out and tapped in the number.

"Spotlight Property Management," a woman on the other end said.

"Hi. I'm trying to reach someone with access to the Step Down…concerning a recent attack."

"Was someone attacked on the property?"

"No, no. Nothing like that," Chase said then balanced his tone, trying to banish the emotion in order to sound official. "Yesterday morning a woman was run down by a man she reported as having seen at the club. There was a *one-off* connection to another incident earlier the night before and I was hoping to talk to the floor manager about a description or possibly even security footage."

"Yes, sir. I'll page the owner and put him in direct contact with you. Can I have your name and a contact number?"

"Chase Grant, but I'm on site now," he said, hoping the additional information after his name would divert her attention away from the lack of an "Officer" or "Detective" preceding his name.

"Oh…you're there now?"

"Yes ma'am," he replied then gave her his cell phone number.

"Alright. I'll page the owner with your number and let him know you'll be waiting for him, Detective Grant."

"Thank you." He ended the call, worried that he hadn't corrected her assumption about him being a detective. But after a deep breath, he decided a miscommunication was easier to explain once the owner arrived rather than muddying the waters before he got the message.

He pulled up an empty crate next to the door and waited. Within five minutes his phone rang.

"Grant," he answered, clipped and gruff.

"This is Robert Herman...I'm the owner of the Step Down. You left a message for me to contact you? Something about an assault on a woman?"

"Yes, sir. To be clear, the assault didn't happen inside the club," Chase said, sounding as police like as possible—he'd certainly had enough police encounters in his life to mimic the tone and language. "But the victim did mention seeing the man in the club when she was there, possibly talking to another individual who *was* involved in an altercation later that night."

"When did all this happen?"

"Two nights ago. According to the victim's account, she left with the third man shortly before, or at closing. I was hoping to speak with an employee who might've been there, or if at all possible, see the security footage if you have any."

"Yeah...it should still be on the computer. So, you're already there? At the club?"

"Yes, sir. Currently at the back door."

"Alright. I'll be there in a few minutes."

Chase waited, worrying how he would introduce himself when Herman, the owner arrived. He was grateful he was still in his work clothes from the day before. They were wrinkled from sleeping at the hospital, but he always wore a shirt and tie to work. With the black khaki jacket, he might be able to pass for a sloppy cop unless someone asked him directly—then he'd have to be honest. It would suck to be arrested for impersonating an officer.

He lit a cigarette and breathed in deeply. It was the first one since he left work the day before, so it made him light-headed. He leaned against the wall to steady himself. A few minutes later a silver Mercedes turned down the narrow back street. He dropped the butt and stepped on it before straightening his tie.

The man got out and didn't even look at Chase. "The video footage only stays on the system for about three days before being overwritten, so if you find anything you need, we better copy it now."

"I understand."

Herman stopped abruptly upon opening the door and looked at Chase. "This isn't gonna come back on me, is it? I don't need a lawyer or anything do I?"

Chase shook his head.

Herman stared at him a second longer then went in. Chase followed him up a narrow staircase at the back of the club and into a spacious loft office above the main dance floor. The darkened glass faced down over the floor and bars. Chase had been in the club before and knew the other side was mirrored.

"Do you have contact information for the people who were working that night?"

The owner began clicking buttons on his computer but paused long enough to point at the wall on the other side of the room. "Schedule is over there. If you'll give me a minute I'll make a copy of it and write their numbers down."

"Thank you. I really appreciate your help with this."

"Ah yep," he muttered unenthusiastically as he looked at the screen over the top of his glasses.

Chase took the schedule from the wall and brought it over, standing behind Herman as he spooled up the video. He got to the last minute of video where customers were present and paused it. "Okay...here's ten minutes after close two nights ago...who am I looking for?"

"The victim is late twenties, tall, attractive, dark hair in a ponytail...she was wearing a gray dress suit the night she met with the third man."

"Okay." Herman wound the video backward at high-speed.

It didn't take long to find Chloe and the guy she left with—they were there until nearly closing time.

"Stop. That's her."

Herman paused the video stream and zoomed in on the couple. "Damn...she could do better than him," Herman muttered.

"Tell me about it."

Herman turned and looked at Chase with a curious expression before returning his attention to the video. "Well, there's the fella she left with." He looked closer at the screen then ran it forward. "Huh."

"What?"

"Don't hold me to it, but she's not moving like she's drunk...she's moving like she's drugged."

Chase looked closer and Herman ran the video back a few seconds before hitting play again.

"How can you tell?" Chase asked.

"I've been in this business for a lot of years and…there, look how she can't hold on to her purse. I'm not saying it for sure, but that looks more like she got spiked with something," he said, turning around and looking at Chase over the top of his glasses. "—like a Roofie or Quaalude."

Chase clenched his jaw and couldn't stop the tight curl of his lip.

"What now?" Herman asked.

"Roll it back. If he dosed her with something I want to see it… And she said he was talking to another guy."

"The one who attacked her," Herman confirmed.

Chase nodded.

Herman rolled the video back and zoomed out, following the backward movements of "Brad". He paused the stream when Brad pushed the check folio across the bar to the bartender. "He used a credit card to pay. I can get you his name."

"Perfect."

Herman wrote down the time stamp from the video then continued the stream backward. A few minutes prior to Brad paying his check, he did, in fact, drop something into Chloe's drink.

"Son of a bitch."

"Yeah," Herman muttered. "I knew that wasn't a booze stagger on that chick…you want me to keep going?"

"Yeah. We've already established that this guy isn't the one who ran her over. But she said she saw him with the guy who did."

Herman nodded and continued the spool backward. They followed his movements for several minutes before he disappeared out of frame, walking backward toward the booths.

"Do you have—"

Herman switched the camera views, cutting off Chase's question. "There he is."

The new video stream showed Brad sitting with two men. The angle was bad and they only had a partial view of one of the men.

"Is there another angle?" Chase asked.

Herman flipped the camera views but only had one other camera that covered that corner booth, and that view was worse than the first. "Sorry. That's the best I can do. Just wait. We'll catch them when they come in."

He sped up the video, running it faster, backward and watched. Brad left the booth and walked backward out of the frame, disappearing out the front door. The men sat there for an hour or so, ordering drinks but never moving otherwise. A second later, the men donned wide brim hats in reverse and walked backward toward the front door as well, scanning the club as they moved—still no clear shot of their faces.

Chloe came into frame walking backward out of the video then out of the club on another view.

"There goes the woman." Herman seemed to be getting frustrated.

"They followed her in."

"Wait a second," Herman said and switched camera views again and ran it forward. They watched as Chloe came in, followed a moment later by the two men in wide brimmed hats.

In a couple of frames, a fuzzy profile of one of the men appeared in the mirrored metal surface behind the bar. He paused the screen and printed it before running the video again. As they left, Herman sighed. "That's the best I can do. It looks like they were staying clear of the cameras on purpose."

Chase nodded. "That's more than I had when I got here. Can you burn the footage from that time stamp forward to a DVD?"

"Sure. And I'll get you that guy's name who spiked the girl's drink."

"Thank you."

Herman walked away and out of the office. Chase stared at the chin of one of the two men who had run down, then dumped his sister. He could feel the hate rising in his gut and took a deep breath to calm himself.

"You seem to be taking this personally." Herman startled him.

"She's my sister," Chase said before realizing he had ruined any illusion he was a cop.

Herman froze with the credit card receipt in his hand, an angry frown tugging at the corners of his mouth. "You ain't no cop?"

He shook his head. "Never said I was. But I am working with the cops. Officer Ortega with Arlington PD and Sergeant James Hall with Fairfax PD. We've been looking for the guy on that credit card receipt since yesterday." He pointed at the receipt in Herman's hand. "Sometimes they just need a clear thinking investigator to give 'em a push in the right direction."

Herman squinted at him for a second before looking down at the receipt. "If the police want anything from me, they can come and get it. For all I know, you're out hunting this girl's ex or something."

Chase leaned over the computer and brought up the Washington Post crimes section.

"What're you doing? Get away from there."

Before Herman could stop him, he clicked on the link and brought up an article about Chloe. There was no picture of her but her name was there—*Chloe Grant was run down by an unknown assailant, then transported to a parking garage in Arlington...*

Herman glanced at the article before leaning forward and reading it. He looked at the video capture of her in his club then back to the article. When he straightened up, Chase held out his phone, a picture of the two of them on the screen, laughing and drinking beer from oversized mugs.

"One or both of the guys in the video ran her over, then beat her and dropped her in a garage to die."

Herman nodded solemnly. "Okay. Here." He handed Chase the copy of the receipt. "Bradley Bowman...but if you want more than that, you'll have to get the police to come and look at it. I'm not handing over the video to you."

"Fair enough," Chase said. "Thanks for your help, Mr. Herman. Officer Ortega or a Detective from Arlington should be in contact with you soon."

Chase was out the door and going down the stairs when Herman called to his back. "Hey kid, I hope your sister pulls through okay."

Chase smiled and gave a backward wave as he bolted down the stairs. "Thanks again."

Chase's phone was out and his web search was running before he reached his car. Brad Bowman's apartment was only a few blocks away.

"Now, Brad...let's see how much you know about the guys who tried to kill Chloe."

He parked a block away and got out, dialing Officer Ortega as he walked to Brad's building.

"Ortega," she answered.

"I hope it's not too early for me to call."

"I'm already at work. Who is this?"

"It's Chase Grant. Look, I have some information for you."

"Good morning, Mr. Grant. What've you got?"

Chase got a sudden chill up his spine and looked behind him. After scanning the quiet street and seeing nothing out of the ordinary, he continued. "Brad Bowman is the guy who brought Chloe to my apartment. And it looks like he may have used a date rape drug on her."

"Okay. Got it. But how do you know he used a date rape drug?"

"I stopped at the club she went to that night and the owner showed me the security video footage."

"You have video footage of them together?"

"I don't. But he does. He said he'd only give it to the police."

"What club?"

"The Step Down... The owner's name is Robert Herman."

"How did you get Brad Bowman's information?" Ortega asked, sounding suspicious.

"The owner checked the credit card receipts for that night."

"Smart. Okay...I'll send someone out to get the video from the Step Down and get a warrant for Brad Bowman."

"Here's the thing. My sister woke up this morning and told me that Brad didn't run her over—"

"Damn... Then it's a dead-end."

"Hold on. She said she saw Brad talking to the guy in the club, the night he brought her home."

"So it may be connected."

"It has to be. There's no way this bastard just happened to dose my sister on the same night he was talking to the guys who tried to kill her."

There was a short pause before Ortega answered, presumably trying to get her head around the strange new information. "I'll still try to get the warrant for Bowman. We'll question him on any connections. If you're correct that he put something in her drink, we could use that as leverage."

"That sounds like a solid plan," Chase replied, though he had every intention of *leveraging* Brad himself.

"How's your sister?"

Chase looked down the street again as he reached the front door of Brad's building. He pulled on the door—locked.

"She's awake. That's a big step in the right direction."

"How are you?"

"I'm okay."

"Where are you right now?"

"I'm on my way to get something to eat," he lied. "Then I'm gonna shower and change before I go back to the hospital."

"Okay. Well, thank you for the information. It's very helpful. Hopefully, we can get a solid lead and maybe an arrest soon."

"Thanks, Officer Ortega."

"Deb, please."

"Thank you, Deb."

"You're welcome. I'll be in touch soon."

Chase stuffed his phone back into his pocket and leaned against the wall next to the recessed door of Brad's apartment building. He waited.

After a few minutes the door opened and a woman left the building. She looked at Chase sideways, eliciting a thin smile and a nod from Chase. As soon as she had passed, Chase grabbed the edge of the door before it closed and slipped inside.

Okay, Brad Bowman, let's do this.

He found the stairs and ran up the eight floors, anxious to get this done before the police could come and spook his target. He arrived and pounded on the door urgently. He could hear movement inside.

"Jesus! What?!"

"Maintenance. The apartment under you is flooding," Chase yelled through the door, gruff, angry. "You need to stop whatever it is you're doing and—"

The door unlatched. "I don't have any fu—"

Chase powered in, slamming Brad into the wall behind the door and pinning him.

"Hey, Brad…remember me?"

Brad tried to shove back, but Chase grabbed the edge of the door with both hands and slammed it again, hard, knocking the wind from him. Chase checked the hallway then punched Brad in the nose, stunning him before closing the door.

Brad's arms flailed as Chase grabbed him by his sweatshirt and dragged him down the dirty linoleum hallway floor. Satisfied they were far enough from the door to not be heard, Chase dropped down heavily on Brad's chest before punching him again.

"You dosed my sister at the Step Down."

"Wha…? I don't know what the he—"

Chase punched him again, skinning his knuckles on Brad's teeth. He shook his hand as he grabbed Brad by the collar with the other. "It's on video, Brad Bowman."

Chase drew back to hit him again. "Nothing happened you asshole! What's the big—"

Chase swung backward, dropping a hammer blow into Brad's groin. He curled up on himself and tried to roll over in the fetal position, but

Chase held him tight.

"Yesterday, she was run down, beaten, then left for dead in a garage about a half mile from here."

Brad shook his head. "Not me... you've got the wrong—"

Chase punched him in the face again. "The guy you met at the club. Who is he?"

Brad's eyes flashed wide and he shook his head, lips pressed together tightly.

Chase looked around for something he could use to persuade Brad to talk.

"I can't. He'll kill me," Brad cried pathetically.

Chase lowered his face to within inches of Brad's and pressed his thumb to the corner of his eye. "He tried to kill my sister. Do you think for a second I wouldn't kill you for being involved?"

"But he'll cut my—"

"Stay focused, Brad...one problem at a time. I'm here now and *I* will kill you if you don't tell me who he is."

Brad screamed as Chase pressed his thumb into Brad's socket—not enough to do damage, but he certainly felt it. "Brick Durggin. He used to be a cop. I was his CI."

A confidential informant? Cop? "What did he want with my sister?"

"I don't know man. He just said to drop the Roofie and take her to your house."

Chase drew back as if struck. "My house? He specifically said to take her to my house? Why?"

"I don't know...he didn't say."

"What were you supposed to do when you got to my house?"

Brad pressed his lips tightly as if that would prevent him from answering.

"Tell me!" Chase screamed, pressing his thumb deeper.

"I was supposed to slip you something too, then leave...that's all he said." He rattled it off so fast with such panic, it took Chase a second to translate. "He didn't know you had a cop neighbor watching."

Chase took a deep breath and let it out slowly before releasing Brad. He stood and stared into space, trying to absorb all the information in that story. "Did he mention me by name?"

Brad shook his head. "No. He didn't even tell me your sister's name. I had to find that out myself."

Chase nodded and went into the kitchen, grabbing a handful of paper towels from the counter.

"Is 'Brick' a real name or a nickname?"

"I don't know, man," Brad said, groaning, cupping his balls and rolling to his side.

Chase nodded and stepped over him on his way to the door.

"I didn't know they were gonna hurt your sister. If I had, I wouldn't have..."

The fact that he couldn't finish his sentence made it clear Brad had no plan B for disobeying *Brick*. Chase wiped the surfaces he had touched before leaving.

"Don't mess with Durggin, man...he's a rabid dog," Brad yelled before Chase closed the door. "And please don't tell him I told y—"

Why would Durggin, an ex-cop, want a douche bag like Brad to take Chloe to my place?

Chase left the building and turned back toward his car. He was halfway there when a scream around the corner set him into a jog. He didn't have to go far to realize what the commotion was—Brad Bowman was lying in the street, folded in half backward at the spine. There, growing wider by the second, was a pool of blood around the heap of meat that had only moments earlier told him the identity of his sister's attacker. *That's no coincidence.*

Chase's heart beat loudly in his ears as a crowd began to gather. A moment of panic hit him as his gaze swept around to the shops that lined the narrow boulevard and caught sight of no fewer than five security cameras.

He dropped his head and went back the way he had come. When he reached the alley leading to the courtyard of Brad's building, he turned, just as the police sirens sounded on the street.

Shit, shit, shit.

He turned at the end of the alley and made his way to his car. Once in, he gripped the wheel and tried to calm his heart rate without starting the engine.

"No, no, no. This is wrong...it's all wrong."

Chase had to assume that wasn't suicide, which meant someone went into Brad's apartment only seconds after Chase had left.

That means they were following me.

Chase moved only his eyes, looking first into his rearview mirror then the side mirrors. Parked half a block away and behind him was a dark blue sedan. Chase thought it looked like a Crown Victoria but he couldn't be sure at that distance.

He started his car and pulled away, keeping a close eye on the car behind him. It hadn't moved by the time he reached the end of the block and flipped his turning signal. But as he was turning, someone ran across the street and jumped into the car. The Crown Vic sped out of its parking space toward Chase.

Durggin.

Chase turned and pulled away slowly, pretending he hadn't seen the sedan. But as soon as he was around the corner and out of sight, he sped up and rushed to the next intersection. There, he cut a hard right, checking his mirrors as he turned. His little Civic was newish but didn't have half the engine that the Crown Vic would.

Once on the next street, he made a hard left cutting in front of a delivery van, forcing it to brake to avoid hitting him. Halfway down the block, a multi-stall car wash offered his best hope of getting off the street. He turned and drove around to the back, parking behind the equipment room, the only part of the wash that couldn't be observed from the street.

He got out and walked to the corner of the wall, peering around the edge. There, he waited several minutes, pulling out his phone and dialing Jimmy's cell phone when the Crown Victoria turned onto the street.

"Sergeant Hall," Jimmy answered.

"Jimmy, it's Chase."

"Chase man, how's Chloe?"

"She's awake…and talking. I need a favor."

"Name it."

Chase looked down the street and saw the Crown Victoria moving toward him. It had circled the block.

"I need you to find out all you can about someone named Brick Durggin."

"Brick?"

"Yeah, I know. It sounds like a nickname to me too, but the guy was a cop in Arlington."

"I'll check. Why…what's going on?"

"That guy you met in the hallway the other night—his name was Brad Bowman. And this Durggin guy put Brad up to dosing Chloe in the club…she wasn't drunk, she was drugged."

"Holy shit, man. Wait… you said Brad Bowman 'was' his name."

Damn cops. "Yeah, about two minutes after I talked to him, he decided he'd try a high dive from his eighth-floor apartment."

"Chase. You're in over your head. You need to get to the Arlington PD right now and tell Ortega everything."

"I might just do that, as soon as this late model, dark blue Crown Victoria disappears. He's circling the block looking for me."

"Looking for you? You're sure?"

Chase peeked around the corner again as the sedan parked. "Yeah. He's parked about a block away now. I won't be able to leave without him seeing me."

"Where are you? Give me the address."

Chase looked around but saw nothing with an address. "I'm in Crystal City, twenty-third south and south Eads Road. I don't know the address. It's a car wash with a Chinese restaurant on one side and an auto parts store on the other."

"Okay, hold on a second. Let me see what I can do."

Chase watched the car at the other end of the street as Jimmy's voice became muted and distant in the background. After a moment the car pulled out of its parking space and drove away.

"Okay. I had a friend in Arlington PD put out a BOLO for a dark blue Crown Victoria in your area," Jimmy said, tension in his tone.

"They left."

"What? Just now?"

"Yeah. I guess they're monitoring police channels."

There was a long pause before Jimmy replied. "Man, I don't know what you stumbled into but this don't sound like a simple hit-and-run."

"I got that feeling too."

Chase scanned the streets for several seconds before returning to his car. "You know what else is funny?"

"There's nothing funny about any of this."

"The guy in the Crown Vic came running back to his car after Brad Bowman took his swan dive…and he came out the back door of Brad's apartment building."

"You need to stop talking to me right now and call Ortega," Jimmy said, agitation slipping into his voice.

"Brad said Durggin is an ex-cop. Brad was his CI."

More silence.

"I'm not sure contacting Arlington Police is a good idea. The guy in the Crown Vic beat feet as soon as you put your BOLO out," Chase added.

"Do you want me to get the State Police involved for you? I'd come up myself, but I'm Fairfax...it's out of my jurisdiction."

"No. But I'll keep you posted, Jimmy. Thanks for the help."

"If you need anything, call."

"I will. Later man."

"Later."

Chase drove home to Fairfax, torn as to what to do next...he had witnessed a murder.

Did I? Was it really murder? Maybe I spooked him. Or maybe he just realized what a pathetic piece of shit he was and decided to end it all.

He shook his head. *Bullshit. The guy in that Crown Vic tossed him out the window.*

By the time he arrived at his apartment building in Fairfax, he was completely paranoid, checking his mirrors every few seconds and wondering what he and Chloe were mixed up in.

His phone rang and he looked at the number before answering—it was Officer Ortega.

"This is Chase."

"Chase, this is Deb Ortega."

"Hi. Did the owner of the club give you the video?"

"No. There was an incident at the club shortly after you called me...a fire. The owner barely got out in time."

Chase felt the blood drain from his face. Someone was cutting a path of destruction along the trail Chase was following.

"Officer Ortega—Deb—there's something going on here that I'd like to share with you, but I'd rather do it face-to-face."

"That's why I was calling. Something else happened."

"What?"

"The lead you gave us on Brad Bowman? Well, it turns out he was murdered this morning."

"Murdered?! How?" Chase asked, doing his best to sound surprised.

"He was thrown from a window in his apartment," she said, but with suspicion tainting every word. "You weren't by any chance near Eads Road this morning were you?"

Chase hesitated. "Can we meet?"

"When?"

Chase looked up at his building then down at his clothes. "I have to change and get cleaned up first. I can meet you at the hospital in about an hour and a half."

"Okay. I'll meet you at the hospital at one o'clock."

"Thanks."

Chase took the elevator up to his floor. Exhaustion having caught up with him, he leaned against the elevator wall and let the hum of the motors pull his eyes closed for a moment. When the bell dinged for his floor, he stepped out and went to his door. He knew something was wrong before he even went inside—only the door was locked, not the bolt. He never left without turning the bolt.

He opened the door slowly, careful to make no noise. When he looked in, he stopped cold—his apartment had been completely trashed. Someone had come in looking for something.

Someone…someone named Brick Durggin.

Near the door, his baseball bat leaned against a small chest. And though the chest contained tools that would make much more deadly weapons, he slipped his fingers around the foam wrapped handle of the aluminum slugger. Opening the chest would be noisy. If his intruders were still in the house, it would give him away.

After peeking into the kitchen, he crept silently through the entry alcove to the living room. All his belongings had been tossed to the center of the room. He looked out his sliding glass door and saw even his cheap patio furniture and planter boxes had been overturned.

That left only the bathroom and the bedroom. The doors were open to both rooms and he could clearly see there was no one in the bath…its cabinets and hutch likewise emptied on the floor.

Tension tugged at the back of his neck as he slowly moved to push the bedroom door wider. Inside, the mattress was flipped and his box-spring slashed. Drawers were pulled out and piled in the middle of the room, his belongings, clothes, and furniture, strewn across the floor—but no sign of anyone there.

He pulled out his phone and dialed Jimmy.

"Sergeant Hall."

"Jimmy, I just got home and my apartment's been broken into. The place is trashed."

"I'll be there in five. Don't touch anything."

"Alright. I'll wait in the hall." He hung up and stuffed his phone into his pocket, about to leave when he remembered he had a bong and sizable stash of pot in the living room. "Shit," he muttered.

He searched the living room, panic building with each moment he couldn't find them. He relaxed with an involuntary exhale after lifting a sofa cushion from the floor and seeing his hand carved box. He snapped it shut and continued searching for his bong.

Minutes passed and he realized he wasn't going to have time to hide the box if he didn't move quickly. Torn, he left the apartment and ran down the stairs to the basement laundry room. There, he tucked the small box behind one of the washing machines. *Safe until the police leave.*

He ran back up, breathless from the exertion and anxiety. He hit the stairwell door on his floor just as the bell dinged on the elevator. Gulping air, his heart pounding in his ears, he forced his breathing to slow as the doors slid aside.

Jimmy stepped out followed by two other officers. "Is the door open?" he asked hurriedly, bypassing pleasantries.

Chase nodded, his lungs burning from the force of artificially slowing his respiration before his body was fully oxygenated.

After they rushed past, he let his breath out in a whoosh and watched as they entered the apartment, weapons drawn. By the time they reemerged, his breathing and heart rate had slowed on their own.

"It's clear now, but you're gonna have to wait until the scene is processed before we can let you back in," Jimmy said, returning to the hallway and holstering his service weapon. His eyes were quick to flash wide and his head snapped up to Chase. "Is there anything in there you need immediately?"

Atta boy, Jimmy.

Chase clenched his jaw in agitation and shrugged, unable to convey the exact message he wanted to.

Jimmy's shoulders slumped, his eyes closed, realizing it was too late to do anything about it. "We'll figure it out later," he said, patting Chase on the shoulder.

Chase sat down on the floor outside his apartment and watched the forensic team and other officers move in and out for more than an hour.

▶◀

OFFICER DEBORAH ORTEGA sat in her cruiser staring at the back entrance of Virginia Hospital Center. The coffee in her cup had grown cold and her mood had grown cold with it. She was about to dial Chase and ask where he was when she got a call on her radio.

"Motor ten, HQ," the dispatcher called.

She rolled her eyes and grabbed her mic. "Go HQ."

"Ten-twenty-one, Detective Sergeant Carl King, Signal one I."

She sighed and shook her head in resignation. "Ten-four," she said, grabbing her phone from the console and dialing.

"Detective Sergeant King," he answered.

"This is Deb Ortega, you left a message with dispatch for me to c—"

"Where are you right now?" King asked, short, clipped.

"I'm at VHC waiting on someone for an interview."

"Chase Grant?"

A chill passed down Deb's back. "Yeah. How'd you know that?"

"We found evidence at the Bowman murder scene tying Grant to the victim," King replied, clearing his throat after speaking as if some of his words got stuck there.

"What kind of evidence?"

"Look, Officer Ortega," King said, clipped and angry. "—I'm not in the habit of verifying my investigations with patrol units. I want you to take Grant into custody as soon as you see him. Is that understood?"

"You do know his sister is in the hospital, a victim of a hit-and-run…right?"

There was silence at the other end of the phone.

"And he did the follow-up this morning at the Step Down…he's the one who hooked us up with the owner and found Bowman's name and the connection to his sister."

"If you say one more word, other than *yes, Sergeant*, you'll be in disciplinary review before the day is done…you got me, sister?"

"Yes, Sergeant."

"Good girl… The Commonwealth's Attorney is already on this one. Bowman was a CI and this Grant punk killed him to cover up his involvement in an ongoing case. It almost got his sister killed."

"What ongoing case? I didn't see anything about an open investigation in his jacket."

"On—going."

Deb clenched her jaw, trying hard not to respond disrespectfully toward the older, and senior detective—despite the low opinion she had for him.

"Besides. I don't know how you'd be able to find anything in that phone book of a record Grant has…he's a low-life punk."

"He's a trade analyst at an investment firm."

There was a long pause before King cleared his throat again. "He can change his clothes but he can't change what's inside."

"You've got the wrong guy, Detective—"

"Thanks for your expert opinion officer. I'll be sure to note your objection for the record."

The call ended before she could respond. "Asshole," she muttered.

She sat, staring at the emergency room entrance, wondering if she should continue to wait or go and find Chase. After taking the last swallow of her cold coffee, she decided to give him a few more minutes then call him.

►◄

CHASE knocked the back of his head against the wall in the hallway outside his apartment. Agitation crept up his spine along with a growing nervousness over his missing bong. He expected it to be found at any moment by the forensics team. After a while, Jimmy came out and leaned against the wall next to him. "Did you notice if anything was missing?"

"I only had one thing on my mind, so I didn't do a thorough search."

Jimmy nodded sympathetically. "Well, we didn't find *anything.*"

Chase's eyebrows shot up in unison.

Jimmy shrugged. "You can go in now and take a look around. See if anything pops out as conspicuously absent."

Chase rose to his feet and went in, Jimmy close on his heels. He searched all rooms, becoming more and more frantic when he discovered his laptop missing. "My computer," he said, flipping cushions, pillows and furniture. "My computer's not here."

Jimmy nodded, jotting it down on his pad. "Anything else?"

Chase looked around at the other techs and officers, making sure they weren't watching before mouthing the words "My bong," to Jimmy.

A crease formed in Jimmy's knitted brow before it dawned on him what Chase was saying. A helpless shrug followed.

"Nope, nothing obvious," Chase said. "But it'll be days before I can go through everything."

"They left the TV, DVD player, and the rest of your electronics except your computer," Jimmy said.

And my bong. What the hell?

"Did you have anything important on your computer?"

"Well, *yeah.* All my pictures, my porn, e-mails…"

Jimmy chuckled.

"It's not funny," Chase said, dropping onto the cushionless sofa.

"Any work stuff on your computer?" Another tech asked, stepping into the conversation, hands on her hips.

Chase shook his head. "No…why?"

"What do you do for a living?"

"I'm a trade analyst for a hedge fund."

The forensic tech nodded. "And you don't bring your work home with you?"

Chase shook his head. "I have web access if I need to do anything on the system, but I don't save any files or anyth—" He stopped cold as something occurred to him.

"What?" Jimmy asked.

"My pass—" he patted his pockets and breathed a sigh of relief, feeling his keys, his system pass code generator and the tiny thumb drive with the secret to his success, all dangling from his key chain. He shook his head. "Nothing. I've got 'em."

Jimmy and the tech nodded as the others started to move out. Jimmy lingered after everyone had left. He looked down the hallway as the rest of them walked away. "I'll be right there."

The other officers and techs waved without looking as Jimmy shoved Chase back into the apartment. "What's the scoop?"

"I don't know, but they took my computer and my bong," Chase replied, his voice barely above a whisper. "The computer I get, but why the hell would they take my bong?"

Jimmy shrugged. "Did they take your stash?"

"I didn't have time to inventory it, but the box was still here."

"This is no coincidence," Jimmy said. "And I'm telling you, they went through this place with a fine-tooth comb."

"Wouldn't someone have heard?"

"Sonya and I are both on twelve-hour shifts. We're not home 'till after midnight, and the apartment next to you is still empty, isn't it?"

Chase turned his head toward the empty apartment as if he could peer through the wall. "Yeah."

Jimmy dropped his head. "Well, shit."

"I know. They—or he—timed it so he could spend as much time as he needed going through my shit."

"That means he knew you were spending the night at the hospital."

Chase's eyes flashed wide. "Chloe! We need to make sure she's okay."

He pulled out his phone and dialed but before he could finish, it rang in his hand.

"Grant," he answered.

"Mr. Grant, this is Officer Ortega. I'm here at the hospital and—"

"Deb, I'm standing here in my apartment with Sergeant Hall. Someone broke into my place and trashed it."

There was a pause while that sank in. "Are the police still there?"

"Yeah, but the thing is, whoever did it took their time and made a mess. That means they knew I wasn't home last night. I need someone to check on Chloe. If this is related to her attack, she could be in danger."

"Hold on a second."

In the background, Chase could hear Ortega talking into a radio. He couldn't make out what was said, but got the sense she was asking for someone to check on Chloe.

"What's she saying?" Jimmy whispered.

Chase shrugged and put his hand over his phone. "Sounds like she's talking to someone on her radio."

Jimmy nodded.

"Your sister is fine," Ortega said. "But we'll put someone on the floor to make sure it stays that way... do you have an uncle who would visit?"

Chase's gut went cold. "No. No uncles, aunts, or anyone else. It's just me and her."

"Someone did try to go in to see her a couple of hours ago, but refused to provide ID. He seemed agitated...said he was her uncle."

"Someone is working hard to hurt her...and me. I'm not sure what's going on but you need to protect Chloe."

"There's something else," Ortega said, hesitant.

"What?"

"There was evidence that you were in Bradley Bowman's apartment. We need to process you."

Shit. They were going to arrest me at the hospital.

"What evidence?"

"I'll ask you this once, unofficial like so we know where we stand...were you at Brad Bowman's apartment this morning?"

Jimmy's radio cracked to life and he went into the hall to answer.

"Is Chloe really safe? You have someone watching her?"

"Please answer my question, Mr. Grant."

Mr. Grant, not Chase. She hasn't read me my rights and they were probably going to arrest me when I got to the hospital—so why is she bothering to question me over the phone?

Jimmy stepped back in the doorway, his face a picture of regret.

Shit! She's stalling until she can get the Fairfax Police to arrest me. Son of a "Bitch."

"I beg your pardon?"

"Just thinking about my problem. Here's Sergeant Hall," Chase said then handed his phone to Jimmy.

As soon as Jimmy put it to his ear, Chase pushed past him and ran from the apartment.

"Damn it, Chase, don't!"

As he reached the stairwell, the door opened and a beefy policeman tackled him, sending the air from his lungs when he hit the floor.

Jimmy ran down the hallway to join them. "Easy, man. He's not going to resist...are you, Chase?"

Chase shook his head, giving up any hope of escaping long enough to get his head around his problem. He went limp and let the cop and his partner who arrived behind him cuff him.

"You have the right to remain silent. Anything you say can and will be used against you in a court of law. You have the right to have an attorney present during questioning. If you cannot afford an attorney, one will be appointed for you. Do you understand these rights?"

Chase nodded as the big cop brought him to his feet.

"I need to hear you say it."

"I understand my rights as you've read them to me," Chase said, letting his agitation add a level of quiet venom to his tone.

"Easy Chase...he's doing his job," Jimmy said as he emptied Chase's pockets into an evidence bag.

"You can decide at any time from this moment on to terminate the interview and exercise these rights," the big cop added.

Chase nodded and looked up at Jimmy. "What was the evidence at Bowman's apartment?"

Jimmy put the phone back to his ear. "Ortega? You still there?"

Chase heard her voice, muted against Jimmy's ear.

"Yeah, he's in custody and not resisting," Jimmy said, looking at the big cop who nodded and winked in reply. "What's the evidence?"

After a second, Jimmy's head snapped up and he looked at Chase. "A glass water pipe with your fingerprints on it."

"Explain it to her, Jimmy," Chase said as the two officers pulled him into the elevator. "Chloe is in danger…enough that I'm being framed for murder."

Jimmy nodded and began speaking again as the elevator doors closed, removing any possibility of being involved in the discussion.

"You're lucky," the big cop said.

"How's that? Because my sister got run down, beaten, and left for dead? Because my apartment's been trashed, or that I'm being framed for murder by the guy who did it?"

He lifted one eyebrow and shrugged, nodding. "Well, when you put it that way…"

▶◀

CHASE was transferred to Arlington police custody and processed hours later. After photographing, processing and finger printing, he was given his call. Under normal circumstances, he'd call Chloe. He wanted to call Jonah, but he was afraid of disappointing his boss/mentor. There was only one other person he could think of—he called Bobby.

It went to voice mail. *"This is the fabulous Bobby Tang. You missed me…your loss. Leave a message at the tone."*

"Bobby I'm at the Arlington police station, I need your help. They haven't set bail yet, but I need to call in every favor you owe me on this. Chloe is in danger."

He hung up and dialed another number. He hated calling Jonah, if for no other reason than he was his boss's boss. But he had been very supportive of Chase since he started working at the firm, taking Chase under his wing even knowing his spotted past.

He picked up on the third ring. "Jonah Harper."

"Jonah, it's Chase."

"Chase. How's it going? Is your sister doing any better?"

"I think so…I'm actually not at the hospital at the moment."

"Are you okay?"

Chase tensed, not sure how to broach his situation. "Remember how you said you'd help me any way you could?"

Jonah laughed. "Yeah. What's going on?"

"Something bigger than I can understand and I need some help."

"Okay. What's happened?"

"Well, somehow Chloe's assault has something to do with me...someone broke into my apartment last night while I was at the hospital with her."

There was a long pause.

"Are you there?" Chase asked.

"Yeah...what can I do? You need a place to stay? Name it. I—"

"I'm at the Arlington police station. Whoever broke into my apartment took something and planted it at the scene of a murder...the guy the police were looking for in connection with Chloe's attack."

Silence.

This was a mistake. Damn it.

"What can I do?"

Chase breathed out in a rush. "I'm about to go have bail set by the night judge. I have the money but I have no way to access it until morning...the banks are closed."

"I'll be there in an hour with my checkbook."

"I know this is a lot to ask, especially from my boss, but someone is really trying to hurt Chloe and I can't protect her from jail."

"I'm not your boss. I'm your friend. If you say you're innocent, I believe you. I'll be there as fast as I can move."

"Thank you, Jonah. You have no idea..."

"No problem, pal. Now relax. I'll be there soon."

"See you in a bit."

Chase collapsed from exhaustion in the chair and closed his eyes. "Thank God," he muttered.

"Come on. We have to get you to the courthouse," the processing officer said then handed him over to two officers. They led him to the rear of the station where he was transported in a cruiser the block and a half to the courthouse. There he waited for almost an hour to go before the judge.

"Okay, what do we have?" the judge asked the prosecutor, a thin, hungry looking young assistant Commonwealth Attorney.

"Your honor, we have the murder of one Brad Bowman, a person of interest in the attempted murder of the accused's sister. We also have the suspected arson of a nightclub that the accused visited this morning identifying himself as a police officer."

"That's not true!" Chase snapped.

The judge turned sharply to Chase, his mouth open and prepared to reprimand.

"Your honor," a man said from behind. Chase turned toward the voice. A man dressed in an expensive suit, carrying a briefcase in one hand and a folder in the other walked into the courtroom, making a hurried beeline to Chase's table.

"Who are you?" the judge asked.

"Roger Talbot, your honor. I'll be representing Mr. Grant."

"Running a little late are we?" the judge said with a sideways grin.

"I apologize your honor, I was given the file less than thirty minutes ago and had to cross town."

"Proceed."

"Your honor. Mr. Grant was a victim of a burglary last night while he attended his sister in the hospital. He wasn't even aware of the break-in until this afternoon when he returned home. Items were removed from his home last night."

"What does this have to do with bail?" The judge asked.

"The item found at the scene of Bradley Bowman's murder had not only my client's fingerprints on it, but those of his sister…who was in a coma last night at Arlington Hospital. Multiple hospital staff can attest to Mr. Grant's presence in her room all night. He slept in the chair next to his sister's bed."

Chase marveled at the finesse Talbot used in waltzing around the subject of the bong or who it belonged to—he had made it a moot point. *Bravo.*

The judge nodded. "What about the arson and impersonating an officer."

"As the Commonwealth is well aware, Mr. Grant had already spoken with the owner of the club and left before the arson occurred. It was Mr. Grant who contacted Arlington PD and informed them of the lead *he* had discovered as well as the identity of the man they were looking for in connection with the violent assault on Mr. Grant's sister. It was Mr. Grant's assistance that gave Arlington PD their information."

The judge looked at the prosecutor. "John?"

The prosecutor began shuffling through his papers, searching for something.

"As to the instance of impersonating an officer, I'm certain that was a misunderstanding, but regardless, it's hardly grounds for detention and bail consideration, especially given the rest of the facts so far."

The judge looked at the prosecutor again. "John. I'm inclined to grant release on O.R... any objection?"

Flustered, the Commonwealth Attorney shook his head. "No objection."

The judge glared at him for a moment. "You could have saved us some time you know. The defendant is released on his own recognizance. Hearing will be—"

"I'd like some time to get a more complete investigation," the prosecutor said, clearly embarrassed.

The judge stared at him with piercing, warning eyes. "Fine…you let me know when you have it together." He banged his gavel.

Chase stood and shook Talbot's hand. "Thank you. Where did you come from?"

"Jonah Harper called my boss at home and my boss called me at home. I got everything I could on the way over here."

"Thank you very much."

"It was nothing. The Commonwealth should have done more research," he said, loud enough for the prosecutor to hear him. The remark was met with a glare.

"What are—"

"Let's get out of here first," Talbot said, guiding Chase out of the courtroom by the elbow.

When they reached the quiet hallway, Talbot pulled him to the side. "There's something fishy about this whole thing."

"You're telling me," Chase muttered.

"There's no way fumble-nuts in there would be pressing for anything but holding you on the flimsy shit they had unless he'd been pressed to do it."

Chase tipped his head to the side, genuine confusion creasing his brow. "What do you mean?"

"They didn't have anything, really, except the bong, and it had your sister's prints on it as well, and we know for a fact she hasn't been in its presence for at least two days—and a break-in at your apartment on top of it. Idiots!"

"I know. Here's the thing, I was—"

"If you're about to tell me anything that might undermine what I just said in there, I need you to think hard before you open your mouth. I'm not your lawyer...I'm Jonah Harper's lawyer."

Chase pinched his lips closed tightly and nodded. "Gotcha."

"Come on. Let's get your paperwork from the clerk and get your belongings from the police station. Mr. Harper is waiting for you."

After collecting a copy of the order and retrieving his personal effects from the station, Chase went outside and found Jonah standing on the sidewalk, grinning like a champion on race day.

"How'd that go?" Jonah asked.

"I can't thank you enough...your guy made the prosecutor look like an idiot."

"My guys are good."

"Yes sir, they are."

Jonah tipped his head to the side. "Come on. Let's get you out of here before you commit another felony in front of the police station."

Chase chuckled and followed.

When they reached Jonah's car, Chase stopped. "I haven't seen Chloe since this morning. I need to get to the hospital."

"I'd take you to your car, but it's been impounded... You won't be able to get it until morning."

Chase's shoulders slumped in exhaustion. The adrenaline had run its course and was now betraying him.

Jonah opened the passenger side door on his silver Bentley. "Come on. I'll take you to see Chloe then you can crash at my place."

"You've already done so much for me tonight. I couldn't impose anymore."

Jonah put his arm around Chase's shoulder, urging him into the car. "After the shit couple of days, you've had? Come on. I'm taking you to see your sister."

He stared at Jonah for a beat, internally debating the pros and cons of bringing his boss further into this mess. Finally, the comfort of having someone who genuinely wanted to help won over pragmatism. "Thanks, Jonah."

Smiling with sincerity, Jonah shoved him toward the open door. Chase let himself sink into the comfortable seats of Jonah's luxurious ride and closed his eyes as Jonah put the car in gear, letting the big engine wind out before shifting up.

They drove to the hospital and Jonah walked up to the ICU with him. Upon arriving, Chase was informed Chloe had become stable enough to move to a regular room so they were directed to the seventh floor. A seventh-floor night nurse cheerfully showed them Chloe's room, seeming genuinely pleased someone had come to see her. Jonah sat in the wide window well at the end of the hallway as he went in.

"I'll only be a few minutes," Chase said.

"Take your time, man. She's family."

It wasn't much of a visit—Chloe was sleeping and Chase didn't have the heart to wake her. He stood next to her bed, listening to her wheezing, bubbling breath. She had been such a beautiful girl and it had made her a target for possessive, dysfunctional assholes her entire life. She'd had no father to show her what a good man should look like. Like Chase, she ached badly for an undefined, missing *something*, leading her to be hurt more times than he could count.

She had been beaten by bad boyfriends before, but never like this—never life-threatening. With her nose broken, jaw wired closed, broken limbs, and wounds across her chest and belly, she would have many new scars to deal with—physical and emotional—once she recovered. *If she recovers.*

He leaned over and kissed her forehead before turning to leave.

He paused outside Chloe's door after closing it, staring blankly at the floor for a moment, organizing his emotions and thoughts. When he looked up, he realized Jonah had been watching him intently. "I'm going to find out who did this and I'm going to kill him." It wasn't an angry threat or an emotional purge. It was a simple, quiet statement of fact—it was a confession.

Chase waited for fatherly advice or even a lecture about "focusing on Chloe", or "accepting things he had no control over". Instead, he put his arm around Chase's shoulder and pulled him toward the exit. "Come on. You need some rest."

THURSDAY
A BRICK TO THE HEAD

CHASE woke in Jonah's penthouse guest room to the sound of kitchen noises. He rushed to put on his pants and shirt, worried he'd miss Jonah if he didn't hurry. Padding out of the bedroom, he buttoned his three-days-stale shirt and turned the corner on the large, open plan living area.

Behind the kitchen island, a woman with dark hair pulled back in a tight bun, looked up. "Meester come out soon," she said with a thick Spanish accent.

Chase looked at the clock on the oven and saw it was only six o'clock.

He nodded. "Thank you." He turned to go back to his room with the intent to shower and clean up.

"Coffee?" she asked to his back before he could leave.

He stopped. *Coffee—that would be great.* "Yes, please."

She smiled and poured a cup from a freshly perking pot. He sat on a stool opposite her, suddenly self-conscious of his appearance and odor. "I'm Chase," he said as she slid the coffee to him.

"Imelda." She had a warmth in her eyes that seemed practiced, easy.

A door down the hall opened and her smile evaporated as she returned to preparing breakfast.

"Melda...are my suits back from the cleaners?"

"They here, meester Hopper," she said, mangling Jonah's name as she walked with purpose to a stack of freshly laundered and neatly wrapped suits and shirts.

"Is my guest up yet?" he asked as he rounded the corner.

Chase smiled and lifted his coffee cup to the air. "Morning."

"Morning," Jonah said with a smirk. "Did you sleep okay?"

"I slept great. Thanks."

Jonah walked over to the kitchen counter and poured himself a coffee. "What are your plans for today?"

Chase waited for him to sit at the island before responding. "I have to see about getting my car back and apartment cleaned up."

"I saw the police photos," Jonah said after taking a sip. "That's one hell of a mess you have on your hands."

"Yeah, I know." Chase had defeat in his voice.

Jonah stared into his cup for several seconds. "Did they get much?"

Chase shook his head. "My computer and a couple of other replaceable items."

Jonah smiled knowingly. "A water pipe and some pot?"

Chase flushed red, embarrassed. He felt like he was a kid again, confronted by an angry parent over some misdeed.

"Don't worry about it," Jonah said, standing and walking into the living room. "No harm in a little natural self-medication."

Jonah lifted the top of his coffee table and retrieved a finely inlaid cigar humidor before bringing it over to the counter.

He set it down in front of Chase. "Some things weren't meant to be kept forever anyway." He lifted the lid and pulled out a clear bottle with some of the most beautiful blue bud marijuana he'd ever seen. "It's good, so you'll probably have to smoke less than you're used to."

Chase laughed, surprised by the candor of his boss. "Thank you. But you better hold on to that for now."

Jonah grinned and nodded, putting it back in the box. He grabbed his cup and sat at the bar again. "They got your computer?"

"Yeah...it wasn't anything expensive, though. Easy enough to replace."

"Anything sensitive on it...? Work related?"

Chase shook his head. "I only used the web interface to do remote work and I never save passwords."

Jonah squinted. "Nothing else important? Taxes? Bank accounts?"

Chase shrugged. "Pictures and videos mostly. But most of the good ones are online already, so..."

Jonah nodded before draining his cup in one swallow. "Well, I have to get ready to go. Senior management meeting this morning."

"I'll be out of your hair as soon as I get cleaned up," Chase said then lifted his arm. "I'm a bit ripe."

Jonah looked over his shoulder at Imelda who was still fixing breakfast. "Melda, see if I have pants that fit Chase and give him one of my shirts...not the Melvins shirt."

"You just keep giving."

Jonah turned to Chase. "Stop acting like it's a big deal. Has no one ever given you *anything* before?"

Chase grinned and sipped his coffee.

Jonah tapped him on the shoulder with the back of his hand. "You're a good guy and helping you is cheap. So don't be such a little girl about it."

Chase laughed and nodded. "Thanks, man."

"My pleasure. Now I have to go get ready for work."

"What about breakfast?" Chase asked.

"I never eat breakfast...that's for you." He disappeared around the corner.

As if on cue, Imelda slid a plate of eggs and sausage in front of Chase. "Thanks, Imelda."

She flashed him a shy smile and went about her duties as he ate.

After Jonah left, Chase went back to the guest room and showered. When he came out, there was an assortment of pants on the bed, along with some shirts, shaving supplies, and an unopened toothbrush.

Chase smiled at the generous gesture as he tried on the pants. In the pile one pair of faded denim jeans seemed to fit well enough, so he buttoned them up and took his shaving supplies into the bathroom. When he emerged the second time, he felt revitalized and refreshed.

Imelda had been instructed to take Chase to the police impound and wait until it was clear he could get his car. After filling out the paperwork, he poked his head through the door and waved at her. "It's okay. They're going to get it now. Thank you."

She smiled, waving back, then drove off the lot.

Chase was motivated again. As soon as he was back in his car and driving down the street, the most pressing matter on his mind—his trashed apartment—evaporated. He wanted to find Brick Durggin.

He pulled his phone out and realized the battery had died overnight. When he got to a stoplight, he plugged it into the car USB. The chime over his radio speakers told him it was connected. After a few minutes, he turned it on. He glanced down and saw there were six missed calls.

He pressed the phone function button on his steering wheel. "Call voice mail."

"Calling voice mail," his car radio replied.

It rang and picked up. "You have *two* new messages. First message."

"Damn it, Chase, where the hell are you? It's Bobby. Call me."

"Shit. I forgot to call him back," Chase muttered deleting the message and moving on to the next.

"Mr. Grant. This is Officer Ortega with Arlington Police. I understand you were released last night but I didn't find you at your apartment. Please call me when you get this message."

"Yeah…that's happening," Chase muttered sarcastically as he deleted that message too.

When he reached the hospital, he scrolled through the missed calls and saw that four of them had come from Ortega, one from Bobby, and one from Jonah last night before his phone must have powered down to conserve the battery.

He dialed Bobby's number. It didn't even ring, going straight to voice mail. "Bobby, it's Chase. I'm sorry I didn't get a chance to call you back last night. They took my phone. I'm out and everything's cool for the minute. Thanks for calling me back."

He hung up and immediately dialed Jimmy.

"Sergeant Hall," he answered.

"Jimmy, it's Chase."

"Man, you're just like a bad penny."

"I know. Hey, did you find out anything on Brick Durggin?"

"Yeah. Hold on," Jimmy said before rustling some papers on his end. "I didn't find any 'Brick' but I did find a Detective Sergeant Grady Durggin, Arlington PD."

"Good...and?"

"Early retirement in 2014 after being cleared in a wrongful death case," Jimmy said. "The department represented him. But as soon as he was cleared, he retired."

"Anything else?"

"He's a private investigator now, security work, corporate type accounts."

"Huh. Okay." He stared blankly for a second as the information processed. "Hey, is it odd to retire after being cleared like that?"

"Nope. It probably means the department knew something or suspected something that didn't come out in trial and told him to retire or else."

Chase nodded. "That makes sense. Okay. Address? Employer? Spouse?"

"That's all I can give you, Chase. No offense, I know you're being targeted, but I can't hand over that kind of information to a civilian. Say the word and I'll turn it over to the state police."

Chase gritted his teeth and took a deep breath. "No. Don't do that. You're right though...hang on to it for now."

"I'll give it to whoever you want me to, but if there's some sort of tie between the Arlington PD and what's happened to you and Chloe, I think you should let me hand it over to the state police."

"Not yet."

"You need to chill, Chase. I know that temper."

Chase laughed. "I'm chill as fuck, dude."

"No. You're devious as fuck. But when it comes to Chloe, don't forget, I know the whole story."

Chase ground his teeth again. *You think you know the whole story.* "Yeah, I was twelve...like more than fifteen years ago. I was just a stupid kid." He clenched his fist, sudden feeling vulnerable. "I wish Chloe had never opened her mouth about that."

"Hey man, I'm not judging you. You were a kid and as far as I'm concerned, you were being a good big brother... a psychotic Viking big brother, but still..."

Chase bit his lip, letting his mind drift back momentarily to the time he had spent in Juvenile Detention. Juvie had taught him more about violence, revenge, and getting away with both than anything else in his life.

"I'm sorry," he lied, contrite. "I just need to figure out what to do."

"Where are you now?"

"At the hospital," he said, dumping the plastic bag with his possessions on the seat next to him. "I've gotta go. I'll call you if anything changes."

"Okay. But do me a favor and at least think about letting me hand over your information to the state police. If you're in the middle of an internal PD issue, you don't want them guiding the message…you'll get burned."

"I'll think about it. Talk later."

"Bye."

Chase flipped through his small pile of returned possessions and grabbed the grainy, printed, security cam capture of the man Brad Bowman sat with in the club. He stared at it for a second before refolding it and stuffing it into his back pocket.

After going into the hospital, he was relieved to see a police officer sitting in the hallway near Chloe's room. *Finally, someone gets it.*

He checked in at the counter and after the nurse nodded, the officer seemed to relax a tick. "Chase Grant," he said, handing his driver's license to the officer.

After logging the visit, he handed Chase's license back and nodded. Chase entered and was greeted by Officer Ortega.

"I figured you'd be by today."

"I came by last night too," Chase said, not even trying to hide his loathing. "There wasn't a guard on her room then."

Chloe stirred then grunted in pain.

"Morning, sunshine," Chase said, pushing past Ortega to get to Chloe's bedside.

"Still?" She rattled through a bubbly throat.

"No. Again. I was here last night and now I'm back."

She tried to turn her head but couldn't, making her wince. "You'll get fired," she said, muted by her wired jaw.

Chase shook his head. "My boss put me up at his place last night. He's cool with it. We all just want to see you get better."

"Mr. Grant, I want you to know I didn't have anything to do with you getting arrested yest—"

Chase turned sharply. "Officer Ortega! If you have something of an official nature to speak about, we should do it in the hall."

But Chloe had caught it. Her eyes flashed wide. "Arrest?"

"Nothing to worry about, Chlo. Someone at Arlington PD had a brain fart and acted on it before thinking it through... Officer Ortega here was about to apologize to me on behalf of the department."

He turned to Ortega with an angry smirk, daring her to contradict him.

Ortega's eyes narrowed and an angry blush rose to her cheeks, but she turned to Chloe and pasted on a thin smile. "It's true. It was a huge mistake and everything is being cleared up. On behalf of the department, I apologize."

Chloe's eyes shifted from Ortega to Chase, questioning.

"See...it's all fine," Chase said sincerely, gently. "Don't worry about it. You just worry about you."

"Can't," she said through a weak coughing sob.

"Yes, you can... It's easy. Just follow my lead." He winked at her, trying hard not to let his eyes water from the emotion bubbling in him.

Ortega looked uncomfortable, shifting anxiously from foot to foot as if she had something to say but was fighting the urge.

Chase noticed this and leaned down to kiss Chloe on the forehead. "I'll be back in a little while. Get some rest," he said, softly and only for her ears.

When he straightened, he jerked his head to the side, signaling Ortega to join him in the hallway. After closing the door, he turned to her, his face only barely containing his anger. "You will *not* drag her through the shit you're trying to drag me through."

Her eyes flashed wide, startled by his directness. "Excuse me? I don't know who you think—"

"I don't know who you think *you* are, but she—" He said, stabbing his finger in the direction of Chloe's room. "—someone tried to kill her. I don't give a shit what you think you have on me. You will *not* drag her into it until she's stable."

Ortega clenched her fists and jaw as another wave of red flashed to her cheeks. "Fair point," she said through tight lips.

"Good. Now unless you plan on arresting me for loitering here in the hallway, I have work to do."

As Chase turned to leave, Ortega grabbed him by the shoulder. "That's not helpful to your sister."

His head snapped around as he jerked his arm away. The other officer who had been quietly watching the conversation stood suddenly and took two quick steps toward them.

Ortega raised her hand to him. "We're fine," she said.

Chase glared at her for a second before storming away, Ortega following close behind. He opted to take the stairs, not relishing the idea of being trapped in a box with her.

Once in the stairwell, she grabbed him again, stopping him on the stairs. "It wasn't my call to arrest you."

Chase stood there, his back to her. "No, but you sure as shit kept me distracted until the arrest was made...didn't you."

He turned to see regret melt the angry glare off her face. "I was ordered to."

"Ordered by who?" Chase asked.

"A detective."

A pattern started to form in Chase's head. "Let me guess... Brick Durggin's old crew."

Her eyes flew wide. "Wait...how do you know that name?"

He shook his head. "My time of sharing information with Arlington PD is over. If you want to know what I know, you'll have to read it in the *Washington Post* crime section after it's resolved."

He pulled away and continued down the stairs, Ortega close on his heels.

"Brick Durggin was the biggest low life this department ever had," Ortega said. "If he has anything to do with this, you'll have plenty of help nailing him."

"That's funny," Chase said continuing down. "Because so far, your department has done nothing but help cover up his involvement in all this."

She grabbed him again. "What do you mean? What does Durggin have to do with this?"

Chase looked down at her hand on his arm then back to her face. "I don't know...maybe something about him on the security footage at the club before it was torched, or Brad Bowman being one of his old CIs."

She ran around in front of him and shoved hard. "No one's heard anything about this. Where are you getting this information from?"

Chase pulled the folded piece of paper from his pocket and held it up to her. "From the security cams at the club. Bowman said Durggin *told* him to drug Chloe's drink and take her to my apartment."

She looked at the paper as a cold wave of nausea swept over Chase's gut—he realized he had just admitted to having contact with Bowman before his death.

"That's not Durggin," Ortega said, her brow furrowed in confusion.

"Not Durggin?"

She shook her head, staring at the image. "It's a shit picture, but I promise you, that's not Brick Durggin...Durggin has a serious beak on him."

He stood there, mouth open but unable to speak. He wondered how long it would take Ortega to realize the other part of what he'd said.

"Who is it?"

She stared a moment longer at the sheet but looked up with an empty expression. "I have no idea, but it's not Durggin."

"This or the other guy he was with at the club, is the one who Chloe said tried to kill her. He's also the guy who gave Bowman the roofie for Chloe's drink. And I think, though I can't swear to it, he's the guy who was following me around in a dark blue Crown Victoria yesterday."

She looked at the picture then back to Chase. "Do you have proof this guy had something to do with Bowman?"

Chase bit his lip and shook his head. "The owner of the Step Down wouldn't give me the video files. I'm assuming they burned up in the fire."

Ortega nodded. "They did. No other proof?"

Chase shook his head again.

Ortega looked down at her feet, deep in thought.

Chase saw his chance to get away before his confession sank in and turned for the door. "Let me know when you figure it out."

He was almost to the exit when Ortega ran down behind him. "Hold up."

Chase kept walking.

"I said *stop!*"

Chase stopped and dropped his head, poised to push through the door.

Ortega stepped behind him. "When did Bowman tell you Durggin was involved?"

Chase turned and looked at her. Her head tipped to the side, but it was concern on her face. "I spoke with him a few minutes before the guy in the Crown Vic threw him out the window."

Anger shaped her face. "So you *were* there yesterday."

"I wasn't the only one there. And I can promise you, I didn't show up to smoke a bowl with him."

"Why didn't you just—"

"Just what? Call? Tell you? I tried to do that with the security footage and it got me blamed for burning the place down. I was arrested yesterday—by a friend, by the way—while standing in the living room of my trashed apartment."

"But you don't—"

"No…you'll listen to me bitch about this."

Ortega closed her mouth tightly, a combination of anger and determination on her face.

He waited to make sure she stayed quiet before continuing. "Someone is coming after me *and* my sister and they have something to do with the Arlington Police. Can you really blame me for not spilling my guts?"

She continued to stare at him for a beat. "You done? Can I speak now?"

Chase shrugged feeling foolish.

"You have valid points. But you can't be out there doing our job…especially with your history."

"My history?!"

"How do you think they matched your prints on the bong so fast? You aren't exactly a model citizen."

He looked away too angry and embarrassed to speak.

She leaned over, trying to look him in the face. "You may not have done hard time since juvie, but you have a fat folder in the police system."

"I can't help it if my life attracts idiots who—"

"*Your* life?" Ortega asked. "It seems to me everyone you've beaten the crap out of has done something to your sister."

His head popped up, anger boiling. "My sister is a good girl who doesn't understand what a bad guy looks like…that's her only flaw."

Ortega lifted her brow smugly. "Her only flaw?"

Chase swallowed the angry bile boiling up into his throat and smiled. "So I suppose you're of the opinion that a woman who's attacked is bringing it on herself."

"No…I'm not. Don't forget, I'm a woman."

"Oh yeah," Chase muttered, sarcastic.

"But there's reality that has to be dealt with outside of how things *should* be."

"Yeah…well they don't teach that in school."

Ortega nodded. "True."

"Look… I want to be as honest with you as possible. But you were involved with them arresting me yesterday."

She looked down at her shoes. "I'm truly sorry for that. I tried to advocate for you, but they weren't hearing me." She looked up and locked eyes with him. "But that's what I'm saying. They saw that nearly every time you've been in trouble with the law, it was in defense of your sister…they put two and two together and came up with their murder suspect."

He shook his head. "I didn't kill Bowman. I knew he didn't do it…Chloe told me. Shit! I told you!"

"I know."

He breathed some tension out of his chest and nodded.

Ortega put her hand on his shoulder. "Now why don't you tell me what you've found so we can start looking for the right guy."

He took a deep breath and put his hands in his pockets. "I don't have much more than you already know and apparently I was wrong about Durggin."

"Let's forget the ID on the security cam printout for a second and walk me through everything…from the moment you left here yesterday morning."

He took another deep breath and let it out slowly. "When Chloe woke up, she told me it wasn't Bowman—except I didn't know his last name was Bowman at the time. I wasn't even sure his first name was Brad."

"How'd you find that out?"

"I went to the Step Down and called the number for after hours contact. The property manager mistook me for the police." He looked up. "I never told them I was a cop."

Ortega nodded, no judgment.

"Anyway, the owner showed up and took me upstairs to look at the security footage. It showed Bowman putting something in Chloe's drink then walking out with her a while later. When we rolled the video back, I saw Bowman sitting with two guys, including the guy on the printout. They had been watching Chloe."

"Did the other guys have any contact with her?"

He shook his head. "Not on the video anyway. But Bowman walked straight over to this guy when he came in." He pointed at the printout. "Like it was a preplanned meeting or something and the mystery guys *had been* watching Chloe the entire time they were there…almost like they'd followed her into the club or something."

"On the video, was there a better image? Something you'd recognize if you saw a mug shot or something?"

Chase shook his head again. "I printed the best angle we had. He knew where the cameras were."

"How did you find out Bowman's name?"

"The owner used the time stamp on the video to find Bowman's credit card receipt."

She nodded. "And his address?"

"Google."

"Then what?"

"I went to his apartment, knocked on the door. When he let me in, I asked him if he remembered me. He did."

"He let you in?"

Chase smiled. "I can be persuasive when I want to be."

She shot him a crooked smirk, eyes narrowed.

He shrugged. "Anyway. When I *politely* asked him what the hell was going on, he told me *Brick Durggin* had him spike Chloe's drink and take her back to my house."

"Your house? Did he mention you by name?"

"I asked the same thing. He said no. In fact, he said Durggin hadn't even told him Chloe's name."

Ortega nodded. "Then what?"

"Then I left. I was almost back to my car when Bowman landed on the sidewalk."

"So he *was* alive when you left him."

Chase nodded. "Yes!"

"What about the Crown Vic?"

Chase shoved his hands back into his pockets. "I wasn't thinking too clearly when I got back to my car. But it dawned on me that whoever killed Bowman must have followed me to his apartment. That's when I saw the guy leave Bowman's building and climb into the Crown Vic. He followed me but I lost him."

"Lost him how?"

"I drove into a car wash and called Sergeant Hall in Fairfax. I told him someone was following me and he put out a BOLO. A minute later, the guy took off like he'd heard the call."

"BOLO's don't go out over the radio unless it's an emergency. They go over a messaging system in the cars."

He furrowed his brow. "So the Crown Vic was an actual police car?"

Ortega shrugged. "It'd be easy to find out. We don't have many left on the force. Arlington switched to the Ford Police Interceptor when the Crown Vic went out of production."

He shrugged.

"What happened then?" she asked.

"I went home to change and found my apartment trashed. That's when you had me arrested."

She narrowed her eyes for an instant, but then she seemed to dismiss the jab. "And what were you planning on doing now that you're out of jail?"

"I was going to see what I could find out about Brick Durggin."

She took a deep breath and nodded. "Okay...can you hold off long enough for me to change into some civilian clothes?"

Chase's eyebrows shot up. "What?"

"You're a civilian—granted, a civilian in an odd bind between the law and a crime—but a civilian nonetheless. You need someone in law enforcement with you."

"No disrespect, and thank you for the offer, but I don't feel comfortable with that."

A crooked smile lifted her cheek. "No disrespect to *you*, but I'm not giving you a choice... you admitted to being in Bowman's apartment before he was killed. I'll arrest you if you don't wait for me." She stood there, grinning at him.

Chase shook his head. "I knew it was a mistake to talk to you."

She patted him on the shoulder. "Just think of me as your alibi if anyone else dies."

"Yeah," he muttered turning for the door. "That only works if I don't actually kill anyone."

"What was that?"

"Nothing."

▶◀

CHASE sat in Officer Ortega's living room and glanced from wall-to-wall as she changed clothes. Her apartment was small compared to his but it was tidy. Hanging on the walls and arranged in frames on various surfaces around the apartment were photos of her family—lots of cops. Judging by the pictures, Chase figured she was the fourth generation to carry a badge.

"I need to make a call before we go," she said as she emerged from the bedroom wearing a pair of jeans and a long sleeved sport shirt under a blazer, feminine but not frilly.

"Wow."

She stopped mid-stride and looked at him. "What?"

"You were right…you are a woman."

She smirked. "Give me a second."

She slipped her service weapon and holster into her waistband as she dialed the phone on the kitchen bar.

She had a short conversation in Spanish then hung up. Chase hadn't understood anything she'd said except "Durggin". He wondered how an officer could simply take a day off for a personal investigation. As he watched her grab her purse and keys, he decided he should ask.

"You ready?" she asked.

"Who was that on the phone?"

She tipped her head slightly and grimaced. "Nosy much?"

"You inserted yourself into my investigation—"

"*Your* investigation? *You* don't have an investigation."

He lifted his eyebrows and nodded. "And you coerced a confession from me without reading me my rights, so…"

She shrugged and shook her head. "So what?"

"So I might not speak the language, but I don't think 'Durggin' is Spanish for 'pick up some milk on your way home'."

Her eyes narrowed and she glared at him for a beat, but then nodded. "My uncle… he's my sergeant."

"Oh! Nepotism in the Arlington PD."

"I can't just take off whenever I want. I had to tell someone."

"And he's okay with you doing a detective's job, looking for a murder suspect?"

She shouldered her purse and turned for the door. "He told me to be careful."

He followed her out and down to the parking lot. "So why would he be okay with it?"

"I told you... If Durggin is involved in this, you'll have lots of support from the PD."

"Then why don't we just go and talk to the detective in charge?"

She stopped before reaching his car and turned sharply. "One... the detective in charge is the one who ordered *your* arrest. *Two,* if we went to him, I'd *have* to report your admission to being in Bowman's apartment."

"And three?"

"What?"

Chase smiled. "I appreciate your enthusiasm here, but honestly, you aren't fooling anyone. This is personal."

"Shut up and unlock the door."

Chase drove them out of Ortega's apartment complex and down Columbia Pike toward Bowman's apartment building.

"What are we looking for at Bowman's apartment?" Chase asked as they neared.

"Why ask me? It's your investigation."

He grinned and glanced at her from the corner of his eye. "My goodness you get snarky when you're out of uniform."

"You haven't seen m..."

"What?"

She shook her head. "Never mind."

He laughed. "You were getting ready to make a joke about getting out of your uniform...weren't you."

She stared forward, stone-faced.

"Admit it. You were going to bump me down a notch with a naked joke."

"Shut up and drive."

Chase laughed. "I'll bet you're super fun when you're off duty."

"One more word and I'm gonna show you how much fun I can be."

"That almost sounds like a proposi—"

She punched him in the arm.

"Ow! Shit!" He grabbed his shoulder. "I'm driving here."

"I warned you."

"No. You said you'd show me how much fun you—"

She punched him again.

"Jesus! That hurts. Stop it."

"Want to go for it again?"

Chase closed his mouth and drove in silence the rest of the way to Bowman's building. They drove to the twelve-story apartment structure with storefronts on the ground level and Chase began looking for a parking spot.

"Where was the Crown Vic parked?" Ortega asked.

"Around back. The 14th Street side."

"Where did he fall?"

Chase swiveled his head as they passed Fern Street. "Right there…in front of the donut shop."

She looked down the street and tapped his shoulder with the back of her hand. "Grab that spot there. We'll walk around outside first."

"Ow," Chase muttered.

She smirked at him as he pulled into the spot.

"What now?" he asked as they got out and crossed the street on foot.

"I want to see where you and the Vic were parked."

Chase shrugged and led her past the shops along Fern Street to the back side of the building. The quiet, less heavily traveled 14th street made it the perfect spot to stay out of sight—the main reason Chase had decided to park there the day before.

"Where were you?" Ortega asked.

Chase pointed at the spot next to the service alley. "There."

"And where was the other car?"

He walked to the corner, pointing across the street and down one block toward the back entrance of a two-story industrial complex. She walked past him without a word.

"Where are you going?"

"To take a look," she replied over her shoulder.

He hurried to catch up. When they got to the space where the Crown Victoria had been parked, she stopped and did a slow three hundred sixty degree scan of the area. Her eyes locked on something at the back of the industrial building.

"Come on," she said, walking toward it.

Chase followed feeling confused. When they arrived at the back of the building, she knocked on the steel door.

The intercom at the door chimed. "Yeah?" answered a man with a bored tone.

She stepped back and looked up. That's when Chase noticed the camera.

"I need to talk to someone about this security camera," she said.

"You'll have to make an appointment at the business offices on Kent Str—"

"I need to talk to someone about this security camera," she repeated, holding her badge up to the lens.

A few seconds passed and the lock buzzed open. In the doorway stood a fierce looking security man wearing khakis, a short sleeved sport shirt and a hat with a security logo. "How can I help you."

"There was an incident across the street yesterday and your security camera may have recorded something useful," Ortega said. "We'd like to take a look if you have a recording."

He pulled a radio from his belt. "HQ, sentry five."

"Go," came the reply over the radio.

"Arlington PD at west door eight wants to look at footage from the security camera."

There was a short pause. "Roger...pertaining to what?"

The guard turned his back on Ortega. "The jumper across the street yesterday."

After another short pause, the radio cracked again. "Roger. Take them to the surveillance room. I'll meet you there."

"Roger," he said then turned to Ortega. "Follow me."

They walked through the warehouse, stacked to the ceiling with crates, boxes, and even a few shipping containers. Down an open corridor, Chase could see through to the other side of the building. Men in hard hats loaded pallets of boxed supplies into trucks with forklifts.

"Busy. What do you do here?" Chase asked.

"I'm security."

"I know. I mean what does the company do?"

The guard looked up at the floor to ceiling racks of equipment then back to Chase. "I'm security."

Chase nodded with a thin smile.

"Right here," the man said after turning into a lower ceilinged office space and opening the door for them.

Inside, the walls were lined with video screens and computer racks. Ortega whistled. "Wow. Impressive."

"Thanks." A man walked through a door on the other side of the room and extended his hand. "Albert Boxer. I'm head of security here."

"This is Chase Grant and I'm Deborah Ortega, Arlington PD."

Chase smiled inwardly at the subtle arranging of the names so that it sounded like they were both with the PD. She showed him her badge and ID.

Boxer looked at them for a beat then nodded, turning toward the table-top control center. "What camera were you interested in?"

"Any facing west that might have video of fourteenth street," Ortega said.

Boxer nodded and sat at the keyboard. "Time?"

Ortega turned to Chase. He wasn't prepared and fumbled for an answer. "Oh. Uh…let's see. It was between quarter to eight and eight thirty. I didn't check the—Oh! Hold on." He pulled his phone out and checked the time of his call to Ortega, working forward for a better estimate. "Yeah…about eight thirty."

Boxer went to work dialing up the various video screens. This was a high-tech system. It looked more like a small TV control room than an industrial surveillance system.

"What do you do here?" Chase asked Boxer.

"I'm security," he replied without turning from his work.

Chase opened his mouth to refine his question but then realized he was getting the identical responses he had from the other guard. He shut his mouth.

Several moments went by as Boxer refined his search, inexplicably shutting off screens due to some unknown trigger, only to turn them back on a few seconds later. Chase realized he was manually "redacting" video footage as he spooled it.

"We're pretty close to the airport here, aren't we?"

"Yep," Boxer said absently as he continued to isolate footage from the west facing cameras.

"And the Pentagon."

Boxer paused the video feed and turned slowly. He shot Chase a bored look. "Your point?"

An elbow to Chase's ribs from Ortega halted his unspoken accusation of the massive industrial structure being some sort of pseudo-military-commercial hybrid.

Chase shook his head. "Just trying to get my bearings," he lied. "I didn't mean to interrupt you. Go on." He shooed Boxer with a couple of lazy flicks of his fingertips.

Boxer continued to stare at him.

"I'm sorry. Really…go on."

Boxer slowly turned back to his work and began a data dump. After a few moments he pulled a thumb drive out of the console and handed it to Ortega, glancing harshly at Chase from the corner of his eye. "This is everything from forty-five minutes before to forty-five minutes after the time your boy here says was the target time frame."

She took the thumb drive and looked at him curiously.

Boxer turned off all the monitors. "Those are full records with the exception of two time periods with rolling blackouts on four of the cameras. If you want those, you'll have to come back with a warrant."

"Can't we just look at the—?" Ortega began.

"That's all I can do for you. I'll have to ask you to leave now."

"Thank you for your help." Ortega grabbed Chase by the arm and guided him to the door. Her tight grip, and the fingernails that dug into his flesh alluded to her anger toward him.

Halfway through the building, the first security guard only steps behind, Chase jerked his arm free from Ortega's grasp. "Thanks, but I'm okay to walk."

His sarcasm drew a sharp glare from her, but she remained silent until they were outside and the steel door closed behind them.

She turned to him, her finger raised in his face. "You really are a piece of work."

He smiled then looked up at the camera, waving at the lens.

Her head followed his gaze. "Come on." She stomped away.

He shrugged at the camera and followed, keeping his distance until they were back at Bowman's building. There, she reached into her purse and withdrew nitrile gloves, handing a pair to him.

Chase looked down. "What are these for?"

"We don't want to contaminate the crime scene."

He stopped walking abruptly. "I'm not going in there. I'm not going to get caught going into his apartment."

"Suit yourself," she said over her shoulder, walking away.

He ran to catch up. "Why are you going up there?"

"To look for evidence." She wouldn't look at him.

Chase grabbed her by the arm and spun her around. "You aren't thinking clearly."

She yanked her arm free and tried to pin Chase's wrist in a standard police restraining move. Chase turned and spun out of it, backing away several feet.

She stepped toward him again, angry.

"Stop! You need to stop now." He put his hand up in warning. "I don't think you've thought this through."

She stopped her aggressive drive but pointed at him. "I'm this close to arresting you."

Chase shook his head but kept his hands in front of him. "I know this is personal for sure now… you weren't this hotheaded befo—"

"Hotheaded?!" She lurched toward him again. "I'll show you hotheaded."

"That's it. I'm gone. Find your own ride back." He turned and left, walking in the opposite direction toward his car.

He was nearly to the corner when he heard footsteps running toward him. He stopped and took a defensive stance half expecting to be tackled from behind.

"Hold on," Ortega said jogging toward him. "I'm sorry. You're right, you're right…"

"I'm right about what? It being stupid for me to go upstairs or that this is personal?"

She took a deep breath and let it out slowly. "Brick Durggin shot a cop…a good cop."

Chase's eyes flashed wide. "And the department represented him?"

Ortega nodded. "Durggin gave some bullshit story about a dirty cop working for a cartel here in Arlington. He said he followed this supposedly *dirty* cop and caught him providing security for a shipment."

"So this dirty cop got caught and Durggin shot it out with him?"

Ortega dropped her gaze and nodded. "Except he wasn't a dirty cop."

"And you knew this cop? The dirty one who got killed?"

Her head snapped up. "He wasn't dirty! Durggin is a lying, filthy piece of shit—"

Chase's hands went up defensively. "Okay, okay. But you knew him?"

"He was my cousin."

A family of cops.

Chase stood there, mouth agape and unable to speak. *This is too convoluted. There's no way it's a good thing I'm here with her.* "So, what do we do now?"

She shrugged. "If the official investigation has been tainted, then there won't be any evidence of Brick Durggin in the apartment. If it hasn't been tainted, all the viable evidence has already been collected."

He stood there for a second trying to decide if the more reasonable Deb Ortega in front of him was who he was working with, or if it was the hotheaded angry cop playing nice-nice. She seemed unstable which in the best of circumstances would be bad, but he was trying to clear his name.

He pointed at her pocket. "We have an hour and a half of video that may show who was here besides me… No one else has that."

She pulled the thumb drive from her pocket. "We need a computer."

"I need to replace mine anyway. There's a computer store across the street. Let's go."

She nodded and followed. Chase began having second thoughts about the benefit of a cop on his *team*—particularly a hotheaded cop with a personal interest in the case.

"Is my case gonna be compromised by you doing this?" Chase asked after a moment.

He looked over his shoulder when she didn't reply.

She looked up, worried. "I'm thinking."

"That doesn't bode well for me," he muttered.

"If I find anything, I'll turn it over to IA."

"And you think Internal Affairs is going to just forget the fact that you took the day off to help a murder suspect find an ex-cop who left the force under questionable circumstances?"

More silence.

"Take your time," Chase said with snide impatience. "It's not like we're in a hurry or anything."

"You really are a smart-assed prick."

"Only with authority figures," Chase said, a crooked smile breaking across his face.

"Ah…daddy issues."

Chase stopped cold and turned, glaring at her. "I'll make you a deal; you don't bring up my dysfunctional bullshit and I won't bring up you being off your meds."

She grinned. "So touchy. I hit a nerve."

"Bipolar freak," Chase muttered resuming his journey to the stores across the street.

"What was that?"

He looked over his shoulder. "I said, 'bipolar freak'."

She laughed. "You forget that I'm trying to help clear you."

He stopped and turned to her again. "No. You're trying to nail the guy who killed your cousin. Helping me is just a byproduct of that."

She shrugged. "As long as it has the same outcome, does it matter?"

"I'm still trying to decide."

"Well, while you're deciding, do you mind getting out of the street?"

He looked to the side and realized he was in the middle of Elm. He resumed his march toward the computer store. "What if the video isn't of Durggin? What if Brad Bowman was lying, covering for someone else?"

"Well, if you questioned him effectively that won't be the case, will it?"

Chase shook his head, hopelessness welling up in him. The closer he got to seeing the security video from the military contractors the more he felt he was making a mistake.

If it doesn't show Durggin...if it shows someone else, will she stop helping? Will she flip and arrest me again?

After purchasing a new laptop and a car plug accessory, they returned to his Civic and unboxed it. He tethered to his phone's Internet connection then downloaded a suitable video player for the files on the thumb drive.

Chase loaded the file and began watching. "Okay, here's the parking space he was in. It's empty at the beginning of the feed, so unless it's in the blackout part of the recording, we should be able to get at least a shot of the license plate."

"Can you zoom in? It's too far to see."

"I can't on this viewer, but the video is high-def, so if there's anything worth seeing we'll be able to zoom once I can load some better software."

Ortega nodded as Chase ran the video through at high-speed. After a few minutes, Chase's car appeared further up the street and though the view was too small to see any detail, he could tell it was him who got out and went around the corner.

Ortega said nothing. Her gaze was locked on the empty parking space. A few moments later, a dark blue Crown Victoria pulled into the frame but parked so that the license plate was obscured by the car behind it.

"Shit. He wasn't parked as far back as I thought he was," Chase said.

"It's fine. When he leaves we should have a clear shot of the rear plate."

The man sat, watching Chase's car and the building for several minutes, then got out and crossed the street. Ortega pushed Chase's hands away from the keyboard and rewound the stream before playing it forward again at normal speed.

She leaned closer to the screen. "No."

"No what?"

She stopped the video and rewound it once more before hitting play. She shook her head, slowly at first but then more aggressively. "No, no, no." It was clear, her mind didn't want to accept what her eyes were telling her.

"What? Tell me what's going on?"

"That's not Durggin," she said, pulling the thumb drive from the computer.

He snatched it from her hand. "Who is it?"

She glared at him on the edge of anger.

"Who?!"

"I'm not sure. Let's go get something to eat. I'm starving," she said, relaxing her expression and attempting a slim smile. "I'll tell you over lunch."

"No. We have video here showing who probably killed Bowman. I want to watch it."

"It just got real complicated and we have to think about what we're going to do next."

Chase stared at her for a beat then tucked the thumb drive into his pocket. "Fine...but you're buying. I just hit the daily spending limit on my card with this computer."

►◄

"Okay, I'm listening," Chase said as he and Ortega sat for lunch.

It was late in the afternoon and the pizza shop was empty except for them and the woman at the counter.

"We can't just go to the department *or* Infernal Affairs with this," she said, toying with the straw in her drink. "We'll get heat from both sides."

He wondered if she had said "infernal" on purpose or if it were a Freudian slip. "Who is on the video?"

She looked up at him, obviously having trouble deciding what she would say. "I need to tell you the whole story."

"It's been my experience that if you have to tell a story to answer a simple question, it's going to involve a lot of subjective fact qualifying."

She reached over and placed a gentle but restraining hand on his arm, pleading in her eyes. "Hear me out."

He hovered, half out of his seat but then dropped down heavily. "Fine. Tell me your story."

"My cousin, Gabe, was a detective…a new detective. He'd only just been brought up from patrol after working hard for years to make detective. Heath was his partner."

"What does this have to do with—?"

She raised her finger to her lips, silencing him. "The entire department hates Durggin and loves—or at least has deep allegiance to Gabe's partner, Bruce Heath."

"What does that have to do with the video?" He said, anger raising his voice above the conversational level.

She looked around to see if anyone had heard or was paying attention. "I'm not sure. I won't be sure until I can have the video forensically analyzed."

"We have to turn it over."

"Not until we have something more solid. If we go in too early, sides will be drawn. And if you thought someone was trying to set you up before, just wait until they find out you're involved in this mess. If it's someone who works for Durggin, IA will be all over your ass, combing through everything you've done for the last two years, and if it's someone connected to Gabe… well, let's just say you won't be able to drive from point A to point B in this city without a police stop ever again."

Any benefit to having a cop working with him just evaporated—for the moment anyway. He could work the edges of this investigation with a cop hanging over his shoulder, but only if the cop wasn't breaking the law too—and this cop seemed to be willing to break every rule for personal reasons. Exploitable, yes, but so dangerous to Chase's future.

He leaned back in the booth and rubbed his face in frustration. "Cops…god damn it."

"It's complicated."

"Who's on the video?" Chase asked squinting at her.

"I don't know."

Chase leaned forward and pounded the table. "Who's on the god damn video?!"

"It *could be* Heath." She wouldn't meet his gaze, speaking down to the table.

Chase could feel his anger rising. "So your cousin's ex-cop partner is the guy who met with Brad Bowman and dosed my sister?"

She just stared at him for a second then returned to toying with her straw. "Can I tell you the story or not?"

Chase's eyes narrowed to slits, balanced on the edge of leaving, then he sat back abruptly. "Finish your story."

"Gabe and Heath were working cartel linked gang activity. Every time vice had a lead, they'd show up and nothing was there…no matter how solid the lead."

"And the department thought it was your cousin—Gabe—who was ratting them out."

She shook her head. "No. That's the thing. No one knew who was giving the cartels help, but they all suspected Durggin since most of the leads came from his CIs. No one was looking at Gabe until the shooting."

"What happened?"

"An informant said there was a transfer of money, weapons, and drugs going on right there, right then and they needed to hurry. They were worried about being blown again so the Captain notified a team himself, no radio, no phone calls…word of mouth only."

"Paranoid."

She nodded and took a sip of her drink. "So they scrape together this rapid response unit using no electronic communications and keeping only those involved in the loop. When they get there, there's already a shootout going on inside. They assaulted the house and inside they find two dead gang members, a wounded lieutenant from the Beltrán-Leyva Cartel, my cousin, and Durggin, laying on the floor bleeding out."

"So Durggin was shot too?"

"Yeah, but he said he followed Gabe there, thinking he was the one working with the cartel."

"What happened to everyone else? Any witnesses?"

"Two of the gang members died on the scene…the rest got away. The cartel rep was already wanted so after he was moved out of the hospital he stood trial for another murder."

"So you had a witness?!"

She shook her head. "He was offered a deal but turned it down. Mexican cartel guys don't roll on anyone…jail is vacation compared to what would happen if they rat anyone out."

Chase chewed on his lip and stared vacantly at the wall. "I don't get it. It was Heath and Gabe's informant who created the lead right?"

"No…that's the thing. It was Durggin's CI."

"Bowman?"

She shook her head. "No. Someone else. But Gabe had already told the Captain he thought he knew who was selling information to the cartel. The Captain told him and Heath to keep a lid on it until they had proof."

"Durggin?"

"That's what we think, but the Captain would never come off the info. Gabe and Heath had something on Durggin, but when it came time for the hearing, Heath couldn't lay his hands on the evidence…he said Durggin must've gotten wind of it and stolen it."

"So Durggin got away clean?"

"Worse…they found numbered bank account information on Gabe when they searched his body. It supported Durggin's claim that he had suspected Gabe and followed him to the meeting. That also explained how he was there when no one else knew."

"And your cousin's partner left the force out of…what? Grief? Anger?"

She shrugged. "He never talked to anyone about it. He just dropped his badge on the Captain's desk the day of the hearing and walked out. No good-byes, no nothin'."

"So did anything change after that?" Chase asked. "I mean. After Durggin was gone, did the cartel information start panning out again?"

"Yeah. Big time. Within a year we had crippled the cartel's presence in the county and all but drove the connected gangs out."

"Awesome."

"No. The Juárez Cartel was right there to fill the power vacuum. They had as much to do with Beltrán-Leyva vanishing as we did."

"You need to tell someone."

"I will."

"When?" Chase asked, incredulous. "My sister is lying in the hospital. She nearly died over this bullshit."

"Don't you want to know why they targeted your sister? And *you*?"

He took a deep breath, trying to resist her logic, but in his heightened state, just the offer of helping find the person responsible for hurting his sister was more temptation than he could withstand. "Before I agree, tell me what you're going to do."

"I'm going to find out who's on this tape and confront him."

"Are you nuts?"

She smiled. "I'm a cop. I'm not stupid. I won't be alone and it'll be done on my terms."

Chase shook his head. "That's awful presumptuous of you. What makes you think I'll go with you to face down an ex-cop or a cartel guy?"

She laughed. "What makes you think I was talking about you?"

Chase's feelings were hurt. He wasn't really planning on saying no, he just didn't like the idea of being volunteered.

Ortega stretched her hand across the table. "Give me the thumb drive and go home. From what I understand, you have a mess to clean up anyway."

"No...the thumb drive stays with me until I can make a copy. It's my only proof that someone besides me went into Bowman's building."

"Fair enough," she replied. "Make a copy when we go back out to your car. You deserve that much peace of mind."

"Alright. Let's go then."

Ortega leaned forward and picked up her fork. "I'm hungry. I'm going to eat my lunch now."

Chase pushed his plate toward her. "You can have mine too. I've lost my appetite."

▶◀

After copying the contents of the thumb drive to his new laptop and dropping Ortega off at home, Chase stopped at the hospital to check on Chloe. The officer there said no one had come to visit since he and Ortega had left that morning, letting Chase relax a little more after the intense day of clue hunting.

Chloe had taken a bad turn during the day, though and was unconscious again. Infection had sneaked in and the swelling in her brain was increasing once more. He sat with her until dark.

Shortly after the evening shift change, nurse Val walked in and put her hand on his shoulder, stirring him from a light doze. "Hi," she said quietly.

Chase smiled. "Hi."

"I'm sorry there's been a setback," she said, squeezing his shoulder gently.

Chloe stirred and Chase got up, nodding toward the hallway. She followed him out and closed the door quietly behind them.

"How are you?" He asked.

"I'm fine," she said, a curious grin spreading across her face. "How are you? You're the one with a crazy life right now."

"Heard about that, did you?"

"Your apartment getting broken into? Yeah."

He grinned. "You didn't hear about me getting arrested?"

Her brow creased hard in confusion. "Arrested? When?"

"Yesterday. The guy the police was looking for was thrown from his eighth-floor apartment…and they came looking for me."

"I hope you had a good alibi." Her hopeful expression couldn't mask her distress.

"Not as good as I'd have liked, but the police were acting on bad info…so was the prosecutor."

"Wait. So you're ou—"

He shook his head. "It's stupid. And it's all taken care of now."

She nodded, seemingly relieved but with a lingering doubt in her eyes.

"The really dumb thing is I'm the one who told the police he wasn't the one who hurt Chloe…he just met with the guy who did."

Her eyebrows rose high. "So they know who did it?"

Chase took a deep breath. "It's complicated. But they're working on it." Chase didn't have the energy to go through the whole convoluted story. He just wanted to relax in his own bed—and even if he left then, it would still be hours before he'd be able to sleep.

She nodded. "As long as they catch him…that's all that matters." She cupped his cheek with the palm of her soft hand. "You look so tired. You really should go home and get some rest. Chloe will be fine. I've seen this a thousand times. She'll probably be back on track in the morning."

Chase nodded. He hated to lose an opportunity to spend time with Val but he was exhausted. "You're right. I should go before I risk falling asleep at the wheel."

She smiled and rubbed his shoulder like the night he came to say good-bye to his father. "Hang in there. It'll be okay. I promise."

"Thanks." He smiled thinly and walked away.

"And Chase," she called to his back.

He turned.

"Don't be afraid to use that number. I don't give it to many people so chances are you'll get right through."

He smiled and nodded before pushing through the door of the stairwell.

The whole drive home, he wondered what Deb Ortega was doing about Heath and Durggin. He felt stupid for trusting her with his freedom—she was clearly in a personal crisis over the situation.

When he got home, thoughts of anything but his trashed apartment flew from his head. "Jesus what a mess," he muttered.

He realized he wouldn't be able to sleep until he had cleaned up some of the mess but he didn't want to face the job in the state he was in. He looked around the apartment and spotted a bag of apples on the kitchen floor. "Perfect," he said and left once more to go downstairs to the building laundry room. Behind the washer was his stash, right where he had left it.

He retrieved it and returned to his apartment. It wasn't the first time he had carved an apple into a makeshift pipe, but it was the first time he had to do it because there were no other smoking options. After smoking two bowls of Strawberry Cough—chuckling over the name when he considered it to be Strawberry-Apple Cough, he realized he was hungry. He hadn't eaten his lunch.

He checked the time—it was still early enough to order a pizza, not even eleven o'clock yet. So he dialed, ordered then set about cleaning while he waited for his pizza delivery.

After flipping the torn box spring back onto his bed frame, he clumsily maneuvered his queen-sized mattress to the edge. It was just about in position to lower when there was a knock at the door. "It's about time," he muttered as he let the mattress drop in place.

He ran to the door and opened it, pulling his wallet from his pocket. He never got to greet the deliveryman. Something hard hit him across his temple and he fell with a thud, his cheek pressed against the cold hardwood floor. He looked across the floor, unable to move as someone stepped over him. Lying there, trying to refocus his eyes, he realized his floor was filthy. *I have to get a vacuum,* he thought, then was struck again, sending him into darkness.

He woke to another knock at the door, later, not sure what time it was. He leaned forward as if to stand but discovered he was taped to his chair.

"WHaha!" *That's not right. I have tape on my mouth too.*

"That's fifteen dollars and thirty-five cents," came a voice from the other room.

"Here. Keep the change," replied another man.

Chase struggled with his bonds, twisting and flexing side to side but ceased all movement when a man of about forty or fifty years and six feet in height stepped into his bedroom carrying the open pizza box. A slice of pepperoni and mushroom pizza hung, sagging from his fingertips, one bite already missing.

He looked up realizing Chase was conscious and smiled. He dropped the pizza box on his overturned dresser. "Hey there, pal," the man said.

"Whahodya." Chase flexed his jaw and opened his mouth behind the tape, undoing the seal on his chin. "Who the hell are you and why the bloody *fu—?*"

The man punched Chase in the nose with his free hand, stunning him into silence.

"I understand you've been asking around about me." He shook his hand out then took another bite of pizza.

"I don't know who you are," Chase said once the full feeling in his sinuses had subsided.

"Right. We haven't been introduced. I'm Brick Durggin."

Chase's intestines flooded with cold and he felt dizzy again, unable to separate the effects of the punch, the pot, or the information. *Oh, shit*, he thought. *I'm dead.*

FRIDAY
CLONED

CHASE had no way to know for sure, but it was certainly after midnight by the time Durggin had his fill of pizza. He looked around the room for some indication of the time, but even his bedside clock was somewhere on the floor under a pile of ransacked clutter.

Durggin wiped his greasy fingers on Chase's shirt—actually, Jonah's shirt since he was still wearing the one he had borrowed the previous morning. Chase looked down at the orange oil stain then back to Durggin.

"What—?"

Durggin put his finger up calling for silence. The smile he had on his face was more disconcerting to Chase than the fact that he was tied up. Though, if he weren't tied up, it probably wouldn't have seemed quite as frightening as it did—Chase was certain he could take the older man if he were free.

Durggin looked around the floor then peeked through the door into the living room. He shook his head and "tsked" his disapproval. "Someone made a real mess, huh?"

"Yeah, I wonder who that could've been?" Chase muttered.

Durggin tipped his head to the side, grinning, then punched Chase in the mouth. "Did I ask for your opinion?"

Chase spat blood but it hung on the loose tape still plastered to his upper lip. The bloody saliva just dribbled down his chin.

"That's disgusting," Durggin said, drawing his lip up in revulsion. He reached over and yanked the partially dislodged tape from Chase's cheek and lip. "There...now you can spit on your floor anytime you want."

Chase popped his neck to the side, trying to suppress another angry, snarky comment—it seemed to be a trigger for a beating.

"Ah. We have a fast learner! It only took, what... three punches? Four?" Durggin said, grinning, then narrowed his eyes to slits as if trying to figure something out. When his eyes popped wide in recognition, he pointed at Chase and laughed. "I recognize you! You used to run with Roughie Harman's old crew...the bookie."

Chase shook his head. "You got the wrong guy."

"Nah...I remember. You're the kid with the head for numbers," Durggin said, shaking his head in wonder. "Small world. Well, hell, that explains a lot."

"Fuck you."

An angry sneer pulled the corners of Durggin's mouth and he punched Chase again, leaving his ears ringing.

Durggin leaned forward and lifted Chase's head by the hair. "Not that bright after all."

"What do you want?"

Durggin smiled. "I want to know why you've been spreading my name around this little dysfunctional family crisis you've been having?"

Chase glared at him.

"Actually...more important than that, I'd like to know *how* you know my name to begin with."

"I heard it on the news," Chase said quietly.

Genuine surprise shaped Durggin's face. "The news?"

"Yeah, when they announced the winners of the annual cocksucker awards."

Durggin punched Chase in the gut, followed by an elbow to the jaw. As Chase recovered from the double strike, Durggin walked into the other room and returned with a chair from the dining nook. He set it down backward in front of Chase then straddled it, leaning on the back of the chair.

"You're a tough one," Durggin said with a crooked grin. "You don't shy away from a beating."

"My sister hits harder than you, old man. You think too highly of yourself."

Durggin drew back to punch Chase again. But when Chase just stared at him, Durggin lowered his fist then slapped his cheek lightly.

He laughed. "Tough as shit…I like that."

Chase remained quiet, glaring.

"I'm going to tell you a story. And in that story, I'm going to reveal some things that…well, let's just say you've been in the loop longer than you know you've been."

"Why don't you jus—"

Durggin punched him in the mouth. "Hush. I'm telling a story."

Chase rubbed his mouth against his shoulder leaving a blood smear behind.

Durggin waited until he was sure Chase would stay quiet before speaking. He nodded. "Good. Once upon a time, there was a kid with moderately good analyst skills who went to work for a moderate sized trading firm."

Chase's eyes flew open wide.

Durggin smiled. "Well, who did you think this story was about…? Me?"

Chase regained his composure. "Go on."

Durggin lifted an eyebrow and nodded. "Anyway. This kid started getting better and better at his analysis…spooky good. Like he had some sort of fortune-teller whispering stock picks in his ear or something. So good, in fact, that his bosses started to suspect something was amiss."

"Amiss…with the analysis?"

Durggin shook his head. "You see, they knew about the market shifts as well. They already knew what was going up and down…they just wanted to know how *he* knew."

"They should have just asked him."

Durggin tipped his head to the side, nodding. "Yeah…maybe they should've, at that."

He continued to stare at Chase for several seconds, trying to peel back his skin with his eyes. He broke eye contact finally and ran his fingers through his hair. "Anyway, they wanted to know what this kid knew. So they hired me to take a look at him when their computer scans came up with nothing of value."

"Why don't you just stop talking about this kid and say what you mean to say?"

Durggin looked up and smiled. "That would ruin the story."

Chase shook his head.

"I didn't find anything. From what I could tell, you found a pattern and refined the tracking. That's not what they wanted to hear, so they told me to have a meeting with you…face-to-face, like…like we are right now."

"So that's why you ran over my sister and trashed my place?"

Anger swept over his face and flushed it red. "I didn't run over your sister *or* trash your place," he said, his voice a low, angry rumble. "But someone…someone wanted you and the police to think it was me."

"What happened when my bosses told you to work me over for information?"

"I told them they were wasting their time. You didn't know what they were doing. I told them you were just a smart kid with a head for numbers with a little bit of dumb luck on your side…that's it."

He's lying. No one would have gone to this much trouble to find out how I was beating the floor average. They could've just fired me if it was a problem. And seriously, who beats someone up to convince them they're innocent?!

Chase nodded. "I see…so you told them no need to tie me down and beat me for information."

Durggin punched him in the side of the head. "You mistake my calm, rational tone for some sort of softness. I don't care if you look like a bloody package of ground beef when we're done…the ladies in your life might, though. You were a good-looking kid."

"Fu—"

"Ott! Don't do it," Durggin snapped, whipping his finger to Chase's face. "When my fist is tired I'll use a book. So if you thought you'd use your face to tire me out, it's a bad plan."

Chase shut his mouth.

"Good boy." Durggin adjusted himself in the chair, folding his arms across the back. "I told them you weren't worth pursuing, but then you managed to empty an entire company of retail shareholders the day before it crashed. That threw up some red flags that my theory wouldn't explain…to them anyway. I still thought you were just a smart kid who also seemed to have a good amount of luck."

Chase nodded. "So who tried to kill my sister? Who broke into my apartment?"

Durggin shrugged. "I don't know…maybe your employers weren't happy with my report, so they went outside and found a third party."

Chase narrowed his eyes to slits.

Durggin tipped his head to the side. "Or maybe something from your past just popped up to bite you in the ass and I just got caught up in it because I've been following you around."

"Bullshit," Chase snapped, but his chest contracted as a slideshow of violence from his past crowded his mind, undermining his confidence in the response. *No. I left my old life clean…there's no one who—*

Chase heard voices in the hall outside his apartment. It took him a second, but he realized it was Jimmy and Tonya coming home from their late shift. There was a light tap on the door. Chase smiled knowing Jimmy would have seen his car in the reserved spot next to his—they knew Chase was home. Optimism swelled up.

Panic flashed across Durggin's face and his hand flew to Chase's mouth, covering it before Chase had a chance to say anything. "Who would that be?" Durggin whispered.

"Muwhmmfump," Chase said beneath his hand, grinning.

Durggin pulled out a small automatic pistol and pointed it at Chase's head. "Who?"

"That would be Sergeant James Hall and his wife Lieutenant Tonya Hall…my best friends and next door neighbors. They've been keeping an eye on things here since—"

Durggin slapped his hand back across Chase's mouth and turned toward the door. "Shit," he muttered then looked at Chase again. "Do they have keys?"

Chase smiled and nodded.

Durggin holstered his weapon and lowered his head, rubbing his face in frustration. "You keep your mouth shut," he said finally before walking into the other room, looking for a way out of the apartment. He'd have to do a serious gymnastic routine to leave by the terrace—that just left the front door. "Shit."

After another, louder, knock at the door, Durggin came back into the bedroom. "Are they going away?"

Chase shook his head, still grinning. "They know I'm here and they won't hesitate to wake me up to get a status update…you're stuck, bucko."

"I'm going to untape you. I want you to tell them you're fine and you'll talk to them in the morning."

Just then, Chase's phone rang on the table with the rest of his belongings. Durggin's eyes flashed to it then back to Chase. "Tell them you'll talk to them in the morning," he said, grabbing the phone and holding it up to Chase's face. He pulled his pistol again and held it next to Chase's head.

Chase nodded and Durggin slid his finger across the phone screen.

"Hey, man," Chase said into the phone.

"Chase...why didn't you answer the door?"

"I'm fine. I'm just getting my ass beat in here by Brick Durg—"

Durggin hit Chase across the face with his pistol at the same moment he heard his front door splinter and crash open. Chase lay on the floor, struck so hard his ears were ringing again, but not so much that he couldn't hear Jimmy and Tonya screaming for Durggin to drop his weapon.

"Did you break my door?" Chase asked, stunned, shaking his head to clear the blurriness.

"Shut up," Jimmy said with a tense grin. "Are you okay?"

"Cut me loose and I'll tell you."

Tonya walked over, her weapon still aimed at Durggin who was on his knees, fingers laced behind his head. "You got him?" she asked Jimmy.

He nodded and Tonya proceeded to cut Chase from the chair. Once free, he relaxed on the floor for a second.

"You okay?" Tonya asked.

"Give me a minute."

While Chase breathed some calm back into himself, Tonya kicked Durggin's weapon away then cuffed him, shoving him to the floor roughly once he was secured. Only then did Jimmy holster his weapon. He pulled his phone out to dial.

Chase sat up abruptly. "Wait...don't call it in yet. Brick was telling me an interesting story before you showed up and despite the beating, he was being pretty convincing."

Jimmy's finger hovered over his phone and he looked at Tonya who shook her head slowly.

"Don't you want to hear what he has to say?" Chase asked. "Before he lawyers up?"

Durggin turned his head at an uncomfortable angle to look at Chase, a strange expression of helplessness on his face.

Chase looked back at Jimmy. "Come on, man...just hold off a minute."

"Why are you looking at him?" Tonya asked, her voice rising a couple of octaves higher than her normal speaking voice. "I outrank him and I said no."

Chase took a deep breath and got up, straightening his shirt and wiping his bloody lip with the back of his hand. "I'm sorry for the confusion, Sergeant...Lieutenant. My friend here was helping me dress my wounds and taped me down because I kept flinching away from his first aid attempts," Chase said, righting the chair then sitting in it. "I won't file a complaint about the door, but I'm going to have to ask you to uncuff my friend and leave now."

"Why you ungrateful little son of a bitch," Jimmy said, glaring at Chase.

"Just a few minutes...hear him out," Chase said, pleading on his face—less effective, he imagined, with the cuts and bruises.

Tonya breathed out in a whoosh and looked at Jimmy, unsure how to proceed.

"Don't look at me...you outrank me."

Chase smiled and went over to help Durggin to a seated position on the floor. Once he was upright, Chase was about to step away but instead paused and smiled. "Oh yeah." *Smash!* He pounded Durggin in the jaw, knocking him sideways to the floor again. Chase flexed his fingers a few times as Durggin struggled back into the seated position.

"Okay...yeah," Durggin muttered.

Chase sat and grabbed a towel from the floor, pressing it to his lip and nose. "Finish your story."

Durggin looked up at Jimmy then Tonya before nodding. "Like I said, I told your bosses there wasn't any indication you were stealing company secrets so they paid me and sent me on my merry way. The next thing I know, one of my old CIs takes a header out the window and my name is getting spread around as a person of interest."

"So Brad Bowman *was* your informant," Chase said.

"Yeah, like years ago when I was still a detective. But I haven't heard from that shit stain since I left the force."

"He said you put him on to my sister...that you told him to drug her and bring her to my apartment."

Durggin shrugged. "He's as big a liar now as he was then."

"No…now he's dead."

Durggin nodded. "It wasn't me. Hell, I thought it was you…I thought you somehow figured out it was me tailing you and offed Brad to frame me."

"Yeah…I suppose I ran down my sister too."

Durggin shook his head. "That's when I knew I was really being set up. As soon as I found out it was your sister in the hit-and-run, then Bowman took his tumble…well, it started making sense."

"How much sense? Enough to know who was doing it?"

"I have some ideas but no…nothing solid."

"So why tape me up and beat the shit out of me?" Chase asked leaning forward.

"Look, I don't know you. But I know you have a nice sized file on you here in Fairfax and Arlington. I also know it was you who dropped my name to the cops, so I wanted to make sure you weren't involved…old habits die hard."

Chase nodded and looked at Jimmy. "Uncuff him."

"What?!"

Chase shrugged. "I'm not pressing charges. Uncuff him."

Jimmy grabbed Chase by the arm and led him into the other room, looking backward at Durggin and Tonya. "Chase…man, you don't want to do that. He's involved in this and you are way, *way* out of your depth here. Let us take him down and at least get a statement from him on the record."

Chase shook his head. "This started because my company was investigating *me*. That means Chloe is lying in the hospital, barely hanging on because of me."

"No, Chase, that's not what it means. It means you and Chloe are being used as pawns in something bigger than even *I* want to be mixed up in. Let me take him down and book him for B&E and assault."

"No. Uncuff him."

Jimmy glared at him silently for several ticks, his face growing angrier, then stomped into the other room. He held his phone up to Durggin's face and snapped several pictures before turning to Chase and doing the same.

"I have pictures of you here and the damage to my friend's face," he said to Durggin. "The only reason I'm cutting you loose is because Chase is a hardheaded asshole who'll *never* listen to reason."

Durggin nodded with a blank expression.

"But if anything—and I mean *anything* happens to him, I'll have you in gen pop so fast you'll forget you ever had a badge... You got me?"

Durggin nodded, trying unsuccessfully to hide his sneer.

Jimmy uncuffed him, more roughly than he had to then turned to Chase, finger raised in warning. "If you get yourself killed, *no one's* gonna be watching after Chloe."

Chase winked despite the pain in his split eyelid and nodded. "I'll bet you'll look in on her from time to time."

Jimmy raised his finger again, briefly shifting his gaze to Tonya then grinned. "Go to hell, Chase. And clean up this damned mess."

Tonya shot Chase a nervous glance before following Jimmy out. Once the front door crunched closed, Chase turned to Durggin. "Tell me what you couldn't say in front of them."

Durggin dipped his head and looked at Chase with the tops of his eyes. "You really are a smart one, aren't you?"

"Time will tell. What couldn't you say in front of them."

"If I'm being set up, then so are you," Durggin said quietly.

"Tell me something I don't know. Whoever trashed my apartment didn't just wreck the fabulous decor, they stole my computer and my bong."

Durggin nodded. "And that bong was found at Bowman's apartment after he died."

"So? That's not news to me."

"But why would the Arlington PD and the Commonwealth's Attorney act on such flawed logic and tainted evidence to arrest you if someone wasn't pulling strings?"

Chase took a deep breath and let it out slowly. "Who?"

Durggin shrugged. "No idea. That's not a grudge issue. That's business."

And it started at work. "Who hired you to investigate me?"

He shook his head.

"You've already told me it was the company I worked for."

"I never said it was the company you worked for...you assumed that. I said it was your bosses."

Chase narrowed his eyes. "So wait...someone at the company hired you but not on behalf of the company?"

A smug grin slid across Durggin's mouth.

"Tell me."

Durggin shook his head again. "I need my ace in the hole. If they're setting me up, I need that information guarded so they don't have time to cover it up."

Chase shrugged. "Fine. I'll just go in tomorrow and start asking executives who hired the slimy PI to trash my apartment and run my sister over."

Durggin lurched forward. "Don't you dare you miserable lit—"

Chase punched him in the nose, sending him flying backward to the floor. "I'm not taped up anymore. Watch those sudden moves."

Durggin rolled over and glared at Chase. After a second his eye went to his pistol, laying on the floor on the other side of the room.

Chase grinned. "Go ahead. I'm sure you'll be able to get out of here before Jimmy and Tonya come back over."

"You prick."

"Yeah, that's me. Who hired you?"

Durggin got up and straightened his jacket. Chase mirrored the move, standing defensively, at the ready. When Chase didn't try to stop Durggin from picking up his gun, the older man snatched it from the floor and tucked it into his belt holster in one swift motion.

"What kind of car do you drive?" Chase asked as Durggin walked out of the bedroom.

Durggin stopped and looked over his shoulder. "Why?"

Chase shrugged. "Never mind. It'll be easy enough for me to get Jimmy to look it up for me."

Durggin clenched his jaw and sneered. "A shitty old Buick. Rust colored."

Chase nodded but wasn't just going to take Durggin's word for it. He'd have Jimmy confirm it anyway. "Did you really kill another cop?"

Chase watched Durggin, braced for violence. But the older man stood there, clenching and unclenching his fists. "I didn't kill Ortega because I wanted to. He was standing there, drawn down on me in the middle of a damn gang meeting...it was on him. Not me."

"Hey man, I was just curious...I ain't never met a cop killer before."

Durggin turned hard and stormed out, slamming the door behind him. Chase stood there, staring at his trashed room then opened the pizza box—half a pizza left. He picked up a piece and took a bite, flinching at the ache it caused his jaw.

As he chewed, a light tap sounded at the door. He shook his head and walked through the living room. "Come on in."

"Not dead, I see," Jimmy said as he entered. He toyed with the doorframe for a moment then closed it with a crunch. "You got more of that?" he asked, pointing at his pizza.

Chase nodded toward the bedroom. "In there."

Jimmy disappeared into the bedroom and returned a moment later with the half empty box. "You mind?" he asked, picking up a slice.

"Help yourself."

Jimmy sat on the cushionless sofa, dropping the box on the coffee table. After picking up a piece of pizza, he looked up. "Oh. I almost forgot." He reached into his pocket and pulled out a packet of rolling papers, tossing them to Chase.

He caught them and grinned. "You forgot? You've been walking around all day with rolling papers in your pocket and you forgot?"

Jimmy grinned. "Okay. I stuck 'em in my pocket a few minutes ago. But I figured you'd need 'em."

Chase looked over at the kitchen counter where he'd left his apple-pipe and his pot. "No. I managed."

Jimmy looked at the apple and grinned. "My man, my man."

"Go on. I know you want to."

Jimmy set the pizza down and walked over to the counter. "You know, if Durggin is being set up, you have a good resource there to find out what's going on." He packed the hole in the apple with some of Chase's pot. "If he don't kill you."

"Yeah. I don't think he's the killing out of spite type."

Jimmy tipped his head sideways as he continued to prep his pipe. "It's your ass."

"I know."

Jimmy lit the apple and drew in deeply, coughing out much of the smoke before his lungs were full. He stepped back and leaned against the counter to balance himself. "Whoa."

"The thing I'm worried about is the rest of the Arlington PD. Someone didn't bat an eye at charging me with murder over nothing."

"Not 'nothing'...you *were* there."

Chase dropped the crust of his pizza on the table and rubbed his face.

"I know, I know…but they didn't know that."

"But obviously, they thought better of it after your lawyer showed up."

"Jonah's lawyer."

"Your boss?" Jimmy asked after taking another hit from the apple.

Chase nodded then pulled at his shirt to look at the bloodstains. "And he dressed me this morning."

Jimmy shot him a smirk, his mouth open ready to ridicule.

Chase raised his finger. "Don't. I'm not in the mood."

Jimmy shrugged and returned to the sofa to start munching on the pizza. "So what're you gonna do?"

Chase shook his head and picked up another piece of pizza. "I'm gonna try to nail my doorframe together then get some sleep."

"You aren't worried someone else is gonna break in here and shoot you in the head?"

Chase took a deep breath then reached for a pad of paper and marker on the floor. He scratched out a message then handed it to Jimmy when he was done. "Tape that to the door on your way out."

Jimmy read it.

"Shhh. The cops next door are light sleepers."

Jimmy laughed. "The budget security system."

Chase grinned and nodded. "I wasn't kidding, though. Get the hell outta here. I need some sleep."

Jimmy got up and grabbed another slice of pizza before strolling to the door. "If you'll wait for me in the morning, I'll help you fix the door frame before we go to work."

Chase nodded and patted him on the back, feeling the body armor beneath his shirt. "Thanks, Jimmy. And thank you for breaking it…you saved me at least a few more punches to the face."

Jimmy grinned and gave Chase a bro hug.

"Thank Tonya for me too, please."

"She thinks we should have taken Durggin in."

Chase nodded. "We'll see. For now, he's worth more to me free."

Jimmy nodded. "Night bro."

"Good night, Jimmy."

Chase closed the door and chained it; the only thing he could do to keep even a passing breeze from opening it. He picked up a piece of his discarded crust and took one bite before tossing it back into the box.

"Who at work screwed me over?" He dropped his head, shaking it.

When Frank's name was the only one that popped to mind, he opened his stash and packed a fresh bowl. After two good, satisfying tokes, he pushed the weed box under his sofa and turned off the lights. As he stumbled to bed, he pulled the blanket from the floor then fell on the undressed mattress.

I'll find out more in the morning.

He was asleep in moments.

►◄

CHASE woke at first light. Not on purpose—he rolled over and his painful, swollen cheek touched his hand, sending him sitting upright in bed. He touched his face with his fingers and winced. "Ow. Shit."

After a deep breath and an aching stretch, he went into the bathroom to get ready for his day. He was going to work—he had some snooping to do there.

By the time he was out of the shower and dressed, a persistent light knock at the door called him into the living room.

"Yeah?" he called through the door.

"It's me," Jimmy replied.

Chase unchained the door and let him in. In his hands, he had a drill, a few long pieces of wood, and a box of screws.

"Morning, Jimmy."

"Oh shit…you look awesome," Jimmy said with a smirk.

It was true. Overnight, the bruises had come in, shiny and swollen like overripe plums, and his lip was split and sore.

He smiled past the ache. "Tried to do my makeup in the dark."

Jimmy chuckled and set the wood down. "Come on. Let's get your door fixed."

Chase started a pot of coffee as Jimmy went to work. While it brewed the two of them made quick work of repairing the damaged doorframe. It wasn't pretty but the door closed and latched.

"We'll fix it proper like this weekend," Jimmy said as he stood back to admire his handy work. "I have three days off."

Chase brought him a mug of coffee as he stared at the door. Several seconds passed before he turned to Jimmy. "When you checked on Brick Durggin's background, who would've known you did it?"

Jimmy shrugged. "It's not a secret or anything. Logs are kept of computer searches, plus I called a friend at ACPD who gave me most of the scoop."

"A friend?" Chase asked after taking a sip of coffee. "A good friend who wouldn't tell anyone what you called about?"

Jimmy smiled and shook his head. "You make friends like that by talking. If the question was juicy, you can bet it got around pretty fast."

"Shit…so there's no way to find out how it got back to Durggin that he was a person of interest."

"You're talking like a cop."

"I've spent enough time with cops recently it's starting to rub off," Chase said, bitter irony coloring his tone.

Jimmy tipped his head to the side and squinted. "You'd make a good cop."

Chase almost choked on his coffee. "Are you kidding?! With my record?"

"Yeah…why not? You don't have any felonies."

"Except the one that sent me to juvie."

Jimmy shook his head. "You were a minor. Not only would that record be sealed but it wouldn't count against you anyway."

"Stop it. I'm not going to be a cop. That whole 'yes sir, no sir' thing would freak the hell out of me. I'd break someone's head inside a week."

Jimmy laughed and nodded. "Maybe you're right…just a thought."

Tonya came out of her and Jimmy's apartment and leaned through the open door. "Oh, baby. Your poor face!" Her sympathetic tone did more to hurt him than the bruises.

Chase grinned. "I'll be fine. Thanks again for last night."

"Did you get anything figured out?" she asked as she reached up and brushed his bruised cheek.

"A bit," Chase replied, wincing at her touch.

"You should've let us take him in."

Chase shook his head. "I think this is better. If someone at Arlington PD is setting us up, it's better that he's out there looking for answers, not sitting in jail."

She nodded hesitantly then looked at Jimmy. "You ready?"

"Yeah," he said then disappeared around the door with his tools.

Tonya looked at Chase with a pained expression. "I hope you know what you're doing. This goes against every instinct I have."

"Only because you're a cop...your brain is wired different."

She winked at him and touched his cheek again. "Be safe and keep us in the loop. You can always call us if you need the cavalry."

Chase nodded and hugged her. "Thanks, Mom. You're the best."

She chuckled and left when Jimmy came back out. As they walked down the hall, Jimmy turned and pointed at the door. "This weekend...we'll fix it right." He glanced at Tonya to make sure she wasn't watching, then back to Chase, making a toking gesture with his fingers.

Chase shot him a thumbs up and went back in to finish getting ready for work.

On the drive into Arlington, Chase dialed Jonah's number.

"Hello?"

"Jonah, it's Chase."

"How's it going buddy?"

"I'm doing alright. Hey, I'm coming into work today but I want to stop at the hospital and see Chloe first. I just wanted to give you a heads up."

"You know you don't have to do that. We're fine here until you get things back together."

"I'm fine. Besides, it's Friday. I need to fix my client list before they all dump me for Bobby."

Jonah laughed. "I think you've earned their trust."

"You know these traders, man. It's all 'what have you done for me lately'?" he said as he turned into the hospital parking garage. "Oh...yeah. I ran into some trouble yesterday. I'm gonna have to buy you a new shirt."

"Trouble? What kind of trouble?"

Chase chuckled. "You'll know when I get there. I'll see you in a bit."

"Later pal."

Chase took the elevator up to Chloe's floor. Everyone he passed gave him a sideways glance. He had gotten so used to the ache in his face he had nearly forgotten how he looked.

He walked past the nurses' station on his way to Chloe's room and her doctor looked up, doing a double take. "Mr. Grant."

"Morning, doc. How's my girl this morning."

He came around and intercepted Chase. "She had a rough night, but she's awake," he said, inspecting Chase's face. "Listen...I don't think you should go in and see her looking like that. It'll upset her."

Shit. He hadn't thought of how his battered appearance might be a problem. He nodded.

"Do you want some help with that?" The doctor asked, pointing at Chase's face.

"No. I'll be fine."

The doctor put his hand in the middle of Chase's back and led him into an empty exam room. "Why don't you let me dress those abrasions."

Chase's first instinct was to resist—he wanted to get to work and find out who had hired Durggin to investigate him—but he relented quickly. Free medical care was a rare luxury.

He sat and let the doctor do his work.

"You know, it's none of my business, but this looks serious... I mean aside from the physical toll. Is there something going on that you'd like to talk about?"

Chase grinned and shook his head. "Just getting to the bottom of what happened to Chloe."

The doctor looked over his shoulder toward Chloe's room as if he could see through the wall. "She's a sweet girl. Strong, too."

Chase nodded.

"It would be a shame if anything bad happened to her due to poor decisions on the part of someone else."

Chase pulled away and looked the doctor in the eye. "I don't know what you think is going on here but Chloe and I are both respectable people. We don't look for trouble, we aren't into anything criminal and I look after her as well as I can."

The doctor tipped his head and nodded. "Okay...I didn't mean to get personal. It's just that between her accident and this—" He waved his hand over Chase's face. "It doesn't seem very ordinary or respectable."

Chase felt his face flush red.

"In that," the doctor said quickly to recover. "It's *abnormal* for people to receive this much negative attention."

"Someone hurt my sister, and I'm doing the best I can to find out who it was...I'm working with the police. I don't know what else you'd want from me."

"Okay, okay," the doctor said, easing his tone back. "I'm just concerned...that's all."

Chase nodded as the doctor finished up on his face. "I get it."

"If that butterfly bandage doesn't keep the gash closed on your brow, you may need a couple of stitches."

"I'll keep an eye on it."

The doctor put his hand on Chase's shoulder. "I know you would do anything for your sister. But she needs you too…you have to be around to help her once she's well enough to leave."

Chase nodded but felt a ripple of agitation over the not so subtle guilting. "I know. I will be."

"Okay."

"Thanks for the first aid," Chase said as he walked away.

"My pleasure. Stay out of trouble."

Another ripple of agitation. "I'm trying."

During the thirty-minute drive to work, made slower by the later start, Chase rolled the mystery around in his head, wondering who had hired Durggin. When he arrived at the office he received more sideways glances as he made his way to his cubicle.

Tammy was standing, propping her breasts on the cubicle partition before Chase had his seat. "What happened to you?"

Her wide eyes and oh shaped mouth made him want to punch her. "I got mugged."

"Oh, my god! And after what happened to your sister…that's horrible."

Chase looked over his shoulder at Bobby Tang's cubicle. "Where's Bobby?"

Tammy shrugged an exaggerated gesture that raised her boobs from the partition then back down again. Chase knew she had to be doing it on purpose—no one could be that oblivious to such a large part of their anatomy. "He didn't come in this morning…yesterday either. Frank came by looking for him too."

Chase looked back at the raised, glass fronted cubicles the floor managers sat in. Frank was there, glaring at him.

"I'll call him later and see what's going on," Chase said.

"I called him already…straight to voice mail."

Chase pulled out his phone and dialed Bobby's number—it went right to voice mail. *"This is the fabulous Bobby Tang. You missed me…your loss. Leave a message at the tone."*

"Bobby, it's Chase. Call me as soon as you get this message."

"Nothin', huh?" Tammy said.

Chase shook his head and pulled up his trade interfaces. "I have to get caught up. I'll try again later."

"Okay," Tammy said, sounding disappointed the conversation was over. "Glad you're back."

"Thanks," he muttered, already absorbed in his work.

As soon as she disappeared behind the low wall, he pulled out his key ring and detached the miniature thumb drive. He plugged it in, brought up a sandbox directory viewer that protected it from network oversight and began expanding the tables. After tracking his customer transactions over the past three days and overlapping it to the tables, he began building his trade actions for the day. He corrected and adjusted the chaotic transactions that had taken place while he was absent, then readjusted the sales and purchases to coordinate with his prediction matrix.

Well, at least my customers will be happy today, he thought as he loaded the matrix into the transaction server.

As his transactions started to execute, he switched screens and began looking for access logs on his system. The list was long with floor managers, senior analysts, and systems techs who regularly accessed the trading floor systems. There'd be no way to find out who had been tracking him that way.

He checked the port logs.

Hmmm. There was a two-hour ghost copy from the USB port with no corresponding time stamp or log on.

"Hey, Tammy?" Chase said.

Tammy's smiling face popped up over the top of the cube, boobs on station. "You rangggg?"

"Did tech services work on my computer while I was gone?"

"Not tech services. But Frank and some guy from HFT came by yesterday and took it for a while. They were at Bobby's station this morning when I came in."

"Did they say what they were doing?"

"OS audit...that's what he said anyway."

Why is Frank working with a High-Frequency Trading server guy? And why would HFT be interested in my system...and Bobby's? "Did they say why?"

Tammy shook her head so expressively, her shoulders moved back and forth. "I guess I don't rate an explanation for managerial gobbeldy gook."

"Thanks," Chase said as he got up and walked to Bobby's cubicle.

Bobby's computer was missing.

He was halfway across the cube farm to the back stairwell when Frank intercepted him. "Where do you think you're going?"

"Downstairs."

"Your calls are still going into the queue. Get back to your cube and log on."

Chase stopped and tipped his head to the side. "Why did HFT clone my system yesterday?"

"That's not *your system.* It's the company's system. Which means it's none of your concern until I say it is."

Chase nodded, chin high, smug. "And Bobby's too, I guess."

Frank looked over his shoulder at the executive window and inserted himself between Chase and the VP's door. "Get back to your hole and do your damned job...I'm not going to tell you again."

Chase stared at him for a beat. "Do you know a guy named Brick Durggin?"

Frank lifted one eyebrow high, his angry sneer vanishing in an instant. "Who?"

Chase smiled. "Maybe the guys in HFT know him." He pushed past Frank and walked to the stairwell.

Frank ran around and blocked the door. "I don't know who you think you are, but this is still my floor and you still work for me."

Chase crinkled his forehead. "Actually, it's the company's floor and I work for them."

Frank's face turned red in a wave of color that closed in from his ears. His mouth opened but he didn't get to speak.

"Frank? Chase? What's going on?"

Frank and Chase turned and saw Jonah standing in his doorway.

Frank stepped in front of Chase. "Nothing. I was just trying to get Chase to log on to his phone bank. His customers haven't heard from him all week."

"His customers are fine in the queue for now. Come on in here, Chase. Catch me up on everything."

Frank grunted something in wordless protest that sounded like a wet fart but walked away with purpose. Chase followed Jonah back into his office and closed the door.

"Jesus, man. What happened to your face?"

"Nothing. It was a disagreement about the investigation. Hey, do you know anything about HFT division cloning mine and Bobby's systems?"

Confusion pulled Jonah's mouth into a frown and he shook his head. "No. That's weird. Why would HFT be interested in trading floor systems? They have those power server clusters down there."

"That's what I was thinking too...Tammy said Frank and a guy from HFT took mine and cloned it yesterday. And they've got Bobby's system now."

Jonah went to his door and opened it. "Frank, can you come down here a minute?"

Jonah went back to his desk and sat. When Frank came in he glared at Chase.

"Close the door, will ya?" Jonah said.

Frank closed it and stared forward, stiff. Chase thought he looked nervous.

"Did HFT take Chase's system and clone it?" Jonah asked.

"I got a request from the server room yesterday. They were looking for a system that might have *inadvertently* downloaded a Trojan. Grant's and Tang's computers were on the list."

Jonah squinted at Frank. "Inadvertently?"

"They didn't say one way or the other. I just assumed if it was on my floor, it must have been an accidental infection," Frank said then looked at Chase. "There's no way anyone in my section would *intentionally* hack an HFT server." The sneer on his face conveyed he meant exactly the opposite of what he was saying.

"Mine and Bobby's computers were on the list...anyone else's?"

Frank looked back at Jonah. "They didn't say."

"Did they find anything?" Jonah asked.

Frank shrugged. "I haven't heard anything. They just took Tang's this morning."

Chase looked at Jonah. "Bobby's not in today and wasn't in yesterday. Phone calls are going straight to voice mail."

Jonah leaned forward and tapped a few keys on his computer then hit the speaker button on his phone. He entered a number and it again went straight to voice mail. *"This is the fabulous Bobby Tang. You missed me...your loss. Leave a message at the tone."*

Jonah punched the key to hang up, then looked at Frank. "Did he call in sick or something?"

Frank shook his head, suspicion on his face. "Not a peep."

"Thanks, Frank. You can go."

"If he and Grant are up to something, he might not come back at—"

"I'm right here," Chase said, staring at the side of Frank's head.

"I said, *thanks*, Frank. You can go."

Frank glared at Chase once more before turning and leaving, closing the door behind him.

"Is there something you need to talk to me about, Chase?" Jonah asked, his head tilted to the side.

"What do you mean? Like about hacking the HFT servers? Really?"

Jonah held his hands up in a defensive gesture. "I'm just asking if you know what's going on."

Chase pulled up the chair in front of Jonah's desk and sat, leaning forward. "There is something really bad going on here and the attack on Chloe was part of it."

Jonah's eyebrows shot high. "Whadya mean 'Chloe's attack is part of it'? Part of something going on here?!"

Chase nodded.

"What happened to your face?"

"I got some information last night that makes me think the firm is tied to something going on with Arlington PD."

Jonah chuckled. "You know...when you question someone, *they're* supposed to end up with the lumps...not you."

"Now you tell me... I'll do better next time."

"Tell me what you know," Jonah said, leaning forward and lowering his voice.

"I went out yesterday with that Arlington cop who's been working my sister's case. She told me a story about the guy who got thrown out of his window and some detectives on cartel cases in the city."

"Cartel? As in drug cartels?"

Chase nodded. "An Arlington detective was killed by another Arlington detective. It was a big stink a year or two ago."

"And you think this has something to do with the firm?"

"Last night I talked to a guy...an ex-cop who was hired by someone here, to investigate me."

"Someone here? At Baxter?" Jonah asked, his eyes wide and mouth agape.

Chase nodded. "That's what he said. I'm not sure how far I should trust him, but it was his informant who drugged Chloe and got dropped on his head from the 8th floor. So... yeah. There's that."

Jonah shook his head. "And now the HFT guys are auditing both computers." He lowered his head and absently pinched his bottom lip between his fingers, lost in thought. He looked up abruptly. "When your apartment was robbed, the computer...is that all they took?"

Chase nodded. "Yeah...well...and my pipe."

"And there wasn't anything on it that might be construed as a system breaching program or anything like it?"

"No...not even close. And that's the thing, this ex-cop...this Durggin guy, he said that whoever it was who hired him *knew* I was winning on my trades...they knew before the trades were executed."

Jonah's brow furrowed in confusion. "Are you suggesting someone at the firm is manipulating the market?"

Chase shook his head. "No! I'm just telling you what Durggin said."

"Durggin, huh?"

Chase watched Jonah closely as the mystery deepened. "I don't know what to do, but I was going to start by asking HFT why they took my computer."

Jonah shook his head. "You better let me do that. An inquiry from me will carry more weight than you anyway."

Chase felt frustrated by that. It felt like Jonah intercepting him, but he had shown his hand—there was nothing he could do about it now. "Okay. Thanks, Jonah."

Jonah smiled. "Don't thank me yet. It sounds too wild to be true."

"I know, I know. But at this point, I just want to know what the hell is going on."

Jonah nodded. "We'll figure it out. Stay low, don't mention it to anyone... If there are illegal trades being made, we don't want to give anyone a chance to destroy the evidence."

Chase nodded. "Whatever you say."

"I do. Now go on back and get caught up. If you aren't too swamped at lunchtime, let's go out...we can talk about it more then."

"That'd be great. Thanks." He got up and left.

▶◀

CHASE and Jonah sat in the bar area of Morton's Steak House at lunch time. As Chase cut into his fifty dollar steak, Jonah was busy talking to someone on his cell phone.

"I don't give a shit that it's procedure. I want to know who ordered it," Jonah said into the phone.

Chase chewed and watched Jonah, anxious to learn something new.

"Well then call the head of security and find out. I want an answer before the end of the day." Jonah ended his call and set his phone down.

"Nothing, huh?"

Jonah shook his head as he sliced a piece from his Porterhouse and stuffed into his mouth. "It wouldn't be so bad," he said as he chewed. "But they don't even know who ordered the damn audit."

"What were you saying about security?"

"Tech security. They seem to be behind it, but can't come up with a name."

Chase shook his head. "That's exactly the kind of response you'd expect if someone was hiding something."

Jonah slowed his chewing and looked at Chase for a beat before nodding. "Don't worry. I'll get to the bottom of it." He lifted his drink to the bartender and shook the ice cubes to get his attention. "Two more."

The bartender set to work on the drinks as he resumed his lunch.

"Is it possible Frank set it up?" Chase asked.

Jonah stopped eating and stared into space. "It's possible." He started chewing slowly as if it was part of his thought process then shook his head. "No. If it were Frank, there would've been a request trail. HFT doesn't take orders from Retail. As far as the company, *and* the SEC are concerned, there's no connection between the two divisions."

"It's just that..."

Jonah looked at Chase and smiled. "I know Frank is an asshole...probably the biggest at the firm. But he's an honest asshole. If he has an opinion, he's not afraid to share it."

Chase nodded. "I guess you're right."

"If you keep going the way you're going, though, you'll be up there in the glass cubes soon enough, and Frank won't be able to break your balls the way he does."

"He'll find a way."

Jonah laughed just as the waiter brought over the drinks. "You may be right, at that. He really hates you."

"I don't know why you think it's so funny. I'm less productive with him hanging over my shoulder. Not more productive."

Jonah nodded then swallowed. "You may be right. I hadn't thought about it that way."

"Well, as long as I'm changing your mind about stuff, how about letting me talk to HFT about who might have hired Durggin."

"Uh uh," Jonah grunted, stuffing another bite in his mouth. "If *you* hit them head on like that, their VP won't come to me to complain, he'll go right to the CEO... then both of us will be in the shit."

Chase shrugged and put his napkin on the table.

"You done?" Jonah asked. "You didn't eat half of it."

"I'll ask for a doggy bag and eat it tonight. I'm not feeling so great all the sudden."

Jonah shot him a worried expression. "Why don't you go home? You don't have to finish out the day."

Chase shook his head. "I'm fine. Besides, the floor matrix screwed up my client list. I'll need the rest of the afternoon to fix it."

Jonah nodded. "Okay. But if you need to, just go. Don't worry about Frank either. He can't fire you without going through me, and that ain't happening."

Chase offered a weak smile in response. "Thanks, Jonah."

"Hey man, that's what friends are for."

▶◀

OFFICER DEBORAH ORTEGA knocked on Bruce Heath's front door. She held no grudge against Heath, her cousin's former partner—she understood how he might feel. The department had all but abandoned him when he couldn't come up with any evidence against Durggin. Heath would have had to face daily glares and lingering doubt about being the partner of a detective who had been tangled in cartel business. It would have cast a permanent shadow on the remainder of his time on the force—she imagined she would have left the department under the same circumstances.

She knocked again then looked down the street to see if there was a car nearby—there wasn't one in the driveway.

Her impatience got the better of her and she walked around the side of the house toward the garage. As she passed the side window of the garage, she looked in and saw a late model, dark blue Crown Victoria. She stopped and dropped her head. "Damn it Heath," she muttered. "Tell me you didn't kill a CI to frame Durggin."

"Hand's where I can see them," came a man's voice from behind her.

Startled, her hand twitched toward her service weapon but then she recognized the voice. "I don't think the department could handle another dead Ortega," she said, raising her hands slowly, her back still toward him.

"Deb?"

She turned, hands still raised. "Hi, Bruce...seen any good base jumping recently?"

He clenched his jaw and holstered his pistol under his jacket. "Leave and don't come back unless you have a warrant."

He turned and walked back to the front of the house, Deb close on his heels. When she reached him, she spun him around by the arm. He lashed out to hit her.

"You son of a—" she blocked his strike and shoved him roughly against the side of the house. "You don't get to act like a cop anymore, you prick...you gave it up, remember?"

He tried to pull away but Deb kicked the backs of his legs, dropping him to his knees. Her own weapon was drawn and pressed against the back of his neck before he could recover.

"Unless you really plan on pulling that trigger, you better put that thing away."

She leaned close to his ear. "Tell me you aren't mixed up in this thing with Brad Bowman."

He didn't answer, prompting her to put her knee in the middle of his back and push him more tightly against the side of the house. "Answer me."

"I'd prefer you read me my rights now so I can call my lawyer."

She shook her head. The video was all she had; no warrant, no reasonable suspicion—and no desire to arrest her cousin's former partner. "Goddamn it, Heath. You're not leaving me much of a choice."

"You can't arrest me. If you could, I'd already be in cuffs instead of all this foreplay."

She kneed him roughly in the back before stepping away. "Screw you. You're doing this to yourself."

"I don't know what you're talking about, officer," he said, keeping his back to her, his hands laced behind his head. "I was just enjoying a chicken potpie for lunch and found you wandering my property."

She clenched her fist, held it tight for a beat, then turned. "Do yourself a favor and don't run. Too many cops in this town might be looking for an opportunity to shoot you on sight."

She walked with purpose and speed to her cruiser, but just before she got in, Heath called to her. "You don't know what's going on here."

She looked at him, grateful her sunglasses covered her watering eyes. "I guess I'll just have to read the court transcripts afterward." She got in and slammed the car door before sending her cruiser squealing from its parking space. "I tried," she muttered, lifting her glasses and wiping her eyes.

►◄

CHASE spent the rest of the day untangling the jumble of confused calls from his customers. The main sales matrices had made a mess of his client portfolios while he had been out and he stayed busy making adjustments. After the trading day was done, he shook his head as he entered the last changes of the day. "It's amazing they can stay in business when the rest of the floor has such shit results."

"Was that directed at me?" Tammy asked, popping her head over the cube wall—no boobs this time. He suddenly missed them.

Chase turned his computer off. "No. Just the default analyst matrix. It seems to be wrong almost fifty percent of the time."

"Oh, I know. I only use it for my quiet customers…the ones who don't complain much."

He was tempted to ask her why she used it at all but thought better of it—it would only lead to more conversation. "I'll see you Monday, Tammy."

"Any big plans this weekend?" she asked to his back.

"Just going to the hospital to sit with Chloe."

She nodded with a troubled smile and waved. "See ya Monday!"

Chase went by Jonah's office and knocked on the door. "Anything?"

Jonah looked up from his computer and shook his head. "They said it was a random audit. That everyone's systems are as eligible for deep analysis as yours and Bobby's…have you heard from him?"

"Nothing," he said, shaking his head and leaning against the doorframe feeling defeated. "Five calls all straight to voice mail and no word from him yet."

"Well. I'm not dismissing the possibility that this just looks bad. It's pretty incredible if it's all connected."

Chase nodded. "I know. Maybe I'm just too desperate for answers."

"Could be. But I'll keep chipping away at it. You go home and get some rest this weekend...spend some time with Chloe."

"I will. Thanks, Jonah."

"You bet. Have a good weekend."

On the way out, Chase again dialed Bobby's number. *"This is the fabulous Bobby Tang. You missed me...your loss. Leave a message at the tone."*

"Damn it, Bobby," Chase muttered as he shoved his phone back into his pocket and got into his car.

He sat there without starting the engine for a moment debating what to do next. As he sat, his phone rang. His heart jumped hoping it was Bobby, but when he looked he saw Ortega's number displayed.

He sighed as he answered. "Yep."

"Chase?"

"Yeah. What?"

"I thought you should know I've handed over the video."

That was a surprise. "Wow. Who'd you end up giving it to?"

"It's in official channels now and being analyzed. That's all I can say."

Chase smiled feeling some of the loose ends tying themselves up in the background. "That's good news."

A long pause followed, making him wonder what else she wanted to hear. "Okay, thanks for letting me know."

"Chase..."

Another pause. *What is up with you, Ortega?* "Yes, Officer Ortega?"

"Nothing. That's it. I'll let you know if anything comes of it."

"Okay then. Bye." He dropped his phone in the passenger seat and left the garage, fighting late Friday afternoon DC traffic to the hospital in Arlington.

When he arrived, he swiveled the rearview mirror around to look at his face, peeling off the bandages and brushing loose scabs away. When nothing began to bleed, he winked at his reflection and went in.

As he walked to the elevators in the lobby, he became aware of hurried footsteps echoing behind him. He turned defensively, prepared to be assaulted.

It was Val. "Whoa...you aren't actually going to punch me are you?"

Val asked, her hands held up in mock defense, but then her eyes flashed wide in shock. "What happened to you?"

He breathed out his stress, embarrassed. "I'm sorry. I've been on edge lately."

She reached up and touched his bruised cheek. "Who did this to you?"

"It's not important. A misunderstanding."

Her eyes narrowed to slits. "Uh huh."

"It's fine, really."

"If you say so."

He smiled thinly, suddenly not in the mood to develop a new relationship. "I was on my way up to see Chloe. I'll talk with you later."

She seemed startled by his brush off but quickly reigned in her expression of disappointment. "Okay. See you around, then."

He turned and walked away, but with each step, guilt crept up his back. Before he reached the elevator, he looked over his shoulder—Val was nowhere to be seen.

"Shit," he muttered as the elevator opened.

On Chloe's floor, he nodded to the officer at the end of the hall before going in to see his sister.

Chloe turned her head slightly and smiled upon seeing Chase, but her expression quickly changed to a frown. "What happened to you?"

Her voice sounded so much better than it had been the last time she spoke to him. His heart surged with optimism. "Fought a lady over the last bag of Oreos at the grocery… She won."

"I can see that." Chloe went back to grinning and raised her bed.

"You look and sound a lot better than the last time I saw you," he said, leaning over to kiss her forehead. "Hospital food agrees with you."

"I can't tell. It all tastes the same."

"That's the meds. Don't worry. You'll get your taste back."

"I'm not sure that's a good thing."

Chase grinned. "True. Your taste in men has always sucked anyway."

She twisted her head but winced at the sudden motion. "Asshole. I meant the food doesn't look appetizing."

He helped her adjust her pillow. "I know. That wasn't fair."

Once she was comfortable, she exhaled out a long breath, then nodded. "Yeah…it was fair. I need to make some changes."

Chase smiled and squeezed her hand.

She looked up into his bruised face. "Did Brad do that? You found him?"

"No...I mean I found him, but he didn't beat me up."

"Who then?"

Chase slid the chair closer and sat next to her. "There's a few things that you've missed the last couple days."

"Like what?"

"Like Brad is dead."

Her eyes flew wide. "Chase," she hissed in a whisper. "You didn't—"

"No. Uh uh." He shook his head vigorously. "But he was murdered."

"Who would've done that?"

"I'm thinking it was the guy who ran you over."

"But why?" Chloe's eyes glistened with fresh tears.

"No, don't cry. It's fine. The police are all over it now."

"What's going on, Chase. Why is this happening?"

He took a deep breath and smiled but remained silent.

She squeezed his hand. "Tell me."

He shook his head. "I think it has something to do with work."

"I'm a restaurant manager. Why the hell would—"

"No, sweetie... my work."

Confusion creased her brow. "The investment house?"

He nodded.

"Why?" she asked.

"I'm still trying to figure that out. Somehow it's all mixed up with dirty cops, cartels, and some asshole private detective who used to run Brad as an informant."

Her confused expression deepened.

Chase shrugged. "I know. I'm still trying to figure it out too." He leaned toward her and fought the building moisture in his eyes. "It's just killing me that any of this has something to do with me. I don't know what I'd do if..."

"Hush. You didn't do anything," Chloe said. "So don't go crying or you'll make me start again...Oh! Look." She opened her mouth wide and closed it again before moving her jaw side to side. "They unwired me this morning."

"That's great. Where'd they put them? I'll hang on to them in case of emergency."

She slapped at him with the back of her hand but the motion caused her to flinch in pain again. "Stop it, asshole."

"Sorry again."

She smiled thinly, clearly not convinced.

"In the meantime, you just worry about getting well. You don't have anything else to worry about…there's a big cop outside ready to tackle anyone who shouldn't be here."

"I've seen him… cute too."

"Jesus, Chloe."

"I'm kidding. Shut up and watch TV with me."

He chuckled, nodding and handed her the multi-remote attached to her bed. They watched an old movie until she fell asleep. When he was sure it wasn't just a passing doze, he covered her with a blanket and turned out the light, leaving the TV playing quietly in the background.

"I'll see you tomorrow, Chlo," he said, kissing her on the cheek.

She stirred but didn't wake.

On the way out, he stopped in front of the officer who watched him as he approached. "Has anyone else been here to see her?"

"A couple of people from where she works came by but the doctor turned them away."

Chase nodded. "Thanks…for keeping an eye on her."

A surprised smile spread across the beefy cop's face. "Just doing my job."

"I know…thanks."

He nodded and Chase walked away, feeling like this whole mess was close to being resolved.

He stopped on the floor where Val worked and went to the desk. "Is Val here?"

The desk nurse looked up. "You just missed her. She took her dinner break."

"Thanks," Chase replied then took the stairs down to the cafeteria.

When he didn't see her, he walked out and across the street to the little pizza shop where they had shared a meal. He saw her through the window with two other women in scrubs.

He watched her, debating whether to go in.

What are you doing? You're a screw-up. A loser. Even if she accepts your apology, all you're doing is delaying the inevitable…she will leave you.

He took a breath and turned away, feeling as if a weight was crushing his chest. He was nearly across the street when she called.

"Chase?"

He turned, smiling sheepishly. "Hi."

"Decided you didn't want to eat here after you saw me?"

"No...nothing like that. I just...."

Her head tipped sideways and she smiled curiously as she tried to decipher his behavior.

"I'm sorry...about earlier," he said. "I just wanted to tell you that."

She grinned broadly. "I figured you were having a bad day... you know—" she circled her face with her finger. "—the cage fighting thing."

He chuckled and dropped his head, nodding. "It hasn't been fun."

"We ordered enough food if you want to come eat with us."

Chase looked through the window to the two women who were now staring at him, giggling.

"Another time," he said. "Thanks for the offer, though. I have a mess to clean up at home."

She nodded, still grinning broadly. "I'll be around."

"Okay...talk soon." He turned and almost ran into a parked ambulance.

While Val was kinder, doing her best to stifle a giggle, her two friends inside were nearly falling over with laughter. He shot her a sheepish grin and walked toward the garage, putting the ambulance between him and the restaurant as quickly as possible.

What is it about her? Why can't I just walk away? I don't even know her. The question haunted him all the way back to the parking garage beneath the hospital. As he swiped his card to pay the parking fee, he realized he hadn't let himself get close to any girl in a long time. It was almost as if he were holding himself in reserve, avoiding distractions so he could focus on protecting Chloe.

He shook his head as he pulled forward. "Well, Chloe *is* almost a full-time job by herself."

He was out of the garage and nearly to Interstate 66 when he glanced in his rearview just as the car behind him passed under a street lamp—a dark colored Crown Victoria.

"You son of a bitch," Chase muttered pulling out his phone.

He dialed Deb Ortega.

"Ortega," she answered.

"Officer Ortega, it's Chase Grant. You know that Crown Vic that we had on vi—"

"Yeah. What about it?"

"It's following me right now."

"Where are you?"

"I'm on George Mason headed away from the hospital," Chase said, glancing in the rearview again. "I was about to get on sixty-six."

"Wait, what?" she asked, muted as if she had placed her hand over the phone to talk to someone else. A second later she spoke more clearly. "You aren't gonna believe this. We just had a tip called in that a dark blue Crown Victoria was seen with blood or red paint coming from the back."

He looked up in his rearview. "I can't see his trunk. Who called it in?"

"I don't know. It came in on the tip line. The captain just stopped it from going out over the radio."

Chase shook his head. *That's too much of a coincidence.*

"Do you want me to try to get behind him?"

"No. Stay on Mason. We're pulling something together. Don't spook him."

"Wait!" he snapped.

"What?"

"Remember I told you he took off after the BOLO was transmitted?"

"Right. That's why we aren't using the radio."

In the background, Chase heard Ortega walking through hallways and knocking on a door. Chase could hear a man talking, but it was too faint to make out.

A moment later, she came back on. "Where are you now?"

"Just crossing North Carlin Springs Drive."

There was further muffled discussion on the other end. "Okay. Stay on Mason and cross Arlington Boulevard. If he's still on you after that, keep going to Columbia Pike."

"Okay…I understand."

"Are you going the speed limit?"

"For the most part," Chase said.

"Drop down to the speed limit and stay there. If you can manage stopping at a light or two without giving yourself away, do it. It'll give us more time to set up our cutoffs."

"You got it."

"Thanks for calling instead of trying to handle it yourself," Ortega said in a quieter voice.

"I haven't been doing too great in the do-it-yourself department lately." *Plus it's better for me if the cops do the shooting.*

"Where are you now?" Ortega asked.

"Coming up to the light on Columbia Pike…it's red."

"Good. We're almost ready."

"How are you communicating with the other units?" Chase asked, worried the trap would be blown if they were using police department communications of any sort.

"We lojacked the six closest units and called their cell phones…conferenced them together. Is he still following?"

Chase looked up in the rearview and panicked—the car was gone. "Shit." He swiveled his head side to side as the light turned green. When the lane next to him moved, he caught a glimpse of the Crown Vic in his side mirror. "Yeah…he's still behind me, but in the next lane now. Hold on and I'll tell you if he follows me through."

"Okay."

Chase moved through the intersection, checking his side mirror in his peripheral view. When he was across, he glanced in his rearview again as the Crown Vic slid smoothly into the lane behind him three cars back. "Yeah. He's still following me."

"Good. You'll pass Twelfth Street, Thirteenth Street then Thirteenth Road South… let me know as you go past each one."

"Passing Twelfth now."

"Okay. When you see the cruisers in front of you, stop and stay in your car."

"Okay…coming up on Thirteenth."

"Thirteenth Street or Road?"

"Oh shit, he's speeding up. He's on to us."

"Damn it! Pull over. Don't get tangled up in this."

"He just passed me. I can see the cruisers behind me."

Chase pressed on the accelerator and pulled up even with the Crown Victoria.

"Chase. Stop your car and let him go!"

Chase disregarded her order and instead pushed down on the accelerator, struggling against the bigger engine of the Crown Vic, to edge him out of his turn. The driver turned to Chase, his face a mask of rage.

As they approached the last street before Four Mile Run Drive, Chase cut into the turn lane and smiled at the other driver as he slid to a squealing halt in the intersection, blocking the way. Rather than stop, the Vic tried to execute a high-speed U-turn in the median. Behind him, Chase watched as two cruisers jumped the curb into oncoming traffic to cut off the escape.

"He's blocked," Chase said, jumping out of his car as a cruiser pulled in front of him. An officer got out and aimed his weapon at him. "They just got here," Chase said, holding his arms out to the side. "Someone's aiming his gun at my chest."

"Drop the weapon! Down on the ground now!" The officer yelled.

Ahead, three sets of blue lights flashed in the grills and on the roofs of the oncoming police cars. The Crown Vic slid to a halt, blocked in both directions. The driver opened his door and got out, lying face down in the middle of the street before the cruisers had stopped their forward motion.

"It's not a weapon. It's my phone," Chase yelled.

"Drop it!"

"Did you hear me, Deb? There's a gun on me!"

"Who?! The guy in the Vic?" Ortega said, her voice now on speaker.

"On the ground hands out to the sides," the officer yelled at Chase.

"No. A cop," Chase replied as he complied with the order.

"Who is that? Who's the officer giving that command?"

"I don't know. My face is on the pavement."

"Not you. The officer. Identify yourself. This is Officer Deb Ortega Arlington PD."

"Officer Farley," the officer said, putting a knee in Chase's back.

"Farley. That's Chase Grant you have on the ground. He called this in. He's working with us."

Farley pulled Chase's wallet out and opened it before releasing him. As Chase stood, Farley handed his wallet back to him. "Sorry. Just being careful."

"That's fine," Chase said, too interested in what was happening with the driver of the Crown Victoria to be angry at the cop. Chase took his phone off speaker and put it to his ear.

"Do they have him?" Ortega asked.

Chase walked closer, avoiding direct eye contact with the other officers. "Yeah. They have him on the ground."

Chase walked around the blockade in the other lane, separated from the action by the concrete and grass median. He arrived at the rear of the Crown Victoria just as the officers opened the trunk. Their expressions told Chase there was something very, very bad contained within. Chase stepped closer—it was Bobby Tang, pale as snow, eyes open and vacant.

"No," Chase said, breathless.

He shoved his phone into his pocket without disconnecting and ran around the Crown Victoria to the man who had been driving. The officers couldn't move fast enough to stop Chase from laying several brutal punches and kicks to the man. "You son of a bitch, I'll kill you, you cock sucking mother f—" Three officers tackled Chase and pulled him to the ground beside the man. "I'll kill you, kill you—"

"What? What's going on?" The man on the ground asked, frantic.

"Nice try, Heath. I guess you were just holding the body for a friend," an officer said, dragging Heath to his feet.

As another cop read him his rights, Heath stood wide-eyed in voiceless astonishment. When the officers let Chase stand again, they inserted themselves between the two men and pushed him backward away from the car. Chase was done yelling—he was watching Heath's face—he wanted that image burned into his memory.

As the police dragged Chase backward to his car, he reached over their shoulders, pointing at Heath, silently mouthing the words "You're dead."

Farley, the same officer who had put him on the ground a few minutes earlier, wrenched Chase from the street, flinging him on the sidewalk.

Chase barely managed to stay on his feet. "Get off me," Chase snapped, shaking himself loose from the cops.

Farley shoved him. "Watch yourself, boy."

Chase stepped forward aggressively and bumped chests with the patrolman, his angry scowl only inches from Farley's nose. A two-handed shove from Farley ended the confrontation as his partner stepped in and separated the two men.

"One more stunt like that and I'll put you in cuffs myself," the partner said, glaring at Chase.

Chase tipped his chin up to Farley, a silent dare to come back. The partner put his hand out, precluding any thought the sneering cop might have had of doing just that.

Chase wrenched his arm away from the partner. "Am I done here?"

"You're done. Get the hell out of here."

It wasn't until he was back in the car and driving away that he realized his phone was still connected.

"Chase!" Ortega yelled from his pocket.

He touched the Bluetooth receiver button on his steering wheel and suddenly Ortega was screaming over his car speakers. "What the hell?!"

"He killed, Bobby Tang. Son of a bitch—"

"Who is Bobby Tang?"

"He's my friend. I work with him at Baxter." Chase pulled over in the first lot he came to and put the car in park. He pounded his steering wheel. "Jesus Christ! What the fucking god damned…" After several punches to his dashboard, each peeling more skin from his knuckles, he realized Ortega was still talking to him.

"Calm down. Please. Calm down."

"Why the hell would he kill Bobby?! Bobby was a good guy…"

"We'll find out. Chase, calm down. We'll find out. Heath is going away for a long time."

Drops of angry tears gathered at the corners of Chase's mouth before running down his chin. The angry sneer he still carried made his cheeks ache which only fueled more anger.

"Virginia still has the death penalty…right?"

"Yeah," Ortega said with slight amusement. "Virginia has the death penalty."

"Good. Because it would suck if I didn't have something to look forward to."

"I'm sorry about your friend. I can't believe Heath would do that."

"Well…" Words failed him.

"Go home," Ortega said, softly, encouraging. "I'll talk to you tomorrow after we find out more."

Chase breathed out a bit of his rage, suddenly feeling tired.

"You did well," she added.

Chase ended the call and sat back in his seat, wiping his eyes with the back of his hand. After several more cleansing breaths, he put his car in drive and drove home. On the way, he regretted not going out with Bobby the night he had asked—it would have been the last time he got to see him. It occurred to him only after the guilt had set in that he would have been at the hospital with Chloe that night anyway. But it was too late—he already felt guilty.

"Now all I need to know is how Heath is connected to the firm."

SATURDAY
PLAYED

CHASE woke at seven o'clock on that Saturday. He lingered in bed trying to fall back to sleep but his grief and his anger built slowly until they filled his mind. After more than an hour of trying to keep his eyes closed, he got up and walked to the kitchen in his underwear. He stood in the center of the floor and surveyed the mess.

He wasn't in the mood to clean but he couldn't stand another minute being reminded that Heath had been through all his belongings, looking for—*for what?*

While the coffee dripped he began shoving debris into piles with his feet—broken stuff on this side, unbroken stuff on that side. Obsessive compulsive triggers kept his feet moving, pushing, piling, long after the coffee was ready, and by the time he got around to using his hands the tone sounded on the coffee pot, letting him know it had tired of waiting for him to pour his first cup—powering down.

He took the opportunity to pour a cup and leaned against his bar as he sipped at the uncomfortably hot, burnt liquid breakfast.

"That's a little better," he muttered, looking across the kitchen, eating nook, and living room. Most of his belongings were back in their places and two large piles of broken or unwanted items sat on his kitchen and living room floor.

He rested on his couch with his mug, enjoying the cushions being in place as if it were new. "Much better." He bounced once, delighted to be reminded why he had bought the couch, to begin with—comfy.

He drained his first cup then went to his bedroom to change into a pair of sweatpants and continue his cleaning efforts there. By eleven o'clock he was satisfied his apartment looked less like a bomb site.

"Time for a smoke break," he muttered and looked around for Jimmy's rolling papers.

He spotted them on the counter and went to retrieve his stash from under the sofa. But when he reached under, feeling around to grab it, his hand brushed something odd—something that didn't belong.

He lifted the skirt on the sofa and looked under it using the light from his cell phone. He squinted, confused as his hand followed a narrow cord that dangled from the springs. But his eyes flashed wide when his gaze followed it to its end and he realized what it was—a microphone.

He dropped the dust ruffle and sat up abruptly, staring vacantly as he tried to piece together the timeline.

The sofa was overturned when I walked in on Wednesday. And the cops were all over the place…no way it could have been there then or they would have found it. He looked down at the cushions and squinted. *That means someone came back.*

"Well duh…" *Brick Durggin came in. I don't know how long I was unconscious before the pizza guy came. I don't know what he might have gone through. I was gone all day yesterday.*

He looked around his apartment, trying to figure out what else might have been touched when his stare froze on his new computer.

The surveillance video!

Chase jumped up and ran to his computer, pushing the start button. As it booted up, he tried to breathe some calm into his mind. He realized if his apartment had been bugged, his computer may likewise be infected with spyware.

He hadn't sct up a password to log into his new computer—there had been no need at the time. He had no personal files on it. The video file was downloaded after he had set it up.

Think...how do I check my computer without letting spyware know I'm checking it?

It came to him in a flash. As soon as the welcome screen was up, he opened a browser and navigated to one of the many free porn sites available. After clicking through several categories, he settled on lesbian home movies and scrolled through several of the links. At the precise moment he clicked one of the video files, he disabled the Wi-Fi and Bluetooth functionality from the keyboard. Anyone who might be viewing his activities would mistake the action for a system crash due to a bad video driver.

He hit CTRL-ALT-DEL and launched the task manager, scrolling through each line and checking the properties. There near the bottom of the alphabetical listing was XSpoolRojEG.exe, sucking up 25% of his processing power. His heart jumped when he saw it was also writing to his drive.

It's a brand new, clean computer... Easy enough to see the files.

After writing down the drive location, he terminated the program, then watched for several seconds to make sure it didn't re-spawn itself. Satisfied he was spy free for the moment, he went to the directory the program resided in. Inside he found nothing—empty.

He set his mouth sideways, thinking, before hitting the view options and setting the option to view hidden files. A log and stacks of encrypted files revealed themselves, timestamps as file names in five-minute increments.

"Gotcha, jackass," Chase muttered then clamped his hand over his mouth and looked, panicked at the sofa.

Keep it together Chase.

The files were easy enough to delete, but he only removed the last set of files, timed to coincide with the faked "system crash". He'd figure out the rest later.

For the next twenty minutes, he browsed the files on his system, looking for any other point of intrusion. He found none. Though he was no security expert, he felt confident he had uncovered the only software set up to spy on him. It would take a real expert to know for sure but he didn't know any he could trust to stay quiet or reach on a Saturday morning.

"Good enough," he said and shut down his computer. The next time he started it up, the spyware would be completely oblivious to his discovery.

Minutes before noon, a knock at the door was accompanied by Jimmy's voice. "Chase, we brought lunch."

Chase opened the door and let Jimmy and Tonya in, hugging Jimmy first with a bro pat to the back, then Tonya with a warmer embrace.

She squeezed him tight then held him at arm's length. "How you doin' baby?"

The motherly warmth and familiarity in her voice permeated his chest, bringing ease where none was present only moments earlier. "I'm doing better."

"Yeah, we heard about Bruce Heath and your friend. I'm sorry about that. Were you close?"

Why is that always the first question… "Were you close?"

Chase nodded. "Yeah…pretty close."

A pained expression washed over both of them and Jimmy shook his head. "I'm sorry man. But at least they caught the guy."

He nodded and helped Jimmy bring construction supplies in from the hallway. As they laid out and measured the door jam replacement, Tonya set about making lunch in Chase's kitchen with the supplies she had arrived with.

"The place looks better than the last time I saw it," Tonya said from the kitchen. "Hopefully with what's-his-face in jail now, that'll be the last of this ugliness."

Chase wanted to tell her what he had found, but he was too conscious of the bug under his sofa to let anything slip. "I'm glad it's over."

Jimmy looked at Chase, an odd expression rippling over his dark, round features. "Don't you still have to find out how it's connected to work?"

Chase shrugged. "I'll tell Arlington PD what I know when they question me. They seem to have it all about wrapped up."

Jimmy nodded but still had a constipated look on his face, as if he were about to pry further. Chase tensed and shook his head sharply, nodding toward the living room. That clearly just made Jimmy more curious, but after staring at Chase for several seconds more, he returned to work, cutting out the splintered wood and replacing the door facing.

By the time they were finished repairing the doorframe, lunch was ready.

"Come and eat," Tonya said, peeking around the corner.

He and Jimmy dropped their tool belts and came into the dining nook. Chase stared vacantly at his plate as Tonya said a blessing. He was forking meatloaf into his mouth before she and Jimmy looked up.

"Mmm. This is awesome."

"Slow down," Tonya said with a warm, rolling chuckle. "You'll choke on your fork."

"Can't help it. I just realized how long it's been since I ate anything."

"Boy…we gonna have to get you married. You can't take care of yourself."

The fact that Tonya and Jimmy relaxed enough to let their folksy dialect slip around Chase made him feel like he had family—for some reason he couldn't quite pinpoint, it made him feel vulnerable and exposed. He looked up at Tonya's smiling face and winked.

Her eyes narrowed in suspicion. "What was that?"

Chase shrugged.

"Oh, my lord. You found yourself a girl."

Chase smiled. "Maybe."

"Well…tell us about her!"

"Val…she's a nurse at Virginia Medical Center."

Tonya leaned forward, hanging on every word. "And?"

Jimmy shook his head. "Let the boy eat, momma. He just finished saying he's hungry."

Tonya swatted at Jimmy with her napkin. "This is more important."

Chase chuckled. "Long black hair, dark brown eyes, and kind of a real light cocoa skin."

Jimmy laughed and almost choked on his meatloaf. "Aw shit…you found you a *black* girl."

"I think she may be Indian or Middle Eastern."

Jimmy shrugged. "Is she cute?"

Tonya slapped at Jimmy again, this time with the back of her hand. "Of course, she's cute. He's got a crush."

Chase nodded. "She's very cute. But man, she's sweet."

"I'll bet." Jimmy chuckled drawing a sour glare from Tonya.

"It's not like that," Chase said after swallowing another bite of food. "I met her, sort of, the night dad died. I was walking down the stairs, still having a hard time saying good-bye, and she walked past me. She put her hand on my shoulder and it was like someone had said 'everything will work out'."

Jimmy lifted an eyebrow. "And that was it? No making out in the stairwell?"

Chase shook his head, grinning. "She just passed me on the stairs and touched my shoulder…that's it."

"That's sweet. That's so, so sweet, baby. I hope it works out."

"I—" Chase's mind suddenly flashed to the microphone under his sofa. *Oh, shit.* "Anyway. Let's finish lunch so I can get the door frame painted."

"You have paint?" Jimmy asked.

"Not so fast. I want to hear more about this girl," Tonya said.

Chase was desperate to change the subject—he felt he'd already said too much about Val. *Stupid, stupid, Chase. You wouldn't even talk about the break in, why would you mention Val?!* He grinned, trying to come across as embarrassed. "That's enough…really. I'd rather get my door painted and finish cleaning up this pig sty."

Tonya looked disappointed but swept her gaze around the apartment. "It doesn't look so bad now. All you have to do is throw out the broken stuff and you'll be set."

Chase nodded, grateful to have successfully changed the subject.

"I need to go get the paint, though," Chase said, taking his empty plate to the sink.

"Don't do that. It's the same white paint they use in every apartment," Jimmy said, joining him and putting his plate in the sink as well. "I'll go down to the manager's office after lunch and get a bucket from her. I've seen inside that closet next to the office. It's full of the stuff."

"Oh. Cool. Well, I can do that. I'll go down after lunch."

"I don't mind doing it," Jimmy said, accompanied by a firm elbow to Chase's ribs.

Chase glared at him, but quickly realized he was setting up an opportunity to smoke some weed.

Chase winked his understanding. "Well, if you don't mind."

"Any excuse to come over and smoke with you," Tonya said, casting a disapproving glare at Jimmy and Chase.

"What?!" Jimmy's face bent in almost cartoonish incredulity. "I'm just tryin' to help the boy."

"Uh huh," Tonya replied, eyes rolling.

Jimmy grinned and bumped Chase with his elbow again. "I'll bring it by later. We can paint it tonight or tomorrow. Whatever works best for you. I'm free."

"Thanks, Jimmy."

"Let Chase finish tidying up. You've got home projects to do next door, too you know," Tonya said.

Chase grabbed the aluminum foil from the top of the counter. "Let me wrap this food for you."

"No, baby. You put that in your refrigerator. It's for you."

Chase smiled then wrapped his arms around her for a warm hug. "Thank you. I'll have it for dinner, too."

"Just stick it in the microwa—"

"He knows how to heat food, Tonya. Leave the boy be."

Chase laughed. "If I didn't know for sure that you two were madly in love, I'd be worried about there being multiple guns in the apartment next door."

Jimmy picked up his tool belts and moved to the door, muttering, "I don't know about *madly* in love."

"Don't you believe him," Tonya said. "We've been together longer than anyone else in either family. It's nice having someone who gets you."

Chase smiled at the sentiment but suspected it was another subtle emotional shove—a hint that he should give it a try.

Instead of pushing the matter, he saw them to the door and helped Jimmy carry the rest of the construction supplies into their apartment. When he came back, he admired the workmanship of the door repair—except for the absence of white paint, it was a perfect match for what had been there before.

He counted himself lucky that in the 90's when those apartments had been divided from luxury, multi-room apartments, his had a wooden frame door added. Had he been in the apartment next to him, the frame would have been metal and not as easily repairable.

He dropped down on the sofa and breathed out in relief that things were coming together. Chloe would be out of the hospital in a few days, work would go back to normal—*except no Bobby. Shit. Damn it all.*

That thought brought fresh anger and grief to his mind. He decided he needed to call the few people he was close to at work and break the news to them. Better that than them hearing it on the news, or worse, first thing Monday morning.

He called Tammy first.

"Oh my God! That's so sad," she said, crying into the phone.

"I know. Hopefully, the police will find out why it all happened."

"It could have happened to me, or Sherry, or even Jake! Oh, my God.

Why would he do that?"

Chase breathed out. "I don't know. I'll let you know as soon as I hear anything."

"Well, do you know when the service is or anything?"

"No. I guess I should call Officer Ortega and find out who she contacted. I don't think I'd know how to get hold of Bobby's folks."

"Let me know as soon as you hear," Tammy said between sobs.

"I will. See you Monday."

"Bye, Chase."

He ended the call and proceeded to call the other few names he kept listed in his phone. After the last employee call, he started to dial Jonah's number but then thought better of it. Certainly, the strange issue with Bobby's computer being cloned would come up in the conversation and he didn't want to talk about that in the apartment with the listening device wired under his couch—just in case this wasn't the end of the drama.

He put on a light jacket and went out, turning the bolt on his front door with a satisfying *click*.

On the way down in the elevator, he dialed Jonah's number—it went to voice mail after three rings. On the way out of the building, he tried again, and again it went to voice mail.

"Jonah, it's Chase. I have some news but I don't want to do it over voice mail. Call me when you get this."

As he got into his car, his mind drifted to the wire under his sofa and the spyware on his computer.

Ortega believes me now…I should tell her. She'll stay quiet until she knows what's going on.

He started his car and linked his phone via the Bluetooth connection as he pulled out of his parking space.

"Call Deb Ortega," he said to his phone and it dialed.

"Ortega," came her clipped reply.

"Wow…someone's in a good mood."

"Chase?"

"Yeah. What's wrong?"

"Why would anything be wrong? It's not every day you get a slam dunk on a double homicide and attempted murder," she replied, her voice conveying anger, not relief.

"So lab results are back?"

"Yeah. It was an all you can eat buffet."

"Tell me," Chase said.

"Your sister's blood and hair were found in the back seat and trunk of Heath's Crown Vic. Bank statements belonging to Brad Bowman were under the back seat and Heath's fingerprints were all over the murder weapon used on Tang."

Chase's chest pinched at the mention of "Tang's" death.

"Bobby."

There was a short pause, then a lowered voice. "Sorry...Bobby."

"What was the murder weapon?"

"Heath's old police flashlight based on early examination. It was in the trunk with the...with Bobby."

"You don't sound convinced."

"There was a lot of damage to his ribs and belly. Someone worked him over hard and for a long time before they caved his skull in."

Chase ground his teeth and shook his head, trying to maintain his emotions—he decided to change the subject. "Who notified Bobby's family?"

"I did. It didn't seem like they were close but they came in to identify him this morning and make arrangements."

"Do you have details about the funeral home and such?"

"I can get them for you. I'll text them to you later."

Chase took a deep breath before launching into his finds. "There's something I want to talk to you about...but I don't want you to do anything about it until we find out more."

"Okay, go ahead."

"I found a wire under my couch and spyware on my new computer."

There was a long pause. For a moment Chase thought he had lost his connection. "You still there?"

"Yeah...when did you find them?"

"This morning."

After another short pause, she grunted something unintelligible in the background.

"I didn't catch that," Chase said.

"I was hoping to put this off, but I don't think we can now," she replied. "We should meet."

"Okay...where?"

"I think you should come to the county jail."

Chase blinked, startled by the answer. "Why the hell would I go there?"

"I'll tell you when you get there."

"No. If you want to talk somewhere private, that's fine, but I'm not meeting you at the jail."

Ortega was quiet for a second then spoke softly. "I know. I understand why you'd have reservations. But there's someone here you need to listen to."

"Who?"

"I'll tell you when you get here."

"If this is another trick to get me arrested."

"It's not. Now shut up and get over there," Ortega snapped, impatient, agitated.

Chase ended the call and debated the order for several minutes. He shook his head then took the next exit.

When he arrived he found Ortega waiting in the parking area in civilian clothes, sitting on the bumper of an SUV and nursing a small cup of coffee. Next to her was an older man who Chase immediately recognized from the photos he had seen at her house.

She spotted Chase and got up with urgency. "We only have ten minutes. We have to hurry."

"Hurry where? Who is this?"

She led them through a side entrance and waited for Chase and the other man to catch up. She peeked through the small window back into the lot after the door closed. "Chase Grant, this is my uncle. Gabriel Ortega Senior."

Chase reached out to shake his hand before the significance of the name struck him. "It was your son that Durggin killed?"

His lips flattened to a thin line and he nodded. "I'm sorry about your friend," he said.

Chase looked at Deb then back to the senior Gabe. "What's going on?" he whispered.

"We don't think Heath did it," Gabe said.

Chase raised an eyebrow. "You have to ignore an awful lot of evidence to make a statement like that."

"Everything would be easy enough for a seasoned police detective to set up...which brings up another point," Gabriel leaned closer and lowered his voice. "Heath *was* a seasoned police detective and yet his vehicle was covered in evidence."

"Maybe he thought he had time to clean it up," Chase replied, clinging to the slim hope that this was over.

Deb shook her head. "Here's the thing. Your sister's hair and blood were in the back seat and trunk...four strands and no more than a single smear of blood. But there wasn't a single ding, dent, smudge, or broken headlight on the car indicating he had ever hit anyone."

"He might have used another car. Maybe he had plastic down in the back seat."

"Do you honestly think he would run over someone, ditch the car, come back with his own vehicle and transport her to another site? Beating her unconscious in between?"

"Maybe someone else was helping him. There aren't enough holes in the facts to suggest Heath is innocent," Chase said, letting a little anger slip. "We know he was at Bowman's apartment. We know he was following me."

Gabriel put his hand on Chase's shoulder, urging calm. "He said he was following Durggin...that's why he was at Bowman's building."

"Well ain't that convenient...'I was there following the *real* bad guy'," he said with a mocking tone.

"The timing on the video supports his story," Deb added. "There's no way he could have gone all the way up, killed Bowman and gotten back down in time to follow you. He said he lost Durggin and was following you, hoping you'd lead him to Durggin."

"This is bullshit."

Deb squinted at him. "Did you see him carrying your bong when he got out of his car?"

Shit! Goddamn! Son of a bitch! "Doesn't prove anything. He could have been carrying it under his jacket.

"No," Deb said, looking over her shoulder through the small window. "Everything the police needed to arrest Heath was in the car...but nothing in his apartment, nothing in his office."

"Look. I'm sorry Durggin killed your son," Chase said to Gabriel. "But you want Durggin so bad, you're ignoring the evidence and are trying to free a murderer. He killed Bobby!"

Deb squinted at Chase, jutting her chin in smug defiance. "Answer one thing for me then, smart guy...Why did he do it?"

"What?!"

"Why would Heath break into your apartment, set up your sister with

Bowman, run her over, and kill Bobby Tang…? And why would he be following you around?"

Chase shrugged. "I don't know. Maybe if you dig around a little more you'll find a motive."

Deb shook her head, agitation rising on her face. "Your apartment is bugged and your computer has spyware on it…what in your life is that interesting?"

"I already know this had something to do with work."

Gabriel inserted himself between the two, inserting a calmer demeanor. "What she means is, what is it about you—or Bobby Tang for that matter—that makes you a target for violence?"

And that was the question, wasn't it. Why indeed? "Shit," Chase muttered. "Something to do with the cartels."

Deb raised her eyebrows noting Chase's "ah ha" moment. "Yeah."

"So why am I here?"

Deb looked at her uncle then back to Chase. "He wants to talk to you."

"Who? Heath?" Chase shook his head. "No. No. Uh uh. Hell, no."

"Just listen to him. Hear him out," Gabriel said. "If nothing else you'll be able to look him in the eye and tell him what you think of him."

Chase's eyebrow jumped up involuntarily. That was tempting. "Okay. I'll hear him out."

Gabriel smiled and nodded. "Come on. He's waiting."

They checked in, showing their badges, then led Chase down a narrow corridor. When they emerged into a larger hallway, Chase knew where he was—he'd been there before on a few occasions. He realized he had just come in the back way; the cop way.

Deb and Chase stood by while Gabriel went to talk with the guard.

"What's going on?" Chase asked.

"This visit is off the record."

Chase shook his head. "How much trouble are you going to be in if you get caught doing this?"

Ortega shrugged. Chase could tell she was motivated by something far more potent than the law and it made him uncomfortable being a part of it.

Gabriel gestured for Chase and Deb to join him. After going into the visitor's "lounge", Gabriel leaned close and whispered. "You only have a few minutes…booth six."

Chase went to the assigned booth and sat, staring at the thick glass, waiting for Heath. When he showed up doing the perp walk, his ankles tethered together with chains, Chase got nervous. The orange scrubs didn't seem to carry the same humiliating air with Heath as it always had with Chase—or perhaps, Heath was just better at hiding it.

The guard motioned to the fixed bench and Heath bent to look at Chase through the window before taking a seat. They reached for the phone handsets at the same time.

"Ortega said you have something to say to me," Chase said, cold, still unable to shake the image of Bobby lying dead in Heath's trunk.

Heath nodded. "I'm sorry about your friend."

"Is that a confession?"

A flash of anger rippled across Heath's face. "No. I was just saying I'm sorry your friend is dead."

"What about my sister?"

He shook his head and dropped it away from the handset. He looked back up after a moment. "How is she?"

Despite the aimless anger Chase felt, the realization that he might be talking to an innocent man tempered his response. "She'll live."

He nodded with a sincere look of relief. "Good."

"Why am I here?" Chase asked.

"Because you need to know I didn't kill your friend or hurt your sister."

"That's easy enough to say," Chase snapped, raising his voice. Gabriel and Deb looked his way. He glanced at them then back to Heath. "It's not me you need to convince."

"I'm not trying to convince you I'm innocent…that's for the police and my lawyer," he said, lowering his voice. "I need you to understand that whatever it is you're mixed up in isn't over just because I'm in here."

That was the first real moment of "truth" he felt coming from anyone about this.

"You see, I don't know anything about what you're into or why Durggin was involved, but I can tell you it has something to do with one or more drug cartels," Heath said. "And if you don't know why then you're in more danger than if you did know."

"Why were you at Bowman's place?" Chase asked.

"I followed Durggin, who was following you."

"Since when?"

Heath looked behind him then leaned closer to the glass. "Durggin is dirty and has been for years. I keep tabs on him when he's in town…I keep relationships with all my street connections."

"When did he start following me?"

Heath shrugged. "I don't know. I got word he was in town and hunted him down. I caught up with him by accident when he followed you from the hospital the morning after your sister was run down."

Chase took a deep breath and let it out slowly. If Heath was telling the truth, that meant Chase had made a huge mistake letting Durggin go the night he broke in—it could have all stopped then. *Bobby might still be alive.*

"I followed him to the club in Arlington and watched him go in after you did," Heath continued. "Then I followed him to Bowman's place after both of you left… I had no idea he'd set a fire while he was in the club."

Chase ran his fingers through his hair, suddenly exhausted again. Nothing was resolved, nothing was over.

"I lost him at Bowman's building but I saw you. I figured if he was tailing you, he'd keep you in sight, so I started following you instead," Heath said.

That made sense to Chase. It explained a good number of things. "What happened yesterday?"

"I hadn't been able to find him again for a couple of days, but I wasn't giving up. Brick is a heavy-handed thug but he's not stupid. He wouldn't be making such a mess of things unless there were big stakes in play. So I followed you again…to the hospital."

"How did Bobby get in your trunk?!" Chase's voice rose again, before grasping a bit of calm. "And all that evidence?"

Heath shrugged. "Honestly, it doesn't take much to hack a key fob. He could have recorded the signal anytime in the last few days then broadcast it at his leisure to open my car… you were in there a long time and I waited until you came down."

Chase nodded.

"I even went up once to make sure I hadn't missed you. You were watching TV with your sister," Heath said.

"So you had no clue?"

Heath shook his head. "It never occurred to me that Durggin might be on to me."

"Where does that leave me?"

"That depends on you... Do you know why he's after you?"

Chase rubbed his face with his hand then shook his head. "No...not really."

Heath tipped his head sideways and squinted. "You're sure?"

"I know it has something to do with work and high-frequency trade server transactions—unless that was all bullshit too. But other than that, I don't have a clue how it's tied to cartels. Not exactly my customer base."

"What's your customer base?"

Chase grinned tiredly. "Blue-haired old ladies investing their dead husbands' pension checks... old guys who sit around all day, following stock message boards but too timid to make a decision without talking to someone first."

Heath shook his head. "Durggin's not into that. It's something else."

"Yeah...I figured."

Heath looked at Chase for a beat, seemingly trying to read the type of person he was. "I don't know anything about you, but the Ortegas seem to trust you," he said finally. "And I don't know what you're into that's got you tangled up with Brick or the cartels, but whatever it is, you need to watch your back."

Chase nodded.

"What the hell is going on in here?!" Chase turned toward the new voice. An older black man, graying around the temples and heavy around the waist, stood in the doorway glaring alternately between Chase, Deb, and Gabriel.

"Nothing you need to worry about, Carl," Gabriel said. "It doesn't concern you."

"The hell it don't!" Carl said, moving toward Chase. "This punk here is part of an ongoing investigation and he's talking to, so far, the only arrest in the case...un—ac—ceptable."

Deb tipped her head sideways toward the door. "Come on Chase. That's enough for today."

"Hold up, sister... Don't think you're just gonna stroll outta here like I didn't see you tampering with witnesses."

"Arrest me then," Deb said, stepping close, her nose only inches from the older black man.

He just glared at her before turning his attention to Chase. "Don't think you're off the hook, punk."

"Yes, officer," Chase muttered, sarcastically.

Carl shoved Chase by the shoulder as he walked past. "That's Detective Sergeant, you shit stain. I worked too hard for some punk ass to demote me."

Chase arched his back, throwing his chest out as he stepped toward Carl. But Gabriel intervened, hooking his arm through Chase's. "That's what he wants, Chase. Just walk away."

Carl grinned cruelly as the trio departed the visitation room. "I'm coming for you, punk…ya feel me?"

Chase turned and grabbed his crotch. "Yeah…I feel ya."

Carl charged toward Chase but Gabriel stepped between them again and pointed at the camera on the ceiling. Carl looked up at the camera then back to Chase, grinning. "Comin' for *you* punk."

Once outside, Chase kicked a trashcan and walked down the ramp to the parking lot. "What was that about?!"

Deb and Gabriel caught up and gestured him to calm down. "That's what he wanted. If you had taken a swing at him in there, he would've had you off the street for years…striking a cop is a felony."

"Cocksucker!" he screamed at the side of the building, his face flushed and veins bulging from his neck.

Deb stepped back and grinned. "You have to do something about that temper of yours."

He was aware he was making an ass of himself—he wanted them to see the hothead. "Who was that?"

"Him? Detective Sergeant Carl King," Deb said with an ironic grin. "That's the guy who convinced the Commonwealth to charge you with murder the other day… Brick Durggin's old partner."

Chase stood there, mouth open but unable to speak.

Gabriel nodded. "So you see, it's a good thing you didn't hit him." He turned Chase toward his car. "Come on. You've heard enough and you're a big boy. You can make up your own mind."

"There's something you need to know…Durggin came to see me."

Deb grabbed Chase by the shoulders tightly. "When?!"

"Two nights ago. He's the one who worked me over."

"Why didn't you tell someone?" Gabriel asked.

"I wasn't sure I could trust anyone in the Arlington PD at that point… My neighbors are cops. They came in and stopped him, but the story he told me was so convincing, I made them let him go."

"What story?" Deb asked.

He proceeded to tell Gabriel and Deb the story as Durggin had laid it out to him, including the apparent regret he carried over killing young Gabe.

Gabriel took a deep breath and looked at Deb. "It's possible. It's possible someone was trying to set Durggin *and* Gabe up—unlikely, but possible."

"But the Beltrán-Leyva Cartel dried up and died after Durggin left," Deb said, almost sounding desperate.

A wave of regret washed over Chase's face. "After Gabe died too."

Deb shoved Chase, two hands to the chest. "The shit with the Beltrán-Leyva Cartel was going on years before Gabe even made detective."

He swallowed hard, letting his anger settle before stepping closer again.

"The Juárez Cartel was in control within months of Beltrán-Leyva disappearing," Gabriel said to Deb in a soothing tone.

Deb shook her head. "Maybe so, but Gabe was dead and both Durggin and Heath left at the same time. So if anyone inside the department was helping the Juárez Cartel, it wasn't any of them."

Chase nodded. "Exactly my point. If someone is setting up ex-cops, maybe it has something to do with the Juárez Cartel. Maybe—just maybe—there was a power exchange and Gabe got caught in the middle. But Heath and Durggin are both out now…civilians."

"No…not out. Durggin admitted to investigating you," Deb said, near desperation in her voice. It was clear she so desperately wanted to clear her cousin's name.

"True," Chase said, giving her a slim concession. "I guess the next step is for me to find out who hired Durggin to investigate me and why."

Gabriel nodded. "Do you need any help with that?"

Chase thought a moment. "No. My boss is a good friend. He's already digging around. I just need to let him know what's happened and try to get him to dig a little faster."

"Thank you," Deb said.

"Don't thank me," Chase said. "I'm trying to get myself out from under this bullshit as fast as I can. It's hard enough taking care of Chloe without a bunch of dirty ex-cops screwing with us… This is purely selfish."

Gabriel put his hand on Chase's shoulder. "It still puts you on the right side of this…whatever this is."

"Just keep our numbers in your phone and call us if Durggin pops up again," Deb said.

Chase scoffed through his nose. "He invited himself in the last time."

"Maybe he'll do it again if we put enough heat on him."

Chase took a deep breath. "And I just fixed my front door, too, damn it." He nodded. "Okay. I'll talk to Jonah. Maybe we can press a few more people from work about who hired Durggin."

"You're sure you can trust him?" Deb asked.

"If I can't trust Jonah, then there's no one I can trust…including the two of you. So you better hope I can."

Deb looked at Gabriel, eliciting a nod from him. She turned back to Chase. "There's one more thing; since the PD arrested Heath, they took the officer off your sister. As far as they're concerned the case is solved."

Chase's eyes flashed wide. "Oh man…I didn't think of that."

"Fortunately, the Ortega family is large and heavily populated with law enforcement," Gabriel said, supportively patting Chase's shoulder. "Until we find all the answers we need we've made arrangements for her to be looked after 'round the clock."

Chase breathed out in relief. "Thank you."

"But that only gives you a little time to find out what's going on from your boss," Deb said. "As soon as the department realizes there's an Ortega family reunion on your sister's floor, they're going to dig in and ask questions… then we're no longer operating in secret."

Chase nodded. "Okay. I'll do the best I can."

Deb smiled. "Go and see your sister."

Chase shook hands with Gabriel and nodded to Deb before getting into his car. As he drove away, he looked in the rearview; the two Ortega's were talking, both staring at him with worried expressions.

This does not bode well.

He drove to the hospital and parked, mindful to check his mirrors for any followers. Satisfied no one tailed him, he went in and upstairs to Chloe's floor. As he rounded the corner to Chloe's room, a young man in jeans and a flannel shirt rose from the bench across the hall.

"Can I see your ID?" he asked.

"That's my brother, Miguel," Chloe said, sitting up. "You can let him in."

Miguel nodded and went back to his seat, resuming his vigilant watch.

"You look so much better," Chase said as he walked in. He stopped short when he saw Val sitting in the chair next to her bed.

"Hi," Val said with a smug grin, batting her lashes. The look said *"I know something about you…and you don't know what it is."*

"Hi," Chase replied, hesitant.

"Val and I've had the best chat," Chloe said, breaking the awkward tension.

"Yeah…your sister has some *fascinating* stories about you."

Chase glared at Chloe. "Oh, shit."

Val walked over and patted his shoulder patronizingly. "I have to get back to work," she said then looked over her shoulder to Chloe. "Great talk. We need to do it again soon."

Chase remained quiet, nervous tension rising up in his gut.

Val leaned over and whispered in his ear. "Don't worry. You're more likable now than you were before…if that's possible." She gave him a quick peck on the cheek and left.

That means Chloe left out the bad stuff.

Chase looked at his sister through slits. "Really?"

Chloe smiled and shrugged. "She's sweet. Your name just came up in passing."

"Yeah sure."

"So tell me…why did the police department pull their guard, but now I suddenly have an off-duty cop outside my room keeping an eye on me?"

"It's complicated."

"I'm pretty smart…I think I'll understand if you tell me real slow."

Chase shook his head. "We don't know if they have the right guy in custody."

"We? Are you a cop now?"

"I'm helping them."

Chloe lifted an eyebrow. "I think that may be one of the signs of the Apocalypse."

"Could be. We're trying to find out who's behind it all."

"You mean the break in and my hit-and-run?"

Chase swallowed hard, not wanting to drop anything too heavy on her—he didn't want to mention Bobby Tang. He nodded. "It's all related somehow. Tied to work. I'll figure it out. Don't worry."

"Why would I worry? Cops outside and a morphine-on-demand button by my side."

"When this is over, see if you can get that to-go."

She chuckled and nodded. "Will do."

He smiled warmly and took her hand. "You really do look better."

"I feel better."

He nodded and patted her hand. "I just wanted to check in on you. I have to go talk to Jonah about something, but I'll stop by again before I head home."

"Don't worry about me. Just get done what you need to get done. I'll be fine. Great people here...and that Val...what a talker once you get her going."

"Really...? Anything about me?"

"It was all about you. And no, I'm not telling you any of it."

"Bitch," Chase said, grinning.

"You know it, babe. Now get the hell out of here before I call my bodyguard in."

Chase winked at her then bent and kissed her forehead. "Love you, sis."

"Love you too, bro."

Chase left and nodded to Miguel on his way out. At the desk, Val was lingering, chatting with the nurse behind the counter.

She looked up as Chase approached. "Have you eaten?"

"I have, but if you want company while you eat, I don't mind watching you." He grinned broadly.

She laughed. "I'd like to get a bite...to eat."

"I just have to make a call first."

She nodded. "I'll meet you downstairs."

She walked away and Chase pulled his phone from his pocket. He dialed Jonah's number again—and again it went to voice mail.

"Jonah. It's Chase. It's *really* important you call me as soon as you get this."

He shook his head and stared at his phone for a second before ending the call. "Where are you?" he muttered as he got on the elevator. "And why aren't you returning my calls?"

Val was waiting when he arrived in the lobby. It was nearly dark outside and he worried briefly that he had let the day get away from him. But Val's warm smile broke his tension as he joined her. "Where are we going for dinner?" he asked as she took his hand, her fingers curling gently, timidly, around his.

"I thought you weren't hungry," she said with a grin.

He shrugged.

She looked at him sideways then abruptly tugged him into an exam room, flipping the "occupied" flag next to the door.

"What are you doing?" Chase asked.

She stood in front of him after closing the door. "You're not good at subtle hints, are you?"

"Well, I thought we—"

She threw her arms around him and kissed him, pressing her body against his. After the initial shock, he slipped his arms around her waist and pulled her closer. Their tongues entwined and warmth flooded to his face and groin.

When she pulled back, only a short distance, she smiled. "Was that too subtle as well or do I need to be more obvious?"

He grinned. "I'm not sure I know what you mean."

"Shut up," she whispered then resumed their kiss.

As they embraced, her hands explored his back beneath his jacket and his hand rose to the curve of her neck pulling her closer.

She stepped back against the exam table before hopping up on it and wrapping her legs around the backs of his.

"Is that flag going to stop anyone from coming in?" he asked softly into her ear as she ran her hands up his chest.

"I don't care," she muttered breathlessly.

He pressed and strained against her, hungrily kissing her open mouth. She reached down and pressed her palm against the front of his pants and moaned into his mouth.

A knock at the door broke them apart in panic before it opened.

"And if she doesn't get the rest she needs when she gets home, there could be complications," Val said, sliding off the exam table. She looked at the gape-mouthed nurse who had walked in and smiled. "Hi."

The new face flushed red. "Uh...hi?"

Val looked at Chase who was doing his best to tug his jacket down over the erection in his jeans. "So is there anything I'll need to know—"

The nurse backed out and closed the door quietly.

Val and Chase laughed their tension away before straightening their clothes. Val bent sideways and checked herself in the mirror next to the exam table before rubbing her fingers along the sides of her mouth. "Maybe this wasn't the best place to do this."

"Ya think?" Chase grinned and pulled her close for a short, but sincere kiss. "I have to go see my boss. But if you aren't too tired when your shift is over, I'll swing by and take you out."

She smiled, bashfully. "So you finally got my hints?"

"I'm slow, but I catch on eventually."

She kissed him again then pushed him away gently. "You're ready?"

He took a deep breath and adjusted his jacket. "Ready."

She opened the door and walked into the hall. "And if you have any questions after she's released, feel free to call her primary care physician—he's already been given all the information—or you can call the hospital and reach Doctor Kapur or me through the switchboard."

"Thank you. I'm sure I'll have questions."

As they strolled past the nurses' station, they received a mixture of giggling smiles and disapproving stares.

Chase leaned close and whispered, "Are you going to get into trouble over that?"

"Over what?" she asked innocently without looking at him, but a pink blush rose to her cheek.

She looked behind them when they reached the stairwell and grabbed his jacket pulling him through the door. She kissed him, bringing his arms around her again.

She abruptly pushed him away. "My shift is over at midnight."

"Midnight."

"Now go away you bad boy before you get me in trouble." She dashed up the stairs, a broad grin stretching her flushed cheeks. She paused at the landing, shooing him away with the backs of her hands. "Go now... Leave before I call security."

"Psycho," he replied, smiling, shaking his head.

"Stalker," she whispered, giggling. "Go away."

He stood and watched as she disappeared around the corner before exiting the stairwell. He left the hospital smiling so widely, his cheeks hurt. *She's a winner.*

He pulled his phone out and dialed Jonah's number again, ringing three times before going to voice mail. "Jonah, it's Chase again. I'm coming over to your place. It's about six o'clock and I should be there in ten or fifteen minutes depending on traffic. Call me if you get this before then."

Traffic was as expected and he arrived fifteen minutes later, frustrated he hadn't heard back from Jonah. He drove down to the underground garage and passed Jonah's car in his reserved spot. "Jesus, Jonah. Why didn't you answer your phone?"

The elevator from the garage was secure and required being buzzed up by a resident. Chase pressed the code for Jonah's luxury penthouse suite, half expecting no reply.

"Yeah." Short, clipped.

"Jonah. It's Chase. Buzz me up."

The glass door to the enclosed elevator and stair lobby buzzed and unlocked. On the way up, he began to relax, feeling now that Jonah was involved, the answers would start flowing. He touched his lip and let his mind drift to Val's kiss.

When the elevator opened on the top floor, he strode confidently, his energy renewed, to Jonah's door, one of two on that level.

The door was already slightly ajar and swung open when he knocked. "Why the hell didn't you answer your pho—" Chase walked in and froze. Jonah was on the floor of the living room, hands tied behind his back and his face bloodied.

"No Chase! Run!"

He turned but something hard and cold hit him across the temple. He dropped to the floor, cracking his head on a hallway side-table on the way down.

▶◀

CHASE slowly regained consciousness hearing his name whispered, over and over.

"Chase… Chase." He opened his eyes to slits as the pain in his temple began to radiate into a massive, vise-like migraine.

His head rolled to the side and a glimpse outside revealed he had been unconscious for a good long while—it was totally dark out.

"Chase," he heard again, whispered in a desperate rasp.

He let his head flop the other direction, his blurry eyesight struggling to focus on the face across from him.

When the muscles in his eyes, slowly, painfully pulled the fog away, it was Jonah's bloody face he saw. "What—?"

"Shhh," Jonah hissed, looking behind him toward the back rooms. "He's still here. Are you okay?"

He flexed his arms against the chair he was bound to. "What? Uh… who's here?"

"I'm here," came a familiar voice from the hallway.

Chase swung his heavy head around and saw Durggin standing there, eating an apple from Jonah's counter. "You…you piece of shi—"

Durggin threw the apple like a baseball, striking Chase in the chest, cutting off his insult. Chase sucked in a ragged breath to replace the air the apple had knocked out.

"That's right…you're the tough guy. You're the one who doesn't mind being knocked around a little." Durggin walked closer before grabbing Chase by the hair and yanking his head back. "This'll be fun." He punched Chase in the gut, forcing his hard fought breath out again.

Chase gasped for breath, his shoulders folded in protectively as far as his bound arms would allow—handcuffs and tape.

"You are just such a smart guy, you mangled the whole plan," Durggin said then yanked his head up by the hair again. "And now a lot of people are gonna get hurt because of you."

"The cops know you set Heath up…they're already putting the pieces together."

Durggin slammed his fist into Chase's gut again, expelling all the air from his lungs. "You don't know when to shut up, do you?"

Chase coughed and wheezed.

"No…the cops *don't* know I set up Heath. The Ortegas *suspect* I did because they don't want to accept a stain on their long, illustrious family history with the department."

"You left too much evidence behind," Chase said between gasps.

Durggin delivered a hammer blow to Chase's ribs. "Shut the fuck up."

"Chase…just cooperate. It's not worth losing your life," Jonah said, struggling against his bonds, the blood on his lip now dried to a dark crust.

"He's gonna kill us both," Chase said. "He's got no intention of leaving witnesses."

Durggin pulled a chair over from the dining room and sat on it backward the way he had a few nights earlier at Chase's apartment. "What makes you think I won't just untie you and let you go if you do what I tell you to?"

Chase shook his head. "Well by my count, it would be the first time you *didn't* kill someone who was in your way."

Durggin took a deep breath and stared at Chase for a second, genuine exhaustion on his face. "Look. I'm not going to get into a debate with you. You can believe me or not. But here's a promise; if you don't do what I tell you to, you will die… and it won't be me who kills you… and it won't be fast."

"Do? What the hell can I do?"

"You remember those 'employers' I mentioned the other night?"

Chase just sneered at him, resulting in a backhand to the cheek.

"We need a dialog here if we're going to get things resolved amicably," Durggin said calmly, smiling.

Chase spat blood on the floor and turned back, still glaring. "Yeah…I remember."

"Well, I wasn't completely honest with you. They aren't *technically* employers—though, with the amount of money they run through your firm they might as well be."

"The Juárez Cartel," Chase muttered.

Durggin's and Jonah's eyebrows rose at the same time.

"You *are* a smart one…how did you figure that out?" Durggin asked, amusement tugging his mouth into a cruel grin.

"The news…right after I heard you named winner of the cocksucke—"

Another backhand across Chase's face sent him to the floor with his chair. Bound as he was, the arm of the chair pinned his wrist, sending a flash of pain up his arm.

"You're just a laugh riot," Durggin said, picking Chase up with the chair, setting him in place. "Keep going with the funny stuff. I have all weekend and your friend here has a refrigerator full of food… I'd only need to stop beating you to nap and take a piss."

Chase rubbed his cheek on his shoulder, glaring at Durggin.

Durggin lifted his eyebrows. "Well?"

"The Juárez Cartel took over the vacuum left behind when the Beltrán-Leyva Cartel went belly up… happened almost to the minute that you killed Gabe Ortega and left the department. I figured you were the one playing cozy with Beltrán-Leyva then got a better offer from Juárez. All you had to do was pin it on someone who couldn't defend himself from the grave then beat feet to help Juárez pick up the pieces."

Durggin shook his head then looked over at Jonah. "This is a real smart guy…whatever you're paying him isn't enough."

Jonah shot him a piercing glare but remained silent.

Durggin looked back to Chase. "Okay…you got me. Yeah, it was me, yeah I set it up to make it look like Gabe was taking the Leyva payoffs…and yes, I helped Juárez clear out the last of the resistance and set up shop in Arlington." He lifted Chase's head by the hair again. "And now, Juárez is really fuckin' pissed that you've been cutting the returns on their laundered money."

Laundered money?! That's what this is about?!

Durggin must have read the surprise on Chase's face. "Oh…? Didn't figure out that part, huh?" He dropped Chase's head. "The only problem is now that you've drawn so much attention, others are gonna start piecing it together too," Durggin said, standing and walking through the living room. He picked up a crystal decanter and examined it closely before dropping it on the floor, shattering it. "So *you* have to fix it…and fast."

"How am I supposed to fix it?"

"First, you need to tell me how you've been narrowing in on the cartel trades and running the matrix against them."

Chase glanced at Jonah out of the corner of his eye then back to Durggin. "Research."

"Bullshit," Durggin said, calmly, amused.

"It's true. I track every sector, every fluctuation and build my own prediction matrix on it."

Durggin turned and looked at Chase, then Jonah. "How many trades per second are recorded from outside the firm?"

Jonah looked back over his shoulder at Durggin then back to the floor. Durggin charged over to him, picking up a corkscrew from the bar as he passed. He grabbed Jonah by the hair and yanked his head up, holding the corkscrew less than an inch from Jonah's eye. "Answer me!"

"We don't have access to the per second trades unless we intentionally record them from the market stream…too much data. We only save one-minute totals."

"Correct," Durggin said. "And with that one-minute total, how many adjustments can you make to HFT server controlled buys or sells…manually?"

Jonah shook his head and muttered, defeated, "None…it can't be done without the fractional data."

"Right again." Durggin walked over to Chase. "Now how is it that a punk kid with a record as long as my arm can walk into a trading firm like Baxter and start beating the HFTs within two months of working there?"

Chase glared at him.

"Answer...? You've been cheating."

"No."

Durggin smiled. "Yes."

"No!" Chase could feel the heat rising to his face. "I used what I had access to...the HFT transactions from our firm."

Jonah shook his head. "Those algorithms are secure. There's no way you could access them."

"Damn it, Jonah!"

Regret flooded across Jonah's face and he dropped his head.

Durggin grabbed Chase by the hair again. "Tell me how you did it."

"The algorithms and matrices are secure but the transactions still have to be loaded and executed. I noticed that stocks on the floor matrices were being run down after the system suggested our customers buy and run up after sells were suggested. No one is that incompetent...not for long anyway."

"How—did—you—get—the—data?!" Durggin's face was flushed with rage.

"The transactions run through the trunk feed like everyone else's. It's raw data. All I needed were the HFT transaction IDs and I could harvest them in bulk. I started doing it a month after I worked there. It only took me two weeks to build a prediction matrix based on our own HFT transactions."

"Like I said...you cheated."

Chase shook his head. "Whatever...at least I didn't kill a—"

A punch to Chase's face left his ears ringing. It was a second or two before he realized Durggin was talking to him again.

"—and set it up to make back everything you've stolen over the last ten months...including what that queer skimmed the other day."

"Bobby? He only had my matrix one day? How much could he have moved?"

"Oh sure...that first night he only moved his customer accounts, but the next morning, he shared it with half the traders on the floor." Durggin sat down in his chair facing Chase. "Apparently, your coworkers were so thrilled to have even one day's worth of your trade magic, they walked away with more than ten million in cartel money... Nothing really compared to what you stole over ten months, but still, a big chunk of change they weren't happy about losing."

"You cocksucker...Bobby didn't know anything about it. You didn't have to kill him."

Durggin smiled. "Who said *I* killed him?"

Chase glared, wondering what that meant.

Durggin shrugged. "Either way, *you* killed him. It was your thieving that involved him...and your sister for that matter."

Chase's rage flooded up and he struggled against his bonds, sending himself and the chair falling toward Durggin.

Durggin simply stood back, watching him fall forward, then delivered a kick to Chase's gut.

"Chase, don't...please don't fight, man," Jonah said, pleading.

Chase lay there for several seconds catching his breath. When Durggin pushed his chair upright, Chase asked, "How is it they're laundering money with stocks...? They're all recorded and regulated by the SEC. They aren't cash transactions."

Durggin grinned and leaned forward. "Did you ever take a look at the companies they were shorting?"

"Penny stocks...small cap. It was all shit."

Durggin nodded. "And if you looked at the companies, you'd know they were all connected by their board of directors. The money came in the front and went out the back to be used as capital for the investments. Losses got bounced down in unannounced bear raids and the profit returns got funneled back in as gains to fuel run-ups."

Chase shook his head. *They're making more money scamming the market than they are on the drugs...using the drug money as capital to hide its source. The perfect way to hide it...right in the middle of everyone else's money.* He looked at Jonah then thought of Chloe still laying in her hospital bed.

"The Securities and Exchange Commission doesn't have enough manpower to keep track of their parking spaces, much less the big firms. How the hell do you think they'd keep track of a million small cap start-ups...most never even report a profit?"

Drug cartels, taking advantage of underfunded federal agencies and lax regulations, shot full of holes by a bought and paid for congress... no wonder this country is dying.

"How am I supposed to fix it for the cartel?"

"You're going to use your magic prediction matrix to preload everyone's trades for Monday. When the HFT servers come online, your matrix is going to work in exactly the opposite direction it has for the past few months. By mid-morning, every retail trade customer account is going to pay back what you took...with interest."

"Yeah, sure. Give me my phone, I'll call that in now."

Durggin punched him again. "Remember what I said before about using a book to tenderize your face?"

"I have no access to the retail floor trade computers, you fucking idiot!"

Durggin smiled and nodded toward Jonah. "But he does."

Jonah shook his head. "No. No way in hell."

Durggin picked up the corkscrew and charged Jonah.

"It wouldn't do any good!" Chase yelled, interrupting the attack. "It wouldn't do any good. He may have the system access but he would need physical access to the floor computers to overwrite the default matrices."

Durggin turned back to Jonah. "Is that true?"

Jonah nodded.

Durggin straightened up and looked at the ceiling. "Shit!" he threw the corkscrew across the room then left, walking down the hallway to the back rooms. When the door slammed, Jonah looked at Chase. "He's in there right now calling the cartel. And when he comes back, he's going to have a plan to get the matrices loaded on the retail floor systems... do *not* fight him on it."

"Jonah, I'll do whatever you say, but he's going to kill us as soon as they get what they want."

Jonah shook his head. "Time...all we need is time to figure something out. Go along with what they want. If we give them an excuse to kill us, they're going to take it. And I don't know about you but my job isn't worth my life."

He had a point. Chase nodded. "Okay."

Jonah smiled. "You didn't do anything wrong...it was smart. And it was smart to keep it to yourself."

Chase nodded. "I think the cartels would disagree."

Jonah shrugged. "Under different circumstances, that would have been the kind of move to make you a partner."

Chase smiled, head down. "I like my nights and we—"

"—weekends free...yeah, I know." Jonah grinned and stared at him for a second. "I'm proud of you."

Warmth flowed up to Chase's face. For a second he almost forgot his throbbing cheekbone.

"I should have told you what the HFT analysts were doing...I should have known the retail base matrix was corrupted. It was so obvious."

Jonah shook his head. "There's no way you could have known. Don't beat yourself up."

Chase scoffed. "I'm not doing the beating."

"Yeah...you need to tone down the attitude. He had me all day and only hit me twice," Jonah whispered. "If you're not careful it's going to leave permanent brain damage."

Chase shook his head, lip curled. "Chloe hits harder than he does."

"Nice...but if you get him pissed, he may start working me again and unlike you, I enjoy recognizing my face in the mirror."

Chase nodded. "Alright. I'll tone it down."

A moment later, Durggin walked back in. "Get comfortable. You aren't going anywhere for at least another ten hours."

Chase sagged against his bonds as Durggin dropped heavily on the sofa group across the room. He put his feet up on the table and tipped his head to the side. "Where's your data?" Durggin asked as if in passing.

Chase looked up.

"It's not on your computer...I searched it. And it's not on your system at work. We went through that with a fine-tooth comb. So where is it?"

Chase nodded toward his belongings on the table. "If it were a snake, you'd be dead already...it's on my key chain."

Durggin jerked forward and scooped up Chase's keys. After tugging on the key chain the top came off revealing a small thumb drive. "You sneaky bastard...you know, if you'd kept it on your computer at work, you would've gotten your ass kicked but none of the rest of this would've happened."

"Well someone should have told me that," Chase said, an angry sneer bitterly pulling the corners of his mouth.

Jonah cleared his throat, reminding Chase he had promised to tone down the attitude. He chewed on the inside of his cheek. "I was trying to make money for my clients and the company."

"And yourself," Durggin muttered as he toyed with the thumb drive. "You have the highest commission rate in the company after the executive officers."

Chase shrugged. "If you say so."

Durggin smiled as he went to Jonah's laptop on the dining room table. "I don't care. Doesn't matter one little bit to me. But in a couple of hours, there's gonna be someone asking you questions who *will* care. And I can promise you this; if you run that smart mouth at them, you're likely to get your tongue yanked through a slit in your throat."

That imagery caused a pinch in Chase's chest.

"There won't be a need for that," Jonah said after seeing Chase's reaction. "We'll do whatever is required to make things right with your clients."

Durggin looked up from Jonah's computer and grunted indifferently. When he returned his attention to the laptop, he inserted Chase's thumb drive. After a moment scanning the contents, he looked up at Chase. "Where's the matrix? All I see is raw data."

"That's all I have. I build the matrix on the fly every day based on the hedge action against the stocks that day."

Durggin shook his head. "Sucks to be you, then. I know my contacts aren't gonna be able to make heads or tails of this shit. I hope you have a backup plan."

Just then, Chase's phone rang on the table next to Durggin. Durggin leaned over and looked at the screen. "Huh…That cute little nurse you've been hanging out with is looking for you."

Chase tensed.

Durggin smiled. "Maybe she should be here too?"

Chase clenched his jaw as Durggin picked up the phone and began typing. "What would that do but make things more violent around here?"

"Leverage…I'm sure the Juárez guys would agree."

"No!" Chase yelled twisting in his chair. "You can't do this without me. If you bring her here, I will make you kill me before she gets here."

Durggin grinned and set the phone down without sending the message. "How exactly do you plan on doing that?"

He tensed his whole body, flexing back and forth then rose off the ground, sending the chair slamming back to the floor. Durggin pulled his gun from his waistband. "Stop it."

He rose up again and slammed down, harder. The frame of the chair splintered and cracked.

"I said *stop it!*" Durggin screamed.

As he jerked sideways against the arms of the chair, breaking the wood, he glared at Durggin. "What are you going to do? Shoot me?! If you want your money, you leave her out of this or so help me god, you're gonna have to kill me as I come to break your fucking skull."

"I'll do it! I swear to fuckin' god, I'll punch your ticket right now."

"Do it!" he yelled, rising from the splintered chair and pulling the last broken piece of wood from the carcass still taped to his arm. The cuffs dangled from his wrist. "You're dead."

"Chase, don't!" Jonah yelled.

But Chase was moving toward Durggin, the arm of the chair held high above his head. "Shoot me you prick!"

"Back off! Back off now!" Durggin rose from the table and circled around, away from Chase.

"You can't kill me. If you kill me your drug dealing buddies will slice your throat when you have to explain killing their only chance at getting their money back."

"I'll take my chances," Durggin said, his voice nothing more than a low growl.

"Then do it! Pull that trigger!"

Durggin circled around as Chase closed in on the other side of the table. When he was close enough to his phone he snatched it from the surface.

Panic and anger jumped to Durggin's face. "Put it down!"

Chase began to dial. "Kill me!" Chase yelled, defiant, angry.

Durggin glanced at Jonah, still tied to his chair. "How about him?" He swung his weapon around and pressed it to Jonah's head.

Jonah closed his eyes and tensed. "Jesus, Chase. Do what he says. Please."

Chase froze. All he had to do was push "dial" and the call would go through to Deb Ortega. But it would most certainly mean the death of Jonah. He stared at Durggin's angry face and the gun pressed to Jonah's temple. When Durggin pulled the hammer back, Chase dropped the phone on the table.

"Smart boy…now get back over there," Durggin said, swinging the gun back in Chase's direction.

He lashed out with the chair arm, bringing it down solidly on his phone. It broke into a dozen pieces of plastic and metal, sliding in all directions. Durggin rushed him, flipping the heavy oak table over on top of Chase. Durggin dove across, driving him to the floor and striking him against the side of the head with his pistol.

As darkness closed around him, his only thought was, *At least he can't trick Val into coming here.*

SUNDAY
HEDGING

CHASE snapped awake as cold water splashed his face. The sky was dark and the air was cooler. He looked up only to discover he was actually looking down—over the rail of Jonah's balcony.

"Whoa! What the fu—"

A quick jerk of his legs smashed the back of his head against the glass wall that served as the balcony rail. He looked up to see two pairs of hands grasping his ankles. He looked down at the street, more than two hundred feet below.

"You have taken something from us and Mr. Durggin says you aren't being cooperative in seeing it returned," said a man with a mild Spanish accent.

Chase twisted his head to get a look at him—a third man standing in the doorway of the balcony. "Dude. The last thing I said to Brick head before he knocked me out was that I'd be happy to fix your problem for you…and if I had known, I wouldn't have changed the matrix, to begin with."

"I am no *dude,* and I'm more inclined to trust our man than you who stole from us."

"I swear, I didn't steal from you. I found a pattern in the stocks and exploited it. I'm an analyst…that's what I'm paid to do."

The two men pulled him back on to the narrow terrace and let him drop on the flagstone with a thud. He sat, gasping, looking up at the men. "I swear. I only want to make things right. I have no reason not to and every reason to make you happy. Even my boss is on board."

The man who had spoken looked over his shoulder at Jonah who was still tied and on the floor. He nodded at Chase. "Okay, I'm willing to take you at your word. But if you give me any reason to doubt your full cooperation, I understand there are several people in your life who are easily locatable…including a sister in the hospital."

Chase struggled to maintain an even demeanor. "There's no need to risk exposing yourself like that or threatening anyone else. I'm cooperating…fully."

"Expose ourselves?" he chuckled, incredulous. "How would we expose ourselves."

Chase nodded toward Durggin through the glass. "You should ask your boy. He's killed or tried to kill so many people recently, he's got law enforcement working double shifts around here. Arlington PD is already looking at him."

The man laughed. "From what I understand, *ex-*Police Detective Heath has already taken the fall for all that."

Chase shook his head. "Brick head in there forgot to plant evidence anywhere but the car then didn't bother leaving hit-and-run evidence *on* the car. It only took forensics a few hours to realize the evidence was planted."

The man looked through the glass at Durggin's back then to Chase once again. "You seem to be well-informed about what the police know."

"I wouldn't be if my sister hadn't been run over, and my coworker and Durggin's old CI hadn't been murdered," he replied, then looked up sharply. "Oh yeah, he also broke into my house and let the police photograph him after he attacked me."

A crease appeared on his forehead as he turned and went inside. Chase couldn't make out what was being said, but Durggin was clearly doing some backpedaling judging by the worried expression on his face.

Chase looked up at the two guys who had dangled him from the rail and were watching him. He smiled and nodded. "How's it going?"

One of the men sneered, but a brief grin flashed across the other's face before he too resumed his stoic watch. The man inside slapped Durggin and a flash of anger contorted his face, but Durggin was apparently smart enough not to cross the cartel representative any further.

After a few more seconds of watching him argue with Durggin, the cartel man returned to the balcony. "Bring him in."

The two men lifted Chase by the arms and brought him inside. After dropping him on the sofa one sat next to him, the other—the one who had briefly smiled—remained standing.

"This has gotten messy," the cartel man said. "It might be best for me to just dispose of everyone involved and accept the loss."

Chase crossed his legs and put both hands on his knee. "Though I have *strong* reason to argue against that particular plan, it really isn't necessary. I've already told your thickheaded employee over there that I can get all your money back plus interest in one trading day...as long as Jonah is willing to loan me his system override codes."

The man tilted his head. "*All* of our money...? All hundred fifty million?"

Chase whistled. "Wow. I didn't know it was that much...but yeah. I should be able to pull that off. It's a triple witching week. That means lots of settled cash getting ready to move on options and pay margin calls."

"Triple witching?" The man asked.

"Yes, uh...I'm sorry, I didn't catch your name."

The man grinned and sat on the table in front of Chase. "You can call me Romeo."

"Romeo. Yes, four times a year, index futures, index options, and stock options all align and expire on the same day. It's called Triple Witching. It's a dynamic, volatile day with lots of cash moved and HFT servers market wide looking for hair-trigger clues to the way things are gonna fall."

"And that happens Monday?" Romeo asked.

Chase shook his head. "Friday. But everyone is hoarding settled cash to make the moves. All the buys and sells from the middle of the week last week until now are going to be sitting in a catapult Monday and Tuesday so any last minute jumps are with settled accounts...no one wants to be caught trying to jump out of a stock that wasn't purchased with settled cash; it's an automatic ninety-day penalty of cash only trading."

Romeo nodded. "And how does that work to our advantage?"

"Your shares have been volatile anyway. A massive run up or run down would trigger all the automatic actions on every HFT server watching them. It *could* be worth as much as two hundred million in stock movement starting at the opening bell on Monday."

"Two hundred, you say?" He smiled though it was clear he was unconvinced.

"That's on the optimistic end, but it would easily cover the hundred fifty you lost with the bad analyst sheets."

Romeo jutted his chin and looked at Durggin. "Have you seen this data he speaks of?"

Durggin nodded. "But it's raw data. I can't make sense of it."

Romeo looked at Chase. "How do I know you aren't lying just to save your life."

"He's telling the truth," Jonah said from behind Romeo.

Romeo turned and looked at him.

"All he needs are my codes and access to the retail trading floor systems before the market opens on Monday," Jonah added. "If you need me to verify the matrix before he goes to install them, I'll be happy to do it. There's no need for violence. We want to cooperate."

Romeo nodded and returned his gaze to Chase. "What do you need to make this happen?"

"My thumb drive. Brick head over there has it," Chase said, drawing a chuckle from the standing cartel muscle. "And a computer." He looked at the dining room table and nodded toward Jonah's laptop. "That one should suffice."

"And you need physical access to the systems to make it happen?"

Chase nodded. "All the floor systems have incoming access filters and browsing can only be done in sandbox browsers…to reduce the risk of hacking the firm computers."

Romeo nodded. "Do it."

Chase got up and walked over to Durggin. "I'll need my data, limp dick."

Durggin threw an elbow to Chase's jaw, sending him to the floor.

"That's enough!" Romeo yelled at Durggin. "I need him more than I need you right now."

"You still hit like my sister," Chase said as he stood and defiantly held out his hand for the thumb drive.

Sneering, Durggin reached into his pocket then handed Chase the drive. Chase closed his fist around it, then jerked his knee up sharply, cracking Durggin in the balls. Romeo's hired muscle moved as if to intervene, but Romeo held his hand up, stopping them as Durggin crumpled to the floor, grasping his groin.

Chase stared at him for a second before turning dismissively and sitting at Jonah's computer.

It took little more than an hour to cross-reference all the stocks and load their current trading prices from the close of market on Friday. After another fifteen minutes building his matrix, he double-checked it against each stock. "Okay. I'm done with the matrix. I need to test run it in the sandbox," he said to Jonah. "I need your access to the system."

Jonah looked at Romeo expectantly. Durggin, who had been sitting in the kitchen, sulking, looked over. "Don't let them brainstorm. Have boy wonder there write down his estimate and see if the boss-man comes up with the same figures. If they don't match, they're scamming you."

Romeo smiled. "As you say."

He nodded toward his men to free Jonah while Chase jotted down his matrix estimates. He got up and walked over to Romeo, handing him the folded slip of paper. Romeo's men sat Jonah down in front of the computer.

"What model should I use?" Jonah asked Chase after logging in.

"Use the house average model for Monday...we should be within a two percent threshold."

Jonah nodded and loaded the numbers before running the simulation. Once complete he looked up at Chase, wide-eyed. "Is this right?"

"I hope so," Chase said.

"What did you get?" Romeo asked.

"Almost two and a quarter million on the floor average. Times a hundred and twenty-five active terminals, that's more than two hundred seventy million dollars," Jonah said, amazed.

Romeo opened the folded piece of paper in his hand. "Two hundred seventy-five million."

"Two hundred seventy-five million six hundred fifty-eight thousand, give or take two percent," Chase said, grinning.

Romeo raised an eyebrow.

"I'll only be able to do it once," Chase said, mildly defensive. "All the SEC required safeguards will go into place within twenty-four hours of us doing it. And there's going to be a mandatory ninety-day cash-only penalty period. But the money will settle without a hitch."

Romeo looked at Jonah. "And the money will be available when?"

"Thursday morning by market open."

Romeo nodded and grinned. "We should have hired you to run our accounts," he said to Chase. "You are—what did Durggin call you…? A boy wonder?"

Chase grinned. "I would have definitely done a better job than the guy you have building your matrix in HFT Division and the default retail matrix."

Romeo smiled. "Perhaps I *will* hire you to do our trading from now on."

"A commission check is a commission check. As long as we're following the trading rules, no one can touch me."

Romeo nodded then looked at Durggin. "You seem to have handled this entire affair incorrectly. And now that your identity is compromised, you aren't much good to us."

Chase's heart contracted. For a moment, judging by the heightened tension in the room created by that statement, Chase wondered if he was actually going to witness Durggin's death.

"Don't forget my import connections," Durggin said, a nervous tick twitching his cheek. "It might put a crimp in your capital flow if your shipments suddenly stopped."

Romeo laughed. "I think you've worked with us long enough to know that our supply lines have multiple redundancies." he shook his head and grinned. "But you worry too much. We always have need of heavy-handed blunt instruments."

"So what now?" Durggin asked. "There'll be warrants out for me by morning if they aren't out already."

"We'll worry about that after we complete the task at hand." Romeo turned to Jonah. "You can do this?"

Jonah shook his head. "No. The matrix works on the average, but each account manager has their own unique list of clients and trades. I can't run that many complex systems in my head like he can…Chase is going to have to do it."

Romeo looked at Chase. "Are you ready to be my broker?"

Chase smiled and nodded. "Happy to. But Jonah needs to come with me to access the building and the trading floor computers."

Romeo glanced at Jonah, then back to Chase. "No. I don't feel comfortable with both of you free. Jonah will give you his access codes and you will go with Luis…he'll make sure you stay on task."

Chase looked at the two men and wondered which one was Luis. When the angrier of the two nodded his head, Chase was disappointed it wasn't the man who had smiled—it would take more effort to smooth the way with this one.

Chase nodded. "Okay."

"You will leave now."

Chase lifted his eyebrows. "Now? It's three a.m. on Sunday morning."

Romeo shrugged. "So?"

"So any entry would stand out plus, backups are running right now. They won't be done until at least nine o'clock…it would be better to go tonight when the indexes update on the servers. No one would notice this little bit of data moving while the index data is populating databases."

Romeo nodded and looked at Jonah.

Jonah looked up, almost startled. "Yeah. He's right. I concur completely."

"Very good. We can all get some sleep then," Romeo said, nodding. "Luis and Franco, stay here and make sure everyone stays cozy."

Both men nodded.

"I'll be back in the afternoon before it's time to go," Romeo said as he walked to the front door.

Durggin followed closely. "What about me?"

Romeo stopped and looked at Durggin. "You should stay here, out of sight. It wouldn't be helpful to our cause if you were picked up for those murders."

Durggin glared at him. "So I'm a prisoner?"

"No," Romeo said, raising his voice. "You are doing what's best for the organization by staying out-of-sight."

"I'd be better off on my own if you don't need me anymore." Durggin moved for the door.

Romeo put his hand on Durggin's chest and stopped him. "You'll stay here like you're told."

Durggin pushed Romeo's hand away, prompting Luis and Franco to pull their weapons.

"Now, now, boys…Brick is a reasonable man," Romeo said. "Aren't you, Brick?"

Durggin looked at Luis then back to Romeo. "Right," he muttered, slowly stepping back.

"You'll stay here and when the trades are made we'll worry about getting you out of the country safely."

As Durggin backed away, Luis and Franco holstered their weapons and relaxed a tick.

"I'll be back later," Romeo said, turning to Luis. "Keep things calm here until I return."

Luis nodded, his face a picture of seriousness as Romeo turned and left the penthouse. Durggin went into the living room and dropped heavily into an overstuffed chair, glaring at Franco and Luis.

The turn of events with Durggin made Chase so happy, he found it difficult not to smile, despite the physical pain it caused. "Well, I'm bushed," he said, stretching. "Let's get some shut eye. We've got a long day of breaking and entering later."

Franco chuckled, but Luis just continued to glare at Durggin.

Chase looked over his shoulder at Durggin, then back to Luis. "I don't blame you," he whispered. "I don't trust him either. A real rat, that one." He made a rat face, complete with gnawing noises.

Luis couldn't help but let a sideways grin slip. Franco burst out laughing.

Good. It'll be an uphill battle but it's doable, Chase thought.

He lay down on the couch and looked around. While Luis kept a close eye on Chase, Franco had disappeared down the hall. When his eyes came to rest on Jonah, he found him staring at Chase, shaking his head nearly imperceptibly.

Chase winked at him then closed his eyes. *Don't worry, Jonah. I'll find a way to get us out of this.*

In his mind, he mapped his way forward, all the while warning himself to be mindful of his anger toward the cartel guys. He realized he even needed to be smarter about his belligerence toward Brick Durggin, antagonizing him only when it suited a strategic need.

He drifted off with the ideas still rolling in his mind.

He woke a short time later to a hand over his mouth. His eyes flashed wide, staring into Durggin's face.

"If you think you can bump me out of the picture by playing sweet with Romeo, then you aren't that bright."

Chase twisted his head trying to free his mouth and nose but Durggin had him well pinned.

"If I get one whiff of you setting me up, you're dead, your sister is dead and that hot little piece of ass you been sniffing around is dea—"

Chase drew his knee up sharply, hitting Durggin in the side of the head. Once free, he threw Durggin to the floor and landed on top, pounding at his face with hammer blows.

Luis and Franco rushed around and grabbed Chase by the arms, dragging him off Durggin.

Durggin launched from the floor, head down and coming hard for Chase. "I'm gonna kill you, you little fu—"

With Chase's arms held up by the two Cartel men, his feet were free. He jumped up and kicked Durggin in the side of the head. Durggin fell, hands at his side, face first, unconscious to the floor. Luis jerked Chase to the ground and slapped him with the back of his hand. The strike opened the cut on his eye.

Chase pressed his sleeve to his face and looked at Luis. "You need to keep a leash on that dog. He just told me he'd kill me if I didn't 'cut a slice' off those stocks for him."

Franco looked at Durggin then back to Luis. He said something in Spanish that Chase didn't understand but he didn't think *"Pinche puto"* was complimentary.

Luis kicked the unconscious Durggin in the gut, answering a question Chase hadn't been quite sure of—had the tension between them been an act? A second kick to the unconscious ex-cop cemented the answer. They really did hate him. *That should make things easier.*

Franco dragged Durggin to the back bedroom and closed the door before returning with a pillow from the bed.

Chase was surprised when Franco tossed it to him. "Thanks."

Franco nodded and took a dish towel from the kitchen, tossing that to Chase as well. He pointed at Chase's face. "You're still bleeding."

Chase pressed it to his eyelid and held it there for a moment before dabbing. It stopped bleeding in a matter of a minute or so.

Luis returned to the upholstered chair next to the sofa and tried to avoid eye contact with Chase. After a moment of staring out the window, Luis turned and pointed down the hall. "You stay away from him. He's bad news."

Chase pulled the bloody rag from his face. "I'm with ya brother."

Luis nodded with a breath through his nose then leaned back and closed his eyes.

Chase smiled inwardly. *This is going to work out just fine.*

▶◀

CHASE woke at first light and looked around the living room. Jonah was still sleeping on the other sofa and Luis was on the terrace looking over the rail at the street below. When Chase sat up, movement in the kitchen caught his attention. Franco was at the counter making coffee.

Chase smiled and wiped his eyes. "Morning, Franco."

Franco looked toward Chase and nodded, grinning.

"Did you get any sleep?" Chase asked.

Franco craned his neck toward the terrace to glance at Luis, then back to Chase, shaking his head. "I couldn't." He jerked his head in the direction of the back bedroom where Durggin had gone.

"Sorry. He's been a pain in my ass all week too."

Jonah stirred and looked around. "You okay?" he asked Chase in a quiet voice.

Chase nodded. "The sofa's not as comfortable as your spare bed, but I'll survive."

Jonah chuckled and sat up. "I meant the damage to your face."

"Oh…yeah. I'm fine."

When Jonah caught sight of Franco in the kitchen he stood. "The good coffee is in the freezer," he said, pointing. "You'll have to grind it but it's worth it…trust me."

Franco smiled and nodded, dumping the filter back into the can before going to the freezer.

Jonah looked at Chase and whispered. "I think you're right to make friends with these guys. It's a layer of protection between us and Durggin."

Jonah obviously didn't understand what Chase was doing and had made his own assumptions. He didn't care what Durggin did, as long as the rift between him and the cartel could be exploited later—Chase had analyzed the personality dynamics, charted the exploit, and was shorting both sides. A margin call on this situation would be deadly, but he was hedging intelligently.

He looked at Jonah for a moment and decided he needed to alter his plan—he needed more time to create a deeper division between Durggin and the drug dealers. "I'm gonna refine the sheet." Chase stood and stretched. "I threw that matrix together in less than an hour and only took into account the floor average. I didn't run the numbers on any of the other securities the retail traders use."

Jonah cocked his head to the side. "How would you do that from here? You don't have the trade lists for the retail floor."

"I know, but I can remember the big ones...they'd be the real paydays anyway. All I have to do is configure the list to each system as I install the matrix."

Jonah narrowed his eyes. "That would add hours to the project...is that a good idea?"

He shrugged dismissively. "What difference does it make if I'm there two hours or six hours? The codes are valid. And if anyone shows up asking questions, they can call you for confirmation that I'm there on your orders...you can tell them you're implementing new studies for the matrices. They'll love that."

Jonah's face pinched in doubtful regret. "I don't know. Seems unnecessarily risky."

"Besides, no one is going to show up or ask. It's Sunday."

Jonah nodded hesitantly. "How much more do you think it would net us?"

Chase looked at the ceiling and squinted, working out the rough math in his head. "Uh...about...another sixty million."

Jonah's eyebrows rose high and he whistled. That got Luis's attention. He turned and came back inside.

"Morning, Luis," Chase said, smiling broadly. "Did you sleep at all?"

Luis grunted with a shrug.

Chase nodded his head toward the back bedroom. "How about the rat...did he sleep?"

Luis stepped to within two feet of Chase, prompting him to sit down on the couch to keep a safe distance. "Don't talk to me. I'm not your friend."

"Sorry," Chase said, holding his hands up. When Luis walked away down the hall, Chase turned to Franco, jerking his thumb in the direction Luis had gone. "What's up with him?"

Franco smiled and leaned over the counter, looking down the hallway. "He is Luis."

Chase shook his head and walked to the kitchen. "I'll do the coffee."

Franco set the bag down and picked his gun up from the counter. He handed Chase the scoop as he tucked the pistol in its holster then walked back into the living room.

Chase ground the coffee in the noisy electric grinder and let his eye wander to Jonah's phone sitting on the counter. He looked up to see Franco flipping through TV channels before he edged over to the phone.

As he picked it up, Luis appeared from the hallway and spotted him. He rushed to the counter and snatched the phone from Chase's grasp, checking the screen to see if anything had been dialed.

Seeing it hadn't, Luis pointed at Chase, his fat finger only inches from his face. "Do that again and you die."

Chase raised his hands innocently. "I didn't want it to get wet. It was right next to the sink."

Durggin appeared behind Luis and glared at Chase before joining Franco and Jonah in the living room.

After coffee, Chase sat at the dining room table to work on the buy/sell matrix.

"Get away from there," Luis snapped.

"I'm working on refining my matrix," Chase said.

"Get—away—from the computer."

Chase shrugged. "Okay, but you get to explain to Romeo why he missed out on an extra sixty million…I realized last night I hadn't included the blue-chip companies in my data."

Luis reached back to hit Chase but Franco stopped his hand, staring at Chase. "Sixty million?"

Chase nodded. "Maybe more. I won't know until I can get the scripts loaded on the computers at work."

Franco looked at Luis. "That's a lot of money."

Luis hesitated, seemingly confused.

"It's true," Jonah said. "When he mentioned it to me this morning I couldn't believe we had left it out. We were so focused on the stocks in the HFT scripts, it didn't occur to any of us that the retail side works with legitimate stocks every day. The volatility of a triple witching week could free up a lot of that cash if the prediction matrix is tight."

Luis continued to stare at Chase, his hand raised.

Chase leaned back in the chair. "Look…that asshole over there spent the last week destroying my life over nothing. All he had to do was come clean to me about what was going on and I would have fixed it so Juarez was making more money than before." He turned the computer so Luis could see the screen. "My share of the commission on these trades is going to be more than two million dollars…and Romeo—I hope he was serious—already said that maybe he should have come to me instead of the guy he has running the funds."

Luis looked at Franco who shrugged. "He wants to work for Romeo."

"You aren't buying this shit, are you?" Durggin growled. "He's lied and manipulated this situation from the beginning."

Chase scoffed and shook his head, looking Luis in the eye. "Look at my face...he did that." He pointed at Durggin. "I didn't know until yesterday what any of this was about, because of that idiot there. He wrecked my life, killed a trader at the firm you guys use, and did such a shit job of covering it, the police know he's involved now...over nothing. I would have fixed it for free if anyone had just asked. I get my commission either way."

"Bullshit, you lying piece of—" Durggin charged at Chase, but Luis pulled his pistol and pointed it at his chest, stopping the big ex-cop in his tracks.

Luis glanced at Chase. "So you wouldn't be upset if I put the *rat* down right now?"

Chase thought for a second. *It's not a real offer, plus it's too early.* He shook his head. "I'm a stock analyst. I like numbers. I love my sister and I'm pissed off enough to want him hurt really bad...but I'm not cool enough to deal with that kind of violence."

Luis grinned at him.

"If you're going to do it, do it in the other room. If you do it in front of me it'll mess with my head so bad I won't be able to focus on the numbers."

Luis laughed. "You're funny," he said, nodding. "Okay. I'll kill him later *after* you make us rich."

Chase winked at him. "Thanks."

Durggin, who had been sweating bullets, slowly backed away and sat in the living room, keeping a close watch on everyone.

"So," Chase said, slapping his hands together and rubbing them. "Can I make the adjustments on the trade matrix?"

Luis nodded. "Go to work, analyst."

Chase got to work on the new sheets, pulling data from all the large companies he could remember being traded at the firm. After several hours of number crunching, macro building, and matrix overlay, he had created his greatest masterpiece.

Jonah brought him a sandwich late in the afternoon. "It's getting late. Are you almost done?"

Chase nodded. "I have to run the parity checks on the averages, but you should be able to run it in the sandbox soon."

Jonah read over his shoulder as Chase took a bite from his sandwich. "That's a lot of numbers. Are you going to be able to make all the changes before people show up to work on Monday?"

"Yeah…the whole reason for the averages matrix is so I won't have a lot of work when I get to the office," Chase said, his mouth full. "It should only take four or five hours."

Jonah nodded and patted Chase's shoulder. "You're really good at this."

Chase smiled and continued to work. A little while later, as most of the apartment occupants watched college basketball, the buzzer rang and Luis went to answer it. On the small security monitor next to the door, Chase saw Romeo standing at the parking garage elevator entry. Luis buzzed him up and a few minutes later, there was a knock at the door.

"Is everyone ready?" Romeo asked as he walked into the living room.

Franco nodded, drawing Romeo's attention to Chase. "What are you doing?"

Luis stepped forward. "He said he could add sixty million to the take…he's been working on the numbers all day."

Romeo leaned forward and looked at the work on Chase's screen. "This is true?"

Chase nodded but then realized Romeo had asked Jonah who nodded as well. Romeo patted Chase on the shoulder. "The boy wonder strikes again."

"Any trouble while I was gone?" Romeo asked.

Luis nodded his head toward Durggin. "We had to pull him off Chase in the middle of the night."

Romeo looked at Durggin, eyebrows raised. "Really? Why is that?"

Durggin just shook his head.

"Something about wanting a slice of the pie," Luis said with a cruel grin.

"That's a lie! I was warning him not to double-cross us," Durggin snapped.

"Chase says you told him you'd kill him if he didn't *cut you off a slice*."

"*Chase* says," Romeo smiled and looked at Durggin. "It seems my men have chosen a side."

"Like I care," Durggin muttered, looking away.

"You should care. They are keen judges of character. If they've come down so quickly against you, they must smell something—" he sniffed the air. "—off."

Franco made a pig noise drawing a glare from Durggin.

"And now the police are looking for you and your connection to the firm," Romeo said, shaking his head and grinning ironically. "Sloppy work, detective. Very sloppy work."

Durggin's lip curled. "I'm telling you, you're making a mistake trusting that punk… He's going to screw you the first chance he gets."

Romeo looked at Chase then back to Durggin. "And what exactly would you do to ensure that doesn't happen? Beat him some more?"

Durggin nodded his head toward the back rooms, indicating he wanted a private word with Romeo. Romeo rolled his eyes and shook his head as if he had grown tired of Durggin, but followed him down the hallway.

Chase's chest tensed but he continued to work as if he hadn't been listening. "Done. Jonah, you can run my numbers through the sandbox now."

Jonah walked over and sat as Chase stepped away from the computer. After a few moments, Jonah looked up with a big grin. "Man…you are a god damned magician."

Chase smiled and nodded. "Thanks."

Durggin walked back into the room and grabbed his keys from the counter. Luis tensed but then Romeo appeared and shook his head. "It's okay. He's running an errand for me."

"I'll need more time than we planned on the original script so we should get moving soon… in case there are any snags getting into the systems," Chase said, sitting back down in front of the computer.

"How much more time?"

Chase tipped his head sideways, calculating. "I'll need about six hours instead of the three I said yesterday."

A worried expression slipped over Romeo's face. "Isn't that cutting it close?"

Chase shook his head. "We should have a couple of hours to spare."

Romeo nodded and walked over to Jonah. "Is there a way to do this faster?" he asked.

Jonah looked nervous, like a deer caught in the headlights. He looked at Chase then back at Romeo. "I don't think so. All the scripts have to be altered manually on site. We wouldn't be able to use the prediction systems to populate the floor computers because the matrix isn't in the main system…plus it would leave a log trail if we tried."

"So we need the six hours?"

Jonah nodded. "If that's what Chase says we need then I have to trust it. I wouldn't be able to make that many manual adjustments in six hours, so it actually sounds fast to me."

Romeo nodded and looked at Chase. Franco stepped over and asked him something in Spanish. Chase didn't understand anything he asked except for the name "Brick".

His heart contracted hard when in Romeo's reply, he said the word *"chica"*.

Shit! Durggin convinced Romeo to let him go after Val!

Chase did his best to remain calm and not show his panic. He sat at the table and started sorting his data sheets into categories as the cartel guys continued to talk in hushed voices. In the background, he opened a browser and logged into his wireless provider's company website. When Luis walked around behind him, Chase quickly pulled up the spreadsheets, obscuring the browser until Luis had passed.

Once gone, he brought up the messaging app for his phone number and typed a message to Val's.

"You aren't safe. Wherever you are, go someplace with people and call Deb Ortega at Arlington PD. ONLY Deb Ortega."

Romeo looked at Chase. "Are you ready to get moving?"

Chase moved the spreadsheets back in place over the browser as Romeo came toward him. "I just have to finish separating the data by category… but honestly, it would be better if we went in after midnight anyway."

Romeo squinted and jutted his chin. "Why after midnight?"

"The access logs. They get closed out at midnight."

"Why is that important?" Romeo asked.

"Oh. Oh wait," Jonah said, moving toward them. "He's right. If there's an open entry on building access—especially on a Sunday night when backups are being run, it'll throw up a red flag to security… We need to go in after 12:01 or the open log will bring eyes on us."

Romeo nodded and folded his arms across his chest. "It would have been nice if that information had been given to me last night. Are there any other surprises I should be worried about?"

A tone on the laptop sounded, notifying Chase a message had been delivered. Romeo looked at the computer as Chase moved his spreadsheets around on the screen, making it look as if it were part of his work. He deftly pushed the function key on the keyboard and the mute button in a flurry of keystrokes, disguising his efforts.

Romeo looked over his shoulder. "A problem?"

Chase shook his head. "Just getting ready to copy to my thumb drive."

Romeo looked at Jonah. "Any other security issues we need to worry about?"

Jonah slowly shook his head from side to side. "I can't think of any...my executive level badge should get Chase into everything he needs access to, and *he* is the real security bypass anyway. Without him doing what he's doing manually, there'd be no way to get the data on the trading floor systems."

Romeo walked away and Chase pulled up the message app. Val's reply, *"Ortega wants to know what's happened."*

Luis moved to let Romeo sit in his chair then came toward Chase. Chase minimized the browser quickly as Luis came around the table.

Luis bent over Chase's shoulder and looked at the screen. His neck flashed hot as the adrenaline began to surge. *Did he see it? Am I caught?* The messaging, though a good idea, had turned dangerous.

When Luis straightened, Chase watched him in the reflection of the screen for a moment as he continued to work.

"Alright," Romeo said. "We'll wait until midnight to go in...who knows, with the extra time, you might find more loose money laying around."

Chase chuckled nervously, drawing Romeo's attention back to him. "Is something wrong?"

Chase looked up and shook his head. "No. But I think it's too late to add anything else to the sheets. As it stands I've had to correct a few numbers in my rush."

Romeo tilted his head toward Chase as if he hadn't heard him. "Maybe we should have another set of eyes on it before you leave."

Shit! "No. I think it's fine now."

Romeo motioned for Jonah to go to his computer. As Luis moved aside, Chase right clicked on the browser window and closed it. Jonah stood behind him, wide-eyed.

"Is there a problem?" Romeo asked Jonah.

He shook his head. "Just a lot of data on this screen." Jonah nudged Chase out of the way and sat in his place. He first brought up the browser.

Chase tensed. "You don't need that. All you have to do is run it in the sandbox again."

Jonah looked up at Chase as the browser window filled the screen. "I see," he replied. "Okay."

Jonah clicked the history button and looked at the links before taking a deep breath. He clicked the link then deleted it. "That probably wasn't the best way to do it, but you should be okay now."

Chase breathed out in relief as the history entry vanished. *Good thinking, Jonah.*

Luis came back around and glanced at the screen. Chase grinned. "You want to check it over too?"

Luis glared at him and returned to the living room. After a few minutes of confirming the data, Jonah stood. "It all looks good."

Romeo smiled. "Alright. Then let's get everything packed up and ready to move out."

As Romeo turned to Franco to say something, Jonah put his hand on Chase's shoulder, squeezing as he leaned in to whisper, "That was stupid. You could have gotten us both killed."

Chase felt his face flush at the reprimand. *Damn it, Chase…he's right. That was reckless.*

"No secrets," Romeo said tauntingly, snapping Chase's attention up.

Chase shook his head. "He's just trying to calm me down…I make mistakes when I'm nervous."

"What's there to be nervous about?" Romeo asked, grinning.

Chase nodded toward Luis. "Well, he's kind of scary."

It was the first genuine grin he'd seen come to Luis's face.

"Luis is a pussy cat," Romeo said insincerely. "Aren't you, Luis?"

"*Minino*," Luis said slowly with a sly grin.

Franco made a noise like a cat and all three began laughing. Jonah chuckled along uncomfortably but gave Chase another squeeze on his shoulder, reinforcing his warning.

Chase nodded discretely. "Sorry."

Jonah smiled and patted his back. "No harm done."

Luis and Franco began packing two black gym bags with equipment. When they were done, they set them on the floor next to the front door and came back, both settling down in the living room. Within moments, everyone was distracted by the basketball game Romeo was watching on TV.

Chase got more anxious as the minutes ticked by. He wished he had something else to keep himself distracted—the long wait had him second guessing every part of his plan.

After more than an hour of basketball, Romeo got up and stretched. Looking out at the now dark skyline of Arlington, he rubbed his belly. He walked over behind Franco and smacked him in the back of the head. "Make some food."

Franco rubbed his head but got up without complaint or even a cross look. He was very tolerant—or very good at hiding his anger.

Chase checked his watch. They would be leaving soon and he had successfully undermined all his own confidence with the long, quiet wait. He looked at Jonah and caught him staring.

"You okay?" Jonah asked.

Chase nodded, though his stone-faced expression didn't convey any sincerity.

Jonah smiled. "It'll be okay."

Chase grinned weakly in response, but his mind screamed, *Are you an idiot?! They are going to kill us as soon as the trades are done!* Outwardly, he remained calm, closing his eyes and walking through the steps in his head once more.

He silently ran through the routines, the scripts, and the transfers in his mind as Franco banged around in the kitchen preparing dinner for the group.

After several minutes of solitude, Romeo sat next to him on the sofa. "Are you sleeping?" Romeo asked, amused.

Chase opened his eyes and shook his head. "No. Just going over the scripts in my head. It's a lot to do manually."

Romeo nodded and smiled. "You'll do fine," he said. He patted Chase's leg but it abruptly turned into a painful grab on his thigh. "But just remember, in case you get any ideas about notifying anyone or escaping while you are on the town, I have Jonah here, and another ace in the hole."

Chase tensed. "What ace in the hole?"

"It's not important right now," Romeo said, patting his leg again. "And it won't be if you do as expected."

"Is that why Durggin left?"

Romeo just grinned. "Just do your fucking job and everyone will be happy…and healthy."

Chase nodded, suppressing a flash of anger building in his gut. Had

Val understood the message? Had Ortega? *Oh no…what if Durggin went to the hospital for Chloe?!*

Romeo got up and walked into the kitchen.

No. Not Chloe. She's on monitors and has a round the clock bodyguard. There's no way Durggin could move her.

"Come eat," Franco called from the kitchen.

Chase remained on the sofa, worrying about what Romeo had meant. *Where is Durggin? Is Val safe?*

"Come eat, Chase," Jonah said.

"Not hungry," he said without turning.

A strong hand grabbed Chase by the shoulder and pulled him sideways off the sofa. As he righted himself, he saw it was Luis. Chase resisted the urge to yank his arm away and instead let Luis force him into the kitchen like a child.

He had never fought so hard to hide his rage. "I'm fine. Fine. Fine!" He said, finally pulling free. "I'll eat."

He sat next to Jonah and ate the frozen dinner Franco slid in front of him.

"That's a good one," Jonah said. "The pasta is actually really tender."

Chase wanted to slap Jonah—he was taking this far too calmly. "Where's Imelda?" he asked instead.

"She's off on weekends. Won't be in 'till noon tomorrow."

"Who?" Romeo asked, pausing his fork mid-way to his mouth.

"The maid."

Romeo nodded and resumed eating.

Halfway through the still-cold-in-the-middle-entree, the chime at the security monitor went off. Luis went over, and seeing it was Durggin hit the buzzer.

Chase craned his neck as subtly as he could to see if Durggin was alone, but the screen went black too fast. Before returning to the counter, Luis unlocked the front door and set it ajar.

The tension built in Chase until he was actually angry at Durggin for taking so long. He fidgeted with his food, praying Durggin would come through the door alone. A moment later Durggin came through the door, alone, like a freight train.

"You son of a bitch!" Durggin yelled, rushing straight for Chase. "How'd you tip 'em off ya prick? How?!"

Chase jumped from his stool and ran around the island counter.

"What the hell are you doing?!" Romeo screamed. "Where's the girl?!"

He did go after Val!

"Somehow this bastard got word to the police that I was coming for her and they swarmed her house as I was ready to go in!" He lurched at Chase.

Chase unleashed his rage and picked up a heavy wooden cutting block from the counter, meeting him halfway through his charge. He swung the board in a wide arch and caught Durggin in the shoulder and ear. Durggin crashed to the floor but drew his pistol, aiming it at Chase's chest.

"Stop!" Romeo yelled, stepping between them and drawing his own weapon, aiming it at Durggin's head. "He didn't even know that's why you were gone! I never told him. If the police came it's because you did something to reveal yourself."

"Bullshit! She ran out of the house just as Ortega and half the PD rolled into her yard. She was expecting me."

Romeo looked at Chase, then to the computer. "That's easy enough to test." He walked over to the computer and brought up the e-mail and the web browser, scrolling through each item several times to verify. "Nothing. Nothing at all."

"That's bullshit," Durggin yelled, waving his pistol in a manner that made Chase imagine an accidental discharge. "I'm going to pop this son of a bitch right now."

Chase kicked Durggin's wrist as he tried to rise, sending his pistol sliding across the kitchen floor. Not waiting to see if he went for it again, Chase jumped over Durggin and rushed to the front door.

Behind him, Romeo yelled. "No! We need him alive!"

Chase was already running down the stairwell before he realized Romeo had stopped someone from shooting him in the back with that comment. He fought back his panic, mindful of the close call and flew down the stairs, skipping steps and jumping the rail on the turns.

His feet barely kept up with his forward movement as he leaned into his decent. The surge of adrenaline lent itself to a feeling of disconnect with his feet, unsure and fearful he would miss a step and tumble down.

He was two flights down before the door above opened and heavy, rapid footfalls engaged in pursuit. His heart contracted and he leapt over the rail, falling half a flight before making contact with the next level. His foot slipped and his body went rigid to catch himself. Only his hand on the rail kept him from tumbling forward.

Without missing a step, he recovered and continued his downward escape. Telling was that they didn't call for him as they ran. Telling was that they didn't call for him as they ran. He could only guess but was fairly confident, if caught he would be killed. His only hope was contacting Ortega, but first, he had to get out of the building.

As he reached the first floor, his breath came in gulps and the sweat pouring down his face stung the cuts above his eye. He pushed through the lobby door but froze when the elevator dinged and opened. Romeo stepped out and looked both directions before spotting Chase.

Chase turned and continued downward into the garage. "Stupid," he gasped, wasting precious oxygen. *If I had just kept going down I'd be at my car already and Romeo still wouldn't know where I am.*

He had opened a five floor gap between his pursuers above, but now Romeo was only half a flight behind him. *Stupid, stupid!*

He hit the door for the garage level and craned to see through the glass door before bursting into the quiet cavern. His footfalls echoed off the concrete, making him feel exposed. He was halfway to his car when another wave of panic crashed down on him. *I don't have my keys!*

Romeo crashed through the door behind him as the realization drilled into a new reserve of fear. He turned between a row of cars and headed for the ramp on the other side of the building.

Romeo's feet weren't moving as fast as his and whoever had followed him down the stairs still hadn't appeared in the garage. *Get to the street. Just get to the damned street. Find a shop, a bus, a crowd…just get out!*

He turned on the ramp at the halfway point and started up hill. Outside, the streetlights beckoned like warm yellow safety shields, begging him to hurry to them. The plane of the street came into sight and a car drove past, followed by a shuttle. *Get to the street.*

He looked over his shoulder and saw Romeo had fallen far behind and the others were still nowhere in sight. *I'm gonna make it.* With that hopeful burst of inspiration, he leaned forward and refocused on the top of the ramp.

Chase's heart contracted as a shadow passed in front of his street view. Luis appeared at the top of the ramp. As if kicked in the gut, Chase stopped so abruptly, his feet failed him for a split second, sending him to one knee. He turned and fled back the way he'd come as Luis charged, full sprint down the enclosed corridor to intercept.

Chase turned and dashed left, up the ramp to the next level. As he rounded the corner, Romeo reached out and grasped at the loose flap of his jacket, clinging to Chase briefly before it slipped, but slowing him down.

"Don't make me kill you, Chase," Romeo said, breathless, gasping.

Chase rounded a row of cars and jumped onto the hood of a Cadillac to reach the split between garage levels more quickly.

Romeo tried to follow but missed the leap and had to go around the Caddy. Dim hope bloomed once more as Chase looked behind him, seeing the gap widening again. Luis bound through the tight opening, running toward Chase like a big cat fixed on the kill.

"Don't kill him!" Romeo yelled to Luis's back.

That's comforting, Chase thought in sarcasm.

He looked over his shoulder again and Luis had closed more distance. "Fast," he gasped. *Damn, he's fast.*

He turned at the corner and sighted the door for the elevators. The slim hope broadened briefly and he found a reserve of speed, driving forward a little faster to close the distance. He looked behind him once more—Luis was only yards away. As he reached the door, he didn't slow, slamming into the wall to stop his momentum.

He grasped the door handle and pulled. It was locked. As Luis's footsteps closed in on him from behind, he realized in sudden horror, *Secure building. No one to buzz me in.* Acceptance of his fate washed over him and he dropped to the ground outside the door, curling his arms over his head.

Luis likewise didn't slow as he reached the door and instead, slammed into Chase with a brutal knee to the side of the head. Only Chase's arms protected him from the full brunt of the assault, but it still knocked the wind from his laboring lungs.

Inside the glass enclosure, the elevator door opened and Durggin emerged, drawing his pistol from his belt as he exploded through the door.

"That's the last time..." Durggin said, gasping for breath.

Chase was certain he was about to take a bullet to the head. But oddly, miraculously, Luis drew his own weapon and leveled it in Durggin's face. "Put it away," he said. He was barely breathing hard.

"Are you fucking kidding me?!" Durggin snapped as Romeo arrived on the scene running right up to Durggin and snatching his pistol from him.

"He almost exposed all of us!" Durggin yelled.

Romeo bent at the waist, hands on his knees, panting raggedly. "He wouldn't have run if it hadn't been for you…I should let…Luis kill you…here."

To reinforce that message, Luis pulled the hammer back on his silenced pistol.

Durggin froze, his eyes darting from Romeo to Luis and back again. "This is a mistake. We need to cap him, eat our losses, and go to ground."

"*Our* losses?" Romeo gasped, rising and putting his hands on his hips, Durggin's gun still held awkwardly by the barrel. "Up until a few minutes ago, we were about to have our losses covered. *You* did this."

Durggin leaned against the glass, still breathing heavily. He slid to the ground and laughed in a breathless cough. "You don't think he wasn't just waiting for an opportunity to run…?" He swung his head around weakly to face Romeo. "He was never going to get you your money… Kill—him—now."

Romeo tucked Durggin's gun into his waistband leaving the grip protruding rudely over his belt like some sort of grotesque erection. He looked at Chase who still sat curled in a ball, pressed against the glass by Luis's knee. "Let him up."

Luis kept his eye on Durggin, the long silencer barrel still trained on his nose. When he moved away from Chase, taking the pressure from his neck, Chase remained still, curling in on himself.

"Get up," Romeo said.

Chase didn't move.

"Get up!" Luis repeated, kicking Chase's hip.

Slowly, Chase dropped his arms and stood, careful to show nothing but absolute compliance. When he was standing, Romeo shoved his head into the glass. "He's right about one thing…I should kill you for that."

"He was going to kill me," Chase said quietly, his shoulder held high to protect the exposed side of his face.

Romeo held him there for several tense seconds, slowly getting control of his breath. "He does as I tell him to."

Chase moved his head under Romeo's elbow and glared at Durggin. "He drew on me after you told him *no*. I panicked…that's all."

Romeo pursed his lips and scoffed through his nose. He lingered there, pressing Chase against the glass for several seconds longer before releasing him. Romeo glanced at Luis waving his hand dismissively, prompting Luis to holster his weapon.

He punched in the penthouse number and pressed the call button. A second later the door buzzed letting the four of them enter, Chase being shoved through the door by Luis.

On the ride up, Durggin glared at Chase through cold, menacing eyes. When Romeo noticed, he shoved Durggin to the wall. "He is my money. You mess with him, you're messing with my money."

Durggin continued to stare at Chase—this enraged Romeo. He grabbed Durggin by the chin and twisted his head roughly. "Mess with my money and it won't be a quick bullet to the head—I will torture you to death over a long weekend."

Durggin jerked his head away but Romeo grabbed it again, twisting it forward.

"Do you understand?" Romeo said with a cool smile.

Durggin twisted away once more. "I got it."

Romeo stepped back. "Good."

When they got back to the penthouse, Romeo looked at his watch. "It's eleven o'clock. Get the gear together and get ready to go," he said to no one in particular.

Jonah sat on the sofa and cast a worried look at Chase when Luis shoved him into the room. As Franco busied himself checking the two gym bags at the door, Jonah leaned over and whispered, "Are you okay?"

Embarrassed, but more determined than ever, Chase turned to Jonah. "Brick wants us dead now," he said quietly. "Don't get caught alone with him."

Luis smacked Chase in the back of the head. "No talking."

Chase dropped his chin to his chest, feigning fearful submission and suppressing the anger that jumped to surface. His ears flushed red from the effort.

"You'll leave in thirty minutes," Romeo said to Luis.

Luis nodded but kept a close eye on Durggin as he circled the room once, finally collapsing in a heap on the overstuffed chair beside the sofa. "He got a message to Ortega somehow," Durggin muttered.

"What?" Romeo asked, glaring at Durggin.

"He got a message out somehow," he replied, louder.

Romeo crossed the room quickly, and leaned over Durggin, forcing him deeper into the cushions of the chair. "He had no way to communicate. There was no message sent. He has no phone…but you—" He stepped back and pointed at Durggin's face. "You are a wanted man because of your heavy-handed, clumsy handling of Bowman and the other broker… the cops were there because you tipped your hand."

"I didn't tip shit," Durggin said, sneering at Romeo.

Romeo kicked out, pressing his foot against Durggin's neck. "I'd rather not get my hands dirty with our prize so close at hand, but I swear on your balls, I will end you now if you don't shut your stupid, *puto* mouth."

Durggin hands reflexively grasped at Romeo's boot on his throat. When Romeo released him, he rubbed his neck but remained silent.

You're as dead as we are, Brick, Chase thought. *All I have to do is outlive you and I have a chance.*

When it was time for Chase and Luis to leave, Romeo walked into the back hallway, signaling Chase over with a wave of his hand. "Let's chat for a second."

Chase joined him, following Romeo to Jonah's bedroom. He put his hand on Chase's shoulder and squeezed, gently, supportively. "Don't listen to a word Durggin says," Romeo said in a quiet tone and held his fingers up separated by about an inch. "He knows he is this far from either being caught by police or executed by Luis."

"I only want to do what I'm supposed to do and get back to my life," Chase said.

Romeo nodded. "That's what I want too… Do this thing, do it well, and that's exactly what will happen."

Chase nodded but then Romeo grabbed him by the neck, roughly. "But one more stunt like what you pulled back there, and not only will you be dead, but so will your sister, your girlfriend, your boss and anyone else you care about… *comprendes?*"

Chase nodded sharply. "I do. I've got it…I promise, no trouble from me."

Romeo smiled and slapped Chase on the back in a friendly manner, though sharply enough to assert his dominance on the moment. "Good. That's what I thought. I just wanted to clear up any lingering doubts."

Chase looked at his bloodstained shirt and jacket. "I need to change."

Romeo nodded and left the room. "Hurry. Luis is waiting."

After changing into some fresh clothes of Jonah's that fit him, Chase returned to the main room and pulled his thumb drive from the computer. He looked at Durggin, holding his hand out. "I need my keys."

Durggin looked at Chase then Romeo.

"Why do you need your keys?" Romeo asked.

"My car has a company sticker on the windshield," Chase said. "It's chipped so the gate opens automatically. Without the sticker, we'd have to go to the public entrance and there's no way to open that from the outside without keys."

Jonah stood and went to the bar, grabbing his keys then tossing them to Chase. "Use mine. The gate won't open for your sticker before six o'clock...only executive level and admin stickers work before then."

Chase nodded and went to the foyer, waiting for Luis to accompany him. As he opened the door, Romeo called to him. "Chase."

Chase turned as Romeo withdrew his pistol and aimed it at Jonah's head. "Just in case you aren't being as honest as you appear to be, remember..."

Jonah looked at Chase pleadingly as Chase ground his teeth, fighting the constriction in his chest. "I understand," Chase said. "No tricks. I swear."

Romeo nodded and reholstered his pistol. "Good luck."

Chase silently counted the seconds from the front door to the elevator, then counted the time required for the elevator to rise from the ground floor.

"No trouble," Luis said as they waited.

Chase shook his head. "Durggin's not with us. The trouble is back there."

Luis grunted in acknowledgment and nodded. "He's a pig."

Chase didn't know if he was using slang for "cop" or a more direct comparison, but he nodded his agreement—Luis obviously had some personal grudge against Durggin, long before Chase started undermining him.

"What's up with you two?" Chase asked as the elevator dinged its arrival.

Luis just curled his lip.

"It just seems more personal," he added.

Luis turned his head slightly to look at Chase then forward again. "It's bad enough to be a cop who can be bought, but a cop who can be bought then switches sides can't ever be trusted."

Ah! Chase thought. *Durggin betrayed Beltrán-Leyva to work for Juárez. That explains the paranoid hatred.*

On the ride down, Chase closed his eyes and resumed his earlier journey through a mental model of his crime. There were a few sticky points he had to figure out, but he was confident that once out of the confines of the penthouse, his creativity would begin to flow to fill the gaps.

"Hey," Luis said, snapping Chase from his planning to see they had reached the garage level. The elevator doors were standing open.

A deep breath and exhale set him in motion toward Jonah's car.

"Which one is it?" Luis asked.

Chase pointed ahead of them. "The Bentley."

Luis whistled as Chase unlocked the doors and slid in behind the wheel. He started the powerful engine and listened to it purr while Luis ran his hands over the plush seats and rich detail of the dash.

"Your friend has good taste in cars," Luis said.

Ah. A car guy…I should have guessed. "What do you drive?"

"Range Rover," Luis said. "But I have a cherry sixty-eight Charger at home in my garage…it's my *amor*."

"Nice," Chase said, backing out of the space. "HEMI?"

Luis smiled and nodded with lust in his eyes. "Four hundred twenty-six cubic inch, four hundred twenty-five horse, twin, four BBL HEMI V8."

"Nice," Chase said sincerely. "Original?"

"Yes…I restored it myself over six years."

"That's the life, man…hands on a set of wrenches, bringing a beauty like that back to life," he shook his head. "I'd love to see it."

A twitch in Luis's cheek before a forced smile told Chase exactly how this was going to play out.

"Get this done, and I'll drive it to your doorstep."

"I can't wait," Chase said quietly.

A short while later, they pulled up outside of the firm's secure garage entrance, only minutes before midnight. Luis pulled his phone out and watched the clock. At one minute past midnight, he nodded that it was time.

Here we go, Chase thought. *And I'm no closer to filling in those missing pieces than I was an hour ago.*

MONDAY
B&E

CHASE tried to remain calm as they pulled into the garage and the gate rose automatically. Luis looked around, his eyes darting from one corner of the garage to the next. He turned and looked back as the gate closed behind them.

"Don't worry. It's automatic," Chase said, pointing at the sticker on the windshield."

Luis nodded, though it was clear he was still on edge. They parked and walked to the executive entrance, Chase strode toward the door as if he belonged there, Luis looking around nervously.

When they arrived, Luis reached into one of the two small gym bags and took out two pairs of black, nitrile rubber gloves. "Put these on," Luis said.

Chase nodded and stretched them over his fingers with a snap. "I need the entry code."

Luis took his phone out and dialed, handing it to Chase as soon as Romeo picked up.

"Okay, I'm ready for the entry code," Chase said to Romeo.

"He's ready," Romeo said in the background before turning the phone over to Jonah.

"Chase?"

"Yeah."

"Okay, put my key card in the slot," Jonah said.

"Done."

"The code is, four, three, four, five, seven, one, one."

Chase punched the numbers in and the reader flashed green, unlocking the door with a hollow clack. "Okay. We're in…is that the same code for the trading floor entrance?"

"Yes. But you'll need my password to access the systems."

"We'll call you back when we get inside."

Chase handed the phone back to Luis who spoke briefly with Romeo once they were inside. The elevator ride to the trading floor allowed Chase the time he needed to get his story straight if they were stopped, but he didn't expect to see anyone for hours. The server room would have been locked tight the night before—no need to pay server admins while a system wide backup was in progress. And the custodial staff would have cleaned the building on Saturday. There'd be no reason to clean again on Sunday.

"So you move money from one stock to another and you make money just moving it?" Luis asked on the ride up.

"Yep. *And* I make money even if the stock is a loser."

"So you could be wrong and still get paid?" He asked.

Chase nodded. "Not only that, I get paid when I buy the stock and I get paid again when I sell it."

"So you could intentionally buy bad stocks to make your customers *want* to sell."

Chase nodded. "Yeah and a lot of firms do just that, but they have to rely more heavily on new clients and new capital all the time. They'd make more if they were right *most* of the time. No need to hunt new capital like that…plus, if you screw around trashing your client accounts for too long, you get a bad rep then the capital dries up."

"So you want to make money for your client."

Chase smiled. "Some…not a lot. Just enough to keep them coming back for more."

"Ah...like cutting product with baby formula, but not enough to kill the high."

Chase laughed. "Yeah...like that only legal."

Luis coughed a weak laugh but avoided eye contact. Chase got the feeling Luis considered laughing, smiling and joking to be less than masculine.

The elevator opened and once again, Chase moved forward as if he owned the place. Luis lagged behind, carefully scanning for any movement. As expected, the door on the trading floor was locked tight and there was no sign of anyone.

Through the double glass doors, Chase saw the workstations and cubicles, lit only by LED stock tickers and glowing exit signs. The occasional screen saver flashed on a handful of computers, but the scene had more the feel of twilight than midnight under the dim glow.

Chase inserted Jonah's key card into the reader and punched in the code, granting them access to the floor. It was the first time Chase had ever been in the space by himself—it seemed odd not hearing hundreds of voices, buzzers, and alarms. On the walls, the trade tickers scrolled the last entries fed to them on Friday afternoon. They wouldn't change again until pre-trade-hours sales began to chip away at the old numbers.

Luis looked around, his hand on his pistol beneath his jacket.

Chase closed the door then tested it to make sure it had latched again. "We're good. We can start on the floor server, up there." Chase pointed at the raised, glass faced cubicle Frank worked from.

"Is that Jonah's computer?" Luis asked in a whisper.

Chase shook his head. "Frank's. The floor manager. His system does the matrix broadcast to the trading floor. But I'm logging in with executive level privileges because I have Jonah's password."

Luis nodded as his head swiveled in a slow, paranoid scan of the floor. "How long?"

Chase looked at his watch. "I'll probably be done around five or five thirty."

Luis shook his head. "What should I do?"

Chase shrugged. "I guess you're here to make sure I don't mess anything up."

Luis stared at him blankly.

Chase shot him a sideways grin. "I hope you brought a calculator."

Luis smiled and shoved Chase gently toward the cubicle.

He booted up Frank's computer and switched to the command screen before the operating system logo had time to flash. "Okay, call them back. I need Jonah's password."

Luis dialed and handed the phone to Chase. "Hi, Romeo. I need Jonah's password."

Jonah spoke immediately. "Lowercase M, the *at* sign, five, uppercase T, three, lowercase R, zero, lowercase F, lowercase A, uppercase L, uppercase L."

"—m@5T3r0faLL... *Master Of All*? You're shitting me. Really?"

"Shut up and type it in."

Chase entered the password and gained executive level control over the floor systems and the main retail servers. "Okay. I'm in... I'll call you back when I'm done or if I hit a snag before then."

"Good luck."

Chase handed the phone back to Luis who pocketed it. Once the matrix interface was up and running he opened a sandbox directory viewer and plugged his thumb drive into the system. "Here we go." He looked at Luis and grinned. "Get comfortable...we're gonna be here awhile."

Luis rolled a chair over and plopped down in it. As Chase worked, Luis got more and more fidgety, turning around in the chair, rolling it slowly to the edge of the platform, then back again. After a while, he made a game of trying to spin as many times as possible with just one push.

Finally, when his foot hit Chase, Chase turned and glared at him. "There's a snack machine at the other end of the room...why don't you go get us some candy and drinks?"

Luis stared at him for a second with his best killer expression then got up and walked away.

"Jesus," Chase muttered.

As the matrix base was loading, he took advantage of being unsupervised to check and see what else Jonah's password would unlock. He started with the security server and was pleased to discover he had access. He looked over the edge of the screen toward Luis and saw he was still fussing with the candy machine, so he decided to push his luck. The more access he had with Jonah's password, the easier this would be when the shit hit the fan.

He queried the executive level directories with Jonah's access and found the executive interface, complete with housekeeping accounts and transfer authorizations. "Nice..." *You'll be useful before this is all over.*

After several minutes of probing while the matrix compiled, Chase realized the light from the monitor had cast a bright blue hue across him and the wall behind him. He looked up to see Luis returning with an armload of snacks and drinks. Chase hastily closed the executive level windows leaving only the scripts running on the screen.

Luis, obviously thinking he was being sneaky, walked around the side of the cubicle to see the screens before stepping up on the platform.

Chase didn't bother looking up. "Did you break into the machines?"

Luis shrugged, dropping several candy bars on the floor.

Chase shook his head. "No one is supposed to know that we've been here. Do you think maybe they might look around for other signs of a break-in if the vending machines have been robbed?"

Luis stopped and thought about that for a second. He grimaced then turned abruptly, walking back toward the vending machines.

"Idiot," Chase muttered.

As soon as Luis was out of sight, Chase brought up the executive interface again, clicking on each function until he found what he was looking for—account transfers.

Insurance. It's just insurance, Chase thought to himself.

Several minutes later, after his script had compiled, he printed out the trade sheets for each computer station in the retail division. After the printer spat out the last sheet, he walked down to the trading floor and began the long process of manually loading his custom matrix on the trader computers.

He had already modified and uploaded the prediction matrix files on three of the computers by the time Luis showed up again, this time with a more reasonable two sodas and two candy bars.

He sat the soda next to Chase then offered him one of the candy bars.

Chase waved him off. "You can have it. I'm in the zone."

"How many is that?" Luis asked.

Chase stood and looked around the large trading floor. "Counting the master server? Four."

Luis's eyes and head rolled back in a gesture of impatience. "How many to go?"

"Counting this one? A hundred and twenty-two."

Luis breathed out an exhausted sigh. "Would it go faster if I helped?"

"Sure," Chase said, sliding a stack of printouts to him without looking. "You can calculate the delta on these and note in the margin what the projected volume is going to be at the opening bell."

Luis looked at the complex spreadsheets then back to Chase. "I don't know how to do that."

Chase pulled the sheets back over to him. "Then no. You can't help."

Luis whacked Chase in the back of the head, playfully, but still hard enough to convey his agitation.

"You asked," Chase muttered as he finished the third system and ran a test on the numbers.

The scene repeated itself for hours—Chase modified the base prediction matrix for each system, taking into account all the stocks for that particular account manager, then ran a test load in the sandbox. Each time, he verified the sheet against each entry then drew a slice across the sheet with a red marker.

He looked at his watch when he had only twenty or so systems left to compile. Luis walked over and stood, hands on hips, glaring at Chase.

Chase looked sideways at him then back at his work. "Almost done."

"It's getting late."

"I know," Chase said quietly.

"When do people start arriving?"

Chase looked at his watch. "The foreign desk traders are already here…two floors down."

Luis turned and looked toward the door, suddenly edgy. "Any chance they'll come up here?"

Chase shook his head as he scanned the sheet he was working on. "Not likely, but even if they did, they wouldn't be able to get in without an executive level key card."

"How long until people start showing up here?"

"Two hours…maybe an hour and a half."

Luis stared at Chase, the discomfort in his stance apparent.

Chase breathed out in exasperation. "Don't worry. I'm almost done. Half an hour at most…unless…"

"Unless what?"

Now? Should I do it now?

"Oh shit," Chase whispered.

"What?!"

Chase looked up at Luis. "Call Romeo…now."

Luis pulled his phone out and dialed. "He says we have a problem," he said then handed the phone to Chase.

"Is Jonah there?" Chase asked, worry coloring his tone.

"Yes, hold o—"

"No. Put the phone on speaker...you both need to hear this," Chase said with urgency in his tone.

"I'm here Chase...what's wrong?" Jonah asked.

"We have a problem that needs to be fixed, like right now."

"What?"

Chase turned his back on Luis and began working on his sheet again. "What happens to all these modified buy/sell matrices I'm building when the main server HFT specs hit the retail analyst servers?"

"Well, they'd...oh shit," Jonah said.

"Right. They'll all get overwritten by the new matrix and distributed to every station as soon as they boot up," Chase said. "All this work would've been done for nothing."

"You can't stop that from happening?" Romeo asked.

"No. I can't," Chase replied, turning to Luis. "Look...not that I want you to show your hand to me, but if you don't get your guy in here to stop those HFT scripts from executing, everything we've done will be a complete bomb."

There was a moment of silence on the other end of the phone.

"Are you still there?"

"I'm thinking!" Romeo yelled.

"Well, whatever you decide, you better do it quick. Those scripts are going to run in about an hour." Chase said. "Also...it would probably be better if you don't mention what we're doing to your guy. The fewer people here at the firm who know what's going on, the better it is for us."

"I know that!" Romeo snapped, then after a long pause, "I'll have it resolved within the hour."

"Don't cut it too close. I need time to bypass the matrix spool on the main retail server before we leave."

"How long will that take?"

"Ten minutes, maybe a little less once all the workstations are set up."

"Okay, I'll call you when he's on site."

"Thanks." Chase ended the call and handed the phone back to Luis. "Keep that close. If it comes down to the wire, we don't want to miss that call."

Luis nodded but didn't seem comforted by the conversation. Chase returned to his scripts and powered through the remaining twenty stations before calling Luis over from his post by the door.

"Can we go now?" Luis asked, sounding more than a little nervous as the first light of sunrise cast an orange and pink glow through the window.

Chase shook his head. "I can't leave until the HFT scripts are shut down and I spool the retail server matrix. You can go if you want."

He shook his head. "Romeo would shoot me."

"Really?" Chase asked, cocking his head to the side and shooting Luis a grin. "I won't say anything if you don't."

The look on Luis's face said he was considering the offer but finally shook his head. "We'll wait together."

Chase nodded and walked to Frank's station in the raised cubicle at the back of the large room. When he got there, he opened a computer window to the security server and brought up the security camera video streams.

"What's that?" Luis asked.

"If we're just gonna sit and wait, I want to know when the HFT guy comes in and wipes the script. It'll give me a few minutes to prep my script."

Luis nodded and watched with him. The camera flashed from view to view, hallways, trading floors, stairwells, parking garage—the loop came to an end then repeated.

"Please be Frank, please be Frank..." Chase muttered as he waited for Romeo's inside man to show up.

"What?"

Chase shook his head. "Nothing." *Please be Frank, please be Frank.*

A few minutes passed and Chase caught sight of movement down a hallway on the server level. He reached up and touched the keyboard, stopping the loop of video feeds. When the man was close enough, he switched views and watched as he passed under the camera. It wasn't Frank—it was just some mid-level HFT server admin.

"Shit," Chase muttered. *Not Frank. Well, this sucks.*

"What's wrong? That's not him?"

They watched the computer admin go into the server room then followed him to his terminal as Chase switched to a different camera view.

"Yeah, that's him," Chase said.

"You sound disappointed."

Chase shook his head. "No. But we're almost out of time. The garage gate should be up by now. It'll take me ten to fifteen minutes from the time he clears the script to finish the matrix spool. We may have people on the floor here by then."

"Here? Before you leave?"

Chase nodded. "So here's what we need to do...as soon as Romeo calls you to say his guy is in and done, you go down and start the car and bring it around front."

Luis hesitated, but just then the phone rang. He answered and nodded.

When he ended the call, he looked at Chase. "Romeo says his guy is in and the HFT scripts are being deleted right now."

Chase nodded. "Okay." He stared at Luis for a moment.

Luis looked back at the door, then down to the video screen. "Alright...I'll meet you out front. You better be there or we're both dead."

"No arguments from me."

Luis nodded once then turned and left. Chase watched him close the door before he returned to work on the scripts. He looked up to check the status of the admin and clenched his jaw. *Damn it all...why couldn't you have been Frank.* He shook his head, his fingers poised over the keyboard.

While the HFT server admin deleted the matrix scripts that would have overwritten Chase's custom scripts, Chase slapped his hand on the desk in frustration before logging back into the executive level menu.

"You have no idea how bad I wanted the inside man to be you, Frank," he said as he worked. "Sucks to be me."

Chase looked up at the screen as the admin left the server room and walked back toward the exit—the deed had been done. Now Chase could spool his special scripts into place, ready for execution upon the opening bell, producing millions of dollars for the cartel.

When he was done, he tucked the sheets down the back of his pants. The rest of his job was more complicated but wouldn't take as long—wiping the video logs and changing the passwords. *Insurance,* he thought. *Time to lower the deductible.*

"Jesus...I can't believe I'm doing this," he muttered as the drives erased hours of video, covering his and Luis's tracks.

A chime at the trading floor main entrance drew his attention. He looked over the low wall to see Frank coming in and propping the door open.

Chase ducked down quickly. "Shit," he whispered.

He was in Frank's cubicle and it was glass fronted, meaning the desk was the only viable hiding place—unless Frank came straight to his desk.

Chase looked up at the screen. The delete sequence was complete, but there was no way he was going to be able to shut down the system in time. He opted to hit the button on the power strip as Frank walked toward him.

Oh shit, oh shit. Chase tensed, trying to think of something, anything that could keep him out of the coming disaster.

As Frank rounded a row of workstations, Chase gave up hope of doing anything but knocking Frank unconscious as soon as he walked around the desk.

"Excuse me?!"

Chase tensed. Ready to spring.

"Hey. No one on the floor without a badge!" Frank yelled, surprisingly, away from Chase.

Chase looked over the edge of the desk and saw Luis, coming toward Frank.

"Where do I fill out an application?" Luis said.

Chase crawled down the short staircase and around the chest height cubical wall behind Frank.

"You'll have to talk to someone in HR and they don't open until eight."

When Chase was next to the door, he rose up so Luis could see him and nodded.

"Oh. Okay then. Sorry. I didn't mean to break the rules," Luis said then turned and walked past Frank.

"What's your name?" Frank asked.

"Jose Lopez. I hope to be working with you soon."

"Fat chance of that," Frank muttered but loud enough that even Chase heard him.

When Luis rounded the corner next to the stairs, he clenched his jaw and grabbed Chase by the arm. "Did you finish?"

Chase nodded. "Yeah. Come on. Let's get out of here." He looked over his shoulder and watched Frank walk away from the door.

They went down the stairs and scanned the front of the building through the glass doors before exiting. Luis grabbed Chase roughly by the arm and yanked him around the corner where he had left Jonah's car.

"Easy, big guy," Chase said, pulling his arm away. "No need for the rough stuff."

"Hurry," Luis said, reverting back to the same snarling glare he had started the relationship with.

Something's changed, Chase thought.

Luis drove away from the building, gunning the engine on Jonah's expensive car and letting the whine ride up before shifting to the next gear.

"Slow down...we're clean."

"No. We have to get back to the apartment."

Something big has changed. And I can guess what it is...I finished my work.

Luis pulled his phone from his pocket and dialed. "It's done," Luis said. "We barely got out, but we're cool now."

Luis looked at Chase out of the corner of his eye then slowed, pulling into a shopping center parking lot. He stopped and set the brake, leaving the engine running.

"He said he did...hold on." Luis hit the speaker button. "You're on speaker now."

"Chase, were you able to get all the terminals updated?"

"Yes. Everything went according to plan except the HFT guy coming in the last minute."

"Good. And all the scripts were verified before you spooled them?"

"Yes."

"Excellent. Luis, take me off speaker."

Luis pressed the phone to his ear. "Uh huh. Okay."

Chase saw Luis's left hand slide down beside the seat.

Oh man, not like this.

"Right. I understand," Luis said into the phone.

"Can you tell him we need to hurry? I need to get back to Jonah's apartment and execute the sandbox push from Jonah's computer."

"Wait. What?"

"Yeah...We only have forty-five minutes for me to push the spool out of the sandbox or it won't run," Chase lied, stalling with his preplanned fiction.

"He says he has to do something else before the scripts will run."

Chase heard yelling over the phone but couldn't make out what it was.

"Yes, from Jonah's system...I don't know! I don't understand any of this shit!"

More yelling.

Luis hung up abruptly and put his left hand on the steering wheel.

"What?" Chase asked.

Luis looked at him with a smug grin. He may not have said anything, but his expression said, *"You are one lucky bastard."*

They raced across town and across the Potomac to Jonah's apartment building. When they arrived, Luis drove smoothly down into the garage and backed into Jonah's spot. As Luis got out, Chase discreetly watched him reach down between the door and the seat. His suspicions were confirmed—Luis holstered his gun when he thought Chase wasn't watching.

This is it. Get ready.

At the door, Luis rang the buzzer and looked up at the camera. "It's me," he said.

The door buzzed and they walked to the elevator, each step increasing the tension in Chase's chest. He pulled the spreadsheet printouts from behind him and loosely rolled them in his hands as the elevator began to move.

"What's that?" Luis asked.

"The matrix sheets for the retail systems... I didn't want to leave them behind."

Luis nodded and watched the numbers on the panel light up as they rose.

Chase's chest contracted and he hesitated, a false start that undermined his confidence, as they got closer to Jonah's floor. *Four seconds between floors, thirty-second pause at a stop,* he thought. His hands twisted and turned the sheets until they were as solid and dense as a metal pipe. When they were within four floors, Chase leaned over in front of Luis and casually pushed the button for the two floors below Jonah's.

A confused crease folded in Luis's brow. "Why did you do tha—?"

Luis didn't get to finish his question. Chase lashed upward with the rolled papers, smashing Luis in the nose and dropping him to his knees, stunned. He followed with a brutal knee to the center of his face. Luis fell to the floor in a heap.

Chase's heart was pounding so hard, he heard it in his ears. He was committed at that point. There was nothing he could do but let events unfold—the first domino had been tipped.

The elevator stopped two floors below the penthouse level and the doors slid aside. Chase looked out to see if there was anyone in the hallway. It was getting late, raising the chances that someone might appear in the corridor, but he had to chance it. He let the door close again, then hit the stop button as the light at the ceiling reached chest level. He pried the doors open as the muted alarm chimed from the elevator speaker, then he reached down and unlatched the outer doors as well. After checking the hallway in both directions, he dragged Luis to the edge.

Luis moaned when Chase reached under his jacket and pulled the silenced gun from its holster. He slammed his elbow into Luis's face to put him out one last time. After taking Jonah's keys from Luis's jacket pocket, he held the cartel strongman's foot and pushed him over the edge of the elevator, letting his weight pendulum his body once. On the swing back, he released, letting Luis fall down the shaft, fourteen floors, and three parking levels to the bottom.

Luis fell silently for a while. Only a slight scuff could be heard once before a distant echoing thud at the bottom of the shaft—Luis was dead.

Chase flipped onto his back and closed his eyes tightly as the doors closed behind him. After several heavy breaths to refocus his purpose, he stood and punched the button to resume his upward movement.

"So much for going straight," he said to himself quietly as he popped the magazine from Luis's gun. "But I guess it's always best to go with your talents."

►◄

CHASE confidently knocked on the door of the penthouse.

"What the hell took you so lo—?"

The door swung open and Romeo froze, eyes wide—Luis's gun pointed at his nose. Chase motioned with his fingers that he wanted Romeo's weapon, his face calm, his movements cold and with machinelike precision.

Romeo reached behind him, slowly.

"Butt first," Chase whispered so as not to attract any attention.

Romeo turned so Chase could see his hands on the weapon, first, Durggin's gun, still in the front of his pants, pulling it out between his thumb and forefingers, then his own. Chase took the guns one at a time and pushed Romeo forward, casually tucking Luis and Durggin's weapons in his belt and aiming Romeo's own weapon at the back of his head.

"You are a dead man my friend," Romeo said with cold detachment.

"Yeah, I figured that out yesterday," Chase said, then swung his gun around to a startled Franco. "Don't do it, Franco. Take it out slowly and set it on the floor."

Franco reached slowly under his jacket, but despite Chase having him dead to rights, the cartel muscle grabbed and tried to draw. Chase fired twice, though once would have been enough—the first shot ripped through Franco's skull with nothing more than a muted pop from Romeo's silenced gun.

Romeo dashed to the side, but in one fluid motion, Chase swung his arm around and fired again. The shot went into Romeo's hip. He screamed as he hit the floor.

Chase stared at him with emotionless calm, his hand steady.

"You are a *dead* man. I will peel the skin off you, then your sister, then that hot little piece of ass, you—"

Romeo's mouth was open when Chase squeezed the trigger again, sending the round through the back of his throat, severing his brain stem from the rest of his body. A second shot split the top of Romeo's head, sending chunks of brain splattering across the floor.

Durggin jumped to his feet, but Chase calmly whipped Romeo's gun around and pointed it at his face. "Hold up, Brick."

"You are one ballsy motherfucker," Durggin said with a sly grin though obviously taken completely off-guard by the abrupt change in Chase's demeanor—and the gun in his face. "You may have just saved all our lives."

"Sit your old, wrinkly ass down."

Durggin obeyed and slowly sat on the arm of an overstuffed living room chair.

"Chase! What've you done? We're all dead now!" Jonah said, finally finding his choked, hysterical words.

"Shut up and cover Durggin," Chase said taking Luis's gun from his belt and sliding it across the dining room table toward Jonah.

"What are you doing? This is nuts. The market opens in—" Jonah looked at the clock on the wall. "—in thirty minutes. Do you think the cartel is gonna be so happy to see their money they'll just forget you killed their men?"

"They don't know I killed their men," Chase said, still holding his weapon on Durggin, who was now smiling.

"No, Chase...don't do it."

"It's done. The market is going to open and those cartel owned businesses are going to liquidate."

"What?! Why?! Why would you bring that kind of heat down on us?"

Durggin got up and moved toward Chase. Chase raised his weapon higher and pointed it squarely between Durggin's eyes. "I don't know if you've noticed or not, but I don't have a problem killing."

Durggin froze. "That was adrenaline...nothing else. You're a second-rate punk. You don't have the balls to cut someone down in cold blood."

Chase smiled. "You seem to know an awful lot about me."

"I've seen your jacket. Nothing but running numbers for bookies and drunken brawls...you're a punk."

"That's the problem with going to the police for a background check," Chase said, taking another step forward and pressing the barrel to Durggin's forehead. "You only see what someone got caught doing...not what he got away with."

"Bullshit."

Chase turned his head to Franco's body then to Romeo. "I think they'd disagree with you."

"Damn it, Chase. What are you talking about?!" Jonah asked on the verge of a full meltdown.

Chase glanced at Jonah then back to Durggin. "Jonah, calm your shit down, pick up that gun and point it at Durggin. I have to send a message."

Jonah picked up the gun. He looked at it for several seconds before raising it. Durggin's expression changed—anger rippled across his face.

Chase walked around him to Romeo's body and took the phone from his pocket.

"What are you doing?" Jonah asked.

Chase looked away from Durggin to scan Romeo's contact list. He breathed quiet relief when he saw Romeo had only called one number in the last two days—the same number registered as having called Romeo four times through the night—Luis's phone.

He zipped his finger down the list of calls made and got to one that said simply *"Patrón"*. Chase wasn't a Spanish speaker but he knew that meant "boss".

"Answer me, Chase...what the hell are you doing?" Jonah asked, turning away from Durggin momentarily.

"Sending a message to *Patrón,* letting him know Brick here, double-crossed Romeo," he replied.

"You son of a bitch!" Durggin jumped up and threw a lamp at Jonah as he charged Chase.

Jonah fell to the floor as Durggin crashed into Chase, plowing him to the ground. Romeo's gun flew from Chase's hand and skidded toward the foyer on the tile floor. Durggin didn't wait to fight, instead, crawling over Chase and scrambling on all fours toward Romeo's gun.

Chase reached behind him and pulled the other gun from his waistband—Durggin's small automatic that Romeo had confiscated the night before. As Durggin's fingers closed around the silenced gun, Chase rolled over and fired two wild shots at Durggin—neither found their mark.

Durggin, now with a weapon, bolted through the door and around the corner. Chase breathed out, pointing the smoking pistol at the door more steadily once on his back. His ears were ringing from the loud *pop, pop* from his weapon—unlike the cartel weapons, it had no silencer. Someone in the building would have certainly heard that.

Jonah scrambled over to Chase. "Are you okay?"

Chase stared wide-eyed at the door until he heard the ding of the elevator in the hall. He stood slowly, still aiming toward the door as he approached it. The motors on the elevator engaged and he peeked around the doorframe in a rapid motion to see if Durggin was lying in wait. The hallway was empty.

He ran back and picked up Romeo's phone before breaking into a run back to the elevator.

"Where are you going?" Jonah asked, following. "The cartel will take care of him now."

Chase pressed the button for the elevator repeatedly. "Chloe's the only one left who can identify him to the police. He's not going to leave a witness."

Jonah tucked Luis's weapon into his pants and grabbed Chase by both shoulders. "Chase, we're still alive...it won't do him any good to kill Chloe. We need to execute those trades or they'll kill us."

"He doesn't care about us. He thinks the cartel is going to finish us off."

Jonah slapped Chase across the face. "They *are* going to kill us if we don't execute those trades."

Chase shoved Jonah in the chest, sending him stumbling backward. "The trades will execute," he said, pressing the button feverishly.

"But you said you had to launch from the—"

Chase knocked Jonah's hands away and rushed to the stairwell door. "I told them what I had to, to get back here and save you," he said. "Luis was going to shoot me in the car... it's all I could think of."

As he pushed the stairwell door open, the elevator dinged its arrival. Chase turned abruptly and ran to it, Jonah following closely. As the elevator descended, Chase browsed to the Arlington PD web page.

He found the number and clicked it, dialing.

"Arlington County Police, nonemergency number."

"I need you to transfer me to the cell phone of Officer Deborah Ortega, now. A murder is about to take place."

"What is your location, sir."

"I'm not at the location! Get me transferred to Deb Ortega, or her uncle, Gabriel Ortega, now please!"

"Please hold."

The on-hold music was a strange, disjointed contrast to the adrenaline pulsing through his veins.

"This is Officer Ortega."

"Deb. Durggin is loose, he and the cartel guys are...never mind. It's too complicated. Get someone to the hospital now. I think Durggin is coming to finish off Chloe."

"Where are you?" Deb asked.

"On my way to the hospital. Please get there or send someone there now. It may be too late."

"I have to hang up. I'll call you back."

"Fine. Go."

In a sudden panic, Chase patted his pockets but found Jonah's keys. He breathed out a rush of breath in relief as he pulled them out then leaned against the doors of the elevator as if that would give him some sort of head start when they opened.

"Where's Luis?" Jonah asked.

Chase pointed at the floor. "In the basement."

"The basement...? Why there?"

"That's where the elevator shaft stops."

Jonah shook his head. "Three dead."

"Four if we don't get to the hospital before Durggin."

"We don't know he's going to the hospital. The cartel is going after him now that you sent that message."

"I didn't get a chance to send that message and now I can't unless we stop him. I'm not taking any chances. I won't let anything happen to Chloe."

Jonah nodded as the doors opened on the garage level. "You better let me drive. You're too wound up."

Chase handed Jonah the keys as they sprinted for the Bentley.

"Strap in," Jonah said. "I'm about to break some speed limits."

Chase adjusted Durggin's automatic in his waistband and snapped the seat belt. Jonah gunned the engine, peeling rubber out of his parking space, then once again as he sped up the ramp, cutting off a BMW that was pulling in.

Jonah flew down the street, weaving through early Monday morning traffic. He slammed the brakes once to avoid being T-boned by a bus when he attempted to run a red light.

"One piece, Jonah. Get us there in one piece."

He slapped the gearshift forward and pressed the accelerator. "I'll get us there. Don't worry."

After a harrowing ten-minute race across the city, they reached the hospital, sliding to a halt in the ambulance zone.

"Go!" Jonah said. "I'll meet you up there."

Chase didn't bother looking back as he slammed the door and sprinted to the entrance. He had to turn sideways to get through the sliding doors then ran to the stairwell. Up seven flights, skipping every other step, he leaned into his climb as if he were going to tackle someone. After bursting through the stairwell door on the seventh floor, he sprinted down the hall wrapping his fingers around, but not drawing the pistol in his waistband.

Rounding the corner at the nurses' station, he noticed everyone seemed calm and collected—no one was freaking out until he ran by.

"Oh, thank. Thank god, I got here in time," he muttered breathlessly then slowed to a rapid walk to Chloe's room. He entered and approached Chloe. She was on her side and the lights were out.

Oh no. Am I too late?

He reached out and touched her shoulder.

"Well ain't that sweet. I got you both at the same time," Durggin said to Chase's back from the doorway.

Chase spun around, a sick feeling welling up in his throat as Durggin raised Romeo's silenced pistol at them. Chase stepped between Chloe and Durggin.

"It's not gonna save you from the cartel, Durggin," Chase said.

Durggin shrugged. "If I'm running anyway, I might as well clean up my mess first."

The next moment happened too fast for Chase to wrap his mind around. The door swung closed, and at the same moment, Chloe reached out and shoved Chase, sending him to the floor with a crash. Durggin fired two rounds into the wall where Chase had been standing only a split second earlier.

It wasn't until Durggin had turned his attention to the person behind the door that Chase realized it hadn't been Chloe in bed who had pushed him clear, but Deb Ortega.

"Ortega," Durggin said and fired into the corner. There in the corner, behind the now closed door, was Gabriel Ortega aiming his pistol at Durggin. Struck by Durggin's bullet, he nonetheless fired his black police Glock.

Durggin twisted, firing blindly as he fell sideways.

"Stay down," Deb Ortega yelled as she fired her pistol, lighting the walls of the dim room with muzzle flashes.

Durggin lurched forward, then slumped to the floor on his hands and knees. He looked at Chase and tried to lift his gun at him, but both the Ortegas fired again, repeatedly until Durggin collapsed on his face.

The smell of gunpowder mingled with the fresh scent of blood as it pooled around Durggin and moved toward Chase. Deb jumped from the bed and ran to her uncle's side as he peeled his shirt away from his bloody shirt.

"Is this the only wound?" Deb asked him.

"Where's Chloe?!" Chase yelled as he pushed himself from the floor.

Deb looked at him then back to her uncle. "She's safe with Val, one floor down."

Chase ran for the door. "This isn't over yet."

"Wait!" Deb yelled at Chase's back. "What do you mean it's not over?!"

Chase sprinted past the station where nurses and doctors were huddled on the floor. "The shooting's over, there's a wounded man in seven ten," he said before slamming his shoulder into the stairwell door.

As he bounded into the hallway one floor down, Val ran over to him. "Oh, thank god, you're safe," she said, wrapping her arms around him.

"Where's Chloe?"

"Down here," she replied, lacing her fingers through his and tugging him forward. "Come on."

Chloe sat up and glared at his face as Chase opened the door. "Again?" She asked.

Chase looked down the hallway and saw Jonah coming toward them. "Shit." He closed the door behind them.

Chloe smiled. "You look like someone used your face—"

"Please don't."

"—to break concrete."

Chase shook his head but smiled as he searched nervously around the room.

"Can I look at those cuts and bruises?" Val asked, stroking his hair gently.

"In a minute. I need to do something first." The sound of sirens filled the air outside as Chase pulled the hospital computer over on its cart and looked at Val. "Can you unlock that screen for me?"

"Sure…but what's going on? And why are you wearing rubber gloves?" She asked as she typed in her password, unlocking the screen.

Chase raised a finger to silence her and turned to the door. He logged into the executive trading screen when he saw a shadow pass on the other side. "Jonah, we need to stop the auto scripts before trading starts."

Jonah appeared, pushing the door open slowly. He poked his head in as Chloe and Val looked out the window at the arriving police cars. When Chloe returned her attention to the door, her eyes flashed wide. Chase's heart sank at the confirmation but he continued to navigate the computer to the admin screen for the firm's executive access.

"Val," Chase said quietly "Can you give us a minute?"

She shot him a curious look then nodded. "Sure. I have to check on someone anyway."

He leaned over and kissed her. "Thanks."

She walked by Jonah who tensed as she left, seemingly struggling with a decision. He clenched his jaw in agitation as the door closed behind her. "It's too late to stop the transactions," he said turning to Chase. "Trading starts in five minutes."

"Plenty of time," Chase replied as he typed.

"I don't think that's a good idea," Jonah said in a quiet, calm voice.

Chase ignored him and continued typing.

"I mean it, Chase. Step away from the computer."

Chase brought up the accounts terminal view and clicked a link, but then felt the cold metal of Luis's silenced pistol against his neck.

"Now, Chase...move."

Chase froze for a second, then hit enter before closing the screen and turning.

"I'd hoped I was wrong about you," Chase said.

"Ha! If you had known, you wouldn't have come back for me after you killed Luis."

Chloe's eyes flashed to Chase but she remained silent.

"As I said...I hoped I was wrong."

Jonah shook his head and looked at his watch. "Three minutes and the cartel will have their money, then we're both safe. All you have to do is keep your mouths shut."

"So you aren't planning on killing us?"

Jonah's eyes flashed to Chloe, then back to Chase. "Your sister recognizes me."

Chase nodded. "Yeah. From the club the night Bowman drugged her."

Jonah smiled. "It was supposed to be simple. All Bowman had to do was drug her then take her to your place and drug you. We would have had your data and that would have been that."

"Not that you would have had my data since Durggin was a world-class idiot. But you didn't count on my neighbor being a cop either, did you?"

"No...and we didn't count on you roughing up Bowman after he brought your drunk ass sister home."

Chase shook his head. "You never plan enough steps ahead, do you?"

"What's that mean, you arrogant prick? You're the one with a gun pointed at your face. Right now, I'm the smartest guy in the room."

"Are you?" Chase asked eyes narrowed to slits, a grim smile on his face.

"What?"

Chase shook his head.

Jonah looked at his watch again. "You were stealing money from my clients." He grinned and shook his head. "But damn you were good at it...I wanted you to come on board with me."

"I suspected it was you when Romeo kept deferring to you on matters of trading... Odd he would do that with someone he had just met for the first time."

Jonah sneered at him. "That money is still getting switched as soon as the market opens, and you are going to go down for the break-in unless you play ball with me."

"Nothing but a low life, cartel flunky for hire...no talent at that."

Jonah smiled but took a step back, raising the gun to Chase's forehead. "Smart enough to get you to do the breaking and entering...you're on the security video, *bro*, not me."

Chase shook his head. "No, Jonah, the security footage is gone...I deleted it with your password."

He squinted, staring at Chase for a beat then looked out the window at the police activity. "It doesn't matter. Your matrix is all over those trades."

Chase shook his head again. "No. It was you who logged in from home and ran them in the sandbox. Not me. The logs won't lie for you."

"I was being forced to, by Durggin and Romeo."

Chase nodded. "Did they force you to transfer the money to your Caymans' holding account?"

"What?"

Chase smiled. "Yeah. And it seems all those blue-chip trades never made it into the matrix." He shrugged in mock regret. "Must have just slipped your mind with all the shooting going on."

"No." His voice was no more than a whisper as panic shaped his face.

"Yes. That means the only trades made were the HFT pump and dumps on the cartel stocks."

"You idiot." Jonah looked out the window once more, seeming to piece together problems in his mind. "That's still enough to pay them back. I'll just transfer the money when it settles on Thursday."

Chase shook his head. "Smartest man in the room."

"That's right. And if you and your girl are smart, you'll let me pin all this on Durggin and pay the cartels what's owed them."

"Except you won't be able to pay them off."

"Why not? You said you ran the trades." Jonah looked at his watch. "And they should be executing right about now."

"That's right. They're executing. But you won't be able to transfer anything...now that your password has changed."

Confusion and anger washed over Jonah's face. He took a step closer and pressed the barrel to Chase's forehead. "What's the new password?"

"I'm afraid I can't tell you that."

He swung the gun around, pointing it at Chloe, who curled in on herself. Chase stepped in front of her and reached behind him, wrapping his fingers around the pistol in his waistband. "It won't do any good, Jonah, aside from the fact that you'd never get out of here if you killed anyone, you need me. Kill her and you could torture me but never get the password."

Jonah pulled the hammer back on the pistol and pressed it to Chase's chest. "Give it to me or I swear to God I'll blow you away right now."

"And do what? Run from the law *and* the cartel...with no money?"

"You son of a bitch."

"That's me," Chase said, his face cold and emotionless. "But Arlington PD is going to be here in a matter of minutes once the excitement upstairs calms down. If you're gonna go, then go. Call me from the Caymans and I'll give you the password."

Jonah looked down, obviously having difficulty deciding what to do.

"It's the only chance you have of surviving this," Chase added to push him over the edge.

Jonah took a step back toward the door and shook his head, grinning. "I guess I wasn't the smartest guy in the room, was I?"

"You never were, Jonah."

He grabbed the door handle but then raised the gun to Chase's head again.

Chase turned his head sideways letting him press the barrel to his temple, but remaining calm. "The password, Jonah."

"Give me my jacket you prick."

Chase took Jonah's jacket off and passed it to him, his head still turned.

Jonah leaned close and put his mouth inches from Chase's ear, continuing to press the gun to his head. "You'll pay for this. I swear to God you'll pay," he whispered.

Jonah lowered the gun and opened the door a crack, peering down the hall before leaving.

Chloe collapsed, crying.

"It's okay," Chase said, peeling off the black nitrile gloves and tossing them into the medical waste container next to the bed. He took her hand. "It's over. He's gone."

She hit him in the arm. "You asshole...he had a gun to your head. How can you be so calm?"

"It's fine...he couldn't have shot me if he wanted to," Chase said, reaching into his pocket. He pulled out the handful of bullets he had taken out of Luis's gun in the elevator. He dropped them on Chloe's bed. "No bullets. I emptied it before I gave it to him."

She reached around to hug him but felt the gun in his belt as he sat next to her on the bed. "What?! You had a gun too?" she snapped.

He smiled and nodded.

"Why didn't you just hold him here and let the police arrest him?" She asked toying with the bullets on her blanket.

"I couldn't. It's better that he left. Trust me."

"Chase..."

Chase shook his head. "Trust me. I thought of everything."

She nodded but started crying again. "Won't the cartel come after you looking for their money?" She asked, wrapping her arm around his shoulder and resting her head on his chest.

"I don't think they know about me...but they'll get their money, so there's no need for them to come looking."

"So you're going to give Jonah the password?" Chloe asked. "That asshole is responsible for almost getting me killed."

And killing Bowman and Bobby Tang, Chase added silently.

Just then, Deb Ortega walked in. Chase stood, pulling Chloe's blanket over the bullets as if he were just straightening the bed for her.

"Are you alright?" Deb asked.

Chase nodded. "Yep...just sitting around waiting for the all clear."

"Okay, we need you to take us to the other site...the one where they held you."

"Okay, but you might want to take this before someone gets hurt." Chase lifted his arms above his head and turned around so Ortega could see the gun.

She pulled a glove from her pocket and grabbed the handle with two fingers. "Whose is this?"

"I think it was Durggin's. There was a lot of action though, so I'm not sure."

"Was this used to kill anyone?" She asked, tension in her voice.

"Not that I'm aware of...not in my presence anyway."

"Whose weapon did Durggin have?"

"Romeo's."

Deb raised her eyebrow. "Who is Romeo?"

Chase shrugged. "I didn't get a resume. Juárez Cartel I think."

"Juaarez?! Now *that*, at least, makes sense," she said as she placed the pistol in an evidence bag from her pocket. "Where is *Romeo* now?"

"Dead...at Jonah's apartment."

She looked around the room. "Where's Jonah? He was with you a few minutes ago wasn't he?"

"He left suddenly. I'm not sure why."

She tipped her head to the side. "That's odd."

"I thought so too," Chase said.

She watched him through slits for a moment, then asked, "Are you okay to travel?"

Chase nodded. "I just have to use the bathroom first."

"Hurry up. We're meeting the forensics guys on site."

"Okay," he said then disappeared into the bathroom. He looked in the mirror and splashed water on his battered face. With the gloves and the jacket gone, there would be no gunshot residue on his hands or sleeves. He turned off the water and dried his hands before pulling a fresh pair of sterile gloves from the box next to the sink.

With the gloves on, he took Romeo's phone from his pocket and opened Google translator. The brief message he typed was clipped and to the point. He copied the translation and pasted it into the texting screen in a message to *Patrón*.

"Durggin traidor huyo.
Harper traidor ido con dinero.
Islas caimanes---contraseña---@SSm@5T3r0faLL
Ahora caza Harper."

As soon as he sent it, he deleted the message from both the phone and the SIM.

"You shouldn't have messed with my sister, Jonah," he muttered as he peeled off one of the gloves and wrapped it around the phone, tossing the other in the trash.

After flushing the toilet, he went back out. "I almost forgot," Chase said, holding the phone out to Deb. "I took this off Romeo to call you with…forgot I had it."

She nodded and took the phone careful to touch it only by the glove that Chase had wrapped it in.

Chase turned to Chloe. "I'll be back in a little while."

"Go," she said. "We'll be fine." She patted the blanket where the bullets were hidden.

He nodded knowingly and joined Ortega outside. As they turned to leave, Romeo's phone buzzed in Ortega's hand.

She looked at the screen and pressed to read. "Huh…looks like you made it out just in time."

"What makes you say that?"

She held the phone up so he could read the message. It was from Patrón. *"Mátalos a todos".*

"I don't know what that means," Chase said. "Non Spanish speaker."

She pulled an evidence bag from her pocket and stuffed it inside. "It says, 'kill them all'."

Chase blew out a breath through pursed lips. "Whoa."

"Yeah," Ortega replied. "Come on. You can tell me what happened on the way."

Or a version of what happened, anyway, Chase thought as they descended the stairs.

▶◀

When CHASE and Ortega arrived back at Jonah's penthouse, the forensics team was already combing over everything. They had apparently discovered Luis's body in the elevator shaft. Two officers were negotiating with the building maintenance staff to halt the elevator so they could recover the corpse.

Ortega and Chase took the stairs up to the penthouse, chatting on the way.

"How many were there total?" Ortega asked.

"There was Durggin, Romeo, and two guys that came with him."

"And you and Jonah Harper."

"Right."

"When did Romeo and his two guys show up?"

Chase shrugged. "I don't know… Late Saturday night or early Sunday. I was unconscious. I woke up and they were dangling me over the edge of the roof."

"That'll wake you up."

Chase chuckled. "Tell me about it. I think I pissed myself."

"So they held you and Jonah there all weekend, from Saturday night till this morning?"

"Yeah."

"And Durggin was definitely working for the Juárez Cartel?"

"I guess," Chase said as they approached the penthouse level. "He was strolling around, armed. Free to come and go as he wanted."

"Well, that would be the connection then…if he was working for the trading firm *and* still working for the cartel, that explains why he had you and Jonah in his sights."

"Yeah, I figured that too."

She stopped at the top of the stairs. "Why would he double-cross them, though?"

Chase shook his head. "I don't know. He had a history of doing that if you're right that he double-crossed the Beltrán-Leyva Cartel…maybe he was trading up again."

She nodded. "How did the guy end up in the elevator shaft?"

"I have no idea. I thought it was weird that Durggin and Jonah showed up alone when they got back from the break in at the firm."

"And that's when everything went to shit?" Ortega asked.

Chase nodded. "Durggin came in and stuck a gun in Romeo's face, shot the other guy—Franco I think his name was—then shot Romeo when he tried to get away."

"How'd you and Jonah get away?"

"Somehow, Jonah got his hands on Luis's gun—the guy in the elevator shaft. He pulled it on Durggin and told me to get Romeo's phone so I could call for help."

She narrowed her eyes to slits but nodded. "How did Durggin get away?"

"He threw a lamp at Jonah, then tackled me. In the struggle, he dropped both guns, his and Romeo's," Chase said, then sat on the edge of the step. "When he ran for the door, he grabbed Romeo's because it was closer and I grabbed his. I fired two shots but missed him both times."

"So you fired a weapon?"

Chase nodded. "I'm a shit shot, though, apparently. I missed his fat ass twice from the kitchen floor."

"Don't feel bad. Unless you're trained, it's hard to stay cool under that kind of pressure." She put her hand on his shoulder as a parent would a child who struck out at a little league game. "Plus, you don't need the kind of guilt that comes with killing someone."

"Yeah…in hindsight I guess you're right."

"So Durggin killed all three cartel guys?"

"I'd think so. I know he killed two for sure. I can't picture Jonah tossing a guy down an elevator shaft…we're number geeks."

She nodded. "And you're sure you're okay with going back in?"

Chase took a deep breath. "If I have to, it's better to just get it over with."

She nodded and opened the door of the stairwell. Chase got up and joined her.

"One more thing, before we go in… Where's Jonah now?" She asked.

Chase shook his head slowly. "I'd really like to know that myself." *At least until the cartel catches up to him.*

LOOKING UP

Friday afternoon, four days later

CHASE held Chloe's arm as she walked from the car to the front entrance of his apartment building. "Stop, stop, stop. I'm getting dizzy," Chloe said, dipping to the side. "Hold on a sec."

Val walked up beside her carrying a bag of medical supplies. "Do you need me on the other arm?"

Chloe smiled and shook her head. "No. I just wanted to see how many times I could make him stop...I'm fine." She walked away from Chase, a little wobbly but grinning from ear-to-ear.

"If you fall and pop your stitches, I'll use a stapler to fix you," Chase said.

She turned, but tipped sideways, grabbing a light post to keep her balance. Chase rushed to her.

Just before he reached her, she straightened up and laughed, walking away. "Sucker!"

Chase shook his head. "Are you sure she's out of danger? I mean, no chance of a relapse or dying in her sleep?"

Val chuckled and shoved him gently. "Stop. You know you love her."

Chase picked up the bag and walked with Val inside. They waited for an elevator as the one Chloe got on rose without them. Chase just grinned—he knew she had done it be a pain in the ass.

"So tell me, *Val.* What does Val mean…in your language."

"Wicked DJ," she said straight faced as they stepped on the elevator.

"Ah…so, an ancient name then."

She punched him gently on the shoulder. "It's short for *Valayi*…another name for the Hindu goddess Parvati."

"A goddess. Hmmm," Chase said, grinning. "No diva here."

Val shook her head. "None from me."

"So what is Parvati the goddess of?"

Val set her mouth sideways, lips pursed. "I don't know if I should tell you."

"Oh. It must be good."

She laughed.

"Is she the goddess of carnal pleasures?" he asked, leaning in and kissing her neck.

"Close… Fertility."

He laughed. "Then I guess we need to have a serious chat."

The elevator door opened and they got out. "Talk? Really? You don't think there's been enough talk already?"

He leaned over and kissed her again. Just then his new phone rang. He pulled it out and answered still smiling. "Hello."

"Okay you prick, I'm in the Caymans. Give me my damned password." It was Jonah.

Chase, put his hand over his phone and nodded Val toward the door. "I'll be right in."

She kissed him and went inside. Chase waited until the door closed before replying. "Hey, pal…how are the tropics?"

"Cut the shit. Give me my damned password."

"Come on, man. I don't want there to be any hard feelings…I covered for you. I told the police it was all Durggin and the cartel guys. You were forced to do what you did."

"I don't give a shit what you told the police. It's not the police I have to worry about. It's Juárez."

"Ah. Yeah. I can see where that would be a problem."

"I had to sneak out of my hotel last night and leave all my clothes behind," Jonah said. "In the middle of the damned night, I had to find a new place to stay."

"Whoa. That sounds rough…really, really traumatic."

"Okay. Enough, smart-ass. My password."

"I never changed it. You stopped me before I could finish."

"You're lying. I already tried my old password."

"What? Oh man. That sucks because I really didn't change it," Chase said, grinning. "Are you sure you didn't give it to anyone else?"

"Cut the shit, Chase. This is my life we're talking about!"

You should have thought of that before you fucked with my family.

Chase sighed in resignation. "Okay. You ready to write it down?"

"Yeah."

"It's your old password with @55 at the beginning."

"You jackass."

"Yeah…like that. Good luck Jonah."

"Fuck you, Chase."

Chase smiled and ended the call. When he went into his apartment, Chloe was already in his bed, arranging pillows.

"Uh…no. You get the pullout sofa," Chase said from the bedroom doorway, hands on his hips.

"But, but, but…" Her bottom lip pouted out in mock disappointment.

"Nope. The pullout."

"But what if I have a relapse or something. Don't you want me to be in the better bed?"

Chase shook his head.

"Why?" Chloe whined, grinning. It was good to see her in such a playful mood.

Val walked over and slipped her arms around Chase's waist. "I have to get to work, but if you'll be up when I get off, I'll come by."

Chase looked at Chloe but pointed at Val. "That's why."

Chloe shivered in mock revulsion. "Fine. I'll sleep in there."

Val kissed Chase passionately before leaving. "I'll see you later, Chloe." She looked at Chase and winked as she left the apartment. "Later," she whispered.

As soon as the door closed, Chloe flopped on the sofa. She grabbed her neck immediately. "Shit. This sucks."

"It's not that bad. And the mattress pad in the closet makes it bett—"

"Not the bed, dumb ass. Being fragile."

Chase sat down and wrapped his arm around her shoulder, conscious of the soft foam collar that had replaced the hard collar in the hospital. "You're only temporarily fragile. And only certain parts." He kissed her cheek. "And thank God your head is so hard or you wouldn't have survived it at all."

She batted him lightly with the back of her hand then sat quietly for a moment. "Chasey…what am I gonna do?"

"Well, I've got a full fridge, lots of popcorn, and ice-cream. We can binge watch something on Netflix and make ourselves sick."

She shook her head. "I mean, I'm so screwed up. You were right…I won't have anyone to take care of me."

"You actually do a really good job of taking care of yourself…with the exception of the parade of asshats you're attracted to."

She began to cry. "I don't know why I do that."

Chase pulled her face to his chest and stroked her hair. "Yes you do, sweetie. Dad was an asshole and made us feel like our lives only have order if we're being treated like shit."

"Why would I want someone like him, though?"

"Because he was there and in charge. We never had to guess about anything because he was always there with a belt or an insult to let us know our place… our model comfort place is in the presence of assholes."

She laughed through her tears. "I'm tired of it."

"So am I. But at least with an asshole, you know where you stand."

She wiped her nose on his shirt and sat up. "So, is Val an asshole?"

Chase shook his head. "No. Val is mom before dad left and she killed herself."

Chloe dropped her head as far as her collar would allow.

Chase lifted it again with his finger. "But I'm not Dad."

She smiled and nodded. "No. You're way cooler. But…"

"But what?"

"But it happened again. That's so heavy Chase… It breaks my heart that you're carrying all those—"

Chase raised his hand sharply, finger in the air. "Stop. You know you can never say that out loud. All of them…every single one of them, including Jonah, were a threat to you." He touched her cheek. "They were dead as soon as they hurt you. They just didn't know it yet."

"But..."

"Family is all that matters. There is no price too high to protect family."

She stared at him for a second and nodded.

"But you can never, *ever* talk about it... Not about this time and not about the other times. Ever," he said more firmly.

She nodded firmly. "I understand."

He patted her leg and smiled. "You want some dinner?" He asked, standing.

"Like what?"

"I don't know...I have pizza, mac and chee—"

"Mac and cheese!"

"Mac and cheese it is."

Chase went into the kitchen and pulled a pan from under the counter.

"Thank you," Chloe said.

"For what?"

"Everything. You're the best big brother a girl could have."

Chase shook his head. *No...I'm a psychopath with only one living family member to care about.* "That's what I'm here for."

▶◀

OFFICER DEBORAH ORTEGA closed her study guide for the detective's exam. She felt strong and more capable than ever before—after she and her uncle had killed Durggin, there seemed to be a new opening for a future she hadn't felt before. She smiled thinking about Chase, grateful he had been there to help her and her family get the closure they had sought for so long.

She didn't even care that there were holes in his story—the evidence lined up, that's all that mattered. But as she sat there, staring at the cover of her detective's study guide, she wondered what really happened in that penthouse. Chase was the only living witness other than Jonah Harper. And it was unlikely they would ever find him—he had disappeared with over two hundred million in cartel money. If he were caught, it would be more likely a cartel hit than an arrest that brought it to a close.

"Did Durggin really kill all those cartel guys?" she muttered.

She took a deep breath then leaned forward, bringing up Chase's record on the computer in front of her. She shook her head at all the close calls he'd had with the law; eight felony assault charges, four of them dismissed, two pled down to misdemeanors, two found not guilty. Five drunk and disorderly, three misdemeanor convictions, probation, never any time served. Three battery charges, no convictions—all related to incidents with his sister.

You've never done a minute of hard time for anything, have you, Chase…smart guy. Deb chuckled and shook her head. "If it weren't for Chloe, you wouldn't have a record."

A name caught her eye; Edward Goff, AKA Eddie. One of the assaults, almost two years ago. For some reason, that name seemed familiar so she looked him up. As her screen produced the file on "Eddie", her eyes narrowed. *Deceased—overdose.*

She clicked to expand the details on the record and tipped her head to the side when she saw the date of Eddie's death—only five days after the encounter with Chase. Chloe had spent two days in the hospital at the same time—three broken ribs and a bruised kidney.

She shook her head, her curiosity piqued and began checking other instances of assault on Chloe Grant. Greg Jared, arrested for aggravated assault after an attack on Chloe; charges dropped—found dead in the trunk of his car a week later. Estimated time of death, though imprecise due to summer heat on the trunk, was two days earlier.

Deb looked at the detective's notes and saw Chase had been dismissed as a suspect because he had been in police custody at the time for a drunk and disorderly, couldn't produce bail until after the discovery of the body.

Deb's eyes flashed wide. She frantically clicked on the search and entered in *"Victim=Chloe Grant"*. There were half a dozen instances of attacks against Chloe Grant recorded in the state police database, and in all but one of them, the accused met some unfortunate end shortly afterward. In each case, whether accidental death or victim of violence, Chase Grant was either in police custody or not a suspect.

Her face flashed hot and her ears began to ring. She shook her head. *He's too much of a hothead to plan like that. If he were a killer, he'd have killed someone, at some point, in the heat of the moment. Hotheads aren't cool killers.*

Deb's uncle, Gabe, walked toward her. "How's it going with the detective's exam."

She nodded absently, staring at the screen. "Piece of cake."

Gabe tipped his head to the side. "What's wrong?"

"Do you think Chase Grant could have killed those cartel guys?" she asked, turning in her chair.

Gabe thought about it for a moment and nodded. "If he or someone he cared about were in immediate danger, absolutely he could have. But I don't think he did...tight shots, premeditation... They scream Durggin."

She nodded, hesitantly at first, then with more conviction. "I guess you're right."

"It was Durggin," Gabe said, patting Deb on the shoulder. "He even came to the hospital to finish off Chase and his sister. No question... Chase didn't kill Durggin; we did."

She rubbed her face, still not convinced.

Gabe smiled. "It would take some sort of evil genius to do all that—kill all the cartel guys then deliver Durggin to the hospital, pistol in hand to be executed, and get out without crossing the cartel himself." He sat on the edge of her desk. "That floor manager from Baxter—Frank what-his-name—he confirmed it was Luis Maniez in the office that morning, and it was him driving Harper's Bentley according to the employees coming into the garage."

"So, Jonah Harper...he's the mastermind and Durggin was just his thug."

"That's what it looks like," Gabe said. "Unless you think Chase somehow resisted the temptation to take two hundred million, killed five guys, and fooled the cartels into thinking it was someone else—including tricking Durggin into showing up, pistol drawn, and tricking us into executing him at the hospital."

She shook her head. "No. You're right—that's stupid."

Gabe grinned at her. "You're sure?"

She nodded. "Yeah. Now that you say it out loud, it's ridiculous. It's what it looks like...his boss got cozy with the cartels, Durggin was the go-between. The two of them cooked up a plan to steal the cartel money and Chase's trade analysis threatened to expose them."

"That's the official story. Can't get much cleaner."

"Yeah...clean."

Gabe patted Deb on the shoulder again before walking away. She continued to stare at the computer screen for several long moments before shaking her head. *Very clean. Super clean...too clean.* "You better watch out for the Juárez Cartel, Chase."

GAT MAN

Monday, two weeks later

CHASE stood over the shoulder of a new analyst on the trading floor, helping her understand the morning matrix load. He looked up to see Frank enter, wearing a suit—a nice suit—a thousand dollar suit.

Chase whistled. "Jesus, Frank! You are one sexy man."

"Kiss my ass, Grant," he muttered as he walked past and toward his new office—Jonah's old office. Frank stopped at the door and looked back across the trading floor. "Just because I'm behind this door now doesn't mean I'm not watching every one of you."

"Frank, everybody… let's hear it for Frank, sexiest man on the floor," Chase said, rising and clapping, creating a spontaneous round of applause from the floor.

Frank pointed at Chase then motioned for him to come into the office.

"Are you set now?" Chase asked the young woman he had been helping.

She nodded. "I think so."

"If you need me, just yell." He left her side and went to Frank's office.

"Come in and close the door."

Chase did as ordered.

"I want you to tell me something and I want you to be honest."

"Honest? Wow. I'll try but can't promise anything."

Frank curled his lip in a mild sneer and leaned forward. "The matrices that Jonah ran before he cleaned out the suspended accounts…that was good work."

Chase nodded. "Yeah. I saw them. Very clean."

"Except Jonah didn't know how to build a matrix to save his life," Frank said, squinting. "He's the one who built the floor matrix everyone hated."

Chase nodded. "Yeah…I can see where someone might think that. But remember, he was using the retail division to pad his HFT transactions."

Frank shook his head. "I saw you all over that data."

Chase sat back in mock astonishment. "Me?"

"Don't give me that. You and he were tight as a tick's ass."

"Such colorful metaphors, Frank. You should write a book."

Frank leaned closer and lowered his voice. "Tell me we don't have to worry about any more infiltration."

Chase shrugged. "As far as I know the SEC-negotiated safeguards are in place and auditor oversight is absolute now," he said, taking a more serious tone. "But I wasn't in on the meetings, so I don't know how much transparency there's going to be."

"I just want a straight answer, Grant."

"You know what I know, Frank. I was as shocked as you when Jonah ran off with those accounts… I had no idea he was intentionally wrecking the retail division to feather his own nest."

Frank's eyes narrowed to slits.

Chase put his hand in the air. "I swear to god, Frank. If I had access to any of that two hundred million, do you think I'd be back here?"

"Two hundred seventy-five," Frank said. "But I'm not convinced."

"I don't blame you. I'd be suspicious of me too, coming back to work for you…my favorite person in the world."

"Kiss my ass."

"I'm trying, Frank."

Frank laughed spontaneously but quickly covered with a cough. "You have a talent for numbers."

Chase's eyebrow shot up involuntarily. *Ouch…that must have hurt.* "Thanks."

"Just don't screw me over."

Chase smiled. "Well Frank, I'll do my best."

"You'll have to come in early to load up your floor matrices," Frank said, leaning back. "I don't want to see you scrambling around here last minute before trading starts and get caught with your pants down."

"Do you have to suck every bit of fun out of everything, Frank?"

"This isn't a game, Grant. Do your damned job."

Chase took a deep breath and let it out loudly. "If you say so."

"I say so!" He stood and slapped his hands on his desk, his face red.

Chase nodded and went to the door but paused and looked back. "Lunch today?"

Frank chewed on the corner of his lip for a second. "Where?"

Chase shrugged.

Frank stared at him for a second and nodded. "Okay. If we're not too busy."

"I'll turn you yet."

"Fat chance, Grant. Now get to work or I'll find a tree sloth to replace you."

"Nice! A joke! See…it's happening already."

Frank grinned and shooed Chase away. "Get the hell out of here."

Chase left Frank's office and walked up on the raised platform above the trading floor. He paused for a moment to admire the sign he'd had made: *The Fabulous Bobby Tang Memorial Trading Floor.*

"He would've loved that," Tammy said, stepping behind Chase.

Chase turned to her. "Hi, Tammy."

"Hi, boss." She looked at Frank's closed door then back to Chase. "Why do you take that from him? You could get a job with any firm in the city…hell, you could go to New York and make a killing."

Chase smiled and looked toward Frank's door. "He's not so bad. And there's one thing I can say for working with an asshole; you always know where you stand with them. No hidden agendas."

"Filterless you mean."

"Even better."

She shrugged, an exaggerated expression that bounced her boobs when she dropped her shoulders. "Do you have today's matrix yet?"

"Yeah," he said, then stepped behind his glass cubicle to pull a thumb drive from the computer. "Go ahead and pass it to whoever wants to use it."

"So awesome," Tammy said, almost manic in her enthusiasm.

"And starting tomorrow, I'll have it loaded on the server so anyone can download it."

"You're the best."

"Six minutes to opening bell," Chase said with a wink. "Have a hot day."

She smiled and waved awkwardly as Chase reached over and picked up his phone, hitting the intercom button. "Good morning traders, analysts, number geeks and fortune seekers. Welcome to the inaugural trading day on the Fabulous Bobby Tang Trading Floor."

Applause and cheers erupted across the big room.

"We have new matrices going around. Feel free to grab a copy and apply your finest analytical minds to them. I think I cooked something hot for you this morning…we'll see."

A smattering of cheers and attaboys flowed up from the floor.

"Keep an eye on copper today…and you know where copper goes, pipe and wire manufacturers will be going the opposite direction." He looked around—every eye in the room was on him. They were all smiling and looking forward to their day—he had done his job.

He smiled. "Five minutes to the bell. Have a good day everyone."

Another smattering of applause filled the room. Frank stood in the doorway of his office, smiling. He nodded at Chase and turned, closing the door.

Though the market opened down at the bell, the traders and analysts stayed positive. By lunchtime, the market turned and moved up. The floor traders found themselves in the zone and company averages were beating the market by as much as twenty percent.

Frank splurged at lunchtime, taking Chase to Jonah's old favorite lunch spot, the Steakhouse. Chase sat and listened to Frank complain about various traders and system shortcomings. He smiled and nodded as the new VP laid out his plan for improving the Retail Division.

On the way back to the office, Frank got a call.

"Who?" he asked the caller. He nodded. "Okay. We're about a block away now. I'll have him up there in five minutes." He ended the call. "A new retail account wants a meeting so they can understand the analysis methods we use."

"Can't the sales guys handle that?" Chase asked.

Frank shook his head. "They specifically requested you. Apparently, you have some sort of reputation."

Chase tipped his head sideways.

Frank glanced at him dismissively. "Don't ask me. I just work here. His name is Martin."

After arriving back at the office, Chase rode up with Frank in the elevator. "Don't get too technical with him," Frank said. "You'll turn him off. And he's got to be a high roller if sales agreed to set up the meeting."

Chase nodded. "I've got it, Frank."

"And don't—"

"I've got it, Frank."

Frank pressed his lips together tightly, a flush of red sprang to his ears. He nodded. "I know. I'll see you when you're done."

They stepped off the elevator and Chase jogged off to meet "Martin" in the retail trade sales reception area. The receptionist nodded toward three men in the corner.

Chase plastered on a sales smile as he walked toward them. "Mr. Martin?"

The oldest man of the three stood, extending his hand. "Just Martin," he said as the other two men rose as well. "Martin Patrón."

Chase's heart skipped a beat but he kept his smile and shook hands with him. "How can I help you, Mr. Patrón."

"I'd like to talk to you about your trade analytics."

Chase glanced at the receptionist, pointing at the small conference room to the side. "Can we?"

She nodded and Chase led Patrón in. The older man motioned for his two companions to remain in the reception area. Once inside, Chase gestured to a chair and took the one on the opposite side of the table for himself, happy to have something between them.

"Where would you like me to start?"

"High-Frequency Trading algorithms," Patrón said. "More specifically, the use of them to create microfluctuations in the market."

Chase took a deep breath, held it for a beat, then exhaled into an apologetic smile. "I'm afraid the retail division doesn't use HFTs. I can only assume you're asking because of the recent news concerning our former Retail Trade Division Vice President, Jonah Harper."

Patrón nodded, smiling knowingly.

"When the SEC auditors went through the systems, they found he used a communications exploit to commingle data between the two systems," Chase said. "The mandatory safeguards that were added, not only here but industry wide, will ensure violations like that won't happen again."

Patrón lifted his chin staring at Chase down the bridge of his nose for a tick before nodding sharply. "That's too bad… I was hoping I could speak to you about replicating an account we had here once before."

"Oh. You've used Baxter before?"

Patrón smiled knowingly once more. "In fact, I've met your former VP of Retail… Mr. Harper."

Chase nodded, continuing to smile despite the growing loudness of the pulse pounding in his ears. "You knew Jonah?"

He nodded. "I actually saw him recently." He leaned forward and grinned cruelly. "He didn't look so well."

"I'm sorry to hear that. No one here knows where he is… Even the SEC is looking for him."

"I'm confident they won't locate him," Patrón said. "Not now, anyway."

That sounded final. "Uh… I'm not sure what you mean."

"He mentioned you…"

Chase felt his guts turn cold. "Me?"

Patrón nodded. "He said you were the mastermind behind the data matrixing, and if I wanted answers, I needed to talk to you."

"Jonah was always kind to me. He flatters me with his confidence."

Patrón shook his head, smiling. He stared at Chase for several long seconds, then folded his fingers and leaned forward. "My associate, Romeo, warned me that Jonah Harper wasn't to be trusted."

Chase nodded as if he were hearing the story for the first time. Patrón tipped his head sideways and measured Chase with a piercing, withering, glare, but Chase remained smiling, unmoved outwardly.

Abruptly, Patrón pushed himself from the table and rose. "Apparently, Jonah was wrong. You don't seem to be properly placed to deal with HFT functions. I'm sorry to have wasted your time."

"Not at all. We're always happy to answer client questions." He reached across the table to shake Patrón's hand.

Patrón gripped Chase's hand tightly and held it there for several seconds. "It's odd... My associate had an unfortunate accident."

"I'm sorry to hear that. Will he be okay?"

Patrón grinned. "No. I'm sorry to say he will not...lead poisoning."

"That's terrible." Chase's face twisted in regret.

"The funny thing is that he seems to have reached out from the grave to warn me about Jonah Harper."

Chase lifted his brows in surprise. "Really?"

Patrón nodded. "I received a text message from him thirty minutes after the police say he died...it saved me from a substantial loss."

Chase nodded, squinting. "Probably nothing more than a delayed message... happens all the time around here when phone towers are overburdened."

Patrón set his jaw to the side and nodded. "I hadn't thought of that...perhaps you're correct... in either case, I wish there was some way I could thank Romeo for the warning. It turns out he was right."

"I've heard believable ghost stories before."

"As have I," Patrón said grinning. He finally released Chase's hand. "It was good to meet you, Chase."

They left the conference room and walked back into the reception area. Patrón stopped and turned slowly, concern on his face. "I understand your sister had some sort of accident recently... she's recovering I trust?"

Chase's face went cold, vacant, his eyes hard and reptilian. Patrón actually flinched at the change as if it were familiar—something one should give a wide berth to.

"She's doing very well, thank you," Chase said. "Once the underlying condition was treated, the rest of her recovery was all but guaranteed."

Patrón nodded. "Good."

Several tense seconds passed, Chase continuing to stare, unflinching, into the eyes of the man. Finally, Patrón broke eye contact and smiled. "It was good meeting you. But I feel confident our paths won't cross again."

Chase smiled thinly and reached out to shake his hand. "Thank you for your visit. And if you see Jonah again, please give him my regards."

Patrón winced almost imperceptibly, then smiled, shaking Chase's hand. "I'm certain I won't be crossing paths with him again either."

"That's probably for the best."

Chase watched as the men left, Patrón looking over his shoulder once before they reached the elevator. Once the door slid closed, Chase reached under his jacket for the pistol in his waistband and flipped the safety on before returning to the trading floor.

Frank saw him walk in and waved him into his office. "How did it go?" He asked as Chase entered.

Chase shook his head. "It wasn't a good fit. I don't think we'll be seeing them again."

"Oh well. Life is full of disappointments."

"I don't think you would've been happy working with him… he seemed the type to micromanage."

"Then great! Crisis avoided."

Chase smiled. "We can only hope."

"Now get your ass to work before I fire you," Frank muttered, staring at his screen.

"You bet," Chase said and returned to his new glass fronted cubicle.

As the traders and analysts answered phones, worked their deals, and moved their clients' and the company's money around, Chase stared vacantly across the trading floor.

He shifted uncomfortably as the gun in his belt poked his back, but then settled down, comforted by its presence.

"Keep walking, Mr. Patrón… Just keep walking."

<<<END>>>

Thank you for reading *Hedged*.

Follow S.L. Shelton at:
SLShelton.com
wolfeauthor.wordpress.com
www.goodreads.com/WolfeWriter
facebook.com/SLShelton.Author

I hope you enjoyed reading Hedged. If you did, I'd like to encourage you to post a review on the site you purchased it from and on www.goodreads.com. Your reviews are the best way to keep an author churning out the work and I'm grateful for every one I get. Feel free to contact me on Twitter and Facebook if you have any questions or thoughts about the stories. I love hearing from you…you make this process a joy for me.

Very best regards,
S.L. Shelton
Twitter: @SLSheltonAuthor

The Garden…

Once upon a time, there was a teacher. He was old and weary, but his wit, seasoned by the years, was the perfect platform upon which to pass lessons to the next generations.

He loved teaching, and he was quite good at it. Young and old alike would travel from far away villages to listen to the old wizard speak.

His insights were simple, and he used plain language to reach as many minds as possible. The people were grateful for his seemingly simple logic and unique storytelling skills, not knowing that the easier it is to understand a story, the harder it was to tell. He smiled when their eyes brightened with understanding, the lesson learned—he could pick out the precise moment when a young mind grasped an ancient truth.

Soon, he was being called on to travel to many new villages. Other communities wanted to learn and be entertained by the old man. But alas, his days were numbered and there were only so many trips, lessons, and stories that could be fit into his remaining sojourn among the living—he had long felt the approaching end of his time.

A wise priest came to him one day. "You should write down your stories and let others share them far and wide," he said. "With your simple words, so artfully arranged, you could open minds in far away places."

"I'm just an old teacher," the wrinkled old man said. "My stories may be something special here, in this small village. But the world is a big place. I'm afraid I'd be wasting my remaining time."

"Nonsense. Your skill is superb, your stories are moving and the lessons are grasped with no effort. You are unique…a rare treasure," the priest said, putting his arm around the old man.

The old man smiled, knowing the priest was artfully stroking his ego. The priest helped him to his chair and patted his shoulder. "Put your words to parchment…share your gift."

The old wizard, worn bone weary from his long and adventurous life, settled into the comfort of his chair—something the old man had grown fond of in recent days; comfort. But he nodded. "If you think I have something worthy to share, I will put the words on paper."

"Excellent," the priest said with genuine joy. "It's a wonderful thing you'll be doing. You'll see."

So the old haggard hands began scribbling words. Hours passed and he didn't even look up from his candle lit writing table—then days passed—then weeks, months, years. He looked up one day and saw a new sunrise outside his window and got up, stretching his back and arms. He walked to the window and felt a connection to the world as he stared into the brightening horizon over his garden. After a moment, he looked back at the piles of parchment he had scribbled his words on.

"That's enough for now," he said and proceeded to bundle the stacks with string before plodding across the village to the priest's home.

He knocked on the door and left the papers on the doorstep. The door opened as he walked away. "So much!" the priest said. "You'll surely touch many lives with your words."

"We shall see," the old teacher replied. "If they like it, I'll write more."

The priest nodded and scooped up the work, rushing it out to be copied and distributed to the far flung edges of the world. Days passed as the old man waited, regaining his strength from the long hours, days and months he had spent hunched over his writing table. And each day, he waited for the priest to bring him news of his stories—*were they well received? Do they want more? Did they like the one about the boy who didn't know he was special?*

But each day the priest shook his head, sadly, having no news to share. With each passing day, the old wizard grew more withdrawn, having had his greatest fears realized; great skill is judged differently when compared to the whole of the world—his gift was small and his unsophisticated, simple language was not world worthy. And worse, he had wasted years of those precious few he had remaining.

Despair overwhelmed him and he left the comfort of his home to sit in the garden that his long passed wife had grown and left behind. He sat at the edge of the fountain and watched the water.

Soon, he came to realize he was being watched. He turned and looked over his shoulder to see a young girl, no more than seven or eight years old, lingering outside the garden gate.

"Are you spying on me young lady?" he asked, grinning playfully.

She shook her head. "I want you to tell me a story."

He smiled and lowered his head. "Later," he said. "After I rest."

She smiled and ran off, obviously excited the old wizard had agreed at all.

As he settled his back against the sun warmed stone, he thought back to those many years ago when he and his wife had built the fountain. Stone by stone, they had worked together to create this beautiful place of peace and warmth. The flowers and trees they had planted had grown large and filled in the once wide open spaces of the courtyard, just as she had planned years earlier.

He closed his eyes and smiled, his eyelids and cheeks kissed by the warm sun. "You planned and worked and look what you've done," he whispered to his long departed wife. "Your work continues to grow and now it has become what you dreamed…even without you here to coax it."

He breathed out softly, grateful to have been a part of her labor of love. "Thank you," he said quietly, then breathed out his last breath.

Hours later when he was discovered, the village fell into despair. And as word traveled, many hundreds of thousands of people across the lands mourned the loss of the great story teller.

The priest stood at the gates and angrily blocked the way of the pilgrims. "You come now to pay your respects because you found his words so moving. Yet, while he lived and ached to know he had moved you, you returned only silence? Selfishly consuming his life's work without so much as a thank you?"

He looked out over the silent masses who suddenly dropped their heads, ashamed to look at the priest.

"Go!" he said. "Walk past his house and say your prayers for his soul. But if none of his lessons pierce your hearts, let this one…give the gift of thanks to those who spill their lives so that your minds may grow…so that you may be inspired. Tell them so they will know their labors were not in vain."

The moral of this story, as you have no doubt figured out, is that if you don't leave a review, the author will die alone in a garden and a little girl will never hear the story she was promised…for reals. ;)

Acknowledgments

A 3:00 a.m. trip to Tysons Urgent Care, followed by a hasty trip to the Emergency Room at VHC can change one's priorities in life. It takes a great staff to calm the nerves and ease the agony. Many thanks to the Nurses, Techs, Doctors and support staff at those two great facilities. Shout out to the seventh floor staff, and radiation oncology. You guys are the best.

I wish to thank Melissa Manes with Scriptionis who stepped in on short notice to stand as primary editor for Hedged. Without her hard work and kindness during this trying time, it might not have been released.

I'd also like to thank another editor—friend and author J.C. Wing, who not only lent her talents as editor to Hedged but who was also the first to read it. Her contribution as well as her unwavering friendship has been a genuine comfort to me as my "Gretel" and I travel this rocky path of her cancer treatments.

To my wife, Diane—my *Gretel*—who remains my greatest supporter. As always, I must point out that I would not have become the person I am had it not been for you. Your presence in my life is a greater gift than I ever imagined possible. Thank you for being you and allowing me to be me—you are a magical creature who quite literally transfigured both of us.

I'd also like to thank all of my beta readers and those who have given me feedback, particularly Jon R, Susan M, Jennifer A, Trudy, Jim F, Jenn M (the coffee lady), James T, Suzanne B, Melissa, Charlotte H, J.C. Wing, Hammond R, Wendy B, and Linda M. Your opinions and suggestions helped me round this story out.

Thanks to my long-time friend, Gabe, who helped me with the Spanish language bits.

For my proofers…thanx a gazillion. I know it's not easy cleaning up after me, but Melissa, J.C., and Margery, you make me look good.

And finally, as always, I'd like to thank our children…grown adults, all of you, and so quick to jump to our aid. Parents couldn't ask for more loving children than you—thank you, Megan, Lauren, and Alex. I love you.

Made in the USA
Lexington, KY
07 January 2017